IN THE WAKE OF OUR MISDEED

GEORGE BYRON WRIGHT

To Cindy;
The artist himself!

CCC

C3 PUBLICATIONS
PORTLAND, OREGON
WWW.C3PUBLICATIONS.COM

In the Wake of Our Misdeed: a novel
Copyright © 2014 by George Byron Wright.

C3 Publications
3495 NW Thurman Street
Portland, OR 97210-1283
www.c3publications.com

First Edition

Library of Congress Control Number: 2014919819

Wright, George Byron
In the Wake of Our Misdeed: a novel

ISBN10: 0-9632655-9-8
ISBN13: 978-0-9632655-9-3

Cataloging References: In the Wake of Our Misdeed
1. Hood Canal, WA-Fiction 2. Wasco County, OR-Fiction 3. Oklahoma-Fiction 4. Child custody-Fiction 5. Marital relations-Fiction 6. Sociopathic behavior-Fiction I. Title

Book and cover designs by Dennis Stovall.
Author photo by Sergio Ortiz: www.sergiophotography.net.

Printed in the United States of America.

NOVELS BY GEORGE BYRON WRIGHT

Baker City 1948
Tillamook 1952
Roseburg 1959
Driving to Vernonia
Newport Blues, A Salesman's Lament
In the Wake of Our Misdeed

"Out beyond ideas of wrongdoing and rightdoing, there is a field. I will meet you there."

—Jalal ad-Din Rumi

–1–

THANKSGIVING 2007

Naomi was at the wheel, Carson merely her passenger. True to her mind-set, she drove aggressively, for the road was there to be mastered, and the rain-pounding darkness provided her the risk she savored. Carson was buckled in, his seat back slightly reclined, his arms folded, his mouth drawn as his wife took on Hood Canal's slickened roadway. In spite of the weather, the passenger window was most of the way down, an act of defiance in the face of Naomi's persistent smoking. Rain spat in at him; he ignored it.

Muddling in his brain was the acidic argument they'd been having since leaving the Barrus family vacation house in Sequim off the Dungeness Spit. It had been another thankless Thanksgiving. Their words, caustic and blaming, had been but a replay begun mere moments after waving perfunctory good-byes to his parents, who stood shoulder to shoulder on the wide porch out of the rain, siblings and spouses, uncles and aunts, aligned behind them. Despite the near midnight hour, tradition called for those leaving first to be seen off before those remaining retired. Featureless images, rear-lit by bright wall sconce porch lights, the group had stood as an obedient choir officially witnessing Carson and Naomi's departure. Carson's father gave them but an upraised palm while his mother offered her typical galloping fingers. Carson imagined, though could not see, the requisite smiles he knew were painted on all their faces. That cardboard cutout of a traditional family cluster held its position until the car was out of sight.

A sudden curtain of water sent up by a passing car slapped the windshield. They both sucked in a breath, but neither spoke. Rather it seemed the opportune instant to discontinue picking at the running sore of their displeasure, one with the other. No ground would be gained by another bristly exchange of the words that only minutes ago had reduced their estimation of each other even further. Carson knew what he knew, and Naomi cared little that he did.

The headlights stabbed fruitlessly into the wet darkness. Wipers hummed, tossing the pounding rain aside, again and again and again. Naomi prodded the silver Beemer SUV forward. Carson tried to doze—but he couldn't. He opened one eye and glanced at the dash clock; it read 1:14, bloody 1:14 a.m. They could have stayed on one more night, but she just had to get to Olympia to see her sister—regardless of the dreadful hour. The argument over their late departure had lasted less than the time it took to shell a hardboiled egg, than the time it took him to catch his father smirking from the kitchen doorway.

He turned his head to study the woman at the wheel: This beautiful woman he'd married on a swell of euphoria. This woman who revealed afterward that she intended to bear no children and who all but willed a miscarriage when her body tricked her anyway. This woman who became so easily absorbed with the lavish lifestyle he afforded her. This woman whom he knew to be attracted to others than him. All of it and more had worn away what had for a brief incredible slice of time been luminous between them.

Her profile was highlighted by the orange glow from the dashboard: the high cheekbones she prized, shoulder-length auburn hair, and the elegant nose that held it all together. Smoke was curling out of her nostrils. Carson was considering one more rejoinder to what had been a lacerating embroilment between them when she drove hard into a curve and a look of horror sprang onto her face. A howl erupted from her throat.

Carson's heart surged. He rose up against the belt across his chest and followed where Naomi's widened eyes were locked; it was in slow motion, even as the car was at speed. The huge semi sliding sideways on the wet pavement, coming at them out of the dark, was a horrific vision. Its gigantic open trailer racked with an assortment of cars was taking the full width of the road. The tractor was jacked hard in the driver's attempt to correct his grievous error. There would be no avoiding the moving car lot; in seconds it would reach and over-power them. Naomi's howl went on. The truck's tractor was hard up against the guardrail, sparks spraying, metal on metal. Crushed by its huge weight, bolts gave way, posts snapped, and a swath of corrugated railing swung away slowly like a massive gate. Naomi wrenched at the wheel, pulling hard left. The car careened across the highway and crashed through the fortuitous opening as the truck bore down on them. Its massive bumper clipped them from behind, sending the vehicle in a carom shot out into the dark. With Naomi's foot jammed on the brake pedal and locked on full throttle, the car twisted out over the canal with its engine roaring.

Carson heard the bray of his own voice seemingly from a long way off. Then silence as they took flight, Naomi and he, in a dream state of soaring. All seemed normal in the car: the inside temper-ature light indicated sixty-eight degrees, the wipers continued to swipe, and the heater still pushed warm air. From the brunt of the truck's impact, the SUV began to turn, as would a dog rolling onto its back. From the shore, the vehicle's impact on the water would have sounded like a rifle shot followed by an immediate reverbera-tion. Within, the sound was buffered, but the impact was not. The car met the water on its top; the seat belt dug into Carson's torso as he hung upside down. His air bag deployed explosively, filling the air with white powder just before water began to find its way in through the open side window.

Like some reptilian beast, the canal slithered into the car. Carson fought off the airbag and thrashed about groping for his seat-belt release. All the while he was screaming her name: *Naomi! Naomi!* There was no response. He clawed at her deflated airbag but couldn't find her, and the canal continued to force its way in, silently invading the space. Before there was no more space, Carson took one last gulp of air and pushed at the door, yanking at the handle. He couldn't open it against the force of the water. He wasn't a swimmer, never had been. Panic tore at him. He stuck his head out through the partially open window of the capsized vehicle and pushed and twisted using a sudden adrenaline surge of strength. But for what seemed like forever his body still could not be forced through the opening. His lungs were burning—maybe this was the end. He was drawn to merely relax, to let his life slip away, when the car shifted in its slow-motion drift downward, allowing him to squirm through and kick his way up. When his head broke the surface, he gasped and felt the canal pulling him away from the submerging vehicle. He thrashed and kicked as best he could just to stay afloat.

The shoreline was rocky where he finally came out of the water, rocky and unwelcoming. He crawled up above the water line, saturated, shivering uncontrollably. After looking about, searching wild-eyed and gasping, he finally made out an eerie light wavering up from the submerged vehicle's headlights. Regardless of this illusory sign of life, he knew she was dead. Up above, from the same spot where the car had left the road, he saw headlights and the outline of the truck, at rest and ruined. Carson could make out silhouettes of people obviously looking for some sign of the vehicle. Someone was waving a flashlight, and Carson could make out the sound of voices loud and dismayed. He raised an arm to wave but slumped down, unable to call out. He could only watch and inhale deeply as his body attempted to regain its equilibrium.

Cold was his immediate enemy. The rain was still coming down, unyielding and drenching; he could feel his core cooling. He tried to stand but kept sagging back down. After a blur of elapsed time, he heard voices of men making their way down over the rocks to the water line. One carried a wavering flashlight. Carson watched them tentatively approach the shore.

It was then, right then, that he made the decision. He remained still and watched.

Whoever held the flashlight moved its beam back and forth above the dark water; the voices were questioning and hyper. Carson lay collapsed in the dark, maybe thirty yards away; he made no attempt to be seen or heard. One of the men futilely yelled, "Hello? Are you there?" None of the men plunged into the cold canal in a valiant effort—*who could blame them,* he thought. One of them said, "Be damned, the headlights 'er still working."

Carson began to crab crawl backward over the rocks, deeper into the darkness. He could feel his body temperature continuing to drop. The shivering brought to bear his limited understanding of hypothermia, of how it progresses until the body gives up. His denim pants, running shoes, and chambray shirt were combined into a saturated heat-draining encasement. The men at the shoreline finally went away and clamored back up the rocky slope, following the bouncing flashlight beam and chattering. More people were standing on the roadway now, looking down. Carson's shivering was more constant. After the two men had gone away and he heard nothing more, he rose up and began to slowly make his way across the rocks, lurching and wobbling away from the accident until he was clearly out of view. His body was beginning to fight his mental directives. His breathing was more difficult. He moved beneath the canopy of a big Doug fir somewhat out of the rain and sagged down to calm himself and think.

The warble of a siren broke in; it aroused him, and he struggled to rise up. With the rescuers now on site making it an official misadventure, Carson knew that he had to move on, leave Naomi behind, and accept the decision he'd made. He crawled over the rocks up and across the scraggly grass and brush until he reached the guardrail. He grabbed onto it and looked back toward the stranded trailer and its askew rack of cars; one was dangling over the side, nose down. The cluster of people milling about had turned as one when the emergency rescue van arrived. Its siren died with a burp while the strip of red and blue lights atop the cab continued to oscillate, the eerie throbbing pulse reflecting off everything and everyone around it. From where he crouched, Carson watched, mesmerized by the scene, finding it hard to assimilate that the embroilment he was witnessing had anything to do with him. Or Naomi. Men erupted from the fire department rescue van and marched forward. The cluster of persons drawn to the drama while on their way to somewhere else met them and began talking and gesticulating. It was fascinating to watch people who were desperate to find, maybe even rescue, people they didn't know—and to be one of those sought was stranger still.

In his dulled state, Carson shivered, watched the activity for a time, then swung first one leg over the guardrail then the other and took a tottering step forward. The instinct to survive welled up; he wanted to live, and those anonymous people could save him. But when he saw the firefighters climb over the railing and begin descending to the canal shoreline, he stopped and took a few halting steps backward. Moments later, a few of the onlookers clamored over and followed the emergency professionals down the slope. Carson came out of the shadows and looked down, following the descent of the rescuers. She was gone—he knew that. There was nothing he could have done to save her. He was convinced—nothing. She'd never worn a seat belt. There had been no response when he yelled her name in the car; she must have died on impact. She must have, he reasoned.

He thought of their last hours together. He thought of what they had argued about and deeper still what he had decided to do about it even then. Now the possibilities he had considered no longer mattered. When he had let the rescuers pass, in his mind there was no turning back. He had to move on; it was done. And yet he remained, standing in the dark and the rain, watching the scene of alarmed strangers scrabbling down to the black water, a collection of the curious, drawn to the calamity of persons unknown. He shuddered with the realization that the woman he'd loved, made love to, and fought with, she was out there—in the water, alone, and dead. A car suddenly approached, spraying water in its passing. Carson flinched, drew close to the railing, and walked away, down the highway, along the stark white fog line. The going was slow, and he had no idea how far he would have to go to find shelter or warmth. And then what? Who was he? Why was he soaked? Whenever a car approached, he turned away, his back to the road. Perhaps ten minutes after he began walking, another vehicle with emergency lights flashing approached. Carson clambered over the rail and hunched down. The car flew by silently, no siren; it was a police car of some jurisdiction. His heart was beating hard, and he had begun to rethink his decision to not step forward and identify himself. Was this idiocy? Of course, but it was done—or it was just the beginning of done.

After what seemed like an hour, but was certainly not, Carson saw lights ahead and plodded up on a low-budget motel called The Waterside. A sign on the office door said to ring the night bell for service. He stood shivering and contemplated a warm room and clean bed, but he had no clever way of explaining his predicament: soaked, no car, no luggage, and no explanation. He went on, passing darkened houses, some with cars crowding the driveways, likely those of slumbering Thanksgiving families such as the one he'd left, which seemed long ago now.

The house he decided on sat among several squat buildings that were dark, blinds drawn, all in a state of nocturnal solitude. He had noted signs offering most for vacation rentals. The one he approached was a small flat-roofed structure with weathered cedar shakes. There was no car in the carport. In the dark, with the rain peppering his already drenched body, he fumbled at a side door, which was locked and unyielding. Then he moved to the deck side facing the canal and found the sliding door there secured. He stood under the overhanging eave out of the rain and massaged his numb hands before shuffling back to the side door and testing it again. His breathing was more shallow and rapid now.

In a desperate thrust he put his shoulder into the door, only to sag down gasping. Then he laughed; no sound came, just the movement of his head and open mouth. The mirth was due to how ridiculous he was at that moment. He could die; in fact he surely would if his muscles refused to respond. They'd find him there, propped up against the door, eventually determine who he was, and speculate why and how the idiot ended up so far from the scene of the accident and his wife's death. He sniffed and knew that Naomi would roar with delight at his pathetic and blundered attempt to get away from her; even when she was dead he couldn't do it. A shudder shook him. His eyes suddenly snapped open wide. He had a clearing of the fog in his head and knew—knew he had to reverse the plummeting of his body temperature. He rolled onto his right shoulder and struggled to a knee and grabbed at the doorknob to pull himself up. He leaned against the building, panting. When the door again refused to yield, Carson backed away and gathered his waning strength. This was it; it had to be. It wasn't; he bounced back. His eyes watered, he leaned on his knees, and he felt the lure of death. Out on the highway a truck hit its manifold brake. The sharp burp of noise broke through; his head shook. This time the doorjamb splintered, and he spilled through, falling onto the floor and losing consciousness.

Awakening was painful. His chest burned with each breath. His head was swimming in a pool of debris he could not make out. It was dark, nearly black. He sat up and opened his eyes wide, trying to see. Just the trace of light cast from some exterior source seeped in through the open doorway. He scooted across the floor, shoved the door shut with a foot, and for the first time since before the accident, felt safe. The evolution of learning where he was came slowly: the floor (linoleum tile), the smell of the cold house (stale odors left behind by others, indescribable scents), the sound of an appliance running (the refrigerator humming), and the impression of refuge (feeling enveloped, walls all around, secure). All was black. He dozed.

Naomi came to him. Her smile was wide and condescending. She was grinning at him through the wavering green of water, shaking her head. Then she drifted down, raising one arm as she sank into the liquid dark. She was gone.

-2-

He opened his eyes. His mind floundered. He moved his stiffened legs, rolled and leveraged up onto one elbow. It came to him with a suddenness that drove him back down. Water was over him again, pulling at him, not wanting to let him rise. He gagged and coughed and sobbed. The sound of his own utterance was strange, hoarse, another's voice even.

He shivered, though not as violently as before, and came up on his feet, where he swayed in the darkness. The small house was quiet and cold. With one hand held out, he began to explore, bumping first into a wall then emerging into the kitchen, where dark gray light stood outside the windows. A clock on the stove broadcast the time in green numerals: 3:20. Carson moved to the kitchen counter and leaned on it, palms down flat, and felt the need to quench a sudden thirst. A cupboard yielded glasses and cups; he picked one and turned on the sink tap and gulped until he was sated. He shivered some more against the clamminess of his clothes.

What was this place? How long before someone came and discovered his break-in? He moved about, finding two bedrooms, a bathroom, and a spacious living room; rustic furniture sat sentry-like arrayed before a small stone fireplace. He closed himself into the bathroom and flipped the light switch; the light over the sink flared on and caused him to blink. The face in the medicine cabinet mirror must have been his, but it was tortured: drawn, eyes shot with blood, hair a damp tangle, a scarlet cut across the bridge of his nose, and a brow creased in an expression of bewilderment. The haggard image wasn't him, not the same thirty-eight-year-old, fit, and reasonably good-looking personage he viewed each morning as he shaved. But for his unique eyes, each of a different color—left blue, right brown—(heterochromia iridum, his eye doctor told him when he was a teenager) and a hairline scar on his lower lip from a bicycle accident when nine, the face seemed that of someone else. He blinked into those eyes then sagged onto to the toilet seat lid and leaned on his elbows and stared at the floor, at the blue and white striped bath mat there. What was this horror story? It couldn't be, it hadn't happened, not like it was coming to him—again. The tears came once more, as did the rack of uncontrollable sobs. Then abruptly he stiffened and sat upright. He reached out, tore off a wad of toilet paper, wiped his eyes, and blew his nose. There was no time to harbor regret; he had to get it together and decide where he went from here.

First he had to get out of the damp clothes. He took the risk of turning on a nightstand lamp in one of the bedrooms and sorted through the clothes hanging in the closet. Not much, but what was there among men's clothes was a close-enough fit. He stripped down naked, laid his wet things out to dry, and put on a pair of jeans and a flannel shirt he'd found. The warmth and dryness was a solace. His leather wallet was wet and slick, and everything was soaked. He spread the contents on the kitchen counter: plastic cards, drivers license, business cards, photos, and cash. The cash was around the five hundred dollars he usually carried. He laid out each bill carefully to dry; it would be his only liquidity for a while. His credit cards would be too easy to track, as well as personal checks; he couldn't use anything that revealed that he was still alive.

Gradually the dark gray turned to early light. Carson walked to various windows and peered out to get a sense of where he was and how safe from discovery. The heavy rain had let up; only a soft drizzle continued. He knew that he couldn't stay long, but he had to rest before he set out to—wherever. When hunger hit him, he looked through the cupboards and the refrigerator and found cans of soup, chili, even eggs left behind by the last inhabitants. He scrambled four eggs, heated up a can of chicken noodle soup, and consumed all as if it was a gourmet meal. There was a coffee maker but no coffee. He did find some stray tea bags and heated water on the stove.

He spent the day regaining his strength and drying his clothes in front of a wall heater in the bathroom, but mostly he wandered the small house fretting over what now? He needed a plan, but none came, certainly not one fully formed. Once he stood at the deck side door and looked out over the canal and slipped into a fugue state: he was again in the car with Naomi, sparks were flying off the guardrail, and then they were in flight above the canal. When, in his mind, the car hit the water, he was jolted back. He leaned his forehead against the cool of the glass door and said her name: Naomi. After he re-lived the horror again, the torment seemed to lessen some—but for how long? He didn't know, just that it would return, that it would hold him in bondage forever. There was no justification for what he'd done—he knew that. Crawling away into the dark, no matter how he could make a case in his defense, was beyond defensible. He repeat-edly wandered the house and peered out of every window. Several times he went to the back bedroom and looked out through the slated shades to determine where he was and to get a feel for any immediate danger of being discovered in the house by its owner or suddenly ar-riving guests. Cars, delivery vans, log trucks moved back and forth on the highway in a continuous motorcade; twice he saw someone walk-ing by on the shoulder of the road, but neither the man in denims and a heavy coat or the woman out for her power walk looked his way. On two occasions, he saw a small public bus with the letters MTA on its side pass by then slow and turn off. He watched and wondered if that could be his way to escape. He raided the cupboard again, finishing the last of the eggs, a couple of cans of chili, even a tin of sardines. When darkness came, he crawled under a quilt and slept on top of the bed. In the morning he took a shower in cold water then cold-shaved using a razor and shave cream found in the medicine cabinet. He was drawing the blade down his neck when his hand trembled; he lowered the razor, and all that he was opting to leave behind him flooded in: how the news of his supposed death would play out, how his family would be affected not knowing he lived, how their deaths, his and Naomi's, would be absorbed. But of course he knew why he had done this thing in this way; he had chosen such an absurd act to avoid one person—his father. To actually do what he intended, he had to do it away from the person to whom he had conceded his identity, his very self. This time it would be different. This time he would set the rules.

He finished shaving and pushed his fears away as best he could for the moment. He put on his dried clothes but kept those borrowed and stuffed them into a small backpack he'd liberated, likewise a lightweight jacket and a baseball cap with *Hood Canal* stitched on it. He shoved the stiff dried money along with his credit cards and driver's license into his still damp wallet and wiggled it into his back pocket. Now he had to distance himself from this place.

About half an hour before the time he'd seen the bus the day before Carson exited the house. He left a note and fifty dollars: *Sorry, I needed a place to be for a bit. A Traveler.* The broken door closed snuggly. He edged out onto the carport, saw no one, and crossed the highway. There was no hue and cry, no bellowing of his name, nor did an elderly man heading the opposite way pay him any heed. He squared the backpack on his shoulders and walked south on the shoulder of the highway, keeping his head down and the ball cap low over his brow. In a few minutes he reached what he thought was the turn off point he'd seen the MTA van use. The bus stop was a short walk up that street at the Hood Canal Visitor Center. Carson stood back from a young woman with a toddler and an older woman who was beaming in grandmotherly fashion. It was surreal to be posing as an anonymous person waiting to board the bus, not as someone thought to have drowned in the canal not so far away. He smiled thinking perhaps he should introduce himself. *Hello, I am the dead man you've been hearing about.* Or had they?

After a short wait, the little bus appeared. A smallish man wearing a billed cap levered the door open and greeted each woman and the child by name. When Carson asked how much, he was told it was free within Mason County. *No charge.* He nodded and took a seat toward the back and held the backpack in his lap.

"So like I was telling you, Steve, they only found but the one body." The speaker, sitting right across from the driver, was a big-bodied man, probably in his seventies, bald, wearing plastic-rimmed glasses that he kept shoving up on his nose.

Carson stiffened and stared at the man. Would he suddenly turn and point to him: *That's him, the one who drowned they can't find!*

The driver checked his side mirrors and eased away. "So you said."

"Yep, a woman, no sign of her husband. Not hide nor hair."

"Maybe she was alone, maybe."

"No," said the old man, leaning forward. "Boys over to the fire station said her husband was with her. Least ways that's what family sources told 'em anyhow. Nope, he's out there somewhere floating or maybe on the bottom I guess."

The driver eased the little bus out onto 101. "Darn shame. How'd it happen, you hear?"

"Yessir, truck carrying a load of cars slid into 'em."

"And the car, it went out into the canal?" asked the driver.

"Sent that fancy SUV flying."

"My stars," uttered one of the women. "Horrible."

"Yessir," the big man folded his arms in an authoritative pose. "Been a long spell since anything's busted through one of them guard rails. They was probably going too fast. Was late, dark, no traffic, raining hard, they was speeding's my guess. Then the truck blockin' the road and all. Yessir, all she wrote."

Carson pulled the backpack closer to his body and turned to look out the side window. *Naomi always drove too fast,* he thought. *So the blowhard had that part right.*

Naomi's death didn't wipe away what had brought them to the edge less than forty-eight hours earlier. Not that it had been the only time they'd approached that same low point. Carson had first seen the beautiful girl who would become his wife when they were in high school, he the upperclassman, she the spirited, leggy knockout he was drawn to—as was every other male in the school. But she chose Carson Barrus. She chose him for her own reasons: he was not unattractive, but the Barrus family had money, deep pockets, and position. Naomi came from a modest background and had always wanted more, so in her self-absorbed, narcissistic way she set out to capture the flag. She had a goal, and she reached it. She followed Carson to the University of Washington by attracting a full-ride scholarship; then she waited while he earned an MBA at Wharton. All the while she kept close to the Barrus family, especially her father-in-law-to-be. Cadence Leland Barrus, known to one and all as CB, had come home to Seattle from Harvard at the urging of his father to help run Barrus Properties, a collection of Class B buildings and parking lots his father had purchased block by block beginning in the 1950s. When Leon Barrus had stepped aside in old age, CB assumed management of the modest company and aggressively plowed ahead, buying up prime real estate, including lucrative downtown Seattle parking lots, warehouses, office buildings, and a dozen or more apartment buildings. When his father passed, CB lost no time in leveraging everything he could from the company's assets and then forcing his siblings to give him total control.

From the sidelines, while playing her hand for Carson, Naomi had witnessed CB's aggressiveness, his success, and his strong personality; she was drawn to the flame and hoped that within his son a similar strength to dominate would emerge.

"Is there a way out of this maze of your devious maneuvers?" had been his face-off with her in late the afternoon of Thanksgiving. They were in the kitchen at the big house on the Dungeness Spit, situated in the closed community of rich folks' playhouses.

Her gotcha smile yanked at his insides. "That your way of saying I'm a bitch?" she came back. "Devious maneuvers? That the best you have?" She laughed.

She laughed, and he wanted to slap her. He wanted to, but of course he wouldn't. Maybe she would have had more respect if he fought back, truly fought back and stood up for himself with her.

"Naomi," he said, exasperated. "What is it you want from me? What?"

He recalled now how she had simply stared at him, how her smirk had just hung there between them. "Something," she had responded. "Anything."

"What?" He knew his voice had cracked and was almost the sound of a petulant child.

He looked out the side window of the bus and heard again her response. "Inner stuff, Carson. Been waiting for some inner stuff. " When his eyes widened, she said, "Hey, you asked. And you know what I mean, too. Don't you?"

Carson remembered standing there amid leftover turkey and ham and yams and pecan pie. He remembered his mother coming into the kitchen just then and seeing her sweet smile fade as she sensed things weren't right. His mother's withdrawal brought tears to his eyes.

He had drawn in a deep breath then and looked into Naomi's eyes again. "Tell me," he'd said, "what besides wealth and status and things have you wanted from our marriage? I'd like to know. What?"

At first her expression blanked, her eyes widening, but then it came back with her mouth opening slightly in that infuriating smile. She gave out with a small huff of a laugh. "Nothing else. You nailed it. Exactly."

That was when Carson saw his father in the kitchen doorway. He shuddered when he saw that CB's mouth held the very same smirk he had beheld from his wife.

The MTA bus pulled off at the next stop and took on another female passenger. The driver called the woman's name as she boarded; she merely nodded. She was maybe forty, wearing denims, a hooded raincoat, and a knit hat. She made her way up the short aisle and exchanged passing eye contact with Carson before taking a seat across from him. Just that brief visual connection sent a chill through him. He turned his head and looked out the window as the bus jostled back onto the highway. The view blurred as he considered himself a fugitive. Can you be a fugitive from your own death? Can you walk away from supposedly being killed and be free and clear if you don't declare yourself alive?

The old guy up front was pontificating about what it was like to drown. "Like them people in that car did," he said, as if from personal experience. The driver just shook his head. From there Carson was drawn back to the last minutes in the car. The blowback from their face-off in the kitchen couldn't be left twisting in the wind. They both knew that. It was a matter of who would pick up the threads. He had.

"So you never actually fell in love with me, is that it?"

In the light cast from the dashboard he could see her face and the tightening of her jaw. "I couldn't afford to fall in love," she said finally. "I had goals. The ones you said. How'd you put it: wealth, stuff, and status?"

"Wealth, status, and things," he corrected.

"Exactly, those are the ones."

"My god, Naomi, where did I ever fit in?"

"Carson, Carson," she chided. "You were the gateway in. So you *were* special."

He'd kicked the dashboard with his foot and cursed. Naomi had laughed hard and hit the horn as if in celebration.

"You wanted me to be my father, didn't you?"

She didn't respond.

"Well, I'm not my father. Never will be, thank god. A controlling, conniving, insensitive, bastard." He waited a beat. "And worse."

Naomi looked over at him but said nothing.

He stared into her face just before she turned back to her driving. "I know, Naomi." He grunted a laugh. "I know all about it. I've known for some time."

She had gripped the wheel and stared ahead. "What's that?"

His laugh was high and sour. "What's that?" he echoed. "What's that indeed? Tell me, is he a good lay?"

"Carson."

"Is it the sex or sleeping with the alpha dog of the clan?"

After a long pause she said, "So you know. Who...?"

"My aunt. Purl, she told me."

Naomi's face contorted into a quizzical expression. "My god," she said. "Were you ever going to...?"

His face burned red. "Pathetic, right?

They fell silent then. Before she could respond, a truckload of cars interfered.

-3-

The bus made one more stop before pulling into a big shopping venue off 101 on the outskirts of the town of Shelton. Carson got off when most everyone else did and stood looking across a sea of cars parked nose-to-nose next to a Fred Meyer supermarket. The busy intersection with retail shops and gas stations on all sides gave him a sense of anonymity—and relief. He walked about for a while, just walked and breathed and felt safe in the turmoil of cars coming and going and people pushing grocery carts—no one seemed to even see him. At a Jack in the Box he ordered a chicken sandwich and coffee from a kid with acne who smiled and gave him the company greeting but never looked him in the eye.

He took his food to a booth, pulled the paper wrapper off, sunk his teeth into the bun, and relished the too salty, too-battered flavor; he was famished. A pile of discarded newspapers caught his eye, and he wondered if the accident had merited any coverage. The local paper was a weekly; it didn't have anything in it. He sorted through the pile and found a crumpled issue of the Seattle Times. There it was at the bottom of page one. He stopped chewing and felt his heart bump. The headline: "Seattle couple die in Hood Canal accident," seemed to float off the page and suspend itself before his eyes. A mouthful of chicken and bread went down in a painful lump. He choked, drank some coffee and stared at the paper, eyes watering. A picture of the two of them together was inset in the article. It was one he knew to be framed and sitting on end tables and mantels. It was taken in a portrait studio maybe two years before. Naomi had wanted a nice picture of them for family to have. He read the story slowly, his mouth drying as he consumed the account of their deaths: *Hoodsport, WA— A couple driving home from Sequim following Thanksgiving with family died early Friday morning when their SUV was forced off Highway 101 into Hood Canal by a truck that had lost traction on the rain-slickened road. Naomi Barrus, 36, and Carson Barrus, 38, apparently drowned after their vehicle plunged into the rain-swollen canal. The body of Naomi Barrus, assumed to have been the driver, was recovered; the remains of her husband Carson Barrus have not been found. Divers have been brought in to search for the missing body. The accident happened Friday morning at approximately 1:30 a.m. The driver of the truck, R.J. Bunter, was not cited. His auto transport truck carried cars destined for Port Angeles. Driving conditions at the time were severe with heavy rains. Bunter reported that his truck lost traction on a curve at the same time as the Barrus vehicle approached. Carson Barrus is the son of CB Barrus of the well-known Barrus Properties Company of Seattle.*

Carson read the article one more time before folding the paper and slipping it into the backpack. He got a refill of coffee and sat quietly sipping and thinking back through the horror show and his crazy choice to fade away. He shuddered realizing again that there was no going back—he knew that. How could he explain his actions even if he decided to come forward? Amnesia? A confused state of mind? He downed the coffee in two quick swallows and left the fast food milieu. It had begun to drizzle again, but he barely noticed it. His mind was on his further exodus. He had to get a ride, hitch a ride, something he had never done and had even disdained when passing a hitchhiker with a thumb out. He'd decided to approach some long haul truck drivers, see if he could get a lift that way. But before trying that he went into the supermarket and found the electronics department. He bought a prepaid cell phone for ten bucks, entered a fictitious name, address, and zip code, purchased fifty minutes of time, and went out to look for a friendly big rig driver.

A young guy wearing a hoodie and pumping gas at a Chevron service station mumbled something and pointed when Carson asked if there was a truck stop nearby. It took about fifteen minutes walking on the highway shoulder to reach the Puget Tide Truck Plaza. Carson approached the truck stop store, stood under the overhang by the front entrance out of the wet, and looked out over the array of trucks: some parked, some being fueled, others departing. Drivers in all shapes and sizes, ages and attire, men and women alike, went in and out of the plaza shop. Carson went inside, filled a coffee cup from a vending machine, picked out a ready-to-go ham sandwich and a package of Oreo cookies, paid a big-bodied woman with dyed blonde hair and an attitude, then milled about like he belonged. Mostly people ignored him and went about their business or chatted it up with a fellow driver. It was like a high school reunion in some respects.

When he'd ramped up his courage, he went outside, took in the scene, and began walking among the trucks. The first driver he approached drove for a big name brand transport company. He just laughed and pulled himself up into the cab. "No way pal. Against company policy to give rides. They'd have my ass." Carson discovered quickly that all the established haulers had hard and fast rules against hitchhikers. Besides, where did he want to go? Had to have a destination. East, he would go east. The first trucker that looked like an independent, a squatty guy with a big gut and long gray hair, was hauling apples south and had his own rule: no riders. Carson kept trying. He chose the white trailer declaring *Irv's Fast Enough Freight* in faded red lettering because it had a sad-sack look to it. Carson conjured a big smile and made his approach. The signage on the door of the aging Kenworth tractor read: Irv Montee Trucking, Cross Wind, Missouri. A thin man wearing a cowboy hat, worn Levi's, and a plaid shirt with the tail out was hitting his tires all around with a ball peen hammer checking for soft ones, like a wrangler checking his horses hooves for a loose shoe. The sound of the idling diesel engine was that of logging chains rattling in a barrel. The rig was tired. Its once bright red cab was oxidized to a dirty pink, its massive chrome bumpers were scuffed and scarred and its wheel rims were covered in road grime. But it still boasted twin bright chrome exhaust stacks that rose up behind the cab. When the driver came back around, he tossed the hammer in a toolbox and pinched a cigarette from his mouth, dropped it, and let it smolder. He was grabbing a handle to climb aboard when Carson came up. The driver looked down and squinted but didn't say a word.

"Howdy," Carson said. All he got back was a cast-eye look. "Question. You ever take on riders?"

The man stepped down and pulled a pack of smokes from his shirt pocket. "Nope."

Carson nodded. "Okay, just wondering."

"Usually, that is. Mostly my old lady is with me. But this time she ain't." He thumbed a butane lighter and held it out in front of a fresh cigarette until it glowed. "Laid up."

"I see." Carson brightened.

"Broke her ankle. Been a bitch 'cause she splits the driving. Not to mention our conjugal events." He hooked a thumb up over his shoulder. "In our sleeper there. Sure miss them." He cackled a raspy bark, showing a missing front tooth.

Carson looked up at the big box of a cab and managed an awkward nod.

"Where you headed?"

Carson coughed. "East, I guess," said.

The man laughed another hoarse chuckle. "East, you guess. Now that takes in a large bit of real estate. Can you dial that in some?"

Carson rolled a kernel of gravel with a toe and smiled. "To tell the truth, I'm just setting out. No destination."

"Shit, you're one of those." Man dipped his head and shook it side to side. "Gonna be a man of the road, are you?"

Carson's face reddened. "Don't know about that. Just needing a ride and saw you were from Missouri and thought you might be heading back that way."

"Uh-huh." The man took another draw on his smoke. "Well, I am heading that way. Took on a load of pallets and wood stove pellets so I'm not deadheading back home. Have to pay the rent."

"Would you like some company for a spell? My name's…Bill, Bill Tolliver, by the way." Carson sort of choked the name out, the one he used when buying the prepaid phone.

"That right? Well, you can be Peter Pan for all I care. I'm Irv Montee, as you can see." He flipped his smoke away and studied Carson. "You running from something—or someone?" When Carson stared back wide-eyed, the man said, "I was just joking. As long as you're not running from the law, we're good. You aren't, are you?"

Carson felt his throat tighten. "No, not that I know of."

"Guess a fella would know if he was. Okay, climb aboard. Guess I can handle it for a spell. But I ain't looking for a Chatty Cathy. Get enough of that with my wife. Been enjoying my solitude."

Carson nodded. "Understood."

"Okay then, how far you wanting to go? Not all the way to Missouri, I 'spect."

Carson hesitated, looked straight in the man's eyes, and shook his head side to side. "No, not going that far, I don't think. Which way you heading out?"

"Oh, I'll go on down to Portland then out I-84. Can drop you off most anyplace between here and Crosswind, Missouri."

"How about I let you know?"

The man shrugged. "Whatever. Unless I tire of you before that."

"Fair enough," Carson replied.

"Fair won't have nothing to do with it."

-4-

The lavish room, excessive in its furnishings, was becalmed in anguish, stunned disbelief written on every face. A plate of Vienna finger cookies sat neglected and irrelevant. Cups of coffee had cooled. Occasional hums of grief caused eyes to look down or mouths to be drawn in. CB Barrus surveyed those assembled, a bemused expression on his face, and cleared his throat.

"They may never find him," he said. When heads turned and eyes widened, he added, "They often don't."

BeBe Barrus, still in deep shock, looked at her husband, seemed to consider what he had uttered, then raised her hands to cover her face. Her small body shook as she cried silently.

"For god's sake, CB, can't you just keep your cold analysis to yourself for once." Purl Strutt, CB's sister, glared at her older brother.

"I was only suggesting…"

"We know what you were suggesting," Purl retorted. "Just put a cork in it for now, will you?"

The room grew quiet once more. All eyes remained fixed on CB as his jaw muscles flexed from Purl's rebuke. She was the only person who ever got away with challenging his autocratic hold within the family.

"There's nothing new, then?" Rove Barrus interceded in his soft voice. Rove was the younger brother to CB and Purl. Their playful father had given each a name depicting motion: Cadence (beat of rhythmical flow), Purl (gentle movement), Rove (to wander).

CB looked at Purl and gave a condescending smile. She lowered her eyelids before saying, "No, Rove, nothing new."

"They've brought in divers, right?" asked Stuart Barrus, Carson's older brother, looking toward his father.

CB eyed his son, studied him for a moment as if the questioner and the question were out of order; he merely nodded and looked away as he was wont to do whenever his oldest child addressed him. What else would he do with this progeny of his who had divorced some years back, declared himself a gay man, and had been in a so-called *relationship* for ten years with an accountant the name of Ned Kind?

The devastating news of the grisly accident had pinned the family beneath a blanket of disbelief. Sadly sweet BeBe had been the one who took the call from a Mason County sheriff's deputy; she was the one asked to verify that she had a son named Carson and he a wife named Naomi; she had been the one to first hear the words: *There has been an accident.* CB had picked up the phone from the floor after it had been shocked from her hand in a spasm of agony; he listened and coolly confirmed the worst news ever. He had then contacted the family one by one, recounting the mishap, as he put it, in exactly the same words each time as if reporting the weather forecast.

Now they were gathered to do the only thing possible: be together and keep asking why. That and wait for the unlikely outcome of finding Carson alive, or at least recovered. What else to do besides congregate and swim in the unbelievable?

"What of Naomi's kin?" Lillian Barrus's octogenarian voice rose strong and clear. She looked first at Purl and then between Rove and CB. "They have to be beside themselves with grief. Have you heard from them?"

CB looked at his mother and saw his nose and his eyes on loan from her. He noted the lines and etchings of her skin that he was sure to assume from her genes sometime soon. "The Saunders have asked to be left alone to mourn the loss of Naomi," he said. "We won't be combining our grief or services, it seems."

"My word," Lillian responded. "Why is that? What a sad thing."

"No idea," CB responded. But of course he knew exactly why Jack Saunders had called with that ultimatum. He recalled clearly the day Saunders had barged into his office downtown and roared his wrath over the revelation that CB had had an affair with his daughter. It had been most amusing to CB to see this big, red-faced man emanate spittle with each word of vitriol as he berated CB for something the man's daughter and he had thoroughly enjoyed. "So what now, Jack?" CB had asked calmly. "Going to tell Carson? Is Naomi going to tell Carson? I thought not. You and Alice coming out to Sequim for Thanksgiving? We have lots of room, love to have you." Even now, CB had to smile remembering the scene of Jack Saunders standing in rigid apoplexy before his shoulders sagged in defeat, shaking his head at CB's smugness and leaving quietly. They didn't come for Thanksgiving.

"Well," Lillian said, bobbing her head in self-approval. "We'll certainly send flowers."

"No," CB enjoined. "We won't do that, either. Mother, now that's just the way it is."

The old woman clamped her mouth shut and pursed her lips and the room was quiet once again. The only sound was that of bottoms shifting about on fine leather furniture until a young woman wearing a starched white blouse and black slacks came into the room and approached CB. She leaned over and whispered to him. He nodded and pushed himself up out of his wingback chair.

"Okay, food's on," he said calmly. "In the dining room. Need to keep our strength up." He and Purl exchanged dissimilar expressions: his self-satisfied, hers reproaching. He led the way. The long, polished black walnut table, now covered by a white tablecloth, was laden with salads, platters of sliced meats, bowls of vegetables, and bottles of wine with barely room for people's dinner plates. Each person found a chair and settled down in silence.

"Nice feast," Purl said as she spread an elegant napkin over her lap. "What are we celebrating?"

CB shot her a frozen rope stare. "You're welcome."

"We could have each brought something," Purl said. "No one's hungry anyway."

"Speak for yourself," CB responded, stabbed a slice of cold prime rib, and dropped it onto his plate. "Guess grief makes me hungry. Surprisingly."

"Not really," Purl retorted.

All eyes around the table were locked open, looking back and forth between the two. No one else spoke. Only Rove filled his plate with food, his expression one of bland disregard. He'd tried being the buffer between his siblings when they were kids but had given it up years back for his own sanity.

"Where are my great-grandchildren? That's what I want to know." Lillian held a silver fork in the air and stared at her empty plate. "They should be here. Carson loved them."

Silence. The lineup of absent grandchildren was rarely spoken of. There were three of them: Rove's two sons, one living in DC and the other in Chicago, and Purl's daughter, living in San Francisco. Rove had two grandchildren from one son, none yet from the youngest, and Purl had one grandchild from her daughter. None of that Barrus generation ever returned home to Seattle with any frequency. All three of them had left town as soon as they were able, saying goodbye to their roots and especially their grandfather and the control he claimed over the family's life, pursuits, and their very souls—as Purl's daughter Katie had proclaimed when she packed everything she owned right out of college and followed her eventual husband to the Bay Area.

"Mom, I can't come," had been Katie's response to Purl. "Not yet, anyway. It's awful, I know, and I love Carson...well loved him, I guess. But I'm not into sitting around that mausoleum listening to grandpa tell us all how we should handle this family crisis."

"I know, Katie," Purl said.

"I mean it. I couldn't take it. I won't take it." She hesitated. "Not anymore."

Purl laughed lightly. "Aren't you the lucky one?"

"Besides, when did CB ever show a smidgen of compassion for anyone? I'll bet before you know it, it will be Carson's fault for dying."

"Katie."

"It's true, and you know it." She promised to make the trip up when a service was actually scheduled. Rove had similar calls from his sons, so no great grandchildren for grandma Lillian, let alone great-great-grandchildren.

Food was picked at. The only sound was the modest ting of silverware against plates. Even with a gray sky outside, a field of light came through the skylights set in the vaulted ceiling and gave iridescence to the room. Stuart Barrus looked up while chewing a piece of ham and studied his father; the light reflected off CB's forehead where his hair had receded. Stuart, who had inherited his mother's genes for hair, smiled knowing how his father deplored losing his hair. He who made cynical comments about his son retaining a lush shock of hair from his childhood as if it was akin to keeping baby teeth—and of course the unspoken implication was that keeping one's hair was due in part to being gay.

Stuart put his fork down, set his elbows on the table, and interlaced his fingers. After a moment he said for all to hear, "This is ghastly." The faces around the table turned his way, and everyone ceased their eating—as if stop-action in a film. "He's...he's gone— my little brother." Tears formed, and he raised a hand to his mouth. "I feel cheated. We were really just getting to know each other, to really know what's inside," he managed to get out on a breathy gasp. "That's selfish, I know but...we were just getting there—"

"No," Rove said. "That's okay. We all...well, we just screw up."

CB smiled and took a swallow of beefy red wine from a big-bowled wine glass. "Eloquent, Rove. Couldn't have said it better myself. Well, I could have but..."

Rove's wife Louise, a pleasant woman of small stature and a loving nature, patted him on the arm and cast CB a withering look; in return she received one of his patented smirks.

"Damn it!" Stuart expelled the words in a harsh burst. "He's gone, don't you get it? And we're sitting here eating catered food and saying nothing."

Ned Kind, the accountant and Stuart's partner, had been quiet and unobtrusive from the moment they had arrived. He had said nothing, merely smiled softly and held his own counsel and stood back. Now he raised an arm and laid it across Stuart's shoulders and squeezed his support. Down the table, CB winced and took another drink of wine.

"Yes, you could call him a good boy," CB said. "A good man. But weak, I'd always hoped for more from him."

The silence was thick, like every ear had been covered. No one even looked toward CB. Most stared at the food on their plates. BeBe's face slackened, and her eyes filled once more.

"Weak?" came Stuart's voice. "What the hell does that mean?"

CB looked toward his son, noted the dead calm, and said, "It means weak. What do you think it means? No backbone."

"My god, Dad," Stuart snapped, "is there no limit to your callous disregard?"

CB twisted his wine glass by its stem and shrugged at Stuart's allegation. "The truth by its very nature is callous."

"The truth?"

With a nod, CB alleged, "Take this…this miserable incident. If Carson had had a bit of backbone, he and Naomi would not have set off in the dead of night. It was obvious he didn't want to go. But he caved, and here we are."

"My god," Purl said with a burst of laughter. "My daughter was right. Katie was right."

"Oh? How so?" CB inquired, retaining his detachment.

"She predicted that you would say it was Carson's own fault for dying." She snickered behind a hand and shook her head.

"Astute is Katie," CB said. "She knows as I do that Carson lacked will."

"No," Purl responded, pointing at her brother, "she knows you are a bastard and wants nothing to do with you. She'll grieve in private and be here when we celebrate Carson's life."

"So be it." CB poured more wine and sat back, comfortable in his isolation.

Later, after the food had been picked over and everyone had suspended grief and willed brave optimism, the sheriff's office called once more. The car had been pulled from the canal; Naomi's remains had been retrieved and collected by a funeral home from Seattle at the behest of her parents. But there was still no sign of a body for Carson Barrus, the assumed other passenger of the vehicle.

BeBe broke down; CB had another glass of wine. Optimism faded.

–5–

Irv Montee pushed the old Kenworth and his load of wooden pallets and stove pellets south down 101 before merging onto I-5 near Tumwater, blaring country music out of his dual-speaker CD player all the way. He smoked non-filter Lucky Strikes one after the other, growled along to the music, and ignored his passenger. Carson held his lip about booming music and smoke floating in the truck's cab, pulled his cap down, and tried to doze. But he couldn't really sleep; at the slightest provocation an endless loop of recurring images ran amok: Naomi crying out, his own yowl, the collision in the canal. When the Kenworth suddenly rocked and Montee cursed and yanked his air horn lanyard, Carson jerked upright, heart pounding.

"Hey howdy," Montee chortled. "You okay there, bub?"

Carson nodded and mumbled. He reset his hat and settled back.

"Ya see that? Dang bonehead up there, one driving that silly-ass Tinkertoy minivan? Pulled right off the shoulder back into this lane without looking. Idiot. Most ran him over."

Carson nodded again and leaned back. Montee eyeballed him, shoved in a different CD, and soon Johnny Cash was singing out of Folsom Prison. In Portland the truck turned east on I-84. On the outer edge of the city, Montee used the Troutdale exit to drop off the freeway near a cluster of roadside gas stations and truck stops. Carson waited in the cab to hold onto his ride while Montee topped off his tanks at a Love's Travel Stop, bought himself a sack of food and more smokes, then hopped right back on the road and ran through the gears back up to speed.

When they were in first sight of the Columbia River, Irv Montee

34

came out of his taciturn shell and yelled, "Big mama," over the top of Cash singing "Dirty Old Egg Sucking Dog". He nodded toward the river and snubbed out his smoke.

Carson jerked out of his nap and knuckled his eyes.

"Looka them whitecaps. Winds really whipping out there today."

"Yeah," Carson coughed and attempted to look interested.

"You been catching a bucketful of zees there, man," Montee said. "Nice having your own chauffeur huh?"

Carson cleared his throat. "No, I mean yes. I just didn't want to cut into your solitude. Like you said. And your music."

"Solitude, huh? Guess I did at that," he said and fell quiet again for a few miles. "Columbia Gorge is a dang wonder," he said suddenly and looked over at Carson. "All that green, them high rocks, prom-ontories they's called, and water gushing down them rock walls. Amazing, man. Right?"

"Uh-huh," Carson responded. "I agree."

"You agree. Wow to that." Montee punched the cigarette lighter on the dash and one-handed another Lucky out of his pack. He took a drag and exhaled out over the steering wheel. "So, you decided? Where you're getting off?"

Carson looked over into the man's lined face and his now humor-less eyes. "Not really. Just thought it would come to me down the road."

"That right? It'll just come to you. Down the road. Well, while you're figuring on that, I've already done figured out where yer gon-na step off." When Caron's eyebrows shot up, Montee chuckled and said, "Yeah, this having company's not my thing. Miss my old lady, but otherwise been enjoying my *solitude,* as you put it."

Carson scooted up in the seat and looked out the windshield. "Okay," he said, caught off guard. "Where you have in mind?"

"There's a spot up ahead right by the Bonneville Dam. I'll drop you off just after we pass through a long tunnel there."

Carson turned in the seat. "What's there?"

Irv Montee snorted and blew smoke. "Nothing. That's the fun

35

part. Think there's a fish hatchery—that's all."

Carson twisted around in the seat, looking ahead and out the side window. "I'll be needing a place to stay for the night and food."

"Look, travelin' man, this'll be a nice test for you. You know, wangle another ride and make your fucking way on down life's highway. What you wanted isn't it? I'm not nobody's wet nurse. Yer a big boy." Montee pulled his eyes back to the road as the big rig passed through a long tunnel. When they emerged, he began braking and pulled onto the shoulder near an exit ramp. Air brakes hissed, and the truck rocked to a stop. "All out for Bonneville Dam," he laughed and held up a small revolver.

"What the hell?" Carson sputtered and leaned against the door. "Man...are you crazy?"

"Could be," Montee grinned. "Whatever. Been giving me some amusement deciding how to eighty-six an airhead wanting adventure on the big bad road. Figured on dumping you somewhere where there's no comforts and let you try and thumb your way outa Dodge. This here's a good spot. So right here's where I off-load you, you putz."

"Put the gun away." Carson clicked out of his seatbelt and gripped the door handle.

Montee's cigarette had burned down; he rolled it to the side of his mouth. "It ain't loaded, you dumb shit." He chuckled and dropped the gun into a cup holder. "Now get your ass outa my rig."

Carson grabbed his backpack and hit the door. As he scrambled out down onto the roadside gravel, Irv Montee flicked his burning cigarette stub out the door at him and shouted, "Shut the damn door, fool."

The truck tugged its trailer back onto the highway, and Carson listened as Irv Montee moved through the gears again. It was sprinkling and cold. He pulled the jacket out of his bag, slipped it on, zipped up, tugged his hat down, and looked back the way they'd come. Cars and trucks emerged from the tunnel's mouth into the rain, raising clouds of mist when they passed. He stepped deeper onto the shoulder away from the wet and took stock. The Bonneville

Dam was north across the freeway, and a ramp ran down from where he stood; a sign said it went to the Cascade Hatchery.

He slipped his arms through the backpack straps and began to walk down the ramp. A stand of conifers, their needles glistening in the mist, buffered the constant drone of cars, RVs and big-rig tires pushing through water up on the freeway. As the vehicular wall of sound fell away, he gained welcome comfort in being alone and in a cloak of some quiet. At the base of the ramp there was a compound of buildings comprising the hatchery: an array of holding tanks, rearing ponds, and something labeled a pollution abatement pond. He gratefully located a public toilet, relieved himself, and stepped back outside thinking only of what lay ahead. The visitor's parking lot was empty, and the facility itself was quiet. He wandered about for a bit and read an information sign that led him to assume that somewhere in the ponds were likely thousands of young Coho salmon fingerlings or smolts waiting to be transferred to some other body of water.

The rain suddenly abated, the sky brightened enough that he felt less cold, and his coat and hat began to dry. He sat on a curb near the exit road and prepared to flag down a ride from someone passing through on the way east; he even practiced a couple of times, once propping up his thumb, the other just waving and pasting a sincere smile on his face. He was dozing in the sparse sun when an older maroon Buick appeared and pulled to a stop in the hatchery parking area. He approached the car and raised his thumb to the elderly shrunken man at the wheel, who looked out through bugged blue eyes and blinked a couple of times before he gunned the car backward and sped away. Carson erupted in laughter and waved his thumb in the air as the car disappeared onto the freeway exit. He had the same luck, though none as explosive, from several other cars that made the detour past the hatchery; in every case Carson was the invisible man.

He paced, sat again, paced some more. The sun reemerged; he stood in its brightness and had the strange sensation of being outside his own skin. It was as if he was standing back, observing himself in the guise of another, someone who just a few hours ago should have died but didn't. He closed his eyes and shook his head. No, it wasn't hours; it was longer than that, but how much longer? And it had been him, not this other self, hadn't it? Yes, of course. He shuddered and wondered what must be going on back where his life should have been. What was happening right then? What about things he would have been a part of: business appointments, the daily routines he would have been engaged in, and what of the house, Naomi's plants, newspapers piling up, the yard man or house cleaner—what of all that? And how were the families handling their deaths and the jarring way they died—supposedly? He imagined there had been a family gathering. He'd already seen news coverage of the car in the canal. Had there been more of that? Had it been it big news? Were they still looking for his body? What plans were being made to memorialize their deaths—the real and the hoax? This plan of his, was it worth the disruption of his feigned demise?

He turned, thumb out, as another car drove by, and he thought it had to be worth it. He had crossed the Rubicon. He had gone this far. If he went back and absorbed the fuss and furor over his no-show death, would he ever have the courage to do what he intended? He knew the answer. It was now that he had to act. Whenever he thought of her, his pain was always the same—always the pain of loss, of course, but mostly the pain of guilt. His baby sister, Aleta Anne, had been gone for two years—that was all, just two years. It felt much longer. His mother found her in the tub. It had been a dark, cold December day in 2005. Aleta was still living at home then; even at the age of 21 she hadn't found the strength to leave and become her true self. She had a modest secretarial job at Barrus Properties; that was the extent of her self-determination. Aleta was beautiful almost beyond description: flawless creamy skin, exquisite cheekbones, her mother's luminous blue eyes, beautiful mouth, and gleaming ash-blonde hair. But more than that, she loved people, and all who knew her adored her. Her sweetness was genuine to her core. There had been many boyfriends in her teen years, but none were good enough, and her father in turn had run each one off. It had been great sport for him. CB's aversion to the young males who came around eventually became legend, and the lovely girl was left alone, isolated from her own life.

Her pregnancy, when revealed, was beyond reversal so had to be concealed—the secrecy enforced by her father. The rest of the family never knew, except for Grandma Lillian who learned of it later and suffered greatly from her knowing. A child was born somewhere. Carson and the rest of the family, unaware of the pregnancy, thought only that Aleta was on an extensive trip to England with a girl friend, as told to them by CB. A birthday gift was the story. That December day in 2005, Aleta drank too much vodka, as she had been doing for some time, ran a warm bath, settled into the tub, and ended her life. It was her son's second birthday, wherever he was. The official cause of death was exsanguination. She had very carefully drawn an X-acto knife up each forearm, had another drink, and slowly drifted away, her life pooling out into the bathwater. BeBe came for her after she didn't come down for dinner. The scream and the wailing of a mother is a sound like no other. CB didn't even climb the stairs, just called 911. They came, the EMTs. They found a pale beautiful young woman soaking in a crimson bath of her own blood. They could find no trace of life to save.

Carson raised his face to the sun and closed his eyes, paying no mind to one more car that passed him by. He said her name on a breath: *Aleta. Little One* he'd called her from the time he was a teenager. She was twelve years younger than he, *a beloved accident* her mother had said too many times to not become a joke in the family. He pulled out the handkerchief that had been in the canal with him, dabbed his eyes, and blew his nose. The guilt he carried with him for Aleta was because he had become aware of the truth when it was too late. He knew that there was a child of hers somewhere, and that child was the source of her decline into depression and alcohol. He knew, and other than grieving her death, did nothing. Grandma Lillian had been his source of information. Ever since he had been a boy, his grandmother was the person he sought out for support and the inside story. Mostly she told him stories of his mother and father that made them laugh. It made him feel better to know those things in the face of a dogmatic father who relished in controlling everything and everyone. When CB wielded his iron hand, Carson could look at him and think of something awkward that he'd done once. It had eased the pain.

Not long after Aleta's death, Carson had one of his regular visits with Lillian. She lived in the city in the historic Proffer Arms, a Barrus property; she'd lived there rent-free for twenty-eight years, ever since Grandpa Leon had died. Carson loved having those little conspiratorial meetings with his grandmother. It seemed to help keep them both from succumbing to the dysfunctional proclivities of the clan. This time the import of their conversation changed and would never return to the trivial vein.

They had shared some of her favorite chamomile tea and Lorna Doone cookies and once more lamented the loss of Aleta. Carson remembered that he broke down again and had to gather himself in his grandmother's restroom that always smelled of flowery potpourri. When he came back out, she had refreshed his tea and added more cookies. She sipped her tea and waited for him to sit back down. He nibbled on a cookie.

After studying him for a long moment, she said, "She had a *child*, Carson." She spoke those four words softly and watched his face.

He leaned forward, still holding half a cookie between thumb and finger, and fixed his eyes on hers. The seconds ticked by; still he stared. "The trip," he said finally.

She nodded. "Yes, the trip."

"It wasn't to England."

"No, it wasn't to England."

"You've known all along?"

She nodded again. "For a long time, anyway."

"And kept it to yourself."

"CB insisted. Carson, I only went along to protect Aleta."

He dropped the cookie remnant onto the plate. "Well, that worked, didn't it?"

"No, it did not." She turned her head toward a sash window letting in gray winter light and sighed. "I thought it best…at the time, to keep quiet—to let CB dictate my silence. To protect her. I spoke with her often and tried to soothe her sorrow. I took her on little trips to the coast, to Victoria—sweet times actually, but not enough. She was tortured, that's the only way to describe it. In her own private hell. Often she would disappear for days. No one knew were she was. CB would put out what amounted to a dragnet until she was found."

"My god," Carson gasped. "I…I never knew. How could I have not known?"

"Because," she said, before swallowing a quavering breath. "Because you weren't supposed to know—ever. No one was. I only knew because of my attempts to be close to her and because I knew about the child. CB was compelled to tell me."

"Where did she go? When she disappeared, where had she gone?"

Lillian drew her fingers beneath her eyes wiping at the tears that had come—again. "Different places. After she'd consumed enough alcohol, she would end up in a motel out on Aurora Avenue or in Belltown. Once they found her in San Francisco."

"Was she alone? When they found her."

She held her lips tight for a moment. Then shook her head. "Not always. No."

Carson looked into her eyes, tears running, and cried silently. His body shook.

Lillian waited and watched and cried with him. "There was nothing I could do to soothe her despair. Nothing. I remember the moment I became convinced that she was lost. It was the first day of December. Two weeks later she was dead."

Carson stared at the floor into the red and purple Persian carpet beneath his feet. He cleared his throat. "What became of it…her child? What is it?"

"A boy."

"A boy," he echoed. "Who was the father? Do you know?"

"I don't. We'll probably never know for sure."

"Was she seeing someone? Aleta, was she seeing anyone?"

Lillian studied his pained expression. "I think for a while," she said slowly. "Vaguely remember a young man…but it was so far back and not for very long." She raised a hand. "Of course, old granny here, I'm not ever in the loop with you young folks. She could have been seeing a dozen men, and I'd never have known." Lillian squeezed her hands together in an attempt to mollify her lie. Of course she had never forgotten the young man; after all, back then he had been the one who made Aleta glow. He had been her future; Lillian was certain of it.

Thomas Shepherd was his name. *Tommy* Aleta had called him, her *Tommy*. Without warning, he vanished from her life one day and she spiraled down from there.

"Any name you can remember? The guy you're thinking of?"

"Carson, no," she perpetuated the falsehood. "I don't. Besides, seems like you should have been more aware of something like that than me. I mean you and Aleta were close."

He closed his eyes for a moment. "Yeah." He spoke on a breath. "We were, just not close enough for my time. I was too preoccupied."

She raised her teacup and sipped tepid chamomile. "You can do that, go on beating up on yourself, but what good will it do?"

"Where is he, the child? Any idea?"

"No. CB won't say and forbids me to ask about the child ever again."

"That right?" Carson remembered jumping up kicking the chair back until it flipped over with a thud. "Forbids you," he said, his teeth clenched. "That son of a bitch." His grandmother started, leaned back, and gazed up at this grandchild who had never shown anger in her presence.

Carson picked up the chair and sat back down. "Sorry, Grams," he said.

"I've always wondered," she responded.

"Wondered what?"

"What it would take to put fire in your belly. Is this it?"

-6-

The *it*, or whatever fire flared up that day, soon cooled to embers before degrading to ashes. He hid his anger and his self-loathing and went on as if the tragic life Aleta had led was behind a mirror and merely illusory. Only when he looked into his grandmother's eyes did he feel the revulsion of guilt over the secret page of shame they shared. And like a car wreck, the immediate horror he felt when first learning of Aleta's child, and the rage that came with that, gradually dimmed into far-removed family lore allowing him the pseudo-peace of no obligation; therein lay his sin. Aleta had borne a child, a son, and he had been taken from her. Why? And why had he never confronted his father once the revelation came to him? More than confronted, why had he not demanded that there be reconciliation, that his grandson be united with the family?

Now the masquerade of his death was giving him the cover to act, to override his cowardice and set out on a course he'd conjured and executed in his head many times. But of course it never went anywhere beyond plying his anger in secret, damning his father, damning the conditions under which Aleta had existed, a life fraught with paternal limits and the passivity of siblings and the other relations who stood by and watched from within their own controlled lives. In the mind game he played, he always projected exactly how he would find the child and conjoin him with his family. But then his imagined plot outline and the course of action he might attempt never occurred beyond hallucinating after several stiff drinks of Maker's Mark. Even in his stupor he never told his wife what he knew about Aleta, although he suspected she knew somehow, and he hated her all the more because of that—that and her snide reminders that getting drunk wouldn't bring his sister back.

The sun was ebbing, shadows were spreading over the hatchery, and a few more cars had rolled by, ignoring Carson's expectant smile and the happy little wave he'd begun to use over his upraised thumb. He'd never been much of a salesman; he was confirming that fact all over again. He was lost in thought when a vehicle actually did crunch to a stop, gravel popping beneath its tires. It was a factory-made pickup on a car chassis—a Ford, sixties maybe. Through the streaked glass of the windshield, Carson made out a wide face with a white and gray beard. A big hand protruded from an open window, waving him over. As Carson approached, the driver smiled, showing a row of big yellow teeth; a line of tobacco juice dribbled down into his beard. He looked up at Carson through smudged aviator-shaped glasses.

"My man, you wanting a lift?" The voice was low, thick, and pleasant.

Carson leaned down. "I am."

"How about my ride here? Will she do?"

Carson stood back and took in the vehicle. It was orange with a black swatch on the hood, had an air scoop built in and a pickup bed; the engine rumbled at idle. Carson smiled. It shone as a polished gem. "I'd say she'll do just fine."

The man hooked a thumb up. "Climb on in, then."

Once in the car, Carson set his backpack on the floor and held his hand out. "Thanks, I'm...Bill. Tolliver."

"Cecil Nash," the man said and took Caron's hand in his immense grip. "You looked a bit lonely out there."

"Yeah, I'm not much of a hitchhiker. Must look suspicious."

"Well, you're on board now," Cecil Nash said in a loud voice. "Where you headed?"

"Not sure, just heading east."

"Ah, you know I did that once, years ago. Wandered. Just a kid. Had a grand time."

Carson laughed. "I'm not a kid anymore. Not sure where this'll end up or if it will be grand."

"I hear ya. Well, I can take you a ways. Far as The Dalles anyway, about another forty miles. That work?"

"Sure. I'm needing a place to stay over for the night. Might as well be there."

"All right then, here we go." Cecil pulled onto the exit ramp and merged back onto the freeway. The man moved through the gears with a floor shift; the engine spoke with a throaty conceit.

"What is this vehicle, anyway?" Carson asked.

The man laughed. "This here's my baby. Marigold. A 1970 Ford Ranchero."

"Marigold?" Carson chuckled, realizing that he was only a year older than the car.

"Yep, we go way back. Bought her new when I was young, single, making good money working the pot line for the old Martin-Marietta Aluminum plant. Marigold and me, we ain't never been apart. Had her longer than my wife. Get along better, too." He gurgled out a belly laugh, tipped his head down, and spit a stream of tobacco juice into a paper cup wedged in his crotch. "We're out for a spin. Didn't figure on getting caught in the rain. Looked nice before I set out. Now I'll have to chamois off her hide before tucking her back into bed." He steered the car with one hand low on the wheel and eased on up to freeway speed.

"Traveling light, I see." He glanced down at Carson's backpack.

"Got most of what I need. I pick up things along the way."

"Sure. Where you hail from, Bill?"

Carson felt that chill again of the innocently asked question. He was feeling more like a nonperson all the time—an illegal alien. Just the asking was like shoving a knife into his gut, a cold blade reminding him that to family and friends he was dead. Imagining their needless pain tore at him. But he had his plan. The only way to consummate it was to work from anonymity.

"North, not far. Up in Washington," he answered.

"That right? Just getting underway then."

"Started out yesterday," Carson said carefully. "Picked up a truck ride, but the sucker dumped me out on the freeway about right where you found me. Took a dislike to me."

"Do tell." Cecil spit into the cup again. "I remember some hairy moments when I was thumbing rides. Can be edgy. Never know if you're getting hooked up with a serial killer. Hell, you don't know my plans for you now, do you?" He bellowed a laugh. "Like the bodies I've carried off in the cargo bed back there."

Carson chuckled. "Can't imagine you doing anything bad in front of Marigold."

"Ha, good one. Don't worry, sweetie," Cecil said, patting the steering wheel. "I'll be good." The Ranchero pulled out and passed a semi with a Walmart logo emblazoned on its trailer. Cecil guided the car back into the right lane and exercised his curiosity again. "So when you're not wandering and hanging out at fish hatcheries, what's your day job?"

"Real estate." Carson had expected the question and was ready with a nonanswer. It was true just not explicit. He wasn't about to spell out Barrus Properties when he was committed to being a nonentity.

"Real estate," Cecil said as he slowed behind a big RV towing an SUV on which was attached a motorcycle trail bike. "Now there's a gig I thought about doing once. Until I found out you had to study, take an exam, get licensed and all. Never any good at taking tests, you know?" He laughed. "So I made aluminum. No tests."

"Everybody can do something, and we can't all do the same thing," Carson said.

Cecil spit again and turned his big head to look at Carson. "Damn, that's downright poetic."

"My grandfather used to say that." Just not the way it turned out, Carson reflected, what with everyone in the family working for Barrus Properties under CB's thumb.

"My granddad had a few of those bits of wisdom." Cecil fell silent. "Miss him."

"Me too."

"Yeah, my gramps used to say all the time to us kids, *Anything you get in life will be because you went out and got it.* Boy, been a while. How long your granddad been gone?"

Carson pondered and felt a stab in his stomach when he realized how long ago Grandpa Leon had passed. He looked straight ahead through the windshield but didn't respond.

"Sorry, man, didn't mean to..."

"No," Carson shook his head. "Just dawned on me that it's been nearly thirty years. He died young, massive heart attack. Only fifty-two. I was about eight, I guess. He was a good man."

"Mama's side?"

"No. Never knew my mother's father. First wife died of TB. Married a younger woman and left town. End of story."

"My mom's dad was closest to me," Cecil said. "Took me fishing, taught me to build stuff, and went to my football games. Lived a good long while, was 81 when he died."

They fell quiet in their memories. Cecil fingered the glob of tobacco from inside his cheek and dropped it into the paper cup. When they cruised by the town of Hood River, Cecil bragged about that leg of the Columbia River being one of the top windsurfing sites in the world.

Carson looked out over the river and glimpsed a few colorful sails attached to boards darting like water skippers among the wind-whipped whitecaps in the November day's fading light. The sight of the wide, cold current caused him to shudder, and he was drawn involuntarily to the sensation of being engulfed. He looked away.

Dusk continued to erode the daylight; elongated clouds hung in the sky, reflecting pink variegated underbellies. The gorge had shed its tree-covered grandeur in favor of a wide view of the rock-strewn hills with sparse vegetation. Cecil pulled on the headlight switch, and the dashboard lit up.

"Be dark soon," he raised his voice over the road noise and ran fingers through his beard. "You know where you'll be bunking tonight?"

Carson inhaled and let out a slow breath. "Not really. I'll just pick out a cheap motel. Must have a few."

"Oh yeah, we got a bunch of 'em. Some cheap, some not so cheap. Take your pick."

"You can just drop me at one you think is free of bedbugs. Or let me off in town, and I'll find a bed. Whatever is most convenient for you."

"Nothing is convenient. Leastways that's been my experience. But then again, sometimes inconvenience can be interesting, if you get my drift."

Carson smiled at the man. "No. Afraid that one passed me by."

"All right then, how about you grabbing a cot out to my place?"

Carson looked sideways and wondered about that.

-7-

Lillian Barrus knew what she knew about Aleta's frightful death, what they all knew. And she was cognizant of the child—that there was one—but nothing else; the rest of the family was totally without knowledge of it. Now with Carson likely gone, only she, BeBe, and CB knew of Aleta's son. At that moment, she looked into the eyes of her oldest offspring and the sweet face of his ever-enduring BeBe. They had come to visit before a determination about Carson was made, what to do: wait for his remains to be found, wait for the family to assimilate his loss, wait for the Saunders to bury Naomi—what?

"We'd like your opinion, Lillian," said BeBe with her little smile. "We'd value your viewpoint. Should we wait or—"

"No sense waiting," CB interrupted. "He's gone. That's a certainty."

Lillian tilted back slightly in her platform rocker. "Your son. You're speaking of Carson here, Cadence." She'd always used his full name whenever she wanted to make a point.

CB smiled, lowered his eyelids and opened them. "Don't do that, Mother." He glanced at BeBe. "We're only here because BeBe thought it best."

"As a courtesy, then."

"If you...yes, as a courtesy. We all know the score. I say let's have a service of some kind and let our lives move on."

"A service of *some kind*?" Lillian studied her son and felt the same twinge in her stomach she'd withstood since he was a young boy; from the first time she had witnessed his lack of empathy. He'd snatched a ball from another child, and she'd noted the cold amusement that exuded from her child over the pain caused to another. All

49

attempts she and Leon made to amend his behavior went nowhere. She had grieved for Cadence then and did so now, though there had never been a solution. "How generic," she said and offered but the slightest of smiles.

CB bit down on her sarcasm and reached for the cup on the low table between them, then pulled back when he remembered it was his mother's chamomile tea; he hated chamomile tea. "Look, Mother," he said. Hearing the tension emanating from his voice, BeBe reached out and put a hand on his arm. She patted, and he pulled away. "Look," he said again, "we have to take action. We can't just wait around with everyone moping."

"Oh, and why is that?" Lillian asked, took a sip of tea, and waited for his response.

"It's a distraction and counterproductive."

Lillian winced over the word *distraction,* looked at BeBe, into her anxious eyes, eyes reddened from days of sorrow, and said in a whisper, "Time, CB, time. Your son, and my lovely grandson, has been missing for just a moment, really."

"He's gone...Carson is. He won't back. Maybe he will never be found."

BeBe pulled a small hanky from a pocket, dabbed at her eyes, and blew her nose. The three of them fell silent and looked into their own thoughts. Lillian pushed up out of her chair and went into the kitchen to heat more tea water. When she returned, she filled BeBe's cup and her own but not CB's, which sat cold and ignored.

She settled back into her rocker and shifted until her back didn't complain as much. She reused her tea bag, dipping it several times. "You know," she said, "I still grieve for your father." She smiled between them, at two very different faces. "All these years later I expect Leon to come through the door from work. Sometimes." She added. "Sometimes I do."

CB studied his mother's lined face; the thin skin stretched over her arthritic hands, her sparse white hair, and inhaled the stale smell of an old person's home. This woman, the one called mother, had he ever loved her? And what would that feel like?

"I know," BeBe responded. "The loss never leaves us, does it? I...I think of my Aleta every day." She raised a hand to her mouth and was suddenly engulfed in sobs.

CB sucked in a deep breath and stood up. He walked over to a window and looked out, his shoulders hunched and hands in his pockets. When his wife's crying softened, he turned and stood behind his chair. "This is maudlin," he said, his voice flat. "People die. We pause for a moment to remember them, and then we move on. We have to move on. That's the way of life."

"Carson is your son," Lillian said. "How you handle his loss is up to you." CB nodded. "But since you made the trip to hear my opinion, I'm going to give it. It is too soon. Give it longer. Let more time pass, perhaps until he is found or the authorities say they've given up." She folded her hands beneath her chin. "Give us more time to accept that Carson is truly gone."

BeBe smiled and wiped at her eyes again.

"And there is something else," Lillian said.

"What?" CB asked as he sat back down. His exasperation was barely concealed.

"The child. Where is the child?"

The gasp from BeBe froze CB. He stared into his mother's rheumy eyes with their yellowed whites but said nothing. For once he couldn't. It was the forbidden question, the one never to be asked, the one no others even knew to ask. She had known for a long time; she had been given a hint by CB but was admonished to let what little she knew pass, never to be discussed again. At the time it had been to protect Aleta, a gamble that she could make a life after all if given time and privacy. It was a wager that never took. Since her death, Lillian had been conflicted, especially after she had shared the child's existence with her grandson. The knowledge that a child, a boy child, with Aleta's genes running through him was alive and living some place unknown to her was a torment. That she might never see him or know him in the time she had left had eaten at her since the moment she'd learned the truth. Now she raised her teacup again, drew the light flowery liquid over her lips, and let the moment stand. CB stared at her; she could see his jaw muscles pulse but was not intimidated by the callousness she saw and knew—she was beyond being bullied.

CB looked aslant at his wife, saw her paralyzed expression, and licked his lips. "We agreed that we would never bring up—"

"You agreed," Lillian cut in. "You agreed, but those ground rules no longer apply."

He scooted up in his chair. "No. No, nothing has changed. That chapter is over and can never be opened. Never."

BeBe's eyes remained open wide and unblinking; she sat so still Lillian wondered if she was breathing. Lillian took in a breath to compensate and said, "Aleta, bless her sweet soul, is gone. The further torture she would have felt went with her. But part of her remains…and we need to know him. Her child, where is he?"

His face reddened, CB raised his voice. "No, Mother. Don't even ask. It is confidential— never to be breached. Whatever…whoever the child is, we cannot interfere with the life he is living, has been living, and will be living. It was agreed."

A clock on the mantel chimed twice. CB looked at his wristwatch and crossed one leg over a knee. "We have to go soon," he said. "After two already, I didn't realize."

Lillian studied her son's sullen expression. "But you know where the boy is."

"Beside the point."

"Why's that?"

"Just is. It was agreed. Papers were signed." He sighed audibly. "To disrupt his life would be unconscionable."

Lillian smiled. "Empathy, CB? Is this new behavior?" BeBe jerked back and turned to observe her husband's reaction to such a question.

CB laughed too hard. "Cute, Mom. Legal. Agreement was made."

"What is it really, CB? You wanting to protect the family name? My stars, it's the twenty-first century. I read somewhere that one out of every two mothers in this country is having a baby before they get married, if they even do. So you don't have to defend the Barrus name over an unwed mother in the family, if that's your intent."

Her son's cold gaze was one she had learned to deflect many years ago. In return she gave him the pliable smile she had perfected for moments like this and waited. His retort came as, "Don't be ridiculous, Mother. Protecting what I've built always gets top billing." He sniffed. "Regardless of eroding social mores."

"What you've built. Does your father get some credit?"

"You know what I mean."

Lillian reached out for a cookie. "This is most revealing," she said. "What a day it is when I discover to my amazement that I'm more progressive than my eldest child."

In a matter of minutes Lillian was alone in her apartment remembering the squeeze BeBe gave her arm in passing as she hastily followed CB out the door. She stood still for a moment watching the closed door as if it might burst back open. But it didn't, and her back hurt. She fetched the extra large bottle of Ibuprofen she kept in the bathroom medicine cabinet, unscrewed the cap, took two pills, and went back to her rocker. It came to her then that there had been no consensus on what to do about Carson. But then she knew there wouldn't be; she'd given CB her feelings about waiting. He had parried her point of view as if it had been an undesirable business offer, easily and without emotion.

Lillian stayed in, not as if she went out often anyway, but that evening she wanted to be alone with her heartache, which was bundled with Aleta, her missing child, and now Carson gone and unaccounted for. The cupboard displayed the array of soup she kept there for uninspired meals; she chose clam chowder, in which she floated a handful of oyster crackers. She spooned deliberately until she wanted no more. She dumped what she didn't eat in the sink and ran the disposal.

She was preparing for bed when the phone rang. It was BeBe. She apologized for CB, something she had been doing for a very long time, a fact he would deplore if he knew about it. She said they would be waiting to hold a service for Carson after all.

Then BeBe said one word before hanging up: *Oklahoma*.

-8-

Cecil Nash nosed the Ranchero down the first exit ramp off I-84 into The Dalles and trundled along on Sixth Street as it paralleled the freeway. It was one of those routes that put the typical commercial strip on display, the kind that had abandoned a town's inner core to sprawl out to the edges and pave big parking lots: competing supermarkets, gas stations, the usual mix of fast food and motel brands and accompanying drive-by coffee kiosks. Carson offered to get out when they approached a motel declaring itself to be low-cost. Cecil shook his head, muttered something indecipherable, and drove deftly from street to street as one does who knows where he is without having to think about it: passing a church or two, then a cemetery before finally entering the old neighborhoods, streets with houses that had aged in place through a steady progression of decades. Some had been added onto. Others were shrouded in replacement sidings: metal, vinyl, asbestos. Once proud houses of the thirties and forties were tired or refurbished to a newness that gave them revived respect. An occasional grande dame of a house stood magnificently restored and able still to represent a piece of the historical past of the town.

Dusk had edged its way in, forcing streetlights to pop on block by block, but soon they were into the dark of the countryside. Cecil drove one-handed out Mill Creek Road, spat tobacco juice, and expounded about his town. In the fading light, Carson listened with one ear as they passed clusters of houses amid the cherry orchards that more than anything defined The Dalles and the county of Wasco. Cecil boasted that over thirty-six thousand tons of cherries were produced annually, varieties with names like Bing, Lapins, Skeena, and Sweetheart. Carson attempted to take it all in, but he was fading. It had been one long, traumatic day. Cherry tonnage and colorful fruit names were floating illegibly in the gauze of fatigue. He dozed to the drone of Cecil's narration until the car abruptly left the road and jounced up a gravel lane. He blinked and raised his head as the headlamp's yellow beams exposed a narrow drive that curved to the left and revealed a big, two-story farmhouse. Cecil wheeled the Ranchero off to an outbuilding and pulled up in front of it.

"We're home, my girl," he said and patted the dashboard. "So." He turned to Carson. "Here we are. I'll put Marigold away, and we'll go in and surprise Ola Mae."

Carson hopped out and stood in the cold post-dusk air while Cecil stored the car, buttoned it up in the big garage, and motioned for Carson to follow him into the house. His wife was in the kitchen stirring a pot of something. Ola Mae Nash was slender and had silver gray hair that hung down below her shoulders. She wore a blue and white checked flannel shirt with the tail out, faded blue jeans, and some sort of moccasins. Her face reminded Carson of Audrey Hepburn in her later years. She was lovely.

"Howdy, love," Cecil called out. "Got company."

She looked up first at Cecil then focused her smiling brown eyes on Carson. "That right?" She lifted a big spoon out of the pot, sipped a taste of whatever was in it, licked it away, and asked, "So, who do we have here?"

"This here is Bill," Cecil said as he sidled up behind the woman, pulled her hair back, and planted a kiss on her neck. "Found him looking lonely out at the Cascade Hatchery. Marigold and me, we were needing company, so there you go. Bill, this is Ola Mae, my ever-loving."

Carson set his backpack down, pulled his cap off, smiled, and raised a hand. She nodded a warm smile in return.

"Staying the night," Cecil said. "Now I gotta go out and give Marigold a rubdown before she catches a chill." He laughed and slapped

Carson on the back on his way out the door.

With Cecil's energy out of the room, it was suddenly quiet. Carson looked around the big kitchen, which had the feel of a working farm where you might see several earthy, ravenous men come in from the fields to a big lunch. There was a long oak slab table with half a dozen ladder-back chairs on either side of it. A butcher block stood on thick legs in the middle of the room. There was a double porcelain sink with faucets that looked like they were the originals, lots of counters and cupboards, backed up by a huge modern stainless steel-clad Sub-Zero refrigerator.

Carson squeezed his grin a bit too hard and said, "Hope this is okay. I mean, I was just grateful for the lift. Didn't intend to…"

"Sleep over?" Her laugh was light and genuine. "Don't you worry, not the first time. Whenever he takes Marigold out for one of his one-man poker runs, as he calls it, I never know what hand we'll be dealt." She laughed at her own predicament. "Must say we've met some very unique people. How about you? What's your fascinating story?"

Carson breathed out a self-conscious laugh. Her question kick-started an instant flashback of the past two days. He felt a slight shudder but tamped down the disturbing reverberation as best he could. "Nothing fascinating about me."

Ola Mae Nash studied him for a moment before reaching up into a cupboard to bring down several soup bowls. "That right? Nothing at all interesting about a good looking, thirty-something I'd guess, inexperienced man on the road, with the look and sound of someone unused to hitchhiking and traveling light?" She looked at the thinly packed backpack at his feet.

Carson felt his face warm. "Not really."

She smiled more deeply and gathered some silverware out of a drawer and took the bowls and soup spoons over to the table. "What's your itinerary? Heading someplace in particular?" When Carson didn't respond quickly she added, "Sorry, interrogation comes with the hot and the cot. Not required to tell us anything, but we get to ask."

"Fair enough," he said regaining some confidence. "I've only been traveling a couple of days, just started. Only looking really."

"For what?" She was back stirring the pot again and adjusting the gas flame beneath it.

"Places. Places to be, I guess. Places where I might like to take time out."

Their eyes met. "See there now," she said, "you are fascinating. I can think of a lot of questions about what you just told me. Places to be. Time out. What's that mean? Time out from what, for instance?"

"Time out for food." It was Cecil stomping back into the house. "What's in the pot?"

She winked at Carson. "Road kill goulash. Roasted a possum I found up by the Carter place, added some sagebrush and young pinecones. You'll be wanting seconds."

"My favorite. Bill, you'll love this concoction." Carson smiled as Cecil picked Ola Mae up off the floor and twirled around before giving her a long, passionate kiss. She pushed him off and glanced over at Carson, red-faced but smiling.

It actually was goulash but of a very savory nature with beef, onions, carrots, and seasoning. Carson managed to consume two bowls before noticing his hosts' pleased expressions. The last real meal he'd had was on Thanksgiving up in Sequim before his life was yanked out of its groove. He enjoyed the feel of this place and these people who had come out of nowhere and invited him in. Mostly he was taking pleasure in the amatory tie between the man and woman, the connectivity he had wished for with Naomi, the ease of being in love and confident in it being the real thing. It had never been so and now could never be.

Afterward, they cleared the table and adjourned to a sprawling living room anchored by a big soot-tinged stone fireplace. Cecil brought in a half-empty bottle of brandy with three snifters clutched by their stems and poured generous portions.

He sat on the couch next to Ola Mae and declared, "Here's to fellow travelers." They all raised their glasses.

Carson took a sip and leaned back in his chair. "How many fellow travelers have you brought home to Ola Mae, Cecil?"

She laughed out loud. "Yeah how many, Cecil?" She jabbed his big shoulder.

Cecil took another swallow and set his glass down. "Not so many." When his wife snickered, he smiled and nodded. "Okay, more than a few."

Ola Mae looked at her man with warmth. "For a spell there, back two years ago, thought we were running a hostel. Was considering taking the rotor out of Marigold's distributor just so he'd stop. Cripple the beast. You see, he only drags people in off the freeway when he's out driving that Ranchero."

"What's the reason, Cecil?" Carson asked.

Cecil poured himself more brandy. "The intrigue," he responded. "Curiosity, I guess. Curious about people. Mainly why they're out there on the road taking shank's mare to get someplace. And in that run up and down I-84, I've run into some interesting folks."

Ola Mae laughed out loud. "Mildly put. There's been some odd ones, even a few scary ones."

"Scary?" Cecil seemed offended. "Who was scary?"

"Like that creep said he was from Georgia. Wanted in my undies, I'll tell you."

"Ha, good taste is all. Did he scare you, love, truly now?"

Ola Mae looked into her brandy glass. "He did."

Cecil clamped a big arm around her shoulders and drew her in. "You never said. You shoulda told me. Whyn't you say anything?"

She put a hand against his hairy face. "Afraid of what you might have done to him."

Cecil studied his wife, his wide face sober. "I guess that's it then," he said. "Bill, you're the last one." He raised a meaty hand. "And don't you be hitting on my woman here, either." He roared and kissed Ola Mae on the cheek.

They put Carson in an upstairs bedroom. The bed had a heavy hand-sewn comforter on it and a mattress as hard as the floor. He opened a window a few inches and fell asleep in minutes.

—————

The next morning, he was roused from a curious dream of walking in an endless corridor by the sound of voices wafting up from outside his window. Car doors slammed, a vehicle drove away, and all was quiet again; then it came to him where he was and why. He stared at the ceiling as it forced its way in; he covered his face with both hands and waited while for the surreal replay of his death to die away. Of course he knew it would return again and again; regardless of the nightmarish paroxysms, he had to make the call. Today he would.

Ola Mae had left a bath towel and washcloth for him on the dresser. He basked under the showerhead, put the same clothes back on, and found Cecil sitting in the kitchen reading a paper over a cup of coffee and empty cereal bowl.

"Ah," Cecil said raising his eyebrows. "The dead man rises. Sleep well?"

"Never better." Carson said nothing of the hard mattress and the pain in the small of his back—let alone his demons. "And the shower was a gift from the god of road travelers. I'll have more empathy for those I see out traveling far between clean sheets and a bath. Many thanks."

"Our pleasure."

"Where's Ola Mae? I'd like to thank her before I head out."

"She's out with a friend. They go out for a walk every Sunday. Be gone for hours."

"Sorry I missed her. What time is it, anyway?"

"Going on nine, my friend. You were zonked."

"Those two shots of brandy," Carson said.

"Could be. Breakfast? I can offer you Cheerios, corn flakes, or you could scramble yourself a couple of eggs. Toast, too, can make toast if you like. And orange juice I got."

Carson settled on Cheerios and juice with coffee. A better breakfast he couldn't remember. Cecil poured himself another cup of coffee, and they sat in silence and sorted through an assortment of newspapers spread askew on the table, mostly the local daily, The Dalles Chronicle. His curiosity on high, Carson found the front section of the Saturday edition while Cecil perused the Sunday paper. The front page was devoted almost entirely to local news, but inside he found sections for World news with a piece about the US suffering 852 casualties in Iraq in 2007, more than in any other year, the highest total since the war began in 2003.

There was a sidebar labeled "Briefly". That's where he saw it: "Body not found". It was mostly a rehash of previous coverage. He felt a flutter in his stomach reading again about his own supposed death. The only thing new was that efforts to find his body would continue. He felt a sense irony and a twinge of guilt over all of the effort and resources being expended.

There was nothing further about the accident in the Sunday paper. Carson took his cereal bowl to the sink and rinsed it out, refilled his coffee cup, and told Cecil he was going outside for a bit; Cecil, engrossed in the news, mumbled his acquiescence. Carson stood outside the house and looked into an orchard across a fence line but didn't really see it. After draining the cup, he set it on the ground at his feet and pulled out his cell phone. His hand shook slightly as he considered what he was about to do. How would she react, hearing his voice? From the grave it would seem to her. He put the phone back into his pocket and walked a ways down the gravel drive, stopped and imagined the implications of what he planned to do. It had to start somewhere. He turned and walked back. The sun had come out, filtered through breaks in the overcast, and the top of his head felt the warmth even in the coolness of the morning. No choice. He had no choice, and she was the one to start with. He needed a co-conspirator; she was the one.

He pulled his wallet out and extracted the bit of paper and studied the phone number. Once it was listed in his cell phone contacts; now he needed prompting. He pressed the numbers. She should be awake and up, unless she'd gone to church, which she rarely did anymore.

The cell phone rang in the warbles and surges common when calling from the fringes of a service area. On the third ring she answered. A cold knife hit his stomach when she said hello in a voice so familiar. He listened as she said hello three times before he said anything. He had a script in his head, one he'd fabricated just for this moment.

"Hello," he said, using a dry, throaty voice.

"Hello," she said. "Who is this? I can't hear you very well."

He raised his voice, using the same alias tonality. "Is this Lillian Barrus?"

"Are you selling something?" she asked. "I'm not interested in buying anything."

Carson smiled. "No, not selling anything."

"What then? Who is this? Speak more clearly."

He held the phone up against his mouth. "What is the news of your grandson, Carson Barrus? Have they found him?"

"No," she said after a pause. "They haven't. Now who is this?"

His heart pounding, he spoke distinctly, careful to maintain the gravelly tone. "I'm a friend of his—of your grandson. Bill Tolliver is my name."

"Don't know any such person. You're a friend of Carson's you say?"

He inhaled and asked the question of all questions. "Do you think he's really dead?"

"What did you say?" Her voice rose and seemed to tremble.

"They haven't found him, have they? Maybe he's still alive." A door slammed; Carson turned and saw Cecil coming toward him. He gently patted the air and pointed at the phone next to his ear. Cecil nodded and walked off toward the building where he kept the Ranchero.

"What a horrible thing to ask me," Lillian literally squawked into Carson's ear.

"But what if he were alive? How would you know? How would you recognize him, his voice and all? How would you?"

He could hear her crying softly. It was a terrible thing to do to her, but he had no choice. He pressed some more. "What could he say, for instance, that only you would know? Some secret you have, maybe?"

The silence was so long he felt at first that she had hung up. Then she spoke. "Mr. Tolliver is it? This is most painful. Shame on you."

"I'm so sorry. It's just that…I can't help wondering, you know."

Again a long silence. "Well, all I'll say is that if Carson were still alive…oh, my god." He heard her blow her nose. "If," she went on, "he would know of those things only he and I shared." The sound of her tears went on for a long moment, then it was over. "Never call me again, sir." There was a click, and she was gone.

Carson looked at the phone and squeezed it before slipping it into his pants pocket. He wandered over to the fence of the orchard and stared at the orderly stand of cherry trees with their shiny striated bark as he struggled to regain his composure. What would he do next? He would call her back. But when, what would he say, and could it be as himself? He heard the Ranchero start up and turned as Cecil backed it out of the storage building, made a wide turn, and pulled up beside him.

"You said something about getting back on the road," Cecil said out the open driver's window while he stuffed tobacco chew into a cheek. "If so, let me give you a lift into town. Be a bit of a walk."

Carson was still shaky, but he nodded. "Sure. I'll get my pack."

"It's in the car. Climb in. I'm giving Marigold another outing. I meet up every Sunday with some buddies at Spooky's. Local pizza joint. Always take Marigold to that meet up—if the weather's okay."

By the time Mill Creek Road became Mt. Hood Street, Cecil was headlong into the story of his summer hitchhiking across the Midwest back when he was in his freewheeling twenties; colorful accounts of brushes with the law, stealing food, and sleeping with a whore in Omaha. Carson listened quietly, chuckled and nodded in silence, until Cecil pulled up at Second and Union. "Anyway, that's the way 'twas. Helluva a trip," he said, slipping the transmission into neutral. "And now here you are on your journey, smack dab in middle of downtown The Dalles."

"That I am." Carson reached over, and they shook hands. "Thanks for everything. Best to Ola Mae."

"Sure 'nuff." Cecil stroked his beard. "You know, I'll be done with my cronies in about and hour and a half, maybe less. If you're still around, maybe we can meet up right here on this corner about then. Just in case, you know."

Carson looked into the face of this man he barely knew and felt a connection of some sort but wondered if there was anything more to it than a short ride, a hot meal, and a bed.

"I mean if you're still around is all I'm saying. You know, check on you before you get lost out there on 84. Being new at this and all." Cecil seemed to read Carson's ambiguity. "Hell, you may be all the way to Boardman by then." He slapped Carson on the shoulder.

"Where's Boardman?"

"My man, you better stop by the bookstore and get yourself a map. Anyway, I'll come by to this corner on my way back home—just in case. Happy trails." Carson got out of the car, pulled his backpack out with him, and Cecil drove off. A block away, the Ranchero's horn sounded once, and a big arm rose up. Carson smiled and raised his hand in response.

He slipped the backpack on, looked up and down the street, and felt the pull of a small town where everything one needed was once all right at hand. The historic complexion of the buildings made him imagine a time when friends and neighbors saw each other on these streets and sidewalks and felt comfort in that familiarity. Now this part of the town brandished colorful banners that labeled it historic, as if it had received a pat on the head and been left to weather economic change alone while it aged. Meanwhile all that would be new left the dance partner that got it there and expanded out to where the game could be played beyond the confines of tradition.

Carson sensed all of that, even though he'd never lived in a small town. At that moment it felt like he actually had lived that way. He pulled on his Hood Canal cap and set out along Second Street. There was the cross-streets grid, on-street parallel parking, block after block of retail fronts: NAPA Auto Parts, J. C. Penney, a jeweler, a furniture store, an old movie theater called the Granada, a few eateries, and everything from office supplies to florists. There was a smattering of empty storefronts, the toothless windows with the For Lease signs taped to them. One handmade For Rent sign said *See Chuck next door at Security Lock & Key.*

He paused at the sidewalk sign that declared Klindt's Booksellers to be the oldest bookstore in Oregon; 1870 it boasted. Something. He went into the store, again sensed the ambience of history, bought an Oregon map, and rejoined his reconnaissance of the town.

-9-

Carson held the folded map in his hand and walked east, continuing on Second Street past more storefronts, but he wasn't seeing much of it. His mind had returned to his grandmother, to Lillian, to the phone call and how he'd deceived her. There'd been no choice in spite of the pain he'd heard in her voice; he needed her now. His decision to dematerialize may have been irrational, but it was taken with the clarity of something decided long before. The losses Aleta and then Naomi may have crystallized into a preposterous conclusion, but now he needed to act.

He kept walking until he reached a roundabout where a historic old flourmill's grain silos dominated the skyline. He turned back onto Third Street. At a convenience market he bought toiletries and a ready-to-go ham and cheese sandwich with a cola, and sat on an outside bench. The uninspiring sandwich went down in dry lumps and with it the hint of plastic wrap. He finished quickly, tossed the empty soda can and plastic wrap in a waste can, and walked on. A few blocks on, he paused by a closed insurance office, set his bag of toiletries on the sidewalk, and considered that what he was about to do was unconscionable. But it was his only option. He pulled out his phone and rolled it in his palm. He knew what he would say; he'd decided. His heart rate rose. She answered on the second ring. Her voice was strong; he was glad of that.

After she said hello, he waited a beat before saying, "Aleta's son." Behind her nonresponse came a murmur that brought tears to his eyes. Just as he reached up to wipe his eyes, a man wearing a cowboy walked by and eyeballed Carson but continued on as if real men in ball caps don't cry.

"Grandma?" He waited and sucked in his breath. "It's me. It's Carson."

The inhalation was ragged and alarmed. "What? No. It can't be. No."

"Yes it is. It's me. It's Carson. Really."

"Oh," she moaned. "Carson. Oh." He could hear her shocked crying and felt monstrous.

"I'm sorry," he said. "So sorry."

"But...what...we all thought you were gone, with Naomi." She sobbed.

"I know. But I'm not."

Her voice faltered. "How...I don't understand. What...where are you?"

He took in a deep breath and let it out. "Grandma," he spoke carefully, "I'll tell you everything, but for now I just want you to know that I am alive. I'm okay. But you can't tell anyone else. No one."

He could hear her blow her nose and give out a whimpering sound. "I don't understand, Carson. Why? I mean...I can't, this is so hard, I don't know..."

"Please trust me."

Another pause. "Is it you, really?" she asked her voice faltering. "Someone called earlier and asked..."

"That was me, Grandma."

"You?"

"Uh-huh. I thought maybe if I could put the idea in your mind that I might still be alive, it would be easier. Less of a shock."

"Well it isn't...less of a shock." Her voice firmed. "Oh my. My heart is beating so."

"Mine, too."

"This has been a nightmare, the accident, Naomi's death...you. We all thought you were dead, too. Oh, I'm...my head is spinning." She took in a breath. "Your parents, do they know? You called them first, didn't you? Oh, poor BeBe, how is she?"

"No, Grandma." He stepped away from the building as a truck drove by. He waited until the sound had dissipated. "Mom and dad don't know. No one else knows."

"But…"

"Grandma, listen please." A young woman with two reluctant children in tow came by. He stepped back and leaned against the building again. "I need you to keep this to yourself. Can you do that?"

"Carson, I don't know. Why?"

"I'll tell you everything, but I need you to promise me. Can you do that?"

He could sense that she was regaining her composure. Her voice settled. "If this is some kind of cruel game, Carson, it is an absolutely horrible thing you're doing. And I refuse to be a party to it."

He cringed. "It may be horrible, and it is, but it is not a game."

"What then?"

"What were my first words when you answered the phone?"

She hesitated then hummed. "I can't remember. Oh. Oh, you said Aleta. Aleta's boy."

"Aleta's son," he reminded.

"Yes. Aleta's son. What did you mean?"

He pressed the phone hard to his ear. "You wanted to know why? Why I'm doing this? That is the answer. Aleta's son."

"I…I simply don't understand, Carson." She sounded exasperated.

"You will, Grandma, you will. Please trust me. Do you…trust me?"

"Well, I…can you promise me this isn't…you aren't playing some strange, awful game of hide-and-seek?"

He laughed. It felt good to laugh. "I am hiding for right now, but it is not a game."

"All right then, my love, I will trust you. But my, how you've put me through the wringer, let me tell you." Even she laughed a bit. "So, what are you doing, and where are you, for heaven's sake? Where have you been? You were in the car, how…"

"I can't tell you about any of that right now. Let's leave it this way for now. I just wanted to do the hard part first, letting you know I was alive and okay. That was really hard, right?"

"Yes. What a shock on this day that all I had planned was a walk to the market to pick up some greens and watch *Sixty Minutes* later on—and mourn for you."

He cringed. "Okay, you digest all of this and get used to the idea, and I'll call you again tomorrow."

"But Carson, your parents, they need to know. You must..."

"No, not yet. So I'm trusting you to keep this just between us for now."

She sighed, agreed, cried again, and they disconnected. Carson stood on the street in a town called The Dalles and contemplated where all of this was going. He decided that he had traveled far enough to give him separation and room to operate. No need to go farther.

He stood next to the building for some time rewinding the conversation with Lillian. He could only hope that his grandmother would hold to her word. He knew that the maternal drive to care and nurture family is an intense force, one difficult to hold at bay. If she aborted her promise, he would have to operate alone and away from any familial contact.

He continued on along Third Street into the face of a cold breeze and came across a Salvation Army Store where he could have bought some of what he needed cheap, but it was closed. Sunday. He headed back into the center of town retracing his path to J. C. Penney's where he bought underwear and socks and a pair of Wrangler jeans off a clearance table; he added a pair of off-brand sneakers, which he put on with his new socks once he'd left the store. He stuffed everything else in his pack and was waiting back at Union and Second looking at his Oregon map when the orange and black thing pulled up into an empty parking space nearby and Cecil tapped the horn. Carson raised a hand refolded the map and walked up to the car.

Cecil was squinting up at him from behind the wheel. "So?" he said.

Carson laughed. "So? So what?"

"Staying or going?"

"Well since I figured out it's at least eighty miles to Boardman, guess I'm staying. For now, maybe longer. I kind of like the feel of the place."

"Guess it could grow on a person. Okay good enough." He hooked a thumb across this body. "There here's Frisco."

Carson leaned down and could make out a man waving at him: about fifty, thin, with a shock of black hair, and a toothy grin. "One of our gang of seven. Frisco and me was thinking that if you weren't set on leaving town just yet, we'd get us a brew to help digest the pizza we put down at Spooky's. You up for that?"

"Guess so. Ate a stale sandwich that could stand a bit more washing down."

"All righty, then," Cecil said. "See that old brick building with the clock tower on it next block over? Well, that's the old courthouse. It houses a pretty decent pub. That's where we're going." He pushed open the car door, reached up to grip the edge of the roof, swung out, and lurched off up the street with Frisco and Carson in his wake.

The brew house was warm and quiet inside. The men stood at the bar and scanned a couple of dozen tap handles of fresh brews. Cecil said he was buying and ordered three pints of his favorite, an ale called Free Range Red. When their drinks arrived, Cecil lifted his glass. "Here's to our gentleman of the road." They touched glasses, and each took a long drink.

"You know," said Frisco, setting his glass on a paper coaster, his grin displaying a row of square teeth, "this here was a mortuary once. A funeral parlor. Ain't that right, Cecil?" he said, looking at Cecil.

Cecil nodded and stared at Carson. "It was."

"If you think on it," Frisco went on, " the same plumbing that they used to embalm all them bodies is right where the kitchen is now." He snickered and swallowed more ale. "Hey, Cecil, your beer have a strange taste to it?"

"Can't tell, but it's okay with me if they embalm me with it." Cecil took another swallow and looked aslant at Carson. "So you truly thinking on hanging around for a spell?" he asked.

"Might. For a time at least," Carson answered. His mind swirled, thinking about what he was about to set into motion.

Cecil leaned on his forearms. "If that's the case, I have an idea for you. Of a place to hang yer hat. You gonna be wanting something reasonable, I expect."

"Cheap is the operable word."

"Think I've gotcha covered then. A friend of ours is wanting to rent a trailer on her property. A travel trailer, a fancy one, too. It's out Mill Creek Road, not far from us."

"A trailer? How much?"

"Think she's just wanting $195 a month. Like I said, reasonable."

Carson smiled. "Maybe too reasonable. What's the catch?"

Cecil raised a shoulder. "No catch, nice lady, clean trailer. No catch really, just a minor thing," he said, looking into his empty glass.

"Minor. Like what?"

"Well…the plumbing's not fully hooked up yet."

Carson laughed. "That's not a minor thing. Meaning no water?"

"Oh there's water, all right. You'd have water. But just water."

Carson laughed. "Just water. Meaning?"

"No toilet or shower hookup. Yet."

"But there's water?"

"Yeah, garden hose from an outside spigot." Carson laughed and slapped the table. "Wait," Cecil raised a hand, "she's gonna hook up to the septic tank soon as she gets a regular renter. Could be you."

"In the meantime I hose off in the yard and pee in the brush?"

Cecil shook his head. "No, no, no. You'd use the shower in her house. And there's a john off the back porch. You know, one of them they used to put in so Farmer Jones didn't have to tramp through the house to take a dump. Hey, it's cheap."

"Sounds fine by me," said Frisco. "Who needs to shower up more'n once a week anyway?"

"Who is this person?" Carson couldn't keep a straight face.

"Name's Marla Snow. She works same place as Ola Mae. Fact is, Marla's the gal she's out walking with now." Cecil pulled out a pouch of Beechnut and stuffed some chew into his mouth. "Nice lady," he repeated while pushing the tobacco around with his tongue. "I'll take you out there if you're interested."

Frisco begged off on seeing the trailer with no working toilet and stayed behind to finish another pint of ale.

-10-

It was small for a farmhouse: a square two-story box of a thing probably built early in the last century, Carson surmised, calling on his
real estate knowledge of old buildings. Two white wicker rockers
rested calmly on a narrow front porch, lessening the structure's lack
of character to some degree. The original wood shingle roofing had
been replaced with asphalt composition the color of dark slate. Un-
fortunately, the previous owners had covered the house in Johns
Manville asbestos siding then painted it ash gray. To Carson, that
gave it the look of someone who wore the wrong outfit to the school
dance, clean but out of fashion. White window trim helped some,
and the place was well kept. Rose bushes grew along the front of the
house, a couple of flowerpots with pinkish winter kale in them sat
on the porch at the top of the stairs, and several gnarled white oaks
stood side-by-side at the edge of the yard, proud but stress-marked
with the passage of time. A patch of grass was kept cropped but had
as many weeds as fescue, and a cluster of bunchgrass had grown a
collar around the post for the rural delivery mailbox out by the road.
All in all the well-worn presence of the place was a comfortable scene.

Cecil had pulled the Ranchero up next to the house on a short
gravel drive and killed the engine. "So," he said with a nod, "this
here's Marla's place. Still called the Cunningham Orchard by the
long-time locals. Once had over thirty-five acres of Bing cherries and
good bit of pasture. When the old folks passed on, the kids sold off
the orchard and pastures but kept this old house. Nostalgia, I guess.
They rent it out. Marla, she moved here from Central Oregon in
about 2001 as I recall, from Redmond. She found this place available

a few months later and has been renting ever since." He drew his mouth in and stared at the house. "Sad story, really. Hers."

Carson turned his head and gave Cecil an inquisitive look but didn't ask.

"Well come on then," Cecil said, offering nothing more and squirming out of the car. He pulled up on his pants before tromping out to the mailbox and extracting a handful of assorted envelopes and catalogs. "I'll take these in for her," he said, brushing past Carson.

After he'd gone into the house and come back onto the porch, he waved for Carson to join him. They settled into the wicker rockers, the joints creaking as they distributed their weight. Cecil took out his pouch of Beechnut and stuck another wad of moist tobacco into his mouth.

"She'll be along soon," he said. "After she drops Ola Mae off to home."

He folded his hands on his stomach, and things grew quiet except for the crankiness of the chairs whenever one of them would rock a bit. Carson zipped up his jacket and folded his arms against the cold. During moments of calm it had become impossible for his mind to not to be sucked back into the enormity of all that had transpired. The kaleidoscope of the tumult took over: a laughing Naomi flashed by, the sinking car, even the sensation of being submerged. He gasped and sat up straight.

"Hey, man," Cecil stopped rocking and reached over. His big hand gripped Carson's arm. "You okay?"

Carson blinked and stared out at nothing, then felt Cecil's grip and inhaled. He shuddered and cranked out a smile. "Yeah, sure." He tried to laugh. "Must have dozed."

"Something got at you."

"Guess so." Carson massaged his face. He forced a grin and jabbed Cecil on the arm.

"So *sad story* you say and then leave it hanging."

"I shouldn't of said nothing. Marla, she's like family. And let me

74

tell you, I wouldn't be bringing you out here if I thought you was a flake." He stood, spit over the railing, and sat back down. The chair groaned again; he eyeballed Carson like he was having second thoughts.

Carson raised two hands. "You done assessing my worthiness? And me being the one who'll have to march in from the back forty to take a shower or..."

"Okay, okay." Cecil laughed before going on.

———————

They were still sitting on the porch when a light blue Honda Civic pulled up next to the Ranchero. Carson halted his rocking and waited for the woman to emerge. He had been mulling over Cecil's telling of Marla Snow's story: that she was in The Dalles because she couldn't stay where she had been, that she had removed herself from where she had been—intentionally—after her husband hung himself. According to Cecil, Marla Culver had earned an English literature degree from Oregon State, eventually was offered a job teaching language arts at Redmond High School, and moved there in the mid-nineties. There she met and fell in love with Glen Snow and his farm, which had been in his family since 1911; they married in 1996. Less than five years later the farm had spiraled down into bankruptcy. Evidently Glen Snow couldn't face that he had lost what had been the Snow Farm for nearly ninety years. The night before the farm's holdings were to be auctioned off, he wrapped a length of hemp rope over a beam in the barn, cinched a hitch around his throat, and stepped off of a fifty-five-gallon oil drum. She found him hanging there before the opening bid the next morning, dressed in his best pearl-button shirt, fresh Levi's, and his favorite Tony Lama cowboy boots. That summer, after living with the aftermath as long as she could, Marla left everything in the hands of Glen's siblings, packed up her personal belongings, and had the trailer towed from Central Oregon up the Gorge to The Dalles.

"It's all she wanted, that trailer," Cecil said. "The only thing she asked to be excluded from the auction. Told me she didn't know where she was going to end up and wanted to make sure she had a place to sleep."

Carson watched closely as the woman got out of the car. She looked curiously toward the two men sitting on her porch. Cecil stood and told her he'd already brought her mail in. She nodded and came toward them, all the while studying the other man, and the other man was looking at her. She was maybe five-foot-eight, slender, even wiry. Brown hair was pulled back in a ponytail. She was wearing jeans and a red all-weather jacket; a light blue flannel shirt showed beneath it. She was carrying an insulated lunch bag in one hand and a paper sack in the other. As she drew closer, she flashed a smile that revealed a slight gap in her front teeth.

"I'm not buying anything," she said in a voice that was lower than Carson was expecting. Her response reminded him that his grandmother had said the very same thing when he'd called her.

"You haven't heard our offer yet," Cecil responded.

"Coming from you," she chided, "I'm almost doubly sure I'm not interested."

Cecil waggled a finger at her. "Don't be so sure there, Missy."

"That so. And who do we have here?" she asked looking again at Carson.

"Sassy," Cecil to Carson. "I shoulda told you—she's a sassy one."

She stopped at the foot of the steps, looked back and forth between them, and shook her head. "Been a long hard day, Cecil. Just tell me what you're up to."

"Okay, okay. This here's Bill Tolliver. Might be he's the renter you been looking for."

She set her carryings on the bottom step, sighed, and looked up at Carson. "That right? And where'd you find him?"

Cecil eased down the five steps and swooped her up in a bear hug. She allowed it with a tolerant smile before pushing him back. "Watch your big feet—fresh tomatoes in that sack." She raised her eyebrows at Carson. "Worrisome if he has to give me a squeeze before telling me who you are. Where did he find you?"

His face reddening, Carson said, "Out on the freeway."

Her smile fell away. "Oh gawd, you're the one. Ola Mae told me you and Marigold were out on 84 again, Cecil. Stayed the night with you and Ola Mae, I understand."

"Well yeah, but…"

"And after she thought she'd put the kibosh on you bringing home any more strays." She looked at Carson again. "Sorry fella, nothing personal."

Carson shrugged.

"Marla, damn it now," Cecil said. "Will you just give me a minute, please? Bill here is no bum, not a drunk, he's educated I can tell, and the man is just taking a trip, hitching his way and has decided to spend time here in The Dalles."

"Here?" she said, pointing a finger down. "In The Dalles?"

"Right," Cecil said. He strung the word out. "And…and he'll be needing an inexpensive place to bed down for a time."

Marla Snow fell quiet and looked between the two men for a long moment. "It's cold out here. Come on in, and we can discuss why this isn't going to happen."

The interior of the house was a smaller version of Cecil and Ola Mae's place: big kitchen, smaller living room, but a nicer rock fireplace, with a mix-and-match set of furniture. They followed her into the kitchen, where she put a teapot of water on a gas range and fired it up. The men kept standing until she motioned for them to sit at a big square table covered in a blue-and-white checked tablecloth. She brought over three hand-turned pottery mugs and a basket of tea packets.

She sat down pushed the mugs across to the two men, and said, "I've decided that I'm not going to rent the trailer after all."

Cecil snorted. "Now that's a dang lie, Marla, and you know it. Just last week you were fussing about needing to get a renter. You can't keep turning prospects away. This is what, three or four you've rejected?"

She stared at Cecil then Carson.

Carson chuckled. "I must really look unsavory."

Her eyes met his. She didn't crack a smile.

"I showered this morning, shaved and everything."

This time she did smile. The teapot began to breathe into its whistle. She brought it over and poured them each a mug full of steaming water. They pulled out their tea selections; Carson saw chamomile, took it, and thought of his grandmother.

"So you showered and shaved," she reentered the conversation. "What else can you offer?"

Carson dipped his tea bag a few times and raised the cup while looking her in the eye. "Well, I'm willing to make the crossing in all kinds of weather to use a toilet and a shower and also get my drinking water strung in from a garden hose."

She laughed. "You knew that much before even coming out here. What else?"

"I'm on a limited budget, have to keep my costs down. This could work. You'll get a flexible renter, and I get a place to bunk for a spell."

She gave Cecil a dubious look. "For a spell, he says. How long's that? I'm not wanting to run a motel."

When their eyes met, Carson noted that hers seemed hazel to him beneath full eyebrows.

She was smiling slightly, displaying the gap in her teeth again and bringing out fine lines at the corner of her eyes. "How about I pay a full month's rent, and we see how it goes?" he said. "If neither of us likes the setup after a week, I pack up, and you keep the money."

Marla Snow looked first to Cecil then back into Carson's face. "What did Cecil quote you for rent?"

"Said one-ninety-five. That right?"

She nodded. "Where's your gear?" She looked at the backpack next to his chair. "That it?"

"That's it." He pulled out his wallet. While she watched, he took out five twenties and slid them across to her. "Keep the change," he said.

"Crispy," she said, fingering the bills. "Been wet."

78

"Road warrior money gets wet sometimes. Not to worry, it'll spend."

They finished their tea, and Marla Snow offered to show Carson his new quarters. Cecil said he'd seen the inside of the trailer, had it memorized, but he would drop by later in case Carson needed a run into town to buy some groceries and such.

The trailer was up an incline behind the house, hidden by a couple of ponderosa pine trees and a small Quonset building covered in blotched corrugated metal. A green garden hose led a circuitous route up and disappeared beneath a polished aluminum-sided trailer house; alongside the hose ran a heavy-gauge power cord. A tow tongue with two propane tanks attached to it jutted out from the front of the trailer to a leveling jack that had been cranked up and rested on two wood blocks. Marla Snow stood back, hands in her pockets, and dug a toe into the carpet of needles on the ground.

"This is her," she said. "My home on wheels."

Carson stepped forward and patted a hand against the siding. "It's beautiful," he said. "How old is it?"

"It's a 1974 Avion Travelcade," she said. "She's old but in great shape. Hardly ever used. My husband's parents kept it in Santa Fe. Lived there in the winter months. It was towed back to the farm after his father passed. No one in the family could bring themselves to use it or sell it. So there she sat under a big lean-to attached to a barn on the farm property." She smiled. "Every once in a while I'd take a cup of coffee and a book and sneak inside her unnoticed to just get away from the farm hubbub. My haven. Fell in love with her."

Carson nodded and walked off along the trailer's length. Marla Snow stood watching him as he studied the wood blocks and stabilizer jack stands Cecil and his cronies had used to level the trailer—as if he knew what he was looking at. He walked all the way around and approached her again.

"Looks great," he said. "What do you call her?"

"What?"

"Her, you keep calling the trailer her, so you must have a name for it."

She ducked her head and laughed. "Silly," she responded. "Hazel. I call her Hazel. After my grandmother."

"Seems to be the norm around here, naming all things mobile." When she looked confused he added, "Marigold?"

Her laugh was light. "Oh yes, Marigold. Well, I'd named Hazel before I ever met Marigold."

Carson studied her for a moment then said, "Don't want to invade your privacy, but Cecil did tell me some about how you ended up here in The Dalles. Sorry about the circumstances."

Her eyes sparked for an instant. "Cecil is worse than Facebook."

"My apologies."

"But I love him, so it's okay." She looked off into the trees for a moment. "Yes," she said, turning her eyes back on Carson. "It has been hard, brutal really. When the ground beneath you shifts then goes away, and you lose everything you counted on, the horror is beyond belief. I don't know if you can relate to that."

"Maybe." Carson connected viscerally with what she said but quashed it as best he could.

"Maybe," she echoed. "Who are you, anyway?"

"Who am I? Just a guy who decided to hit the road."

She cocked a smile at him. "No."

"I'm not?"

"Thinking there's more to this than Joe citizen deciding to stick his thumb out."

Carson felt a twist in his gut. For an instant he wanted to dump his horror story on her—all of it. It rolled in on him like a video, like a wave, forcing its way in—again.

"Hello?" Marla Snow was leaning forward to make visual contact with him.

He blinked and met her fixed gaze and regenerated a weak smile.

"Where did you go, Mr. Tolliver?"

"Drifted, didn't I?" To her raised eyebrows he said, "How about

80

we take a look inside, give Hazel the once-over? Before I fall asleep standing up."

It was compact, just twenty-four feet but spectacular. There was wood trim, a small kitchen, colorful upholstery, double bed, cozy dining area, and a restroom with a claustrophobic shower. Carson felt connected immediately. "And you're going to let me move in?"

"It was close, but yes," she kidded. "For now."

"I'll be good."

"Whoever you are," she responded.

-11-

It was in the paper, Naomi's obituary and funeral notice. The service was to be at the University Presbyterian Church in Seattle, but of course no one from the Barrus family would attend; it had been so decreed. Lillian Barrus, still staggered by the sudden revelation that her thought-dead grandson was actually alive, called her son and pleaded with CB to not let Naomi's funeral pass without some acknowledgement from their family. But he callously upbraided her: "Leave it alone, Mother. I mean it. They want nothing to do with us."

Lillian felt righteous anger begin to warm her body, a sensation she had packed away long ago—until now. Several days before the funeral, she went against the edict and called the Saunders' home; Naomi's mother Alice answered. She said nothing in response to Lillian's greeting but could be heard mumbling, probably with a hand over the mouthpiece.

"Mrs. Barrus," said the raspy male voice that came back on. "Jack Saunders. What can I do for you?"

"Hello, Jack. Who is this Mrs. Barrus person?" She threw in a little laugh.

After a pause Jack Saunders said, "All right, Lillian." His voice remained wooden. "Is there something you want?"

"Just to say that I know what you must be going through."

"I doubt you do," he responded.

Lillian held her words for a moment. "Oh but I do, Jack. Very much I do." Her recall of Aleta's death lay dormant most of the time, but it sprang forth at that moment.

He could hear Jack Saunders inhale his regret before he spoke.

"Of course, Lillian. Forgive me for that shameful oversight."

She was not sure if the man meant her granddaughter or her still-thought-to-be-missing grandson. She went on the premise it was Aleta he meant. "Nonsense, Jack. That was then, this is now. Your pain is much more acute—how could it be otherwise? Forgive me for calling. I know it is your wish that we Barrus's stay clear of your celebration of Naomi's life, but I simply had to call and express my own sorrow for you and Alice and the rest of your family."

"Thank you, Lillian. We have no quarrel with you."

"You will be in my thoughts."

There was another short pause before Jack Saunders asked the obvious. "Is there any news of Carson?"

Lillian caught her breath, and the presence of Carson swirled in her head. "No," she breathed finally. "We have heard nothing from the authorities in the last few days."

"Sorry. That's not good news."

Knowing the opposite truth but withholding it was causing her heart to beat noticeably. "One can only hope," she said, abetting the deception.

"Yes," Jack Saunders said softly, "one can only hope."

"Well," she said, "while the sympathy of others, though well meant, may do little to ease the pain, you are still in my thoughts." And there they left it.

———————

Lillian and Herbert Roe, a man she'd met in the elevator six months ago, were eating small tuna fish salads for lunch when the call came. These days her few phone calls were mostly from among her small circle of female friends, usually someone from her book club or the garden club that no longer did any gardening. Herbert Roe lived on the same floor of the apartment building, so he never called, just ambled down the corridor and tapped on her door. Since Carson's first call, every new ring sent a chill up her back that it might be him again. And each time she wished as hard as she could that it would be him. This time it was.

With the sound of his voice she spoke excitedly. "Oh, wait, wait." She waved a hand at Herbert Roe and pointed at the phone. He bobbed his head in understanding as she picked up the bulky land-line phone and walked it into her bedroom with the extra long extension cord trailing along. Herbert just kept on placidly eating his salad and sipping V8 juice. She closed the door, sat on the bed nervous and breathless, and said his name. "Carson."

"Hi, Grandma. Did I interrupt something? You have guests? I can call again."

"No, no. Don't you dare hang up. It's just a neighbor friend. He and I were having a bite of lunch."

"He? Something I should know? Who is this guy?"

"Don't be silly. He's just a nice man who moved into the building a few months ago. We met in the elevator, actually. Herbert Roe is his name. Retired architect, it seems. And he's younger." She giggled. "We're sharing tuna salad at the moment."

"Life in the fast lane for Grams."

"Carson, I've been waiting."

"I know, and I'm sorry. Had to find a place to settle in."

"Where are you? I have to know."

"Not right now. Later. I need you to be my undercover agent for the time being."

"Oh," she sighed. "This is awful. Carson, this can't go on. Don't ask me to keep this to myself. I can't do it. I just can't."

"Hey, you are the toughest person I know. Of course you can do it. I need you to do it."

She hesitated. "I spoke with Jack Saunders today. Naomi's funeral will be this weekend."

"This weekend." He fell silent. She listened. "Naomi." His voice grew thick when he breathed her name. "I have hallucinations," he said. "When I can see her. Literally see her. We're in the car...it's the last image I have. We were arguing...before it happened." She heard him pull in a ragged breath. "Now she's gone, and I'm not."

Lillian's nerves were on edge, but she held them in check when she spoke. "But you survived, dear one."

He didn't respond.

"Tell me," she said, "could you have saved her?"

"No." He choked it out. "No. I couldn't have. I knew she was dead as soon as we hit the water...from the impact. Died right then. She never wore her seatbelt, and I couldn't reach her. I tried. I tore at that airbag, but I couldn't get through it. I was going to drown and—"

"Carson," she interrupted. "Stop. I'm sorry. I shouldn't have asked you that. Naomi died of head injuries. There was nothing anyone could have done. They said so." She waited for him to say more, but when he didn't, she asked what she had been waiting to ask. "Now you have to tell me—why did you do this? Why disappear?"

"I told you when I first called."

"You mean about Aleta's son? Really? You actually meant it? My word, Carson. You were drowning. How in heaven's name did you come out of the water and at that moment think of her child and go into hiding?"

He inhaled. "Because I've been filled with self-loathing ever since you told me about her baby and that she wasn't allowed to have her own child. I've had this rage in me." He barked a laugh. "Listen to me—my rage. That's rich. Remember you asking me if knowing of that injustice would be the thing to finally put a fire in my belly? You remember that?"

"Yes." She spoke softly. "I do."

"Well, that fire has languished, smoldering in my gutless belly. Never did I summon the courage to act on it. And I'm not acting on courage even now, far from it. I came out of that canal soaked and crawled away and realized I could do what I want to do without having to fight for it. To act out of the shadows, I guess.

"I...I couldn't get her out of my mind—ever. Damn it, there's a little boy out there somewhere with strangers. It clawed at me that he would never know Aleta and that she was never allowed to live the life she should have had."

"But what now, Carson?"

"Find the child and bring him home. Where he belongs."

Lillian stared at the bedroom wall, at the watercolor of an iris hanging there, and didn't know what to say in response.

After a moment, he said. "Whatever it takes, I'm finding her child."

"Oh, Carson. You can't..."

"Will you help me?"

Lillian held a hand over her mouth and gripped the receiver with the other.

"Grams?"

"My sweet one," she began, "you can't just go steal a child from its legal parents. I know you loved Aleta. We all did. But this...what you intend, it would be impossible. There are laws and attachments."

"I know it could be a fool's errand, and it will require careful steps, but I am determined. Do you know where he is? The boy, do you know?"

She stood up from the bed. "Carson, this is worse than a fool's errand. You must abandon this idea. You must. And come back to us." She paused then said, "No, I won't help you. I won't help you because I love you so. It would be tragic for you to attempt."

"You do know, don't you? Where he is."

"No, I don't." She rationalized that she wasn't really lying, she'd only heard BeBe say one word: *Oklahoma*.

"I don't believe you. Think about it. I'll call you again. And as you promised, keep all of this between us. Grams? Please."

After a long moment of regret she gave in. They disconnected, and she went back to finish her tuna salad. There was a new hole in her heart.

"Who'd you say it is?" Vincent Horne leaned back in his desk chair, phone to his ear, and looked out his office window from thirtieth floor of the Rainier Tower. The view was spectacular, but he had grown used to it. "Wouldn't tell you? Look I haven't got...say that again. Watermelon? Holy...put him through."

Horne sat up straight, planted his elbows on the desktop, and waited to be connected. His mouth had gone dry; he stared at nothing and took in a deep breath.

"Vince?"

"Geez," Horne blurted and stood up, shoving his chair back. "It's you. Isn't it?"

"Yes."

"My god, I'm having a stroke here. What the hell, Carson." He dropped back into his chair. "It can't be. My god, my god, my god!"

"I know. Sorry to drop in on you like this, Vince. But it's me—really."

Horne blew out a breath. "I've been following things nearly every day, in the papers, TV, radio. You know, waiting for the news, expecting your..."

"For my body to be found?"

"Yeah," Horne said softly. Vincent Horne, partner in the law firm of Jefferson, Caldwell, and Horne, had met Carson Barrus when they both attended the University of Washington, before they went separate ways, Horne to earn his law degree and Carson his MBA. They had become inseparable friends and kept in close but sporadic touch as the years went by. They were among those friends who may not see each other for months, years even, but when one calls the other, it is like they had talked the day before. Neither had contacted the other for nearly nine months—now this.

"Guess they haven't. Found my body."

Horne burst out with a laugh of relief. "Guess you'd know."

"It's been surreal."

Horne laughed again. "I bet. And just when I was thinking this was going to be another routine day." There was a moment of quiet while each considered the other. "Man, you've got me off balance, Carson. I'm reeling. What...I mean, how can this be?"

"First, I need you to know that only you and one other knows I'm alive. I need it to stay that way for now. Okay?"

"You mean your family..."

"Except for one of them, no. Vince, you have to keep this to yourself, will you? And I mean no one else, not your wife, your partners, no one. Will you?"

Horne's heartbeat had leveled off. He expelled a nervous chuckle. "Are you sane? That would have a big bearing on things."

"Hell, I don't know. Might not be. I've considered that myself. Still, I need your help."

Horne's office door opened, and a middle-aged woman came in carrying some file folders. When she laid them on his desk, he gave her a signal she knew to mean that he was not to be disturbed. When she was gone, Horne said, "Okay. First, tell me why you did this? What did you do…just walk away from the accident or something?"

"That's right. That's just how it was. Came out of the canal after nearly drowning and decided to walk away."

Horne spun his chair around and looked out the window again focused on nothing. "This is so bizarre. Where are you?

"Can't say."

"Okay, again, why did you do this?"

"Can't tell you. Not yet, anyway."

Horne laughed. "I've had clients like this—want all kinds of help but won't tell you anything about what and why. All right, what do you want from me?"

"Vince, I need to know that you trust me. I'm not working some kind of scam to avoid debt or evade business obligations or family responsibilities—nothing like that. I didn't steal a huge sum of money. And I don't think walking away from your own death is a crime, not sure though. And before any insurance policy on my life can be activated, this will all come out, and no claim will have been paid out. Those are my disclaimers."

"Okay, I trust you."

"Can I trust you in return? Will you keep this in confidence?"

"Haven't I kept *watermelon* in confidence all these years?" The word *watermelon* was code between them for a moment of sexual frolic they had succumbed to years ago when they were both engaged. "But man alive, *watermelon* is a but a silly moment of no consequence compared to this."

Carson laughed. "Okay, I can trust you. Go back to work, and I'll be in touch when I need your help. Tell you more then."

Horne had opened his mouth to ask something, but Carson was gone.

-12-

To Carson, his first night in the trailer was akin to being in a very comfortable cargo container: an elegant box with windows and a tolerably good bed. When the temperature dropped, he burrowed into the sleeping bag loaned to him by Marla Snow and slept fitfully but warmly except for a protruding cold nose. It was pitch black when he awoke abruptly once, sensed the closeness about him, and shivered, but not from the cold. He slept in snippets until daylight began to emerge as a gray smudge, then scooted up out of the sleeping bag, breathed in the smell of the cold trailer, and slipped barefoot into his shoes. He stepped outside, wearing only a tee shirt and Jockey shorts and leaned against a ponderosa pine tree to pee. Steam rose from his vigorous stream, and fog puffed out in bursts from his nostrils. Later he would negotiate going into the old house to shower and use a toilet, but for now he would just pee outdoors. In the trailer's chill, he rinsed his face in cold water, brushed his teeth, combed damp hair, and dressed. Slipping on his jacket, he stepped outside into the growing daylight and looked about him. It was quiet and still except for the twittering of a chipmunk that scampered by and ran up a tree. At the sound of a vehicle passing out on Mill Creek Road, he turned and saw Marla Snow standing next to the Quonset building, arms folded across her red coat, looking up at him. He gave a small wave and walked toward her.

"Morning," she said, offering him a bland smile. "How'd it go?"

"Okay." He nodded. "Cold, but comfortable. Thanks for the sleeping bag."

"Sure. I'll get some propane in those tanks and show you how to use the furnace. If the propane costs too much, you may have to chip in on it."

"Thought I was going to use the shower in your house."

She shrugged. "You may do that. We can work out a schedule for now. Toilet on the back porch is yours to use. If this renter bit works out, I'm thinking of maybe plumbing the trailer."

"Okay." Carson smiled and considered that he could tell her a bit about being a landlord. "What time is it, anyway?"

"Little after six, I'm getting ready to go to work. Since this is your first day, how about you come on in? Coffee's on, and I can offer you a Welcome Wagon breakfast with a choice of wheat toast or a bagel. I eat light."

She turned abruptly and walked off in long strides toward the house. Carson followed her inside and sat at the kitchen table when she asked him to and waited patiently until she brought over a cup of coffee and set it in front of him.

"Where do you work?" he asked.

She spoke over her shoulder while loading the toaster. "For a company called Boyd Organics," she answered. "Big farm operation located in Boyd, in what used to be a town up until fifty years ago. Listed as a ghost town these days. It's about ten miles south of The Dalles. We farm about 3,500 acres of chemical-free crops, grains, produce, and fruit—all organic. Grind our own organic flours, have big greenhouses to raise fruits and vegetables year around, plus we sell a lot of organic and natural products from other producers, things we don't grow or make." She brought over a plate of toast, no bagels after all, and a jar of blackberry preserves.

"Sounds like a big change from teaching high school English."

She sat down and began spreading jam on her toast. Her expression was nonresponsive until she had covered the bread. "Yes, but I'm doing what I went looking for," she said without looking up. "Something worth doing without a set of expectations undermined by people who haven't a clue what it takes to do the job, like teaching young minds. I earned the training, knew what I was doing, but they always knew better. The stupider they were, the more they thought they knew."

Carson ate his toast without preserves and sipped the coffee without commenting. They ate in silence for a bit until she went to refill her cup and brought the pot over to top off his as well. She looked down at him until he met her eyes.

"You know the rest I guess, from Cecil," she said.

"I guess I do, maybe. Some. None of my business."

She ignored his disclaimer. "Thought I'd put it all together: college, teaching job, and the man to spend my life with. It worked right up until it didn't." She sat down again and cupped her hands around the mug.

Carson studied her: hazel eyes, dark eyebrows, and rose mouth without lipstick. He wanted to say he understood, that losing your mate is hell and that he had lost his as well, even if they had suffered a torturous marriage. But then, he wasn't Carson Barrus; he was Bill Tolliver with no interchangeable history to share.

She picked up her plate and cup, went to the sink, and came back. "I have to go pick up Ola Mae now. We both work for Boyd. Guess Cecil's coming by to see if you want a lift into town. Expect you have some errands."

"I do," he said. "First thing will be to find me a set of wheels to use."

"Can't help you there. But I'm sure Cecil will have some ideas. Usually does." She smiled pleasantly. "Have to go now. Feel free to use the shower."

He stood at the front door window and watched her drive off, marveling at being taken in by a group of unlikely strangers, his world totally awry from only days ago. Was he truly crazy?

———

After taking a shower, he sat on the front porch in one of the rockers, zipped his jacket against the cold, and waited until as seamlessly as a breath the questions came again. Why not return home, appear contrite before the family, lament Naomi's death, endure admonishments for disappearing, and then merge back into life as it had been? Could he do that? Of course not. There would be a price, and it would be bottomless. No, preposterous as it was, he'd made his decision and intended to see it through. He wondered if he could *ever* go back.

He had his cell phone out, ready to call Vince Horne again and prevail on him to take the initial covert step, when Cecil drove up. He rotated his bulk out of a white Ford Taurus, stood up, yanked on his pants, and raised a hand.

"I'm not walking up there," he shouted, "if all we'll be doing is walking back out here. You wanting a ride into town?"

"Where's Marigold?" Carson asked as he walked down the porch steps.

"Resting. This here's my run-around vehicle," Cecil said, patting a fender on the car.

"Name?"

"No name, just a car. Things you need to get in town? If so, I'll run you in. I've got a couple of errands myself. Where to?"

They got into the car and slammed doors simultaneously. "First off," Carson said, "where can I get a car on the cheap? I need to borrow or rent some wheels."

Cecil brought the engine to life, spit tobacco juice out the open window, and let a flatbed farm truck pass before pulling out onto Mill Creek Road. "A car," he said. "Our best bet is Frisco. He carries on a kind of used car business out to his place. On the side like. We can start there. Owes me a favor or two, anyway."

Frisco's place was out Chenoweth Creek Road: a sturdy ranch-style house with a metal-walled pole building set off from it. Cecil pulled up a concrete drive and tapped his horn. Frisco wandered out, after a bit, holding a coffee cup. He sidled up and looked down at Cecil through the car's open window.

"Morning," he said, sporting a toothy grin. "What's got you fellas out roamin' the back roads at this hour?"

"Come to look at your cars." Cecil slid out, reached inside his cheek, levered out a glob of used tobacco, and flipped it out into a clump of brush. "You remember Bill, he's in need of some wheels. A loaner like." Cecil shoved a fresh round of chew inside his cheek. "You holding on to any good rides?"

"Now, wait a minute," Frisco stuttered as Cecil started off toward the pole building. "Whatcha meaning by loaner?"

"You know, like borrow." Cecil shoved at the big door, it grumbled open on rollers. "Lookie here, Bill," Cecil shouted. "There's some sweet cars in here. How about that Honda?"

When a verbal shoving match ensued, Carson stepped outside away from their sparring and considered that he'd never had to borrow a car, or anything else for that matter, ever. Somehow an arrangement was made and a sober-faced Frisco watched Carson drive away in a mid-mileage ten-year-old silver Toyota Camry. He would have free use of the car.

In town, he went by the Salvation Army store and spent some of his limited resources on some cheap bed linens and a frayed bath towel with a garish Hawaiian design on it. He followed up with a stop at Safeway for a stash of food and two cans of Pabst Blue Ribbon then returned to the trailer to set up housekeeping, as it were. For the first time in his life, he was under financial pressure for the basics. It was a strange, unsettling feeling.

A fuel company delivery slip was stuck to the trailer's door. He would have to wait for Marla Snow to show him how to use the propane furnace. Once he had made up his bed and put away his modest store of groceries, he stepped outside and felt the odd sensation of having nothing to do, no demands, and yet he knew what had to be done. He checked his phone, still had plenty of minutes left, and called his grandmother. She answered, turned down her television, and after another round of hearing about the distress she was enduring, he persuaded her to reveal where she knew Aleta's son to be. Oklahoma. That's all she knew, she told him emphatically. But where in Oklahoma? He had to know, and if the family that had the boy was even still in Oklahoma. And he needed names: an adoptive family name, a foster parent name, any names that could help him connect with the child. He implored her to find out. She resisted, still thinking his quest to be an untenable, even sad, scheme; but when her regrets had been again fully vented, she acceded to her grandson's wishes. She promised to proceed at once; he would call back in a couple of days. By that time he hoped that she would have managed to wrest what he needed to know from his mother. Although not told so by Lillian, he felt certain that had to be her source.

-13-

Carson slid into the trailer's kitchen nook that evening, stared at a blank piece of paper, and considered everything he would have to ask of Vincent Horne. Just how far could he push old college ties to help him decipher the legal, custodial, even moral, issues that were sure to arise when trying to find and rescue a sequestered child? The steps he wrote down were at once measurable, point-by-point actions while remaining nebulous, indistinct, even frightening in their possible outcome. Later it came to him that never once as he prognosticated his future action, had he thought of Naomi. She only came to mind now in the throes of shuddering hallucinations as he slept. That part of his life was by that time beyond bereavement.

He redrafted what he theorized needed to happen, but no matter the variations, he felt no greater clarity, or a heightened degree of certainty that he could make it all happen. He would do what had to be done and hope that Vince would sign on. Finally he set his notes aside and set about to appease the hole in his stomach, only to discover that he had no can opener, no dishware, nor any utensils— worse yet, he didn't have a clue about how to light the stove burners. So except for cereal and milk, all of the food he'd purchased was sealed in tin, unreachable, reminding him that his skills as a home-maker were sorely limited. He didn't feel like settling for breakfast cereal, so he finally slipped on his jacket and went knocking at Marla Snow's door in search of culinary tools. When she came to the door, he stood there with the rolled up sleeping bag he'd borrowed under one arm and grinned like a door-to-door salesman.

"Evening," he said to her noncommittal face. "I'm working my way through college selling magazine subscriptions. Could I interest you in *People* magazine? Comes with this free sleeping bag."

She looked him up and down. "How about *Trailer Life for Dummies?*" she answered and took the sleeping bag from him.

He laughed loudly and bent at the waist. "Got me there. This dummy is here confessing his ignorance."

"Like?"

"Like not thinking about having something to open cans with or plates to put food on. That is, unless the landlord has such items and intended to provide them to this neophyte renter."

Marla Snow smiled, waved her hand, and invited him in. "Takes two dummies to make dumb work. I'm a neophyte landlord, so we're even. I had planned on providing the basics you mentioned, simply forgot. So, in lieu of enjoying what was surely to be a gourmet meal you were about to prepare, what say you partake of a little steamed broccoli and a hamburger patty followed by some ice cream? Not gourmet, best I have."

He easily accepted her offer and eagerly downed the food while she watched him eat with interest. When they had finished spooning small servings of vanilla ice cream, he helped clear the table and wash the dishes. While he dried, she opened her cupboards and pulled out an oddball assortment of plates, cups, a frying pan, pot, old teapot, and silverware. Finally she reached into the kitchen tools drawer and withdrew a can opener.

"This is an extra," she said, holding it up, "although I hardly ever eat anything out of a can anymore."

"I can only aspire to be able to prepare meals not in a can. Thanks for feeding me, again."

She nodded and offered him a glass of wine, which he accepted. Then they had a second and talked in generalities: mostly about the trailer—was it working all right? Yes, but heat would be nice. She took his humor in stride and offered that she was considering running gray water and the toilet into the septic system. Cecil and some of his buddies could do it, she surmised.

"You think so?" Carson asked.

She laughed, her eyes bright from the wine. "He's actually pretty handy, and he knows a bunch of guys. Among them they can do most anything."

"If you say so. It'd be great to have the trailer plumbed."

She took another sip of wine and looked at him quizzically. "Think you'll be around long enough to justify all of that?"

He hesitated. "I think so." When he saw her eyes narrow a bit, he added, "I may be away for a time, but I'm figuring this is home base for a while."

"How long is that, a while?"

"Not sure. Longer than a month, less than the rest of my life." He pushed out a little laugh.

She held the wine bottle up again; he put a hand over his glass. She poured herself a little more. "Guess we could all say that—the life part, anyway."

Carson smiled. "Yes," he said, thinking that up until a brief tic of time ago he would have told anyone interested that his life was set for the long term.

Marla Snow drank the last swallow of wine and set her glass down gently. "Tell me," she said, "if I may ask again, what are you doing here? In this town? In good old Wasco County?"

Carson sat back in his chair and looked into the face of this woman he had only just met. Now wasn't the time to reveal his plans.

"I'm on this odyssey," he smiled. "Just seems like a good place to get my bearings."

Her face grew questioning. "What does that mean?"

"I...well, I found myself going through the motions, everyday exactly like the next."

"Been there," she slipped in.

He looked at her face and saw the resolve written there. "Like a lot of people, looking for something missing in their lives, I guess. But it was like I'm not me...I know, weird. And really I cannot explain it in a way that would make any sense to you."

"Uh-huh. You have family?"

He nodded.

"Married?"

"Was," he answered after a beat then said it: "She died." Those two words left his mouth on a whispered breath and spun in his brain— the first utterance acknowledging Naomi's total absence to anyone.

Marla Snow's eyes widened; she took in a deep breath and swallowed a hum. "Wow," she said softly. "Two peas in a pod we are. Sorry."

He just nodded again.

"You know how many times I heard that bloody word after Glen died? Too damn many. So I apologize for saying it to you. What else can one say?"

"I understand," he answered. "It's okay."

For a moment they shared small intuitive smiles, each sucked into their own version of loss. Marla Snow traced a finger around a square on the tablecloth.

"You said you are going to be away for a time," she said.

"Uh-huh."

"Getting away from it? The loss?" When he didn't answer she went on, "That's what I did. Ended up here."

"That working?"

She tipped her head to the side. "Mostly. Work in progress."

"That's the way of it, never finished," he said as if he knew.

She smiled. "Agreed. So this place is the jumping off-point for your odyssey?"

"Guess so. Wherever it leads." He laughed.

Marla Snow stood and took the wine glasses to the sink. "Well," she said with a note of resignation, "since I'm not going to hear your life's story, let's go see about lighting Hazel's furnace. Get you some heat."

She marched out of the house; Carson trailed behind matching her long stride. He watched as she opened the furnace door, turned something, depressed a button, and lit the pilot light with a kitchen match. She showed him where the thermostat was, and soon heat was coming out of a vent. Next she showed him how to light the stove burners.

"Got it?" she asked. He nodded. "Okay, then let's go out to the Quonset so I can show you where the circuit breaker is, just in case you turn on too many things and the lights go out."

When they entered the old Quonset hut she reached out in the dark and found a light switch. The semicylindrical building was suddenly illuminated with a row of overhead lights that shown down beneath white enameled light shades. She showed him the breaker box and the switch that controlled the circuit for the trailer; but it was the big open room that caught Carson's attention and held it: the size, the contents, but most of all the aroma.

"What is all this?" he asked. "And what's that smell?"

She waved an arm out. "Oh, it's just my candles." She shrugged. "Just something I do on the side to make extra income. A hobby that got out of control."

"Smells nice."

"That's Bing cherry fragrance. My claim to fame," she said. "My own special formula. Anyway, that's the circuit breaker box," she turned. "In case you overload things. It also runs the lights and outlets in this building. Okay?"

Carson walked forward beside a long worktable lined with shipping cartons and rows of tall candles, short candles, candles in jars, votive candles, and candle-making equipment. Every candle was a deep maroon color.

He picked up a pillar candle and smelled it. "Nice," he said. "Really, you make these?"

She folded her arms across her chest. "Yep, I'm the candle lady. It is mostly a pain, especially now trying to fill Christmas orders and come out on top financially. "

"Interesting."

"You think so?" She stepped over and pushed a small shipping carton for no reason. "I'm getting out of it after this season. Getting more hours out at Boyd Organics, so maybe that'll be enough so I can stop this candle gig."

Carson listened and looked around the building some more. "Special formula?"

She stepped over and picked up a candle, rolled it on her hand, and put it back down. "Yeah. Wouldn't be in this up to my waist if I hadn't come up with a formula that worked. Most cherry fragrance candles smell like flavored cough syrup. I bumped into a better way is all."

"Like what?"

She expelled a grunting sigh. "A guy that runs a distillery in Portland told me I ought to try using the volatile alcohol that comes out of the distiller first when they're making cherry liqueur. It is called the 'heads.' Nasty stuff they have no use for, but it's real aromatic. Got some, added it to my own formula, and it worked. But I'm tired of it."

"Really?" He picked up another candle and smelled it. "Seems like it would be a nice little business."

She stepped over, took the candle out of his hand, and threw it in an overhand arc. It thudded against the metal-ribbed wall. She stared at where the cherry pillar had fallen then turned and walked out of the building. Carson waited a bit before following. He looked back over the array of candles, turned off the lights, and went back to the trailer. It was warm inside, too warm. He turned off the furnace, stowed the dishware and utensils, and stepped back outside to cool off. He looked down toward the house and wondered about his landlord and her demons. He surmised that what had just occurred wasn't really about cherry candles any more than he was a free-spirited nomad.

A few snowflakes began floating down and shown up bright and white in the light coming from a trailer window. He shivered, pulled the trailer door open, and stepped inside. With the click of the door latch, he felt a sense of comfort he hadn't had for a while.

———————

The *Seattle Times* carried the story in the "Local News" section the following day. The headline was neutral and yet sobering: "Seattle man presumed drowned". The brief article read: *A Seattle native last seen November 22, Thanksgiving Day, is now presumed drowned. Carson Barrus, 38, and his wife Naomi Barrus, 36, were lost when their SUV plunged into Hood Canal near Hoodsport in the early hours of Friday, November 23, after being struck by a semi truck and trailer. Naomi Barrus's body was found in the submerged vehicle, but the remains of Carson Barrus have not been located following extensive searches by Mason County Sherriff's department by boat, divers, or foot patrol along the canal shoreline. Officials have declared that Barrus is now presumed to have drowned as a result of the accident. Memorial services for Naomi and Carson Barrus are pending.*

Carson awoke from a deep sleep the next morning feeling rested for the first time in many days, not knowing that he had been officially declared dead. He arose, lit the heater, had cereal and milk, no coffee (he'd forgotten to buy any) and went to use the shower in the farmhouse. Marla Snow's car was gone already; he was relieved that he wouldn't have to face her after the candle-throwing incident—not yet anyway. He scurried back to the trailer in the cold, noticing that the snow flurries of the previous evening had left only traces of white on the ground. He dressed, sat at the kitchen nook table, and retrieved the note pad on which he had outlined his intended course of action.

He studied it again and decided it was time to make the calls.

-14-

BeBe Barrus agreed to meet with her mother-in-law and suggested her favorite teahouse just north of Pike Street Market in downtown Seattle. BeBe was already seated at a small scalloped white marble-topped table in the Dragon Mountain Tea Shoppe when Lillian arrived. It was early afternoon in between the busier hours, so the little place was pretty quiet. Lillian gave a wave as she entered slowly on complaining legs and eased down, as best she could, onto one of the wrought-iron chairs. BeBe returned Lillian's greeting with a tight smile and pretended to be looking for something in a large leather purse. Not finding whatever it might have been, she set the purse by her feet and rested her hands on the table.

"I just love this place," she said. "Smells so good, don't you think?"

Lillian repositioned herself on the chair's small seat and looked about. "I guess so," she answered. "You know my smeller isn't what it used to be, but I'll take your word for it."

BeBe squinched out a tolerant smile. "What would you like, Lillian? I'm having oolong tea."

"I'm a chamomile drinker. You know that. Maybe I'll try something different this time. Make a suggestion. What about one of those green teas?"

BeBe's smile stayed in place. "All right. Let's see...I think you might like jasmine pearl green tea. It's another of my favorites."

"Fine. Jasmine. I'll take that."

BeBe caught the eye of the waitress on duty and gave her their order, adding a small plate of English biscuits. "There," BeBe said, "this will be nice, and it's my treat."

Lillian folded her hands in her lap. "Thank you." She looked around at the array of gifts and the wall of teas in jars and nodded. "It is a nice shop, very nice."

"I think so," BeBe said, laboring to paint over what she anticipated was coming from Lillian. "Though it's been a while since I've been here. I used to come here quite often."

"Uh-huh." They fell silent for a long moment before Lillian spoke. "I saw the piece in the paper. About Carson. Presumed dead is official, isn't it?"

"Yes." The little smile on BeBe's face faded. "No sign of him so…so, oh Lillian," she choked and raised a hand to her mouth.

Lillian watched her daughter-in-law crying and drew her mouth into a sad line, attempting to show remorse for the one lost. BeBe's pain was obviously so earnest, the guileless agony of a mother for a lost child, that Lillian was near blurting out that her son lived just to relieve her pain. But she didn't; it was ripping away at her innards, but she held fast and thought of her mission. She watched BeBe dab at her eyes with a paper napkin and looked away to gather her thoughts and rehearse the script she had devised in her head.

She was about to foist an intrusion into BeBe's grief when the tea and biscuits arrived. The fragrance of the Jasmine tea came out of the metal teapot; Lillian liked it. BeBe told her to let it steep a bit; she did and bit into a shortbread biscuit as she waited. When BeBe began to pour her oolong tea out into a porcelain cup, she did the same. In unison, they sipped cautiously of the hot teas, set their cups down, and smiled the smiles they had developed over the years. They were never truly close as daughter-in-law and mother-in-law largely due to their discomforting understanding of the nature of CB. The mother had known her oldest son as a cold and insensitive child from the early years and felt regret for BeBe from the first realization that she might marry her son. Over the years, through their exchanged glances and careful conversations, they shared the realization that the man they knew as son and husband was hard to love and from whom they received no love in return. When with her daughter-in-law, Lillian was forever drawn into memories of the dark days when BeBe entered a private mental health facility after Aleta's death. Her recovery had been slow and agonizing for the family and virtually unsupported by CB. Lillian feared for BeBe's mental state now with Carson's loss and felt a sense of wretchedness for what she had to do.

"I like it," Lillian said. When BeBe looked up she added, "the tea, the jasmine."

"Oh," BeBe responded. "Yes, it is very nice, isn't it?"

Lillian smiled as best she could and took another sip. "So," she said after setting her cup back down, "when will there be a memorial service?"

BeBe's eyes widened. "Oh. I'm…well, we haven't decided. You know CB. He's not one to rush such things."

Lillian harrumphed a grunt. "What? Just days after the accident he was all for having a memorial right then and there before there was any conclusion of Carson's presumed drowning. I've known him to rush a business deal through in one day or evict a tenant thirty seconds after the law allowed."

BeBe fell silent and looked away only to turn her eyes on Lillian with fire in them. "I know. But he is…was our son, your grandson, so we'll take the time we need to."

"Yes, of course. I'm sorry I spoke out of turn. Forgive me."

BeBe nodded and raised her cup again.

They sat sipping their tea and finished the biscuits. BeBe raised her hand and asked for more hot water for each of them. After the waitress poured steaming water into each pot, they were left with just each other and the quiet between them.

When Lillian sensed that BeBe was uncomfortable with the silence, she opened her script and spoke. "You said Oklahoma."

BeBe's eyes opened wider, her expression one of dread. "What?" She tipped her head forward. "What did you say? No don't…just don't."

"Don't what?"

"Lillian. You know. And you know I can't."

"Can't what?"

"What are you doing? Is that why we're here?"

"BeBe," Lillian said slowly, "I want to know all there is to know."

"No."

"I insist."

BeBe emitted a short sharp laugh. "You insist?" She stood up.

"Don't leave," Lillian pled.

"I'm going to the ladies room. I'll be back, but don't expect me to say anything about that." She stood looking down at her mother-in-law. "Just don't."

Lillian drank tepid tea and stared at nothing, thinking of what to do next. Carson was expecting her to work a miracle and draw the truth out of his mother, his mother who didn't know he was alive. She moaned and held a hand to her face. She would have to torture this woman to find out what she knew.

BeBe returned and sat down. She was flushed and damp. She had evidently washed her face. Her blue eyes shone brightly from behind the stylish glass frames she wore. She was ready to resist. "I can't stay much longer."

Lillian squeezed her hands, feeling the arthritis complaining; the cold damp weather always exacerbated the aching. "Of course you can. Besides, what's more important between us than the losses we've endured? First Aleta, then her child, and now your son."

BeBe squeezed her eyes shut; tears came out from the creases. "Lillian, how can you do this to me?" She spoke with her eyes shut.

"How can I?" Lillian scooted around on the little chair; her rump was getting numb. "Because, my sweet one, because you know what I want to know, what I need to know."

"No, you don't need to know anything. Let it go, Lillian. Whatever it is you think I know, I don't. I'll never know."

Lillian looked about then whispered, "Damn you. You do know. Don't shake your head—you do. Otherwise, how did you know to say Oklahoma to me?"

"I shouldn't...that was a mistake. I don't know if it's Oklahoma anymore than I know if it's Chicago."

"BeBe." Lillian used her name as a cudgel. She hit her with it. "BeBe," she lowered her voice and repeated her name.

"Why are you doing this?"

"Why?" Her head swam in the reality of that question. "Because... because since you lost Aleta, since we *all* lost her, my heart has agonized over that beautiful child's tragic life and what drove her to end it."

"Tragic life?" BeBe sat up and clutched a balled-up napkin in her hand. "She had a wonderful life. We gave her everything."

Lillian leaned forward and under her breath said, "No."

"No? How can you say that? Lillian what a horrible thing to say."

Lillian felt nasal moisture gathering. She reached down and pulled a tissue from her purse and brushed at her nose, all the while looking into BeBe's pleading eyes. "BeBe," she said, taking the edge off her voice. "She was a caged bird. You know that." BeBe's eyes grew wide. "A caged bird never allowed to fly. She had all the material things, but she was watched over and held away from real living." Lillian felt her throat draw shut hearing her own words. "You know that," she whispered.

BeBe stared, glanced at her tiny gold wristwatch then looked up to stare some more. "I have to go." Her voice was a whisper. She started to move her chair back, but Lillian reached out and took hold of a forearm.

"Not yet." BeBe stiffened but didn't pull away. "I intend to find out where the child is, and you will tell me what you know," Lillian said. "Right now you will tell me."

"No." BeBe shook her head slowly side to side. "I won't. You know I can't."

"You will, or I will blow this family up. I'll pull the scab off this. I will."

BeBe's head drooped to almost resting on her chest, and she sobbed. Lillian waited patiently. When they left the tearoom, she knew all that BeBe knew; there was much more to learn, but she had done what she promised. It was raining hard. They each opened their ever-present umbrellas and walked away in opposite directions. No hugs were exchanged.

———————

After a dinner of canned chili and crackers, Carson cleaned up, promising himself that he had to get some greens back into his diet, and stepped outside to escape the sauna-like temperature in the trailer. He was still learning how to adjust the heat and had set the thermostat too high. The cold night air felt good for a short while until his body temperature lost ground to the east wind coming out of the Columbia Gorge. He stepped back inside, made sure the furnace was set on low, picked up his cell phone, and stared at its face, half expecting it to speak to him: *Are you sure about this?*

"Yes, Carson, I talked with her, and it was painful," Lillian responded to his question. "Very painful."

"I'm sorry I had to ask you to do that. How is she?"

"She, you mean your mother? BeBe is, well BeBe. Sweet as ever and feeling the pain of your loss, damn you. Carson this is so unfair—you're holding me hostage. I wanted to tell her. I almost did."

"But you didn't, right?"

"No." Her chin trembled, and she held the phone away from her mouth for a moment. "No I didn't. I kept my word."

"Thank you."

"Yes, well…it's done, I guess you can say. Not that I learned much."

Carson inhaled and held it for a beat. "Did you ask her about what I want to know?"

"Of course." Lillian sounded testy. "I'm not senile, Carson."

"I didn't mean that. I'm just anxious to get on with this." He hesitated. "So what did you find out?"

"Generalities, mostly just generalities."

"Like?"

Lillian had been watching the *News Hour* on PBS; she'd muted the sound when the phone rang. As she collected her thoughts to respond, she used the remote to turn off the set. She put her feet up on a padded footstool and sighed. "Okay. Well, we already know the location is somewhere in Oklahoma, maybe not."

"What do you mean?"

Lillian sighed into her grandson's ear. "Carson, I'm…really I'm not wanting to do this."

"Grams, I already know that part. But you will. You said you would."

She laughed but not a happy laugh. "In a weak moment. I was so elated that you were alive I would have promised you anything. Guess I did."

He laughed back. "I could be back in Seattle all settled in, dealing with Naomi's death and getting on with my life, you know?"

"Then why aren't you?"

He took in a slow, deep breath. "I made a decision when I survived. I'm stuck with it."

"Nonsense," she said. "It's crazy what you're doing. Come home. We'll say it was temporary amnesia. You can still do what you want about the child."

"No, he'd block it."

"CB?"

"Yes."

"Just go round him."

"Have I ever? Has anyone ever gone against him head on? Has anyone in our family?"

"This can be the first time then. You can do it."

"Grams, I've been gutless. We all have." He paused. "I need this space and this anonymity…for now I need it. I know, not courageous, but I need this head start. It's the only way I can do this, the only way—for Aleta and her son. I'll be tough in my own way."

"Carson," she spoke softly, " you don't have to be tough, not for me. I love you for who you are, for your caring self. Be strong, no need to be tough."

After a long moment of quiet between them, he said, "Okay. But I have to do this, get on with it. What did you learn from Mom? You confirmed somewhere in Oklahoma?"

"Yes, she remembers CB saying it was outside of Tulsa, a small town. But doesn't know the name, just that it sounded Indian. Thinks it started with a T. She really tried, Carson, but after all she doesn't press CB any more than the rest of us. Besides, it's been several years, the people involved could be somewhere else."

"What else? Anything? Need leads. Names, any family names?"

"Maybe. BeBe gave me a couple of tidbits that might be something to work on."

"What?" Carson had a prickly chill.

"Don't get your hopes up now. Might be nothing. More than likely isn't anything."

Carson leaned forward on his elbows. He was almost afraid to hear what his grandmother was set to tell him. There had been comfort in hiding behind his blustering intent to retrieve a lost nephew; it was a case of backbone not being put to the test. What if Lillian actually gave him specifics on which to act? He waited for her to unwrap the package, to lay open what she'd learned.

When he didn't press her, Lillian asked, "Are you still there?"

"I'm here," he answered. "Just waiting. Tell me."

Lillian brought a foot up onto her knee, slipped off a slipper, and massaged the bunion of a big toe. "Okay," she said and winced at the pain. "BeBe thinks the family who ended up with the boy were named something like Brown or Braun, maybe Bronson. She couldn't be any clearer than that."

Carson scribbled the names down on his note pad. "What else, anything? Any first names?"

"No, no first names. But there is one interesting thing. A midwife delivered the child."

"A midwife?"

"That's right. BeBe thinks it was a home birth."

"No hospital, what the hell? Ah, not traceable."

"Could be the reason I suppose."

"Anything else?"

"Not really. BeBe said only that at the time your father gave her what she called a terse summary of what happened then told her it was all done, clean with no one the wiser, and for her to put it out of her mind."

"No one the wiser? Manipulative bastard," Carson said.

"Yes," she said on a breath. "As we know. But now what?"

He said he would let her know and left it at that. After the call he sat transfixed, staring at the sparse bit of information he'd written down; it wasn't much, but he had actual facts. Now he could try and do something. The reality of that caused a stir in his head. He thought of his father, as he had all of his life whenever he considered a course of action, whether as a child or as a grown man. It had always been that way: How will Dad react? What will Dad do? The shudder came in that moment, the familiar signal of apprehension he had withstood so many times. There had been countless painful showdowns with his father, times when CB upbraided his middle child and relished in disemboweling his son's plans, his son's dreams, even the smallest of his son's intentions. Among the most hurtful showdowns happened when Carson was thirteen; he had purchased a kit from the All-American Soap Box Derby organization with his own money and built a racer, all by himself. For weeks he worked on assembling the car until proudly he asked his father if Barrus Properties would be his sponsor. CB had gone out to the garage to view his son's project, something he had not known was being built, and stood staring at it. Carson remembered the cynical smirking laugh more than anything. Then his father had squatted down and yanked on the front right wheel until it wobbled and came loose. He did the same to the steering wheel and handed it to his son saying: *Guess you're not ready for the big time yet.*

Carson stumbled out of the trailer, the memory of that sickening moment still so clear, and wrapped his arms around his shoulders. Tears of the boy came again, and suddenly he emitted a yell out into the darkness. He stood still as the sound rose then dissipated. The porch light down at the house came on, and he saw the figure of Marla Snow silhouetted in the open front doorway. He stood still, and so did she; soon she went back inside, and so did he.

The anticipation of what lay ahead kept him awake until he had processed his intended next steps again and again and again. Finally he drifted into an insensible sleep.

-15-

The banging on the trailer wall the next morning startled Carson from an irretrievable dream of a sort he often had—color and light, nothing else. He jerked awake, stumbled out of bed, and opened the trailer door; cold air wrapped itself around his legs. Cecil Nash stood there grinning, a lump of chew bulging in his cheek, his hands jammed into the pockets of a heavy canvas coat.

"So bucko, how's trailer life? Sleeping okay in this tin can?"

"I was until..."

"Sorry. Wake you? Hey it's past eight o'clock, time to be up and about. Let me take a look inside. I'd like to see the layout since you took up residence." He stepped up and motioned Carson back inside. "You mind?"

Carson stepped back. "Yeah I kind of do, as a matter of fact. Still in my skivvies as you can see."

Cecil pushed on in. "I've seen worse," he laughed. "Cute little abode, ain't it? You done any cooking yet?"

"Nothing fancy, mostly heating food out of a can. Going to try more inventive cooking now that I'm settled in."

"How's the showering working out? Using the house? Using the john too or the tree outside?"

"My personal hygiene of particular interest to you, Cecil?"

"Don't get your shorts in a knot. Marla wants me to see what it would take to hook this bucket up to the septic and the like. So I'm just doing some research, seeing what your needs are, if you don't mind."

"I do mind. Give me time to wake up and get dressed. May want to take one of those showers you're fussing about."

"I'm not fussing. It's called recon. Now throw on some clothes. You can shower later. I'm taking you to breakfast in town. Pretty Pearly's. Best buttermilk pancakes on the planet. My treat. Even drove Marigold."

"If you'll drop me at the library on the way back. Need to get on the Net."

"I can do that."

It was on the edge of December and getting colder in the Columbia Gorge. Carson zipped up his lightweight jacket against the east wind and pulled on his cap, vowing to drop by the thrift store again to pick out a heavier coat, maybe even gloves. Cecil coaxed Marigold to life and drove through a cold sun into town out Third Street to a diner extracted right out of the fifties: Pretty Pearly's, complete with red laminate counters, chrome swivel stools, booths with inoperable coin-operated music boxes, and a glass-enclosed pie holder with banana crème, lemon meringue, and Oregon cherry pies.

Cecil raised a hand and called out, "Two of the usual."

A husky woman wearing plastic-rimmed glasses and a red apron echoed: "Two of the usual" and from the kitchen pass-through a raspy male voice responded: "Two of the usual".

Two of the usual arrived minutes later: a stack of four huge buttermilk pancakes, four link sausages, two eggs sunny-side up, and coffee. Cecil finished his order off humming with satisfaction while Carson managed about half of his serving.

"What'd I tell you? Good, huh?" Cecil beamed.

Carson merely smiled.

Cecil pushed his plate aside and leaned on his forearms. "That you howling at the moon last night?" When Carson raised his eyebrows, Cecil said, "Marla told me she heard someone yelling late last night. Said sounded like it was coming from up around the trailer. You're not going all weird on us now, are you?" He craned his neck forward. "'Cause I feel responsible like, you know, hooking you up as a renter out there and all."

"Look who's talking. What's weirder than trolling the freeway in that orange and black thing of yours, picking up strange characters off the road and bringing them home to your wife?"

"Well...ya got me there. But still, I can't be worrying that I've put Marla at risk." He tilted his head. "Was you, wasn't it? Yelling."

Carson sagged back and laughed. "Everyone's weird, Cecil. Take your friend, Marla. She went strange on me the other night herself. Swelled up in a huff and threw one of her luminaries the full length of that Quonset building. Pretty good arm."

"Luminaries? What you talking about?"

"Her candles. The cherry-scented ones."

"Oh. Our lady of the lights," Cecil teased. "Snow Lady Candles, that's what she calls her little enterprise. Got a bit riled, you say?"

"She did. Was showing me the power box, and when I expressed interest in the candles, she took exception. Like I said, heaved one with some heat behind it."

Cecil let the waitress refill his coffee and dumped some sugar in it. "Candles was just a hobby 'til she figured out how to really give some ring-a-ding to the Bing. Things really started perking along, gave her some extra income—seemed to enjoy it. Guess she's soured on the whole thing. Go figure."

Carson nodded. "By the way, it was me doing the yelling. So count me among the rest of you weird ones."

Cecil took a long drink from his cup. "Looking for blood after dark?"

"Just childhood memories of goblins in the bedroom, I guess."

Cecil turned his head to look out the window onto the street. When he looked back a low level smile parted his lips. "You know," he said, "I been suspecting that Bill Tolliver's not truly your name. Am I wrong?" When Carson just looked at him, Cecil added, "Figured not. So who are you, really?"

"Cecil, don't..."

"I know, none of my business. It's just that...are you in trouble? No, wait," he held up a hand, "because if you are, well, maybe there's something I could do. You know, something."

"Look," Carson said, "I'm not in trouble, not like you are probably thinking." *Not unless you think walking away from your own death to be trouble*, he thought.

"Not thinking anything. Well, I'm wondering. That's a better word, maybe. Wondering."

"You can put that on hold. You're wondering."

Cecil pulled out his tobacco pouch once more. "I was just hazarding an opinion, you know, like we all got problems, not the same or nothing, just saying." He thumbed a pinch of Beechnut chew into his cheek. "And I may be poking where I shouldn't be, but—"

"You are," Carson said and flinched as a woman walked past on her way out of the café: shapely, nice face, brunette, a near image of Naomi, enough to cause his heart to thud. He half-expected the woman to spin around and come at him snarling in Naomi's throaty voice, *Aha, Carson, so there you are! Left me to drown, you bastard.*

He sat back, shaken, and saw Cecil staring at him.

"What is it?" Cecil looked around.

Carson suddenly stood and left the café. Cecil threw down money for the meals and traipsed along behind, keeping a distance between them. Nothing more was said as he drove up Court Street to the library except to mumble that he was going to the building supply store and would be back in half an hour or so. Carson stepped out of the car, waved a hand, and walked away. Cecil watched this stranger he'd brought home to roost then spit in his cup and drove on.

In the library, Carson took a chance and used his Washington State driver's license to get a guest pass to use a computer when one was available. After less than ten minutes, a beefy man who'd been leaning in close to a computer screen stood up, wrestled on a denim jacket, and sauntered away liked he solved all his problems. Carson slipped into the vacant chair opened Google and began his first search for towns in Oklahoma that began with the letter T. Wikipedia had a list of twenty towns beginning in "T". Populations ran from merely 106 in a place called Terlton to over 390,000 in Tulsa—and everything in between. Most of the T towns were small, a few hundred with an occasional one over a thousand. Tulsa would be an obvious place to begin, but after that the people he wanted could be anywhere in the state. Add in BeBe's blurry memory of supposed last names, and he knew that he'd have to bring in local help, perhaps a private investigator.

After less than twenty minutes, he closed out his search and went back outside, zipped his coat closed again, and sat on a bench in the library breezeway. Vincent Horne took his call at once.

"I've been on edge since your call, you dufus," Vincent said exuding a tight laugh. "I was beginning to think I'd imagined it. It is you, isn't it?"

"Watermelon."

"Okay, okay. My god, Carson, do you know that they've declared you officially dead? It was in the paper. Officially. How's that feel? Weird, I bet."

"Yeah, I heard. If you can imagine having an out-of-body sensation, that was it. I feel like I'm Warren Beatty in that movie *Heaven Can Wait*."

"Better look in the mirror again. It'll be a big improvement if you look like Warren Beatty. If that works, I may go jump in Hood Canal." They both hummed their laughs. Vincent swallowed at the knot in his throat. "God, this is so bizarre. I haven't slept the night through since you called. My wife keeps asking what's wrong. She probably thinks I'm having an affair."

"Are you?"

"What?" Vincent looked toward his office door; it was open. He turned his chair to face the windows.

"Are you having an affair?"

The pause was an indictment. "What's that got to do with this?" he whispered.

"Not a thing. Unless you think it does. Who is it?"

Another pause. "You wouldn't know her. And it's mostly over."

"Mostly? Isn't that like being somewhat pregnant?"

"Hell, how'd we get into this? Forget that—where are you?"

The laughter and jabber of three children running up the library walkway with their mother caused Carson to fall silent. He smiled at the woman as the tribe scurried past; she was too harried to reciprocate. Vincent Horne was asking if he was still there. "Yeah I'm here. Can't tell you where I am. I will, just not now. Bear with me."

Vincent waited a beat or two. "Okay compadre, I'm with you. What's next?"

"I need your help. Like I said."

"I'm nervous here. Hope you know that." Vincent felt his right knee vibrating kinetically beneath the desk. "I have been imagining what you might want from me. Won't tell you all the weird possibilities that have gone through my head. I mean, what could a supposed dead man want after he's been officially declared expired? I've been freaked."

Carson stood and walked the length of the walkway and stopped at the stairs that led up to the library parking lot. He inhaled slowly. "I know, outlandish," he responded.

"No kidding. So what is it...you want?" Vincent got up from his chair and approached the office windows. He looked down from thirty stories, his eyes playing on the pill-shaped top of a Metro Transit bus creeping along, and waited for the answer.

"I...Vince." Carson's knees weakened, and he had to sit on the steps. "My god," he uttered on an exhaled breath. "This is... my head is spinning." He leaned on his knees.

"You okay, man? You there?"

"Yeah, here."

"What's happening? You okay?"

"No, I'm not okay. What is...it must be you."

"What? What do you mean?"

"Vince." He shuddered. "I've had all of this bottled up is all I can figure. I'm shaking like a junkie here." He felt the tears coming and could do nothing to stop them. He gulped and choked out a sob and another and another. He sucked in a deep breath and felt his body shaking in this new explosion of grief.

"Are you all right?" The voice was that of an elderly man carrying several books. He leaned over and placed a hand on Carson's back. "What is it, young man?"

Carson snuffed his nose and wiped at his eyes and sat up straight. He smiled at the man. "Some bad news," he responded. "I'll be okay. Thanks."

The old man rose back up erect, looked down, patted Carson, and walked on up the stairs.

"Vince, you there?"

"Yeah. What's going on?"

"I lost it. Must be that with you for the first time since it happened I can let down. I don't know—it just happened. Naomi, she's gone. Vince, she is really and truly gone. I guess I had put her in a sort of limbo, on a shelf like maybe I could go get her down again." He paused and bit down. "But I can't, can I?"

Vincent hesitated. "No buddy, you can't. Gone is gone."

"Yeah." He squeezed his eyes shut. "She...she...there's a hole. No matter how we were together, there's this hole with nothing in it."

"You were good though, you and her, right? I know you were crazy about her."

"I was...once," Carson answered. "It'd been a while since those days. You know, Vince, it actually makes it worse in some ways. Who am I grieving for? The love that had been my life or the life that was no longer my love?"

Vincent dropped back into his chair and leaned his forehead into the palm of a hand. He considered how to respond, or if to respond. He had never been exposed to anything like this in his life or his law career. Of course he had heard of people going missing or disappearing on purpose but never someone he actually knew, and certainly among all known to him, Carson Barrus would never have made any list of probables. All these years he had never felt closer to any friend than this man. Back in those college days at U-Dub, they'd become unwavering amigos because the chemistry was there, the result being an exchange of magnetic DNA. Not that they connected regularly; they didn't hold Huskies football season tickets together or participate in cigars, whiskey, and poker nights. It was more than that, even though Vincent had no ready definition.

"Carson," he said finally, "I've never had any loss like that. I can't... I don't know what to say. I want to help you with it, but I...I simply can't."

"Vince." Carson stood and looked out onto Court Street. Marigold was sitting at the curb. He raised a hand and saw Cecil do the same. "Vince, I don't need you to do that. That's not why I am coming to you, not even close. I know you care and would save me from this if you could."

Vincent released a quiet sigh of relief. "So what, then?"

"I want you to help me find my dead sister's child."

-16-

Stuart Barrus first learned that his brother had been declared officially dead when his Aunt Purl called and read the news article to him; they swallowed their heartbreak together and endured a painful acceptance of an unwanted reality. Usually strong-willed and fearless, that day Purl had been inconsolable. That day, Stuart had been the one to remain calm, letting her pour out all she had been holding back; all along she had convinced herself that her youngest nephew had not perished, that he would somehow reappear. Purl's face to the rest of the family had been stoic, but with Stuart she could reveal unrestrained grief without concern of being judged for lacking fortitude. She was so aware that Stuart knew what it was to take body blows for one's decisions of how to live your life. She had never asked him how he had weathered the disdain from his father and the hesitant, mostly lacking, support from the rest of the family. But he had endured and enjoyed a warm and loving life with Ned Kind.

Now she had called him again.

"Stuart," Purl's voice was tight. "We have to do something."

"What do you mean?"

"For Carson. We have to do something. A service, a memorial service. We have to."

"Of course we do, Purl. Is something being planned?"

"No," she snapped. "CB is forbidding it for now."

"What? Forbidding...I thought he was all for holding a quiet ceremony and having done with it."

"He was." Her voice had its edge back. "Until the newspaper came out with the authorities throwing in the towel. You know how he is

121

about negative publicity."

"Negative publicity? This is about his son, for crying out loud, and my kid brother. How ridiculous."

"Since the word got out, his phone has been ringing steadily. People only want to express sympathy, yet he thinks it will affect the company's image. He's decided to wait until the whole matter is cold and old. That's just what he said: *Cold and old.* Then hold a private time in Sequim with just family."

"Cold being the operative word." Stuart looked up when his partner came into the room and mouthed the word *Purl.* Ned Kind nodded his head and shrugged. "So, Purl, what do you want to do? What does my mom think about all of this?"

"Oh, you know, BeBe is and always has been caught in the middle, the poor dear. She's not going up against my brother, I'll tell you that."

"And Grandma?"

There was a pause from Purl. "She'll go along with whatever we decide," she said after a moment. With the hesitancy in her voice, Stuart could almost see her running her fingers through the strands of her gray hair that she kept short. She did that when she was unsure or uncertain, which wasn't that often. When Stuart didn't react to her prediction about Lillian, she added, "I've discussed the options with her."

"Options? Does that mean doing something without Dad's blessing?"

"Exactly." He heard her take in an audible breath and let it out into the phone. "You good with that?"

Stuart leaned back in the armchair he was using and crossed a leg. "Of course," he said. "I'm in. Who else? Rove?"

"Yes, in his own fashion."

Stuart smiled at her depiction. He could imagine his uncle's hesitation, his wondering way, asking what everyone else was doing. "So outside of Mom being a maybe, we're all agreed then? Who's going to tell CB our decision? Small item."

"I'll do it. Been taking him on all my life."

"And resilient you are."

"Yeah," she breathed. "Except for when it comes to losing family younger than I am. Not right, Stu, not right at all."

"I'll be listening for the thunderclap. Then I'll know CB has been invited."

They laughed. It was a good laugh.

CB Barrus set the phone receiver down in its cradle and tapped it with a finger. He looked at the man seated across from him.

"That seemed to go well," said David Haack. Haack had his legs stretched out in front of him, arms folded across his chest; he wore a smirk. He was counter to CB's sartorial standard of starched shirts, cuff links, rep ties, and creased expensive suits. Haack last wore a suit, without a tie, at his father's funeral. At this moment he was dressed in khakis, a black tee shirt that stretched across his chest, and tasseled brown loafers.

"My sister, Purl," CB said.

"So I gathered."

"About Carson."

"Uh-huh. And?"

"Family is going ahead with a service."

Haack sniffed and looked to the side then back. "Not waiting, then?"

"No."

"So you gonna just let it ride? Like that?"

"I don't know."

"You want me to do something?" Haack was on the payroll of Barrus Properties. His only job was to be at CB's beck and call for *special duties*. And no one called him Mr. *Hack* but once: It's *Hawk*, he'd say in a tone that tendered no humor.

"Like what, David?"

Haack raised his arms above his head and clasped his hands; his biceps swelled. "Intervene."

"It's family, for Christ's sake. Get a grip, will you?"

"Whatever you say."

CB glared at his fixer. "You speak to the Vietnamese?"

Haack nodded. "I did."

"And?"

"Like I said, his restaurant is pulling in bigger numbers. Good reviews. Wants to expand, so looking at some other locations. Got a superior offer, seems like."

"From Sullivan, anybody else?"

"Haven't heard of any other offers because Sullivan's is very good: more space, nice build-out budget, bigger kitchen, and rate per square foot that will be tough to beat. Plus Sullivan will lock in the rate for a long-term lease."

"Location?"

"Good location. Just a few blocks from where he is plus a corner, nearby parking. It'll be hard to match, CB."

"So we're toast."

"Seems like. I gave him your offer. He just smiled. Little pissant. Never liked him."

"Really?" CB gripped the arms of his chair and shook his head. "Gee, don't suppose he might have picked up on that." He cleared his throat. "Well, kiss it off. I'll tell leasing to start looking to fill that spot. When's the lease up?"

"Six months."

"Okay. Damn, I didn't want it to go this way."

"Can't win 'em all."

"No, I mean the memorial for Carson. Quiet, just family, that's the way it ought to be. What Purl wants to do will cause a real commotion. Don't want that."

"It'll blow over. Life moves on."

"The real philosopher, are you now? Of course it will blow over— that's not the point. It's about Aleta."

Haack's brow crinkled. "How so?"

CB laid his hands on the desk and squeezed them together. "It's about losing people before their time. Gets people thinking, gets my family thinking. Upsets family when the young ones die. That's why I wanted to control this thing. Purl mentioned Aleta's death just now when she told me about doing this thing for Carson."

"What's it been… two years since the suicide? Time flies."

"David." CB's tone grew cool. "Are things still like we set them up?"

Haack crossed his arms again. "The boy?"

"Yes, the boy, you fool."

Haack locked his eyes on those of his employer. "Not respectful for you to talk to me like that. I don't appreciate it."

"That right? Get used to it." He inhaled hard and waved a hand. "Forget it. So now reassure me, is the set up still working?"

Haack bobbed his head. "Far as I know, working fine. I've been sending out the payments on schedule. No feedback of any problems being reported from that end."

"Same family, nothing's changed?"

"Yep, the Brawners. Same ones."

"Make sure it stays that way. With all this fuss over Carson, she'll come back into people's minds, my mother's for one and now Purl's. We solved that mess once and for all. Need to keep it that way."

"Don't worry. All's quiet in Oklahoma and has been from day one. No one is going to risk messing up the money tree."

"Damn it, David, this isn't about the money. It's more than that."

"Not to the Brawners it isn't. The money is what keeps them in line and taking care of the kid. Don't forget that."

CB picked up the Mont Blanc pen on his desk pad and rolled it in his palm. "You're probably right. Still, now may be the time to double-check things back there. Discretely."

"Whatever you say." Haack raised his six-feet-four body out of the chair, looked down at CB and ran a hand over his buzzed head. "And I'm always discrete."

"Yeah? Well, take your discrete self over to the Sempler Apartments and have a chat-up with the manager there. What's his name, Samson? Complaints have been funneled to me that he's been hitting

125

on a single parent mom there, threatening eviction if she doesn't give him a roll in the sack. Tell him to get his pussy somewhere off the property or look for other work."

"I know that dude. Thinks the low-income residents are his little kingdom. You oughta dump him."

"No. He's tough, doesn't fall for sob stories, and has the best record on late rent payments of any of our properties."

Haack shrugged and turned just as the office door opened and Mary Dickens, CB's executive assistant, entered. She came carrying a sheaf of papers, placed them on the desk, and looked up at David Haack. He smiled at her, spoke her name, and walked out. She followed him with her eyes. When she looked back at CB, his face held a passive smile.

"I know," he said to her. "You don't like him. You don't have to."

"Good," she said.

"He does things I need done. You know that. Things no one else can or will do."

"That must make you very happy," she said.

-17-

Carson stuffed his cell phone into a jacket pocket and shivered. Vincent Horne had agreed to everything: the money, the plan, Carson remaining incognito for a while yet—even finding an investigator in Oklahoma. It had begun—for real.

He walked down from the library to where Cecil sat in the Ranchero, its engine at idle. The bed of the vehicle carried lengths of PVC pipe and assorted supplies. Carson knew what it all was and he hoped, properly applied, he'd end up with a shower and toilet in the trailer. He slid into the car just as Cecil spat into his omnipresent paper cup once again.

Cecil drew the back of his hand across his mouth. "You know, should of thought of this before, Marla, she's got a computer. Online all the time for her candle business. Bet if you asked her real nice she'd let you use hers."

"Real nice. How would that sound?"

Cecil looked over his shoulder out the back window and eased Marigold out from the curb. "Maybe if you started out squelching her fears about a wolf man living in her trailer. That'd be good."

"You don't think she'd throw a candle at me?"

Cecil chuckled. "Can't say for sure. She can be forceful."

Carson smiled to himself. "Okay, I'll give it a go. Now would you mind running me by the Salvation Army Store? I need to get a heavier coat. Then a quick stop at Safeway so I can expand my grocery inventory."

"No need for the coat. I have a closet full, and I'd especially like to get rid of the ones I used to fit into. Embarrassing. Groceries, you're on your own. I'll wait in the car. No place to spit in the store."

The "Reduced for Quick Sale" small tri-tip steak curled when he cooked it a bit too long, but still he savored it well beyond canned chili. Along with frozen green peas thawed in a pot and a Pabst, he felt he had truly dined for the first time in his aluminum box. Cecil had come by earlier, carrying a broad smile, and presented him with a split-leather suede coat with a wool fleece lining; it was well broken in, but Carson accepted it gratefully. Now he settled down with a full stomach and a warm coat, heated water for a cup of instant coffee, and recalled his conversation with Vincent Horne. Each time he thought of what they had agreed to, his doubts reemerged.

"Are you sure about this?" Vincent had asked at least three times. "I mean, I'll do whatever you ask, Carson. I'm just saying…"

"Yeah, I'm sure." He'd said that, but he wasn't sure about any of it. He only knew that he had to do it.

"Okay then. Let's go over it again." Carson remembered Vince as being the methodical one between them: organized, systematic, on time, and always followed through. In some ways he'd driven Carson up the wall with this detailed mind but not now—now he needed those very qualities.

"First thing I need is cash," Carson said. "Don't want to use my credit cards, and I'm running on fumes, buying clothes at the Salvation Army store and eating expired-date food."

"Can't imagine," Vince laughed. "You're probably safe using the credit cards. I mean everyone thinks you're dead, right?"

"Still not taking any chances. No credit cards, no checks."

"Okay. I can advance you the money. Cashier's check for ten-thousand, right?"

"For now."

"That's a good amount. Won't draw any undue attention."

"I may need more later, but you'll get it all back with interest."

"Never mind the interest. So we'll meet in Tacoma in two days?"

"Right. I looked online and found a Starbuck's in Tacoma just off I-5 located on Seventy-Second Street. I'll leave The Dalles by six.

Factoring in commuter traffic in Portland, I should hit Tacoma right around ten give or take."

"Got it." After a pause Vincent said, "You know, just a few days ago my life was stuck on ordinary, except that my college roomie had drowned. Now here I am up to my Jockey shorts in intrigue, a dead man walking, and absolutely no interest in anything else."

"Tell your wife yet?"

"About you? Of course not. Oh, you mean the other matter. I broke that off. Not an issue."

"Except that your wife is still suspicious, right?"

"She wouldn't be if you'd let me tell her about all of this."

"Not yet. In the meantime, I need to stay on track, Vince. I know I'm asking the moon."

"My wife I can handle. But my law partners, that's another matter. I can't taint my reputation, not even a little bit."

"Your name will never come up. Promise."

"Item two," Vince answered. "Secure a private investigator in Oklahoma. I can do that through a law school colleague who lives in Tulsa. I'll have him find someone good but off the grid."

They fumbled around for a few minutes more; then Carson said, "Give me hope?"

"Sure," Vince Horne said, swallowing his misgivings.

After contemplating the call for a moment, Carson drank down the dregs of cold coffee, set the cup in the sink then stepped outside and slipped on his new old coat—nature was calling. He stood in the dark, hands into his pockets, and looked down toward the house. It was lit up; she was home. With his breath gusting out ahead, he strode down the slight incline, relieved himself in the porch toilet, then stepped out and rapped on the kitchen door. A moment later the latch clicked. She opened the door slowly, like one would to keep a house cat from escaping. Her expression was one of indifference or suspicion; he couldn't quite tell which.

"Good evening," he said, attempting a pleasant moment. When she didn't respond, he added, "I am the werewolf from just upslope."

A smile flickered on her lips.

"I understand that I caused you some alarm last night. We werewolves have our moments. Sorry if I disturbed you."

She didn't open the door any wider. "It was strange," she said finally.

"Indeed," he said and rocked his torso forward and back. Her hair was pulled back in a ponytail. "I like your hair that way."

A mere nod was all she offered in response. "Is there something else?" she asked.

"You mean other than ponytail and werewolf talk?"

"I suppose you could say that, and it is cold out."

"Oh, and my standing here is letting cold air in. Forgive me." He stepped back to leave.

Again she asked if there was something he needed, if the trailer was functioning satisfactorily, or if he was merely using the facility.

"There was that," he answered, "the facility. But I really came to ask if you could see your way clear to allow me access to your computer."

"My computer?"

"Yes, you see..."

"Come in, I guess." She opened the door wider and went on into the kitchen. He followed, closing the door, wondering if he was welcome or just being tolerated as a tenant.

"Coffee?" she asked.

"If you have it." He slipped off his coat and hung it on the back of a chair and sat down.

When at last she sat down and they both had mugs of coffee, Marla Snow surveyed her renter and took at least two swallows before speaking. "By the way, Cecil and a couple of his cronies are coming over tomorrow to run a line from the trailer to my septic system. Your nights of cold runs to the toilet and waiting to use my shower will soon be over."

"That will be good."

"So what's this about my computer?"

"I need to get online to do some research. Cecil said you had Internet access."

She studied him without expression. "I do." She picked up her mug and held it. "Use it for business mostly."

Carson took a risk. "The candles. Is this a busy time? Christmas and all?"

If a look could relay that you've said something completely empty-headed, the statement held in her eyes claimed that honor. "It is hectic," she said, her voice low. "Spent every hour after work out there packing shipments. Fact is I should be out there right now, but I'm flagged."

"Flagged?"

"Tired, pooped. *Flagged* is a word my grandfather used." She rose and retrieved the coffee pot and poured each another round. "I'm using my computer a lot when I'm home: processing orders, taking new orders, and just all-around communicating with customers. Doesn't last long, but when it's the hot season, I don't do much else."

"I understand," Carson said. "I can use the library."

She studied him for a moment. "This about your odyssey?"

He felt his face redden. She smiled at his reaction. "You could say that," he answered.

She leaned forward on her elbows. "Just noticed your eyes."

"Heterochromia iridum," he said. "That's what it's called, having two eyes of different color: my left being blue and the right brown." He opened his eyes wider.

"I've never heard of that before."

"Well it is less common than that gap between your front teeth." He showed his own teeth and tapped a forefinger against an incisor.

She reached a hand up to her mouth. "Got me," she said. "I kept my mouth closed most of the time when I was growing up, especially around boys. Guess you couldn't keep your eyes closed, though."

He laughed. "No. But I looked away a lot. Found things to focus on instead of the person staring at me. We learned our little tricks, seems like."

"So here we are with our mutual flaws."

"The ones that show, anyway."

"You suggesting that there are others?"

"Aren't there?"

She turned her head and looked away for a long moment. He waited her out. The face she showed him when she turned back was a flat canvas. They studied one another, neither giving any sign of where their mind was.

"I could find that comment offensive," she said. "I could, but then what?"

"Yes," he smiled, "then what? We're sort of trapped, aren't we? Each taking a road of deviation, each with our own justification to be living a life of separation."

"That is very heady. I just thought we were both running away from where we were before. Isn't it simple as that?"

He finished what was left in his mug. "How can it be simple when the person you were closest to is gone? One minute there, the next there is no answer when you say their name. How is that simple?"

"It isn't," she answered, "but we're still running…aren't we? Trying to get away?"

Carson blinked at the image of Naomi as it flashed by. "What was your husband's name again? Glen?"

She inhaled and held her breath. "That's right. Glen," she said on exhalation.

He nodded. "She was Naomi. We were married for thirteen years."

"Glen and I only had five years before, well, you know what happened."

"Suicide is horrible for those left behind." When she stared at him like he didn't have a clue, he said, "My little sister took her own life. Two years ago." He paused. "That's incredible, two years ago right now, this month. Just before Christmas." He closed his eyes and thought of how wooden and hollow it had been; the glitter of the holidays had no relevance, no joy, no caring—nothing. The only release came when a new year took over and in its bullying brashness managed to muffle the wound in a minor way.

When he opened his eyes, Marla Snow's face had softened, and a knowing smile had taken over her mouth. "It's still hard to imagine," he said to her.

"I know. I wonder if it will it ever go away—the pain?"

He coughed at the lump in his throat. "Ask me again in twenty years."

"Twenty years," she said after a time. "I was hoping…"

"What do I know?" he said. "Maybe never." When she held a hand up to her throat he put a hand out on the table and said, "I just meant we would never forget."

She nodded and leaned back in the chair. After a moment she asked, "When did your wife die?"

It was all he could do to keep from gasping and shouting: *Don't ask me that! Please don't ask me that!* But she had. It was a direct hit on his house of cards. He shuddered and smiled into the quizzical look that came into her eyes when he didn't respond. How should this fellow Bill Tolliver answer this question? Could he risk telling her the truth, the real truth, or should he invent a made-up story for a made-up Bill Tolliver? He looked into his empty mug.

"Not long ago," he said finally.

"How long is that?"

He made a choice right then. "Thanksgiving." His ears rang, and his face flushed.

"Thanksgiving? A year ago, two years ago?"

"This one." He tapped a finger onto the tabletop for emphasis.

She looked into his two-colored eyes in disbelief then turned her head away as if she could clear what she'd heard. "You mean this Thanksgiving?" she asked when she brought him into focus again. "Just, no, not…"

"Yes that's when."

Her shoulders dropped. "Bill, my god. I…I don't know what to say."

He shrugged and blinked at the tears he didn't want right then.

"I've been talking about Glen like we were seeing things from the same perspective maybe...that's been over six years, but..." She stood up and paced a few steps and back. "Forgive me."

"It's okay. You didn't know. Really, it's okay."

She sat back down. They looked at one another, at the tablecloth, and at other things in the kitchen. Sounds from the old farm house came into the quiet between them: the creak of the chair he was sitting on, the murmur of the refrigerator compressor, the thunk of the second hand moving on an old electric wall clock.

"You know," she said. "I wanted to get out of town the moment the funeral was over. Almost did it, had a suitcase packed, but duty first—the schoolteacher in me, I guess."

"I wasn't at her funeral," he interrupted bluntly. "Naomi's service. I wasn't there."

Her expression was priceless. He had to stifle a laugh. "I guess we handle grief, each in our own way," she said.

"And I'm not Bill Tolliver. Not my name."

He didn't get back to the trailer until after two in the morning. Not until he had told her all of it. At some point she opened a bottle of red.

-18-

He drove away from The Dalles an hour before sunrise the next morning after scraping a light layer of frost from the windshield with a credit card. The only person to take note had been Marla Snow carrying a lunch cooler out to her car ready for another day at Boyd Organics. She gave him a raised-hand salute, which set off a flutter in his stomach. Because of their late-night truth-tell-all influenced by too much wine, she now knew everything. Everything. He was swallowing back the sour taste of confessor's regret when he pulled onto Mill Creek Road.

He arrived in Tacoma before the appointed hour, ordered a cappuccino, and waited. The room swam for a moment when he saw Vincent Horne's roundish body finally enter the coffee shop; seeing this human remnant from his past was unnerving. He waited until their eyes met, raised his eyebrows, and spread his mouth in a conspiratorial grin. Vincent stood in place for a disbelieving moment before shaking his head and going for his own drink. Carson nursed the last of his cold cappuccino until Vincent approached and stood looking down. After another shake of his head, he slid onto a chair and let out with a chuckling hum. Carson revisited the memory chip of his friend: he saw the same oval face and the same bright blue eyes, but the hair, once lanky and black, was now close-cropped and tinged with a hint gray; and the college wardrobe of baggy khakis, U-Dub tee shirts, and boat shoes with no socks had been replaced by an expensive dark blue suit, stiff white shirt, and accoutrements.

"Great to see you, Vince. Thanks for this." Carson offered his hand; Vince hesitated then reached out with both hands to squeeze the flesh of the man he once thought dead.

"Same here. No thanks needed—yet. You've put some punch in my days of routine. To say the least. This is downright spooky." Vince chuckled and took in his classmate's appearance. "So much for the button-down shirt and pressed suit image, my man. And the facial hair is well beyond five o'clock shadow."

"Hey, I'm beginning to like the comfort of jeans, serviceable shirts, and this broken-in leather coat. Besides, along with the whiskers, this outfit may just keep me from being recognized."

Vince looked around. "Hadn't thought of that." He drank from his latte and studied the face of his former college roommate. "Do you have any idea how unbelievable this is? I mean…well I was half expecting this to be a ruse." He laughed under his breath. "I'd show up, and no one would be here, or some of our old classmates would be pulling the ultimate gag. For which I would have killed them, hope you know."

"Nope, it's me."

"I can see that. I can see that. It still doesn't make any sense, but I do recognize you and you are alive." He reached over and pinched Carson's arm.

They both sagged back in their chairs and smiled. Then they started laughing and didn't stop until they were getting cold stares. Vince swallowed his elation, patted the air, and they settled down to minor chuckles.

"So now what?" he asked.

"That's the big question. Gives me knots in my gut," Carson answered.

"I can't even imagine." Vince canceled his smile and leaned forward. "So tell me. All of it. Don't just shrug, damn it." When Carson merely looked back at him, he insisted. "Not kidding, man. If I'm going out on a limb here, I need to know what the hell happened."

"That's fair. First let me ask you this. Are you okay with this, what I'm up to?"

"Yeah," Vince said with some hesitancy. "For now I am. But I need the whole story."

"Uh-huh, freaky, I know."

Vince leaned back and loosened his tie. He put on his lawyer face and studied his witness. "So I'm sitting there in my office, freaking out, trying to get my head around you...you dragging yourself out of Hood Canal, with your wife dead in the car, or so you thought, and just deciding to disappear? At that very moment? That right?"

"She was. Naomi. She was dead."

"How'd you know that?"

"I knew."

"Okay, you knew. But even with that, why did you just leave? What was going on in your head? That's what I don't get. Were you out of it? Looney Tunes? What?"

Carson smiled. "Outside of hypothermia sucking the life out of me, my mind was clear. I knew moments after I came out of the water what I was going to do. I sat on the rocks, shaking, and I could see the car's headlights shining up through the water. People came down to the water's edge. They were right there, but I didn't shout to them or anything. Then I...well, I just decided to leave."

Vince drew his lips in and shook his head. "Unbelievable. Why? That's the big question."

Carson rubbed a hand over his stubble and considered the days he and Vince had spent together, the outrageous things they'd done, the secrets they held (including *watermelon*), and the trust he had in the man across from him. How deeply could he now call on that trust and the glue built between them when the only real stressors they had ever shared were college pranks?

"It had been on the back burner for some time, Vince. The decision to leave my life behind wasn't dependent on just happening to drive off into Hood Canal one day."

They chuckled at that but it was self-conscious. And for the second time, subsequent to telling it all to Marla Snow, he unveiled the story. When he had finished, Vince sat quietly studying his friend before handing him an envelope containing a cashier's check and the name of a private investigator in Oklahoma. Carson handed him a dollar bill and retained him as his attorney. He also told him where he was living and how to contact him. Their hug was long and hard. Carson watched his new attorney drive away from the coffee shop, wondering if all of this would lead to the conclusion he imagined and if Vincent Horne actually trusted his sanity. Before getting back on the freeway, he stopped at a nearby K-Mart and bought a new disposable cell phone plus an additional 100 minutes. He broke the old phone into pieces and scattered its parts among a couple of trash bins in the parking lot.

———————

Back in The Dalles he went directly to a community credit union he had scoped out earlier to set up a checking account. His story to the new accounts clerk was that he had just moved to the area and needed to transfer funds. She examined his out-of-state identification, new local address, the cashier's check, and then asked him to wait. Carson rubbed at his stubble and wondered if he'd be found out. He imagined the manager marching over to declare: "We know who you are!" But a minute or so later, the clerk returned smiling; all was well she just needed her manager's approval to accept the check. He took the small pad of temporary checks provided, shook hands with the very pleased woman, and returned to the trailer.

It was already dark at five-thirty when he parked next to Marla Snow's Honda. He saw lights on in the Quonset building and went in; the cherry aroma hit him immediately. Marla was standing at a big table amid a sea of small cartons, rolling candles into bubble wrap sheaths for shipping. She looked up as he entered, her hair gleaming beneath overhead lights, and studied him as if he were a process server.

Carson inhaled and smiled. "Nice."

"Don't even smell it anymore." He watched as she taped a box shut and flattened a pressure sensitive address label on it. "So, how'd it go? Your college classmate, did he buy into your watery grave story?"

Carson hesitated.

She smiled. "I know—what we'll tell someone late at night over a glass of vino. Regrets?"

"No," he said, "no, not really. It's just that…"

"Not sure if you can trust me?"

"No," he laughed, not too sincerely, picked up a candle near his hand, held it, put it back down, and said again, "No. It's just that…"

"It's just that you don't know if you can trust me, Carson. It is Carson, right, not Bill?" He nodded. "And why should you trust me?" she said.

"Do I have a choice?"

Her laugh was what they needed right then. "No, guess you don't. So tell me, did your buddy come through? And can you trust *him* even?"

"Can now. He's my lawyer of record. Gave him a one-dollar retainer."

"There you go." She paused after running plastic tape across another box. "You and your darn story…been in my head all day. Takes a lot to astound me, but you did. Being thought dead. Gad. And then this plot of intrigue you laid out. Haven't decided if you're nuts, a truly noble guy, or a liar."

The sweet smell of the candles filled his nostrils, causing him to brush a hand across his nose. They stared at one another. "I'm none of those," he answered finally.

"No claims of a noble act?"

He waited. "Maybe, back when it would have mattered, but not now. Now I'm merely wallowing in the muck. May not succeed, probably won't, but I have to try and set things right without fucking up a little boy's life even more."

She reached back and retied her hair. "So what's next?"

He thought of the telephone number in his pocket. "Tomorrow I will make a phone call. One that will set everything into motion. Makes my blood run cold."

"Really?" She pulled another box toward her and one more candle and began to roll it in plastic wrap. "And if I may, who might that be?" She didn't look at him.

"Someone unknown to me that I may hire to start digging. I need to know where my sister was when her son was born."

"In Oklahoma, I thought."

'It's a big state. All I know is the letter T."

She nodded and held up a candle. "Want to help?"

They worked side by side packing Snow Lady pillars and slapping mailing labels on boxes, nothing more said about their mutually distorted lives. Finally she held up her arms and called it over. When they stepped out into the night, she pointed upslope and told him that Cecil and his buddies had spent the day laying PVC pipe from the trailer to the septic tank. He could now take a shower and use the toilet without running out into the cold.

He watched her walk away, weary, then levered the door open on the trailer; he sat on the edge of the bed, imagined what tomorrow would be like if he used the phone number, then fell over on his side and slept in his clothes. Around three he arose after sleeping hard, used his toilet for the first time, smiled when it flushed cleanly, and went back to bed. It was light out when he scrubbed his eyes open, assuming it to be around eight thirty; it was actually ten. He brewed some more bitter instant coffee and had a bowl of raisin bran. The small shower actually worked; the water got hot and circled down the drain like it should. He dried off with the hand-me-down frayed towel and felt civilized.

After shaving off his stubble, he dressed in fresh clothes and sat in the quiet of the trailer all set to do something. If he made the call, if he took out that piece of paper with the name and number on it, and if he punched the keypad on his phone, things would be set into motion—then what? He shrugged into the bulky leather jacket, tugged his cap on, stepped out into a cold but clear day, and walked up behind the trailer until he hit a fence line. He stood there for some time just looking out into the orchard beyond the fence before making his way out onto Mill Creek Road. He struck out along the shoulder, plodding over the gravel at the edge of the road. Occasional vehicles, mostly pickups and farm trucks, passed going toward town; more than one driver raised a finger above the steering wheel in greeting—the small town salutation. At first he gave stiff waves back, but eventually he quit looking up; his mind was elsewhere.

His right hand held on tightly to the piece of paper in his pocket; he had memorized the name on it: Ezzard Dale. Ezzard—what kind of name was that? He recalled there had been a professional boxer by that name: Ezzard Charles. After walking for half an hour, he came up on the Mill Creek Grange, an old buff-colored building with a gravel lot between it and the road. He walked up to it, sat on the steps, pulled out his phone to call his grandmother—he dreaded it. The ringing buzzed in his ear six times before there was a click and Lillian's voice.

"Grandma, it's me."

She groaned. "I've been so concerned," she said in a husky, emotional voice. "This has been just awful. I can't sleep the night through. I'm wondering where you are and what you're doing all the time." She sighed. "Carson, this can't go on."

He felt a flush of anger. He had to get her buy-in to make it all work. "I know this is tough. But I'm on the way with this. No stopping. Stay with me now."

"On the way," she echoed. "With what, Carson? Nothing good can come of this. Even now your Aunt Purl is gearing up for your memorial service. And you father is fighting it. It is a nightmare, I tell you."

"What? Why is CB fighting it?"

"Why do you think?"

"I have no idea. I thought he was pushing for it."

"That was until you were reported as presumed drowned in the paper."

"So?"

"In CB's warped way of looking at things, your death being in the news hangs a cloud over the family name and thus his business. He wants to do something quietly, just family up at the Sequim house."

"You're kidding." Carson stifled a laugh. "That's good, actually."

"Good? What on earth…"

"In fact, I need you to agree with him."

"Agree with him?"

"For now, Grams, for the moment. It will give me some time to get my plan underway. Once that happens I will come forward after you've told everyone that I'm actually alive."

"Me?" She sucked in a ragged breath. "Oh Carson, I don't want to be the one."

Carson looked out toward the road as a white utility truck with a lift bucket on it cruised by. He waited a few breaths and said, "You are the only one who can do it. The only one." When she didn't respond, he added, "I'll walk you through it."

"Through what?" she demanded.

"The story. How I came to wander away and so forth."

"When?"

"Soon, maybe by next week. Please, just wait that long."

Again she didn't come right back. After a long moment of silence between them, he asked, "How did the funeral go? Naomi's?"

"Big turnout, I was told. Church was full. One of my garden club friends went at my request since we Barrus's weren't welcome. She said it was a nice service, as nice as those things can be, I guess. I was never close to her, you know, still and all I couldn't just look away."

"Thank you. At least that part of this bad dream is over."

She sighed her regrets one more time; he repeated his assurances, and they left it that way. Afterward he sat on the grange hall steps and stared out at the road, the phone still in his hand. His fingers trembled when he finally tapped in the 918 prefix. When the phone began buzzing, he walked out onto the gravel of the parking area and looked down at his feet. Then a soft middle-range male voice said, "This is Ezzard."

Carson held his breath.

"Hello," came the voice again.

"Yes…yes, is this Mr. Dale?"

"That's right, Ezzard Dale."

Carson looked at the scribbles on his slip of paper. "Ezzard Dale Investigations?"

"Uh-huh, that's me. Who's this?"

"Mr. Dale, my name is Bill Tolliver." He wasn't ready to reveal who he was until he was sure this would work out.

There was what sounded like chewing noises over the line. "Do I know you?"

"No, we've never met. In fact, I'm calling from out of state."

"Outa state. Where outa state?"

"For the moment, let's just say in the Northwest."

"Okay, the Northwest. What's on your mind?"

"Your name was given to me by a local source through my attorney. I have a special need of someone with your skills."

"What is it? Has to be local—I don't work out of Oklahoma. You wanting something done around these parts?"

"Where are you located, exactly?" Carson asked.

"Me? I'm in Sapulpa, about fifteen miles south of Tulsa." More chewing sounds.

Carson inhaled and considered how to ask for what he needed. "Not sure quite how to go about this."

"Just spit it out, man. I'm not gonna bite your head off—yet, that is." Ezzard Dale gurgled a laugh. "Not yet," he repeated.

Carson chuckled in self-defense. "Okay," he said and kept strolling around in loose gravel. "I need you to find some people for me."

"See now, that wasn't so hard. Too bad I don't do that."

"You don't?"

Another surge of laughter hit Carson's ear. "Just pulling your leg, friend. Of course I spend most of my waking days finding people. It's what I do mostly: sit on my keister waiting for someone to stick their head out. Big word we all use for that is *surveillance*. Don't be fooled— it's all just nosing around, hanging out."

Carson laughed. He liked the man's style. "Think I need some of both." He paused. "Can you keep this confidential?"

"Have to, my man, if I want to keep my license. State law says that

I gotta keep whatever I might do for you confidential. Just between you and me. Okay?"

"Okay. What do you charge?"

"Depends. What is it you're wanting, specifically?"

"When does the confidential part start?"

"Started when I picked up the phone. Have to keep a tight lip even if you don't hire me on."

"Okay. Going to take your word for that."

"That'd be good, that'd be real good, us getting off on the right foot here."

Carson sat back down on the grange hall steps and carefully began to unravel the story, leaving out the most painful parts and the Hood Canal horror story, and specified what he needed Ezzard Dale to do. Dale listened quietly except for the moist sounds of eating and the crinkle of something being unwrapped. When Carson had it all out, they both fell silent for a long moment. A dark blue SUV pulled off the road, and a man in Levi's and a plaid shirt got out with a golden retriever, cast a quick look at Carson, took the dog over to a patch of weeds, and let him do his duty. When the dog was done, his owner left the steaming turd behind, had the dog jump back in, and drove off. Carson was used to the city where everyone had to carry around doggie-doo bags and clean up after their pets.

"Mr. Tolliver," Ezzard Dale was saying for the third time. "You there?"

"Yeah, sorry, distracted."

"Uh-huh. So think I get what you're wanting, and I'm interested in your case. I've done my share of child custody work. Not much to go on, but enough to get going."

"How much do you charge?"

Ezzard Dale took in a breath and hummed for a moment. "I generally get between forty-five and fifty dollars an hour, depending on the workload, plus mileage and incidental expenses. I'll need a retainer, say around a thousand dollars, to get things started off here. I'll send you a contract, a client retainer agreement. You sign it where there's some little red arrow stickers, make yourself a copy, and send it back with the check for the thousand. Make that out to Ezzard Dale Investigations."

Carson mulled the matter over while Ezzard Dale filled his ear with positive talk about proceeding quickly to get results. He let the man run on while he willed himself to pull the lever and set it all in motion. When it seemed the investigator had run out of more assurances to offer, Carson stood once again, jammed his left hand into a pants pocket, strolled out four steps and cleared his throat.

"Okay," he said, his throat tightening. "Send me the paperwork." He gave him Marla Snow's house number and the number for his cell phone of the moment.

"Fine, fine," Ezzard Dale said. Carson could almost hear the smile on the man's face. "I'll send it out overnight—today. Should be there tomorrow."

"How soon will you get on to this? My job?"

"Well sir, Mr. Tolliver, I'm going on faith here. I usually don't put any time in unless I have a retainer in hand. You know? I've got burned too many times, and this old boy didn't just fall off the potato truck. But I sense the urgency you have over this matter, so I'll get things rolling. Start making inquiries and doing some background work tomorrow."

Carson let Ezzard Dale ramble a bit more before cutting him off and disconnecting. A sudden gust of cold wind blew across the parking lot; he buttoned his coat up snugly and stuffed the cell phone in a pocket. When he turned his back to the gust, he felt the tautness that had been riding across his shoulders begin to ease as if the mere act of conspiring with a paid fact-sifter in Oklahoma would make everything okay. It wouldn't, of course, but still he felt some sense of fulfilling a self-made promise to Aleta, to somehow reach back to when he hadn't done right by her and doing it now. Too infrequently had he done the right thing when faced with an unprincipled act. Usually he had decided that stepping up to thwart an unfortunate wrong was ultimately the responsibility of others. He learned to do that by observing the one person whom he despised among all others: his father. CB Barrus's example to his sons had always been to let wrongs heal themselves, especially if they were wrongs beneath his own tent; those were under his total control and thus had less pushback from others. Carson had joined in with hollow laughter many times in the presence of his father and those who circled about him fawning when CB was gloating about another victory over an unsuspecting soul. His father's winning hands never included the words *compromise* or *fairness*. Carson was born of his mother's kind heart but had been tutored by his father and his philosophy of winning, winning at whatever was the game of the moment: be it a business negotiation or a golf game. It didn't matter what the playing field was, he was always in it to win it, no matter the price.

Carson had often agonized while smiling like a sycophant, which he had been in every sense. He'd hated himself for it but failed to reframe his *go along* mentality. The comfort of the family business—its monetary rewards and social standing—was seductive; that is where he had chosen to remain. The cost for that was a layer of scar tissue over his inner self; the part of him that had yearned for compassion and fairness had been neutered to imperviousness, an indifference to the mistreatment meted out by his father.

-19-

Purl Barrus was upended when her mother called. Her scheme for Carson's memorial, planned in secrecy, was nearly ready to go public. The University Unitarian Church had been reserved, the date picked, a caterer retained, and plans were being finalized for the reception. All of that was sent asunder when Lillian called that morning. Purl was nursing her second cup of coffee, still in her pajamas and robe, seated at the computer when Lillian broke in.

She listened to her mother from one side of her brain as she usually did, kindly and with the neatly timed uh-huhs yet with her eyes locked on the computer screen. But when what Lillian called to say finally hit her consciousness, Purl jerked fully upright, the *New York Times* headline page blurring before her, and she squawked, "What? Did I just hear what I heard?"

"Now Purl, before you get all het up, I need you to listen to my reason."

"Mom, what in the hell is in your tea this morning? You know that we're on the verge of announcing the service—this week, as a matter of fact. No way are we not going forward with Carson's memorial."

Lillian sniffed into the mouthpiece and cleared her throat, delaying tactics she'd mastered over the years of ameliorating familial discord. "Purl," she said then paused. She had waited several days to call Purl because she knew of the outburst she'd have to endure.

"Mom, don't *Purl* me. I know that tone."

"Purl."

"Mom...okay, what? But you're not going to derail this. You're not."

On the other end of the call, Lillian raised her teacup and

attempted to anesthetize the moment with a swallow of chamomile tea, known for its calming nature. "What if I told you that you must postpone this event for a very important reason, a reason that I am unable to share with you right now? But it's imperative."

"Imperative." Purl's laugh was strained. "Are you telling me that?"

"I am."

More tense laughter. "This had better be good. How do you intend to convince me based on evidence you can't tell me about?"

Lillian inhaled and looked across the breakfast table at her apartment neighbor Herbert Roe, whom she'd asked to come by just to be on hand when she took on her daughter; she valued his even temperament. He smiled benignly, knowing little of what was being discussed, and went back to the morning paper.

"I don't," Lillian said. "I don't intend to convince you based on evidence."

"Mother," Purl breathed her exasperation. "Do you realize how much time and effort I've put into this? My god, I just gave the caterer the final okay yesterday."

"I do realize, and I love you for it. Honoring Carson."

Purl held back for a moment. "Then why...wait a minute—CB put you up to this, didn't he?"

"Heavens no. Give me more credit than that, please."

"I don't get it. You've been all for this. What is it? Tell me, Mom, now."

Lillian looked over at Herbert Roe. He studied her wide eyes then laid the paper down and held her gaze as she spoke. "Purl, honey, I need you to trust me. I mean *really* trust me."

"And this isn't coming from CB?" Purl almost taunted.

"No, I promise you not."

"What, then? Give me something."

Lillian's stomach was churning. She wanted to scream out *Carson is alive! He's alive! He didn't drown!* But she counted to five and told her daughter, "All I can say, dear one, is that your plans for the memorial need to be put on hold for a very important reason. It's imperative."

"Imperative. As in *stop the presses?*"

Lillian chuckled, relieved at Purl's humor. "Exactly like that. You'll understand soon. Just hold off for now."

"How soon is soon?"

Lillian said that she couldn't name an actual time, just that it would be soon. She begged, and Purl finally acquiesced. After a long moment of dead air, Lillian quietly asked about family plans for Christmas, anything to end on a note of normalcy. Purl snorted out a laugh and said *Mother*, in a tone that required no further comment. They disconnected, and each cratered into their own anguish of the moment. Purl didn't get out of her robe until noon, after which she made the calls that pulled the plug on Carson Barrus's memorial. Lillian thanked the man across the table. Herbert Roe responded that he wasn't sure what was going on but that the high color in her cheeks had indicated a matter with a bit of tension to it.

After that she spent most of the morning pacing, looking through the day's mail made up of primarily seasonal catalogs and staring out the window before going out for a long walk down into the neighborhood's collection of boutiques. The Christmas retail displays, festive decorations, and piped-in holiday music, which usually brought out the warmth of the season in her, sparked nothing; not even the tinkle of the Salvation Army bell, being brandished by volunteers from the Rotary Club, aroused her innate nature of compassion. Nothing could blot it out, the entanglement of the real and the unreal—nothing.

———

When Marla Snow left work at Boyd Organics on Thursday, she had signed out for a week of vacation so that, coupled with the company shutdown for Christmas, she could finish shipping last minute candle orders to arrive before the holiday. Her car was backed up to the Quonset building, and she was loading the Honda's trunk and back seat with boxes ready for shipment when Carson wandered off Mill Creek Road and up the drive. He stood back watching for a bit before she stood up and looked at him.

"This isn't a spectator sport, in case you're wondering," she said. "More ready to go if you are keeping score."

He smiled, joined in carrying out boxes until the car was full, and offered to ride along and help unload at the post office. After they delivered the shipment, Carson waited while Marla took care of business. When she returned and dropped into the driver's seat, he was jarred out of a daydream filled with a faceless private detective and an anonymous small boy.

"You with me?" Marla said as she pushed some paperwork into the car's center armrest receptacle. "You looked like a goner there."

"Guess I was. At least my head was out of my body."

She draped her hands over the steering wheel. "Something to talk about?"

"Maybe later."

"Okay then, I have an offer for you."

"That right? An offer?" He smiled a questioning smile.

She lowered her eyelids and raised them slowly. "Stay focused. The offer is simple. Help me pack up my outstanding orders and I'll give you dinner. Take us an hour, well maybe more." It actually took them nearly three hours. It was after eleven when they sealed the last box and stepped out into the night. The security light above the Quonset building cast their shadows out over the uneven ground, each one a long and distorted phantom; their breathing gleamed on white clouds beneath the stark illumination.

Marla swung an arm forward and walked off. "Okay, let's eat."

In the comfort of the old farmhouse, they dined on venison meatloaf along with spinach salad tossed in garlic vinaigrette accompanied by a passable red wine. They ate in silence; at least until their hunger pangs had been calmed. A second glass of wine was poured; they sat back in their chairs and let the food settle.

"Never had venison meatloaf before," he said, breaking into the quiet. "Very good."

"One of the men that works for Boyd's is a hunter. He gave me some of his prized ground venison. All I did was add a recipe of spices my mother concocted long ago."

"Tastes great."

She nodded and sipped more wine. "So, it's later."

"What?"

"You said maybe later you'd have something to say."

He looked straight into her eyes. "I started it today."

"It?" She tilted her head. "Your odyssey. Right?"

A switch was tripped when she said the word again: odyssey. It was still fresh, still close, and yet somehow distant. Now when the dark water immersion came into his head, he no longer let it lacerate his psyche; he was managing to marginalize its harm. And yet it had changed him: who he was and how he thought of himself relative to the blame and unfairness to all who knew him and had known Naomi. But he intended to absorb the blame, however it came down on him, if it meant that Aleta's child could somehow be found and taken from where he didn't belong to be where he did. He had reasoned over and again and decided he didn't really care what punishment would be meted out on him: the man who feigned his own death would undoubtedly be condemned. So be it.

There had been a time, a moment in the summer of 1994, just after he and Naomi had wed and were en route to Paris for their honeymoon, when he had settled back in his first class seat, looked over at the stunning woman he had just married, and had a sense that life was coming together as if it had been divined. Their wedding night in the Sorrento Hotel in Seattle had been luxurious and romantic but with none of the storied first-night pyrotechnics; after all, they had been sleeping together since college. In fact, by that overseas flight, they had already settled into a comfort zone, a pattern that unknown to him was already vexing to Naomi. She had always favored a life of constant stimulation: *party on* had been her mantra. Soon he was viscerally aware of her distancing herself from his predictable manner of living, but he soldiered on, as did she, presenting their marriage as solid and fortunate. Then Aleta had disappeared on the far-flung trip to nowhere only to return a broken creature and take her life in a tub of scarlet water. Nothing had been the same for him after that: not his life, not his self-esteem, not absolving himself of the guilt, the regret of knowing how her life had been marginalized by their father and yet being complacent, doing nothing to help her. Naomi drew further from him and his somber mood, his despair; she pulled away, drawn by the magnetic lure of his own father.

The day his Aunt Purl had taken him aside, her face a mask of regret, and divulged his wife's infidelity and his father's complicity, something blunt and hot bore into his brain. He had staggered around in a daze for months afterward; wretched gut-level anguish was ever-present, but it was when they were both in his presence that the crushing bone-marrow shudder would pass through him. He had gone beyond the hate he'd harbored back then, a loathing he'd kept hidden. He had shouldered the disgrace rather than reveal such an abomination. He was beyond the pain of his wife dying.

Marla Snow had gone to open another bottle of wine and was back. Her voice was trying to make its way into his head. She was saying, "That is, if you feel like sharing more of your saga." She held the bottle above the table smiling. "If you do, this is a very nice California Cabernet from the Napa Valley. Let's see, it's a Burgess Cellars label, and the person who gave it to me says it rated 90 points, if you understand how that works."

"That's good," he said with a nod and raised his glass. "I'll take a pour."

"Ah." She held the bottle aloft. "Is there more to say?"

He looked up into her handsome face and drew his brow into a furrow. "You're especially curious about my little journey."

She settled onto her chair, holding the bottle out, and leaned forward. "Carson, it is amazing, your story. It is truly inconceivable. You get that, don't you?"

"I suppose. I'm so caught up in it I don't think about how it might seem to others. Crazy for sure."

She laughed and finally poured the wine. He watched the glass fill with deep purple until she stopped, lifted the bottle away over her own glass, and poured again. They raised their goblets, touched the bowls, lifted them to their lips, took serious drinks.

Carson turned his glass by the stem and said, "It's beginning."

"Beginning?" She was looking at him as if he might break out laughing, the whole thing being a big joke.

He nodded, lifted his glass again, and repeated, "Beginning."

"Beginning how?"

"Tomorrow a package will arrive at your door. Overnight express delivery."

She blinked and waited.

"Had to use your address. Only one I have."

She waited some more, turned her glass around but didn't drink.

"A contract. It will set things in motion."

She saw his jaw tense as he bit down. She took a drink of cabernet and gave him some time. "So," she came in, "you good with that?"

He didn't respond at first, just looked down at the tabletop. She could tell his mind had gone somewhere into himself. Then he huffed out a laugh. "I'm about to turn on a light in a very dark closet. And today...today I talked to a voice and agreed to pay him to rummage around in that closet with me. But all I have is this voice who says he'll do what I ask for money. Is he real? Will he do what I ask him to? Will it matter?"

Marla didn't try to answer his questions or ask her own. She knew not to. The memory of people lining up to ask her how she felt and what was she going to do after Glen had hanged himself was still with her. The persistence of the well-meaning locals coming at her with a barrage of inane questions, suggestions, and surreptitious prying had in large part been what drove her away. She sat quietly now and gave the man across from her time to consider his self-doubts.

"I'm terrified," he said finally. The frail smile he showed her was short lived. He suddenly reached up to pinch his nose between those mismatched eyes and came away with the dampness of tears. He wiped his hand on his pants leg. "Look at me," he said. His small laugh was but camouflage.

"Why are you terrified?" she asked.

"Yeah, why? How's the poem go? Let me count the ways."

"Elizabeth Barrett Browning," she responded. "A love poem."

He looked up. "Right. Guess I could fudge on that one, couldn't I? I adored my little sister...but not enough."

"Don't you think she knew that?"

"No," he answered raising his voice. "No."

"Why are you terrified?" she asked again.

His glass was empty. He reached out for the bottle. "Because of the most incredibly bizarre decision I've ever made in my life. Strange, stupid, crazy, call it whatever you will, but it's done, and I have to play it out or..." He stopped.

"Or?"

"Right, or what? Fall in on myself? Admit I am a lunatic? Then what? Plead temporary insanity and go back to...to what?"

"Is that what you think you should do, quit this? Give up?"

"The answer is no. I may end up in the loony bin, but I will find him."

She raised her arm, he raised his, they touched glasses and finished the bottle. He woke the next morning with skin too tight for his skull and a head complaining mightily. He struggled to sit up, shoved aside an afghan blanket he'd slept beneath, and rose from the couch in Marla's living room. The walk up to his trailer was slow and meandering. He showered until his head cleared, dressed, took several ibuprofen pills, and scrambled three eggs, which he ate with a slice of wheat toast coated with jelly and washed down with more instant coffee.

Around ten o'clock Marla rapped on the trailer door and handed him the UPS Express envelope that had just arrived. Their eyes lingered on each other for a long moment before she said *Good Luck* and left him to his demons.

-20-

Carson flexed the cardboard envelope in his hands and read the name of the sender, E. Dale with a Sapulpa, Oklahoma address. He pulled the package zip tape open and drew out the promised client retainer agreement. Carson had seen many contracts and this one was little different, except for the part about an *investigative assignment*. A brief cover letter called for filling in the blanks, signing the contract, and returning it with the thousand-dollar retainer. He read the boilerplate language through twice then called Vince Horne's office and left a message for him to call back.

"Damn, Carson." Those were the first words out of Vincent Horne's mouth on his return call. "What have you been up to? That cell number you gave me doesn't work."

"Sorry, Vince. Thought I'd better dump that phone and get a new one."

"Forget that. It would probably take a court order to track your calls. Besides, who's going to bother doing that with everyone thinking you're dead?"

"All the same, I don't want to be leaving a trail."

"If it makes you feel better."

"Vince, I'm going ahead with this."

"Really?"

"Yeah, but it gives me the shakes not knowing how it will turn out."

"Now's the time to call it quits. Take your lumps and move on." Vince's voice grew muffled; he was talking to someone else. "Hold on, Carson."

Carson stepped out of the trailer, walked a few feet, holding the phone to his ear, and stared down toward the farmhouse. Could he stop now? He was drawn back into a dream he'd had two nights ago: he was holding Aleta, embracing her with all his strength, and she was breathing words into his ear, asking him to avenge her child and to save him. In a soft chant she implored him over and over, *save him, save him,* until he awoke staring up into the dark inhaling in harsh gasps.

"I'm back," Vince Horne was saying. "Sorry for the interruption."

Carson hadn't paid any notice. "Never mind."

"So Carson it's…." He stopped midsentence. "Hell, what is it?" He laughed. "I'm a lawyer without words, can you believe? Thing is, you need to know that I'll back you no matter what. If you stop now, take the body blows, and come back to home base, I'll still be your friend. We'll get you through it." After a noise that sounded like he was sucking through his teeth, he added, "Then again, I know you want to find the child and set things right—as right as you see it anyway. Doing that, it'll be sticky. No way of knowing what you'll run into until you do it. What are we talking about here: a child being held and raised illegally on the one hand or abduction on the other? Where this'll all sort out legally is the big question."

After a moment of quiet, Carson said, "I'm not backing away."

"Okay," Vince sighed. "Okay. So why'd you call me if you're all set to go?"

"I've been in touch with that investigator you found for me. Guy name of Ezzard Dale in Oklahoma."

Vince laughed. "I'd forgot about that. I remember the name, Ezzard, just like that old boxer."

"That's right. He's sent me a contract to sign. Plus I'll have to send him a retainer, a grand to start with. Thought maybe I'd run the language by you before I sign. Okay?"

"Sure, why not? I'm just sitting around here waiting for you to call. It's not like I have any real clients or anything. Oh hell, go ahead— read it to me."

After hearing the contract language, Vince said it was straightforward with no real gotchas; it was okay to sign it. He admonished Carson to keep him in the loop and not leave him hanging wondering what was happening. And especially not change burner phones without telling him. Carson left Vince sucking air over his revelation that he would be catching a flight to Tulsa as soon as Ezzard Dale had uncovered some leads. Carson disconnected after Vince said "Oh boy" four times in a row.

———————

That afternoon Carson took the signed contract to a stationary store downtown, made a copy, put the original into a UPS Next Day Air envelope with the check made out to Ezzard Dale Investigations, and sent it off. He'd watched the clerk handle the envelope just like any other then walked away knowing that he'd turned a corner. There would be no reversing course.

With his fate sealed in a cardboard envelope on its way to Oklahoma, he drove downtown, where he wandered aimlessly. He drifted in and out of the stores seeing but not absorbing the essence of the season. Christmas was exerting its full commercial revelry on the community.

He strolled on and felt irrelevant in that scene, an alien watching the rituals of another life form. When he had overdosed on ubiquitous canned music, he wandered down Union Street beneath an overpass and walked down to the edge of the Columbia River. The wind pushed up at the bill of his cap and whipped the water into a scene of agitated whitecaps on blue-gray water. Off to his right a jumble of boulders r32rapped the shoreline; across the water on the Washington side, atop a mesa-like low-level plateau, a white house sat above a promontory of vertical rock formations. Beyond that in the distance rolled the low mountain range known as the Klickitats; the color of brown sugar, they gave the appearance of a gargantuan beast lying on its side taking a nap. Carson took it all in, standing up against a metal railing as the cold wind buffeted his face. From Cecil, he'd heard all about the days before the bridges came, when ocean-going ferries had been a familiar presence on the then mighty Columbia, fighting the powerful currents to carry packets of cars and trucks from The Dalles across to the Washington side and back. The river had once been mighty before The Dalles Dam helped tame it and took away the cherished fishing grounds of Native Americans. Celilo Falls, an amazing collection of waterfalls in the river itself, had served as a fishing ground for native people for over 15,000 years. The story of the dam construction flooding that historical site is part of The Dalles' DNA. Celilo Falls: gone but not forgotten was how Cecil had concluded his history lesson.

After the wash of the river's wind had numbed his face, Carson walked back up into town and sought out a travel agency he'd located earlier; it was time to make plans for the trip, to put it all on the line. He sat at a small desk and told the travel agent, a middle-aged woman wearing half a dozen spangled bracelets on her right arm, precisely where he wanted to go: Tulsa, Oklahoma. When? Soon, he said, but for now he just wanted to know the flights, times from Portland International Airport, and cost. The travel agent nodded, took it all down tapping at her computer terminal, and clucked on cigarette-damaged vocal cords that she didn't think she'd ever booked a trip to Tulsa. He responded that he had never been there himself. They shared their mutual cluelessness until he left with a printout of available flights. Outside on the sidewalk, he paused in the buffeting wind and unfolded the page of flight schedules to read the options again: airlines, departure times, layovers, and arrivals in Tulsa. Just having that information gave him a level of comfort along with a heightened anxiousness: the comfort of knowing how he would get to the place where Aleta had been taken once was coupled with fear of what lay ahead. He refolded the paper as it flapped in his hands and stuffed it into his coat pocket. It was time.

That night, back in the Travelcade, he fried a pork cutlet, sliced up a potato and sautéed it in a skillet, and tugged apart a stalk of Romaine lettuce, which he doused from a bottle of house brand Thousand Island dressing. Along with a budget beer, he felt a sense of contentment, even as his mind bounced around the fact that he would soon be on his way to a place *unknown* to find a child *unknown* now held by people *unknown* and count on the help of a seeker also unknown to him.

Later he went down to the farmhouse to borrow a suitcase from Marla. She invited him in and went looking while he sat in her living room and listened to the CD she had playing, a selection of early Simon and Garfunkel. He had dozed off only to be roused when she dropped a black nylon roller bag at his feet.

"So you're really going, then?" she said looking down at him.

"I am. As soon as I get the word from my sleuth."

"Nervous?"

"Hell yes," he said. "Wouldn't you be?"

She hesitated. "Guess so, can't say. Not my drama."

"Drama." He laughed. "It is that, more than that, it's a damn...you know what, I feel like I'm the face in that painting *The Scream*. You know the one?"

"Edvard Munch. The painter. Norwegian. I used to teach my students about art when I had the chance. Believe it or not, that ghoulish image shook them."

Carson stood and took up the handle of the suitcase. "I know the feeling. Anyhow, think of that painting, and that's how I feel. Except it's not a painting—it's real."

He pulled the bag to the door, its wheels buzzing across the kitchen floor. "You remember the night you heard me yelling outside?"

She nodded. "Almost had Cecil run you off."

"Maybe you should have. You know," he smiled, "if it weren't for an errant truckload of used cars, I'd be engaged in life as usual. Not happy, merely pressing on like always. Up in Seattle my family would be gearing up for another senseless time of spending too much on stuff and acting like it means something. I don't know— maybe they'll do it anyway." Marla didn't respond. "Well, thanks for the suitcase. Soon as I get the word from my man on the scene, I'll stuff it with all I have and go to a place I've never been and try to set a wrong right. But then again, not sure I'm the one that's got it right. Think so, but who knows?"

"You may not succeed, but you're not wrong," she said giving him a tight smile. "You could stop, you know. Stay here, hunker down, and take root like I did."

He studied her face for a long moment then shook his head. "No. Can't. Not sure what the hell I'm doing, but I've made a promise to my little sister. A new promise," he said to her curious expression.

When the call came from Ezzard Dale several days later, Carson listened to the syrupy voice tell him that he had something and that Carson should come to Oklahoma. With a case of the jitters, he packed the suitcase with all the clothes he had, called the travel agent and told her to book him for the first flight possible. She came up with an American flight leaving Portland at around three thirty the next day. He hesitated, used his real name, and said he would drop by with a check in thirty minutes, which he did; by then she had confirmed the reservation. He went to bed early, didn't sleep, and found Cecil Nash waiting outside the trailer the next morning when he emerged carrying the suitcase to his car. He confirmed that he was heading into Portland to catch a flight and accepted Cecil's invite to have breakfast at Pearly's before he left. They were quiet over their orders of the usual until Cecil wiped his beard with a paper napkin and asked, "So Marla says this is all about your odyssey thing. That right?"

"It is. Yes," Carson answered.

Cecil pushed a bite of pancake around in a puddle of syrup. "Too much to ask for a clue of what you're up to?"

"Yes, it is."

"I'm only the one who picked your ass up off the freeway, gave you shelter, and found you a place to live. That cut any ice with you?"

"Some. Not enough. Not right now. Later."

"But Marla, she's in on this?"

Carson drank some coffee and looked at Cecil over the rim. "She is."

"She is better looking than me. There is that."

"Not that, Cecil."

"What then? What's so secret?"

"I owe you, and I'm grateful, but Marla and I have covered mutual ground. That's all."

"Mutual ground." Cecil gave up on what was left on his plate and nodded. "Okay. Not sure what that means, but okay. I'll keep an eye out on the trailer."

"Thanks, and tell Frisco I'll settle up about the car when I get back."

They shook hands in the parking lot, and Cecil stood watching the Camry drive away, his hairy face a mask of puzzlement.

Carson left the car in long-term parking and rode the shuttle bus to the main terminal of Portland International Airport. He went through the ticketing process, checked his bag, made it easily through security using his Washington State driver's license, and looked at his watch: he had a couple of hours to kill before his flight. He stood in a long line at a coffee bar to get a medium Americano, doctored it with cream and sweetener, found a quiet corner, and pulled out his cell phone. The number came into his head easily now.

Lillian was settled in, comfortable with her tea on the side table by her chair, knitting in her lap, and the radio set on the classical FM station, when the phone interrupted her reverie. She set her needles down groaned her displeasure, and reached for the receiver.

"Grandma, it's time," Carson said, his voice calm, but he actually felt lightheaded just saying those words.

"Carson. Time for what?" she spouted.

"You can tell the family. That I'm alive."

There was silence from her end that went on for a moment. "Oh my," she whispered finally. "You really want me to do that?"

"I do, yes."

"Carson," she said. "I'm frightened now. I didn't think I would be, but I am."

"You've been wanting to tell everyone, Grams. Know you can."

"But how? I don't know what I...how I can do this."

"Been thinking on that. What if you call a meeting?"

"A meeting?"

"Yes, a meeting, a family meeting. You could say it is to get this thing about Carson settled. Something like that. You could insist."

"Insist? I suppose I could do that."

Carson tried to laugh. "You're tough, Grandma. Put your foot down."

"But after I spill the beans, what then? They'll be all het up and want to know everything. Where you are and what you're up to."

"Just tell them you don't know where I am but that I will be home in the near future to tell them everything. How about that?"

"I don't know. All along I've pleaded with you to let me tell them, and now I'm nervous."

"You'll do fine."

"Carson, where are you? Can you tell me now?"

He paused. "I am at the airport in Portland. I'm going to find the boy."

She rose and the crossed room, the phone cord trailing along, and turned down the radio. "So you're going to Oklahoma."

"Yes."

"This is outlandish, Carson. Nothing good can come from this. It will destroy you and ruin this family."

"So you've told me. Aleta wants me to do this," he said with the sound of a final call for a flight to Minneapolis in the background.

"Aleta? What do you mean?"

He hesitated, knowing how it would sound, but said it anyway. "She came to me and begged me to save her son."

Lillian sank back in her chair. "Came to you?"

"This comes from way back, Grams. I never did right by her. None of us did. The only thing left is to recover the part of my sister that still lives and restore her child to his own blood."

"Carson, are you sure you're okay? This impossibly tragic time, the loss of Naomi, the horrendous accident, it all must have exacted a heavy toll on you—physically and emotionally. Please abandon this...this fantastic scheme, and come home."

"Grams, call the family together. Tell them I am not dead. You might as well tell them what I'm up to—it will come out soon enough. And remember the fact that Aleta gave birth to a child is not known to most of them."

"Oh my, yes, I'd forgotten that."

Carson laughed into the mouthpiece. "The dust will fly, and CB will have to backpedal and bluster about why it has been kept a secret. Wish I could be a fly on the wall when that is revealed."

Lillian's resolve at first shrank back but then surged forward. She exhorted Carson one more time to give up his objective but then promised to do as he asked. But she insisted on knowing where he was living, having his cell phone number; he gave it all to her and felt a twinge knowing the genie would soon be out of the bottle.

His flight to Tulsa lifted off ten minutes late.

-21-

It was closing in on 11:00 p.m. central time when Carson walked through the Tulsa International Airport amid fellow groggy passengers and mostly closed terminal shops. He followed the baggage claim signs and emerged into a big lobby where the carousels stood; one was already expelling the luggage from his flight. He had wandered over to watch for his bag when he caught sight of hand-lettered sign on a piece of cardboard with the name *Bill Tolliver* scrawled on it; it was being held by a stubby wide-bodied man wearing a wrinkled Harris Tweed sports coat over a yellow polo shirt. His balding head was buzzed short, he stood maybe four inches above five feet, wore black-rimmed glasses, looked to be about fifty and was Black. Carson raised a hand and caught the man's eye. He nodded and ambled over.

"Ezzard Dale," he said when he came close. He held out a hand. "What do I call you?" he asked smiling.

Carson clasped onto a meaty hand and smiled back. "Good question. But I guess we can dispense with Bill Tolliver. He was useful but no longer needed."

Ezzard Dale nodded. "Okay, Mr. Barrus. This may be a more interesting piece of work than I first imagined."

Carson plucked his suitcase off the luggage roundabout as it came by and set it down. "Thanks for meeting me at this hour," he said.

"No need being too nice about it," Ezzard Dale said. "You're paying for my time. As requested, I reserved you a room nearby. My car's right out front. You hungry?"

"Yeah, but I can hold out until the morning. Had peanuts and coffee on the plane."

Ezzard Dale smiled. "Filling. I picked up a couple of subs and some beer if you're interested. Figured you could check in, and then we'd get acquainted over some high cuisine." He laughed in a burst and waddled away. Carson followed the man's swaying posterior and couldn't help wondering where this contractual relationship would lead him.

After a short ride to the airport Hilton Hotel in Ezzard Dale's ten-year-old Ford Crown Victoria, Carson checked in using one of his credit cards for the first time since coming out of the canal. He squinted when the desk clerk swiped it, as if he was about to be hit, but it cleared without a hitch. Evidently no one had gotten around to cancelling his cards since he was declared deceased. That made him wonder about their house: the electricity, gas, newspaper, and Peggy, the woman who cleaned every Thursday. Had their antisocial neighbors noticed that no one was ever home now; were they even aware of their deaths? Ezzard Dale followed him to a room on the second floor. He was carrying a sack of sandwiches and a six-pack of Pabst. The room smelled of cleaner and looked like any of thousands of rooms in thousands of hotels. Ezzard Dale dropped the food on the room table, slipped out of his jacket, raised his thick arms in a stretch, and gave out with a big yawn.

"Sorry," he said. "Been a long day."

"Working other cases?"

"Not so much, just a long day. With Christmas bearing down, people seem to be putting their investigations on hold. Sort of like elective surgeries." He laughed at his own joke. "Anyway, I'll have more time to focus on your case. Besides, I usually do most gift buying on Christmas Eve day. That's my way."

Carson blinked. "Christmas," he said. "Not even on my radar screen."

"I got that feeling," said Ezzard Dale. "It's like that sometimes when a thing gets so big in your head it pushes everything else out. In my line of work, I see a lota that." He pulled a wrapped sub out of the bag and set it on the table. "Here, maybe some food and a beer will help. Got you a turkey and ham sub. Hope that's okay. I'm having a veggie delight." He patted his stomach. "Watching my weight. Can you tell?"

Carson merely smiled. Ezzard Dale pulled the tab on a beer can, took a long drink, and studied his newest client. They ate in silence for a few minutes.

"I've been cogitating and probing since we talked," Ezzard Dale said.

Carson paused in the midst of taking another bite and set the sandwich down. "And?" he said. "Anything?"

Ezzard Dale smiled and pushed up on his glasses. "Not so you'd notice. No forward movement you could measure if you sighted down a stake. Ideas are mainly what I have. So far only just stuck my nose under the tent. This here dilemma's got no corners, no defined shape—not yet."

"So what am I doing here?" Carson asked. He leaned back and held a beer in his right hand. The investigator's expression was almost one of amusement; Carson didn't like it. "I say something funny?"

Ezzard Dale wiped a paper napkin across his mouth. "No, not at all."

"What, then?"

"Well," he said, "we're at that stage, what I call the mating dance. With nearly every client we circle about, dance in and out until we decide what we're really up to. Does Joe really love his wife and want to find out if she's faithful because he loves her? Or does the hard-ass really want evidence of her adultery so he can dump her and save a ton of money?"

Carson drank some more beer and set the can down. "And you're wondering what I'm really up to?"

Ezzard Dale held his arms out. "Hey, I don't care what your motives are. I'm not the archangel of darkness and light. Besides, I get paid either way. I just want to know your agenda so I'll be looking for the real thing here."

Carson stood suddenly and looked down at Ezzard Dale. "All

right, damn it. You want the unvarnished truth?"

"I thought you already gave me that. You mean you didn't?" He raised his hands palms out. "No harm in that, because that's the norm in this business. My clients lie to me first. Then we get down to it. You lie to me, Mr. Barrus?"

"Carson."

"Mr. Barrus until we get down to it."

Carson paced a few steps and back. "I didn't lie to you. Not really. I just left out some things."

"Critical things, would you say?"

Someone slammed a door in the hallway. Carson looked at his watch; he hadn't set it for the new time zone, but he knew it was after midnight. "It's getting late."

"Two hours earlier in Portland. You're still on Pacific Coast time. Critical?"

"Okay." Carson nodded and sat back down and looked into the round face across from him. "Look, Ezzard, there's more I need you to know."

"Okay." He sat back and wiped at the moisture on his forehead. "More is always good."

"There's a freakish reason why I used an alias when I first contacted you."

"Freakish? You don't say. Haven't had that in a spell." He squeezed his empty beer can, collapsing it in the middle. "Okay, man, I'm listening."

Carson met Ezzard Dale's eyes for a moment then inhaled and unveiled more of the story. The investigator's face remained expressionless throughout the telling. When he finished, Carson dropped his elbows onto the arms of the chair; his smile was one of chagrin. Ezzard Dale bit into the second half of his sub sandwich and nodded his head several times.

"You literally…let me get this right," he spoke as he chewed. "You actually, your car actually went into that canal, and you wiggled out leaving your dead wife behind?"

167

Carson squeezed his hands together on the tabletop until they hurt and said yes.

"I mean…I know what you said. Heard it clear enough. Just corroborating things. It's what I do, you know."

"Understand."

"Okay, then." Ezzard Dale finished chewing, eyeing Carson. "So far so good. Well, what I mean is, up to that point it sounds like a man saving his ass. Like most of us woulda done. And you figured your wife was deceased." He wadded up the paper that had held his sub and rolled it into a ball.

"I knew she was dead. I knew it. Saw it."

Ezzard Dale bobbed his head in acknowledgement. "Sure. You were there—I wasn't. But then," he looked straight at Carson, "then you just go on your way. You disappear. You vanish. Suppose when they couldn't find a body they assumed you drowned."

"That's right. It was in the papers: *presumed drowned.*"

They sat staring at the tabletop, both of them looking down at the fake walnut-grain laminated surface. The sound of people passing out in the hallway filtered in: laughter and loud voices.

"You know," Ezzard Dale said, rapping a knuckle on the tabletop. "I've had cases where guys would just disappear. Not that uncommon. Mostly, though, they're running away from something: leaving a wife and kids or maybe stole money from their employer—and like that. This is something of a different ilk." He smiled. "You crazy?"

"Could be. All I know is that, crazy or not, I will find my sister's child and make things right. You in? Or do you want to tear up the contract?"

Ezzard Dale pushed back, stood, and slipped his battered tweed jacket back on. "I'm with you. I'll nose around, see if I can unearth who you want to find—then we'll go from there."

"Fair enough."

"Fair's got nothing to do with it, my man. I do this for the money, nothing else. I can't be a champion of lost causes and feed my kids. Besides, best for you if I remain totally outside the box on this. It's your personal mission. I'll do you a better job that way."

"So what's next?" Carson asked.

"I'm heading home. I've ordered you a rental car that'll be dropped by here in the morning. Like I said, I've begun thinking on this, but working on the thin info you've given me, I haven't gone much beyond the thinking part. Here's my card. Whyn't you drive on out to Sapulpa in the morning, and we'll go to work. I've written down directions to my office." He handed Carson a slip of paper with a crude map drawn on it.

Carson had one more beer after Ezzard Dale had gone and watched the CNN crawl with the sound off. After seeing that New York Mayor Rudolph Giuliani's presidential bid was losing steam and that a fire had broken out in Dick Cheney's office, both positive signs, he turned the television off and unpacked. His cell phone came to life just as he had turned off the light.

"How you doing?" Marla Snow's voice was atonal.

"Just turning in," he answered.

"Sorry, forgot about the time difference. Just wondering if you got there safe and everything's okay."

"Not many landlords would go to the trouble of checking on their traveling tenants."

"Just making sure you'll be coming back. If not, I'll put an ad in the paper for a new renter. Prime property now that I've got it all fixed up."

He was enjoying the sound of her voice. "So am I being evicted?"

"Thinking on it. Since I know this guy renting my trailer is not really who he says he is."

"Sounds like grounds to kick him loose."

"Got to give him thirty days notice is the thing."

"Might be back by then, cause trouble."

"I expect he will." They laughed and seemed to run out of what to say next. "But the real reason I called," she broke the silence, "is about Cecil."

"Cecil?"

"Yes. He came by today saying he'd promised to keep an eye on the trailer for you."

"He did say that."

"That's fine, I guess. No need really, but okay if it makes him feel good. But then he started pressing me on what you're up to. Where you've gone, what this odyssey thing is all about and such. What do you want me to do with him on that?"

Carson looked at the clock radio by the bed; the bright red numerals were declaring the hour to be 1:03 a.m. "He's a good man. I trust him."

"So you're good with him knowing everything?"

He thought it over for a moment. "I guess. Just ask him to keep it between you two...well and Ola Mae. Think he'll do that?"

"Damn well better. I'll lay down the law and lean on him about keeping his yap shut with his cronies." After a little pause, she said, "So you're doing okay then?"

"So far."

"Okay, that's all I wanted. Bye."

The connection went dead. Carson took in a quick breath and looked up into the dark of the room. With her voice suddenly gone, cut off, he was surprised by the visceral response he had just hearing her speak. How long had it been since the voice of a woman had raised pleasurable tension in him? Naomi had been the only one in his mind and heart all those years ago, the one to truly capture his passion, that fervency struggling to mature and perhaps deepen into the love that would surpass others. The deterioration had begun by inches, marked by small treacheries, those so unnoticeable as to be invisible. By the time it was all self-evident, the betrayals they both knew to have occurred had so obliterated his need to be loved that he'd become unaware of the loss. A barrier had built itself up and replaced the part of him that loved and needed love in return.

Now two damaged persons found themselves sharing the same patch of real estate in a place that asked nothing of them. Was either of them capable of reestablishing what used to be open, loving and worthy of love in return? Carson felt a small shudder over the prospect of exploring that part of himself again. Then again, he knew that whatever passion was available to him now must be for Aleta and her son. There could be no other distraction until this thing was done. He palmed his cell phone and laid it on the lamp stand beside the bed. It was another hour of wakefulness until the one-act play in his head ran its course and he fell into some sort of slumber.

Tomorrow it would begin in earnest.

-22-

Lillian Barrus arose early Saturday morning, putting an end to a night that could not be shut off. She struggled up out of her bedclothes and sat on the edge of the pillow-top mattress and tried to gather her thoughts. The tautness that stretched across her chest was exacerbating her sense of unease. She had been begging Carson to let her tell the family that he was not dead, but now that the way was clear, she was uncertain. It should be a moment of wild celebration, an amazing revelation that would be told over and over for decades to come: the kinsman who came back from the dead. She knew clearly that after she revealed the news, after what would be the briefest of celebrations, chaos would prevail.

Breaking out of her rumination, she shuffled to the bathroom, limping from an arthritic hip that disliked being abed, and relieved her bladder. Afterward, with her rheumy blue eyes, faded and floating on yellowed whites, she studied the old woman in the mirror above the sink and grunted disgustedly. Viewing her shriveled self, once willowy, once vibrant, once a local beauty, had become an unpleasant ritual. She washed her face with warm water and soap but decided to shower later once she had orchestrated just where and when the family would be convened.

It was still dark outside when she took tea and toast with a dab of raspberry jam at the kitchen table. She had turned on the radio to the public broadcasting station and felt comforted by the familiar voices of *Morning Edition*. She heated more tea water and had a second piece of toasted wheatberry bread, spread with more jam; she had decided they should meet at Purl's place. She would call her when the hour was more humane and see how her daughter would react, first to Carson being alive and then to her request to have a family meeting at her house—that very night. When her Leon was alive, their home had been the gathering place for all things familial: Thanksgiving, Christmas, the Fourth of July, and any time the children and grandchildren got together. There was no debate about where to gather; everyone knew to go to Granny and Gramps. It stayed that way for a while after Leon died, family coming to the big house; then Lillian was coerced by CB into selling the house and taking up free residence on the top floor of the Proffer Arms. She hated it no matter how she purred her appreciation for the nice apartment. It was a very nice place, just not her place.

By seven-thirty she couldn't wait any longer. Whether Purl was awake or still in bed, Lillian was calling her. She reheated water, set a steaming cup on the end table on which the landline phone sat, cinched up her robe, and lowered into the platform rocker. After a sip of chamomile, she tapped in a number that was among those in her mental directory. It began to ring, and she closed her eyes.

"Mother," said Purl. "You're up early."

Lillian cleared her throat. "It's always a surprise when you say my name before I tell you who it is."

"Caller ID."

"I know. I'm just not used to it. And so we're both up early, it seems."

"Yeah. I didn't sleep at all."

"Nor did I. Guess it's catching."

Purl laughed. "Could be in our DNA. Thanks."

"And the bad news is that it doesn't go away as you age. Just gets worse."

"This why you're calling? Insomnia?"

Lillian closed her eyes again and took in a slow breath. "No, something more than that."

"About?"

"Carson."

Purl inhaled sharply and snorted a laugh. "Back to that again, are we? What? Did CB finally give us the okay to honor his son? Here we are closing in on Christmas, and we still have this dreadful, god-awful thing hanging over our heads. CB is such as ass." She paused a second then added, "That what you called to hear?"

Lillian had leaned forward when her daughter had begun her rant, her eyes closed tightly, and waited her out. When the opening came, she said, "No, and I need you to listen to me. What I have to say is important."

"Mother, I refuse to hear any more inexcusable maneuvering about delaying a—"

"Purl!" Lillian snapped. "Stop now. You hear me? Just stop." Her voice dropped. "I...I just need you to listen. Please."

"Mom." Purl's voice lost its fierceness. "What is it? Are you all right?"

"I'm okay. It's not about me. I'm fine." Lillian had taken a tissue from her robe pocket and was dabbing at her morning watery eyes. "It's just that...I need you to be level headed now."

"You're scaring me," Purl said. "What about Carson?"

Lillian leaned back and tilted her head back and said *Oh God* in her head. "I'm counting on you, dear."

"What is it?" Purl begged.

"He isn't dead." She paused. "Carson, he's alive."

Dead silence. Then Purl sputtered, "Mother, what in the hell are you talking about?"

"He is." A sense of calm came over Lillian. "Alive. Our dear Carson is alive."

Purl was seated at her kitchen table with the *Seattle Times* spread out before her, engaged in her morning ritual when her mother called: half a grapefruit, a bowl of Special K cereal with 1% milk, and a cup of coffee, black. When Martin had died from a massive stroke, their shared breakfasts of everything from his fluffy sourdough pancakes to her fluffy omelets disappeared. She couldn't bring herself to make them by herself, so it was a bare-bones low-calorie menu from then on. The newspaper's headlines blurred in the face of Lillian's bizarre declaration. Purl raised her head as if to blurt out to Martin what she has just heard, but of course he wasn't there.

She rested her head in an upraised hand, elbow planted on the table. "You have a bad dream, Mom?"

Lillian's eyes snapped open. She hadn't thought of this reaction, of not being believed. "No. Purl, you must believe me. Carson didn't drown."

"Didn't drown? You mean you wished he hadn't drowned."

Lillian gasped. "Purl Anne!" she said at the top of her voice, "How dare you suggest that I'm deluded."

"Calm down, Mom. I didn't mean—"

"Just what did you mean, then? And what is it going to take to convince you that your nephew lives? The time has come. He has given me permission to alert the family, and I need your help."

"The time has come," Purl echoed. She stood up from the table and walked to the kitchen window above the sink. It was penetrating that her mother was serious. "And how is it that you know this, Mother?"

"He called me, I don't know, sometime after the accident. I nearly had a stroke."

Purl steadied herself against the counter and leaned on one hand. "You're sure it was him, actually was Carson? People can do horrible things even fake being someone. You are convinced it was him?"

"Yes. Absolutely."

"And why you? Out of all of us he called you. Why?"

Lillian hesitated. "Does it really matter, dear? He made contact but wanted me to keep it secret for a little while. I guess he trusts me. We've always been close."

"This is so bizarre. What happened? How did he not drown?"

"It's a long story," Lillian said softly. "We'll get to it all, but later."

"Later? Where is he? Can I call him?"

"No. Not yet. He's…Purl, we need you have a family meeting tonight. At your house."

"Tonight?"

"Yes, if you will. Please."

Purl grunted like she'd stubbed her toe. "And what reason am I

175

to give? I can't just blurt out that Carson is alive. They'd haul me off as a nutcase."

"Just like me, right my dear daughter?"

"Got me there. I'm still not sure I buy this."

"You don't have to—later you will. Right now just say that the head of the family, the matriarch of the clan, is calling a family meeting for the purpose of finally discussing Carson. That we'll get this over with. But you are not to say anything about him being alive. Just tell everyone to postpone anything else they have planned for this evening. Be at your home by seven o'clock and no excuses."

In the end, Purl agreed to do as her mother asked. She would ask Stuart bring his grandmother. After they had disconnected, Lillian sat quietly rocking. She smiled and considered her directive to Purl: the matriarch of the clan is calling a family meeting, as if she'd ever done such a thing, as if any woman of the family had ever asserted herself in such a fashion. Now was the time, she assured herself; in fact, she felt energized by this family drama in which she was the lead orchestrator.

She showered, selected the dress she would wear, laid it out on the bed, and visited with her apartment neighbor Herbert Roe when he dropped by for their usual tea and cookies; he provided shortbread biscuits this time. They chatted about the weather and the presidential campaign before he left to run some personal errands. She had smiled and engaged with him benignly while her head was a twirl with the performance ahead of her, but she mentioned nothing of the psychodrama to come.

The day wore on. Around one o'clock she nervously tapped Carson's cell number into her phone keypad. He answered while in the office of a private investigator. That gave her a chill, but they shared a breathless exchange of concern for one another then had a good laugh over her ordering the clan to a meeting. They spoke briefly about how she should approach the family. Her confidence was growing even though she still worried over her grandson's pursuit; she feared it would come to no good end.

Stuart Barrus followed his grandmother's instructions to circle the block until they were the last ones to arrive at Purl's house. He got a kick out of Lillian's gumption and enjoyed aiding her in making a grand entrance. Her only response to his curiosity was to waggle a crooked forefinger in the air and tell him: *Just wait.* Her stern facial expression stood in place of the always-smiling woman who showed up at every family gathering; on this occasion, his sweet granny was on hiatus.

Familiar cars were parked in the driveway and on the street in front of Purl's big New England-style house in Laurelhurst. She and Martin bought the house early in his law practice, raised their daughter Katie there, and lived the good life within in those walls until his death. Now Purl moved about the place filled with memories and too much space but refused to sell and move into smaller quarters. Lillian thought of that as she and Stuart approached the front door and bit down on her own regrets of being pressured into giving up the house of her life.

She and Stuart stood on the front stoop beneath an amber porch light and waited for the bright red front door to open. Lillian took in a slow deep breath, hoping that the knot in her stomach would release itself; it didn't. When the door swung in, Purl stood in the opening and looked down on the diminutive figure of her mother. She propped a hand on her hip, let her wide mouth form an insincere smile, and blocked the way in.

"Mother. Stuart." She looked from one to the other. "Well they're here, all but CB, of course. I hope you know what you're doing."

Lillian sniffed and hunched up her shoulders. "Let's find out," she said and stepped in and edged past her daughter. "No CB? Not surprised." She let Stuart help her out of her coat. "But we'll just see about that. He may be induced to join us."

Purl's forehead bunched between her eyebrows. "Don't go too far," she said and looked at Stuart.

"What's that mean?" he asked.

"You'll see," Lillian said and marched off.

They were gathered in the living room, aligned on two couches that faced each other before a gas-fired fireplace log, each one holding a glass of red wine; no one had been interested in tea or coffee. Lillian entered and stood as straight as she could and looked from one face to the other. In return she received only dubious stares and a couple of benign smiles.

She inhaled and let her eyes play over the flickering flames of the pseudo fire. "Thank you for coming," she said finally, giving as much force to her voice as she could muster. "We have something significant to discuss."

"Lillian." BeBe Barrus's voice rose in almost a cry. "What are you doing?"

Lillian clasped her hands at her waist and drew herself up as erect as she could, ignoring the twinge in her back. "Just this," she said. "It's time to talk about Carson." She took in the array of questioning faces: Rove's deep brown eyes stared out from beneath dark eyebrows. He almost looked amused except that the smile on his wide mouth was frozen. And BeBe, she had her face all scrunched up, her rosette lips puckered in anticipation of the moment when she would be moved to tears. Stuart had walked past his grandmother and turned to study her, tilting his angular face in question, not sure what she was up to. Purl hung back waiting, watching, curious to see how her mother would play this out.

Lillian had the floor, but she wasn't quite sure what to say next. She blinked her eyes, stood quietly, and let the moment of silence extend itself. She'd read once that in a group setting nothing is more powerful in gaining attention than silence. The quiet closed in on the room like a heavy quilt threatening to smother their ability to speak—until Lillian finally did.

"No CB," she uttered, cutting through the silence. "Where is he?"

All eyes turned on BeBe. She started and sat upright. "He had a... no, he just decided not to come. That's all." Her smile was self-conscious. "Didn't think it would come to anything—that's how he put it."

"What's that mean?" asked Lillian.

"I guess it means that he's already made his decision, you know, about any memorial service for Carson. We all know that." BeBe smiled pathetically. "So why be here?" She shrugged and tittered.

Lillian took a step forward. "Yes. Not surprised. Not surprised at all. But BeBe," she raised a finger, "you may want to call him in a bit. He might choose to drop by anyway. Good chance of it." Stuart brought a ladder-back wooden chair up behind his grandmother, but she demurred. "I'll stand for now."

Rove had taken a generous swallow of wine and now set his glass down on the coffee table, a long slab of black walnut that had been personally selected by Martin Strutt two years before he died; Rove was careful to use a coaster. "Mother," he spoke up in a voice louder than his usual intonation. "I don't know what your intent is, but I think we all want to treat Carson's loss with love and respect. Right?" He looked around and received nods from BeBe and Stuart; Purl and Lillian remained detached. "So," Rove went on, "with or without Cadence, we can agree on a memorial service and give Carson a blessed send-off. Forget about CB Okay?" He looked over at BeBe, who only pursed her lips and said nothing in response.

Lillian looked down. "No."

"Mother, we don't need CB's approval if that's why you've called us all together."

Lillian looked up over their heads at a painting above the fireplace and paced her breathing and fretted about revealing the unbelievable to them. After all, the strongest among them, Purl, hadn't believed her, probably still didn't. "Rove, there will be no memorial service." She raised a hand with its crooked fingers. "There will be no memorial service because it's not needed." She inhaled once more. "Because Carson is not dead."

Then she slumped down onto the chair provided and waited out their cries of alarm and nervous laughs. Stuart coughed out his disbelief turned to Purl and raised his arms in question; she only shrugged. Lillian didn't reply to the flurry of questions or the incredulity written on their faces; she merely smiled, folded her hands in her lap, and remained calm. When she didn't respond to them, Stuart finally raised an arm to quiet everyone down and turned to his grandmother.

"Grandma," he began, "you know that nothing would make us happier than to learn that Carson didn't drown. That he isn't gone. That said, we have mostly come to some closure now. I hope you understand that."

"Of course," she answered.

"All right then," he went on, "it will be exceedingly hurtful if what you claim is only your wish. Is that what it is, the wish we all have that this horrible thing had not happened?"

She licked at her dry lips, felt her heart quickening, and repeated the words: "Carson is not dead. I assure you, he is not. Please hear me out. Then you will be filled with the same shock and joy I felt the day I first learned of his survival." She looked into the group portrait of dumbfounded faces and began. They listened intently. Their reactions of wide eyes, hands to the mouth, and shakes of the head gave her the release she wanted from being the solo keeper of the secret. When she stopped, the room was quiet; eyes were either staring at her in disbelief or casting about looking to confirm their amazement with someone else.

Lillian saw and felt their uncertainty. She knew that the only way to make them know the truth was for them to hear his voice. She asked Purl for her cell phone and held it up. "Will you believe his voice?" she asked.

"You can reach him, right now?" asked Stuart. "Where is he? Why doesn't he just come to us?"

"He is not here," she answered. "But I think I can reach him. Are you ready for that? I know this is a shock, as it was for me. We can wait until you've all absorbed the news."

"No, do it," Purl said. "If it's true we need to know—now."

When everyone said yes or nodded, Lillian unfolded the small piece of paper she had been holding in her hand and focused on the number she'd scribbled on it. She held the phone up, pressed each number firmly, and put the device to her ear. The dumbfounded expressions on their faces filled her chest with unease; especially BeBe, who was holding her face between both hands, her face wrinkled in apprehension. They must hear from Carson; they must hear his voice. After a brief lag, the ringing buzz filled Lillian's ear; her eyes widened. With each ring she expected the connection to be made and to hear Carson speaking to her. Instead all she got was a brief answering message: *It's me. I'll get back to you.*

Lillian groaned her disappointment then uttered a hopeful few words: "Carson, it's me. I'm with the family. Please call now." She fumbled with the phone before Purl took it from her and ended the call. Lillian looked befuddled; some faces held *I told you so* expressions of doubt. Most took another drink of wine and sank back in their seats.

"He'll call," she said. "He really is alive. He'll call. He will."

Purl put a hand on her mother's shoulder and patted her. "It's okay, Mom. We'd all like this to be true. We know you mean well."

"Mean well?" Lillian snapped reaching up to push Purl's hand away. "You still think I'm off my head. Well, I'm not. If you would all just get past thinking I'm an old fool, we could begin to put this part of our lives back together." No one spoke. "Give it a bit. He will call."

Still no one spoke. Another bottle of wine was opened and passed around. An occasional whisper was exchanged, but no one addressed Lillian. When Purl's cell finally did ring, twenty minutes had passed; the phone's chiming tone froze people in place. Purl pressed the phone and handed it back to her mother.

Lillian held it to her ear and could hear "Hello, hello" being spoken. "Oh," she moaned pleasurably and nodded to all the wide-eyed faces. "Carson, it's you. Thank god."

"Sorry, Grams, I'm in a restaurant and didn't hear the ring." He paused. "So you are really with the family?"

"Yes, we're here," she answered too loudly. "All except your father, that is."

"What else is new? Grams, are you okay? How are they taking it?"

"I'm fine," she answered. "Well, they are shocked, of course, and I'm pretty sure think I'm addled in the head. That's why I'm calling you. They need to hear your voice."

"I understand. I'll do that but nothing else. I am not ready to get into a long drawn-out conversation. You can tell them what I'm up to if you want, but I won't at this point."

"Whatever you say, dear one," she said.

"So, how do you want to handle this?"

"I don't know. I'm not much good with these cell phones. Purl is lending me hers."

"Okay. Ask Purl to put it on the speaker mode. That way everyone can hear."

Lillian held the phone out to Purl, who was still standing beside her. "He says to put it on speaker."

Purl was staring down at her mother, stupefied, as were all of them. She hesitated before taking the phone and activating the speaker mode and handing it back to Lillian. "Just hold it up and talk," Purl said.

"Okay. Carson, can you hear me?" Lillian asked.

"I can hear you loud and clear, Grams." Everyone in the room drew in a breath and leaned toward Lillian.

"Say more, Carson," Lillian said. "They need to hear your voice clearly."

There was a delay, then Carson said, "Hello, everyone. This is really me. I'm sorry for the stress and anxiety my absence may have caused, but I have my reason. I can understand any anger you may have, and I regret that. I won't say more now or take time to answer questions. It is just time to confirm my survival. Goodbye." There was a sound of disconnection.

"Wait!" Rove jumped up. "Oh my god, this is incredible. It *was* him. It was."

It was Purl who asked her mother the question that had to be asked: *Why?*

-23-

Earlier that day, while Lillian was organizing his coming-out party, Carson was two thousand miles away sitting in a cramped storefront office on north Water Street in the old downtown of Sapulpa, Oklahoma, sharing maple bars and coffee with a stout private investigator. Ezzard Dale sat at a steel gray enamel metal desk with a scored laminate top, eyeballed his new client, downed the last bite of a maple bar, and pushed a pastry box at Carson.

"Another?"

"No," Carson said. "One maple bar's my limit."

"My favorite," Ezzard Dale responded.

Carson merely returned a thin smile.

Ezzard Dale wiped his sticky hands on a paper towel and looked intently into Carson's eyes. "Here's the deal. I started with the loosely useful pieces of info you gave me: a town beginning with the letter T, the midwife thing, and the big maybes on the supposed names of the people who might have the child. Right? Now all that piled up is not worth a bucket of warm spit, as the saying goes."

"It's all I have to go on," Carson responded.

"I'm not complaining, Mr. Barrus."

"Carson."

"Yeah, okay, and call me Ezzard. I'm just saying the details are a little sketchy. Course that's okay because otherwise you wouldn't need me. And we don't want that, now do we? If you could have just waltzed into town and knocked on a door and got what you wanted, what's the fun in that?" He laughed and threw the paper towel in a wastebasket. "Have to tell you, though, it will take some creative investigative work. Like to begin with, there's over thirty towns in the state of Oklahoma, big, small, and in between, that have names that start with the letter T."

"I know," Carson said, "I Googled it."

"Damn, Google will be the death of my business. Hear that, Scooter? Bet we hear Google with every client these days. Right, I am I right?"

A sylphlike young woman sitting at the other desk in the office raised her head from behind a computer screen. "That's right, boss." Her voice was that of a child. "Nearly every time seems like." She had long black hair and very pale skin so translucent that blue veins could be seen, and she stared out through thick glasses. Ezzard told Carson that this Scooter was his prime investigator when a fat black man didn't fit the bill, which was often.

"All right, then," Ezzard said, "you done your due diligence, so I can't snow you any about having all those places to look. What else you dug up that I can't throw on the table?"

"Not a thing."

"Okie dokie then, guess we're good to go." Ezzard swiveled his chair in Scooter's direction. "Actually, I turned Scooter loose on this right after you and I talked by phone. And I think we've made measurable progress."

"What's that mean?" Carson asked.

Ezzard chuckled. "What it means is, I grilled Scooter this morning before you arrived and found out what she's found out so far, and now I get to tell you what she said and take the credit." He leaned back and laced his hands across is stomach; his chair complained. "We moved on the midwife angle first. Figured we could narrow the search window by focusing on this part of the state since you had that loose clue about a small town near Tulsa. That right?"

"My mother let that drop with my grandmother. Not sure how accurate it is. For all I know, might even be towns starting with the letter C."

Ezzard lifted his right shoulder in a shrug. "Ash can that thought.

We'll go with T for now. By doing that we cut the number of towns we'd have to scope out in half. Then we can eliminate towns with a T where we can't locate practicing midwives."

Carson leaned forward, elbows on his knees. "Will that work?" He closed and unclosed his hands.

"Might. Course, it'll be a process of elimination, that is, once we decide on what to eliminate. That's where you come in. Scooter has a couple of questions along that line."

The two men turned to look at the young woman. She blinked, her brown eyes appearing large through the corrective lenses. Her small voice spoke with certainty. "Mr. Barrus, from what you told Ezzard, seems like this…this child was born sort of, as we put it, off the grid. Is that right?"

"By that you mean, not in a hospital?"

"More like under the radar," Ezzard responded. "Is it likely your father would have sought out a midwife for your sister who wasn't certified?"

"Certified?"

"You see," Scooter broke in, "there are both certified and lay, or noncertified, midwives. Here in Oklahoma, midwives don't have to be certified. Most are going that route, but there's still what are called direct-entry. They're traditional midwives, the ones who learned from other women: grandmothers, mothers, aunts, or any women who were part of the midwifery culture. Guess you'd call them self-educated, with skills handed down from one generation to the next. Those who see midwifery as a calling and have resisted licensing."

"So you're thinking that maybe my sister's baby was delivered by such a person?"

"Put it this way," Ezzard said. "You think your father was trying to keep this quiet? Keep the birth secret?"

"Of course." Carson blurted, looking from Ezzard to Scooter and back. "Absolutely. That was the bastard's whole intent."

Ezzard chuckled. "Okay Scooter, think you got your answer."

"The thing is," she said, "just where to start looking."

"And what did you decide?" Ezzard asked with an impish smile on his face. He winked at Carson.

"I Googled," she said with a little laugh.

"Aha!" Ezzard expelled, dropping an open palm on his desk. "It's rampant right under my nose. So, what did you find out? And can we generate billable hours out of it?" He roared a laugh. "Just kidding, Carson. Scooter?"

"I found a small direct-entry website and called one of the midwives listed." Scooter dipped her head and smiled. "Told her I was interested in midwifery and wanted to know if she could put me in touch with any local lay midwives. You know, to talk to."

"Isn't she great," Ezzard said. "Sneaky but honest, right? Okay, Scoot, what'd you find out? Where you going with this? Our client is getting antsy. Cut to the chase."

Scooter held her hands together and entwined her fingers. "Okay. So I just started making phone calls and eventually came up with a list of lay midwives in several adjoining counties. Six names actually. All women who are direct-entry midwives." She looked at Carson again. "I gave that all to Ezzard."

"And good work it was," Ezzard said. "From there I made some calls myself and talked with all but one of the names Scooter dug up. Called on my exceptional skills of interrogation and peeled back the onion."

"And?" Carson said. "You find a likely candidate?"

Ezzard held up two fingers. "Picked a couple to start with. One lives out in Tonkawa. The other's in Tahlequah. Home of the Cherokee Nation."

Carson blew out a breath. What would that be like, connecting with the woman who delivered Aleta's baby? Would she cooperate? If so, then what? When he caught his breath, he found that Ezzard was studying him with sympathetic eyes. "Boy, I'm getting this feeling," Carson said. He held out his hands. "Getting the shakes."

"Yeah, most of my clients go through that. You're almost afraid that we've found a link to your goal. That right? It's the old *be careful what you wish for* caveat." He leaned forward, elbows on his desktop. "You want take a break here?"

"No. Hell no. Go on. What do we do now?"

"Face time, my friend. We gotta see these women up close to find out if either is the one we're after. That's our next step. You up for that?"

"Me? I thought..."

"No, you know the little details that I don't. I plan on being with you to give this inquiry a serious tone. I'll use my charm and experience, of course."

"Which one first?" Carson asked.

Ezzard referred to a spiral notebook on his desk, studied a page of handwritten scrawls, and said, "Let's head on out to Tonkawa first and call on Saffron Taylor. Ninety-minute drive."

"Saffron?" Carson said. "That for real?"

Ezzard smiled, and Scooter giggled. "Hippie culture. Lot of lay midwives got into it back in the seventies when flower children were doing their own thing, even delivering babies, I guess."

Carson rubbed knuckles into his eyes and laughed. "Okay, Saffron. See her first, then who's next?"

"Well if this Saffron isn't the one, we'll go out to Tahlequah and meet up with Inola Jeffcoat. If I miss my guess, she's Native American. Older too, by the sound of her voice."

"You think they'll tell us anything?"

"Maybe, maybe not. But I have my ways. Let's not consider failure, just put on our nicey-nice smiles and be all warm and fuzzy. You check out of the motel in Tulsa?"

"I did."

"Okay, friend of mine owns a retro sixties motel not far from here." He slipped a business card across the desk. "Get a room there. He'll give you a good rate. Think you'll like it. Meantime, I'll call Saffron and see if we can get on her calendar, maybe sometime tomorrow."

Carson rose from his chair, thinking of the prospect of actually looking into the eyes of the person who had delivered his sister's child. How would he react? What if that person refused to see him as legitimate, as a person who has rights to a child not his own? He looked down into Ezzard Dale's face.

"You okay, man?" Ezzard asked.

"No. No, I'm not okay. Doesn't matter—let's do it."

Ezzard rose slowly and held out a hand. "We will."

-24-

Lillian was still seated with Purl standing over her waiting for an answer to the big question that hung in the air: *Why?*

"Mom," Purl said, her arms folded. "What is going on? Why did Carson do this?"

"I'd like to know that myself." CB's voice froze the room into a scene of staring mannequins. All eyes turned to him standing in the entry to the living room, his hands deep in the pockets of a heavy navy overcoat. "If it's actually true, that is."

Purl turned to look toward BeBe, whose face was flushed red. "So you made a call, did you, BeBe?" CB was smiling a tight-lipped smile she hated. "Well, no matter. Glad you finally saw fit to join our family séance here, Brother Dear. Didn't take you long to get here. Seems we've succeeded in bringing Carson back to life. Or maybe we just heard from him from the spirit world."

"What's all this nonsense, Mother?" CB addressed Lillian from behind her chair. "Some charlatan convince you that my son is still among the living?"

Lillian remained seated, hands still in her lap. "Say what you will Cadence," she said, using his given name; she deplored the use of CB as a pompous appellation. "Carson is alive. I've known it for some time now."

CB slipped off his topcoat and dropped it on a chair. "Is that so?" He walked into the room, which seemed devoid of air with his arrival. He stood opposite his sister, leaving Lillian bracketed by the two of them, and studied his mother's face. "You've known. For how long?"

"Maybe a couple of weeks."

"Weeks, is it?" He squatted down. "If this is true, why did you keep it to yourself?"

Lillian met his hardened stare without flinching. "Because he wanted it that way. And I honored his request."

CB rose at the behest of complaining knees, despising his emerging arthritis, ruing that his sixtieth year was upon him. He looked into this mother's aged eyes for a prolonged moment; when she didn't look away, he smirked, stepped over to the coffee table, and poured himself some wine. Other than Purl's caustic welcome, no one else had spoken. He took a deep swallow of what seemed a middlingly good cabernet and spotted his brother staring at him wide-eyed.

"So Rove," he queried, "you buying into this fairy tale?"

Rove coughed out a small laugh and looked about him at the others. "Don't think it's a fairy tale, CB"

"Oh, and what makes you say that?"

"We just heard him on the phone."

CB took another drink, looked down into his glass, twisting the stem, and compressed his lips. "You heard him," he repeated. "No, you heard someone say he was Carson. You people are so gullible." He laughed; it was a laugh meant to belittle. "This is one of the oldest scams in the world. Calling families desperate to deny the truth and—"

"It was Carson." The voice that cut in was Stuart's. When his father yanked his head around, angry at being cut off, he repeated, "It was him. We all heard him. Smirk all you want, Dad. This isn't a case of group hypnosis. It was him."

"Really?" He looked at all in the room in turn, focusing at last on BeBe. "And you, my dear," he said to his wife, "what does the mother think? Was it our son?"

BeBe twisted a napkin in her hands and raised her head. "Yes, CB, it was Carson." Then she nodded vigorously. "I'm sure of it." She smiled in relief. "Isn't it wonderful?"

CB raised his glass in the air. "Well hallelujah!"

Everyone seemed to relax and bask in agreement in spite of CB's cynicism.

"So what did he say? Carson. What did he say?" CB asked. "What's the explanation for this dramatic reentry? Where is he, and why did he do this? Mother? You seem to be the keeper of the flame here. Tell me."

This was the moment Lillian had dreaded. All she could do was delay a bit and collect herself for the ultimate unveiling. "Well," she began, "he said it was really him and that he was sorry for causing so much worry."

"How nice of him," CB barked. "Did you hear that, everyone? He's sorry. Well damn him."

"CB!" BeBe burst out. "How can you say such a thing? Our son is alive. Whatever his reasons, he's alive."

CB glared at his wife, repulsed by her cowering naïveté, for being the easily cowed women he had created over years of deriding everything she did. Her little burst of vigor was out of character; he'd driven all such exuberance out of her some time ago. He studied the determination on her face and felt a moment of puzzlement over her behavior.

"Ah, the mother," CB said, holding out an arm toward her. "Ever the believer in her children. Even if they feign death. Now that is the ultimate test of a mother's love."

"Oh for god's sake, CB," Purl said, her exasperation hanging in the air. "Must you always be yourself?"

CB laughed loudly. "As I should be. As I should be."

"Well for once, give us all a break from your persona so we can come to grips with this family situation. Can you? Can you just do that, keep your own ego in check for the moment?" Purl glared at her big brother.

"As you say," he answered, raising his hands in mock surrender. "But we need to know the whole of this, Mother," he said. "Give it up. All of it—and now." He turned and faced Lillian, who still sat calmly in the chair, hands still in her lap.

"All right," she said. "Carson did get out of that canal and walk away." With all eyes on her, she told of his contacting her, pledging her to secrecy, but telling nothing about where he was. They listened, took in all that she told them, spellbound. But when she pulled up short of the full story, they became agitated.

It was Rove who broke in first. "But Mom, you've got to tell us where he is and what he's up to and why. There's more—we have to hear it."

"You're right, Rove," she said, nodding. "There is more. What do you boys call it, the whole enchilada?"

For once everyone smiled. "That's right, Grandma," Stuart said, "that is what we want: the whole enchilada."

She inhaled and smiled at their expressions of anticipation. "But you must promise me to remain calm and level headed."

Purl had drawn up a hassock near her mother's chair. "Mom, you're freaking me out. Has he done something terrible? Is he on the run or something?"

"No dear, he's not a criminal or on the run. However, the judgment of what he is about may well be different among you." She paused, fearful of revealing too much. "Carson has been residing in Oregon."

"Where in Oregon?" CB probed.

Lillian lowered her eyes at Cadence. "Patience, son."

CB shrugged and sat next to Rove on the couch.

"Carson is in Oklahoma right now," she said and watched for CB's reaction. She flinched when his head snapped around.

"Oklahoma?" he said, sitting forward.

Lillian nodded. It seemed that everyone mouthed the word at the same time: Oklahoma. She half expected them to burst into the song from the musical. Mostly they looked at each other with baffled expressions, all but CB; he was studying her with eyes that were mere slits. Off behind him, BeBe's face was frozen in shock, her mouth held open in a small orifice of alarm.

"Oklahoma," Stuart said again and laughed. "Why there, of all places?"

"Wait everyone," Purl said holding up a hand. "Go ahead Mom."

Lillian brushed her dress out smooth in her lap, picked at an errant speck of something, and made a motion of flicking away whatever it was. She raised her head and waited until a sense of calm came to her. She smiled. "Well," she began, "I never thought this day would come. I suppose I was in what is called a state of denial. First, I want you all to know that I feel shame for what I've known but have kept to myself."

"Mother, don't." CB's voice froze Lillian for a prolonged moment. The rest in the room sat immobilized, wary expressions moving back and forth.

"What the hell is going on?" Stuart asked.

CB reached out for a nearly empty bottle of wine in a motion of nonchalance. "Nothing," he answered while pouring out the bottom of the bottle. "Nothing to be aired here, certainly not now. It's out of the past and of no concern and can only hurt where it shouldn't have to. Right, Mother?" He swallowed all in his glass in one gulp.

"Oh, Cadence," she responded, her voice shaky. "Can't you for once act as I've always wanted you to? Please?"

"And how is that, as a simpering, weak-kneed sycophant? Where do you think we'd be if I'd not been the hard edge of this family?"

Lillian raised a finger and dabbed at a tear in her eye. "No," she said, "but as a man of character who makes principled decisions. That's all I've wanted, son. That's all."

Purl looked to her brother, to view his reaction to such a penetrating assessment from the woman who had borne him and endured him. His face was flexed in a mask that accentuated the creases in his brow and in his cheeks. The only sound to be heard was the soft breath of the gas-fired flames in the fireplace.

"Why, Mother," he said at last, breaking the vacuum, "you crush me with such commentary. And I thought that my years of endeavor on behalf of you, my siblings, and assorted progeny would have earned me some semblance of esteem in your eyes."

The breath that Lillian pulled in was both ragged and plaintive.

193

"No, your achievements have always been self-motivated and for your own aggrandizement. Now that must stop."

CB seemed stunned for a moment before his expression turned to one of bemusement. "One might assume your proclamation to be too late and without enough weight to be effectual."

"Nonetheless."

"You must not do this," CB said and stood up quickly, his face reddening.

When Lillian merely stared back at her son, Rove suddenly burst forth, "What the hell is going on? I feel like I'm in a house of mirrors or something. Is this about Carson or what? What are you two talking about? Please!"

"CB, dear, sit down, please," said BeBe. Her face had taken on a kindly air. "It will be all right."

"Mother," Purl said with force, "just spit it out, for crying out loud. What is it?"

"It's about Aleta," Lillian said.

"Aleta?" Stuart's inflection was one of astonishment. He looked around at the others and back at his grandmother. "My god, what could ever take us back to that tragedy?"

Lillian saw that CB was slumped on the couch, looking down, his jaws flexing as he bit down. "Yes, our dear Aleta. You see…before her death our sweet one…" Lillian held her hands prayerlike beneath her chin. "Had a child."

The gasps were as if an inflation valve had been activated on a life raft.

"What?" Purl exclaimed. "No, that can't be."

"Impossible," Rove joined in.

"But true," Lillian said.

"A child?" Stuart said.

"Yes, a boy."

"A boy," several of them said in unison.

Stuart looked up at the ceiling for a moment then turned his gaze on CB "Dad, what's going on? You know all about this, don't you? Is this true, Aleta having a child?" He reached up with both hands and rubbed his face. "This is crazy. How could this be?"

"The trip." It was Purl, her tone resolute.

"What?" Rove said, his voice in a high pitch.

"Her trip to England, remember?"

Rove shook his head. "No. I don't recall that."

"I do." She looked toward CB then her mother. "Was a big deal, CB springing for such an expense. Wasn't in character."

With a grunt, CB rose from the couch. "Come on BeBe. We're leaving."

BeBe stiffened and said, "I'll be along. I have my own car."

"No we're leaving—now." He stared at her until she stood and followed him out.

With the sound of the front door closing, everyone in the room looked about, each assessing the others. Rove reached for the wine bottle, found it empty, and went to get another.

After expelling a long breath, Stuart said, "Okay. Grandma, tell us what Carson's doing."

"That's where Aleta's child is, Oklahoma. Somewhere in Oklahoma. That's what we think anyway. Carson has gone there to find him and bring him back."

Rove stood holding a new bottle of wine. "I cannot believe this. Is this even real?"

Lillian spoke softly. "It is, Rove, it is. But the outcome is yet to be known."

Christmas lights outlined the house behind him. He stood in the driveway, wearing a coat against the chill and waited as David Haack exited his Cadillac Escalade and approached. Haack had a cigarette in his mouth, which he tossed aside before closing on CB Barrus. He assessed the body language of his employer, a skill he'd perfected over the years. Whatever had brought him to the Barrus residence without explanation, it was not about happy holidays.

"Nice lights," Haack quipped.

"Cost a fortune to have them put up," CB responded. "BeBe's thing. But forget that."

"Okay. What is it?"

"Oklahoma. The child."

"Yeah, what about it?"

"My son is there now looking for him."

Haack was wearing only a tee shirt. He folded his arms and studied CB, his face placid as usual. "Stuart is in Oklahoma?"

"No, it's Carson."

Haack lowered his arms, his mouth opened, closed then opened again. "How can that be? I mean he's..."

"Not dead," CB interjected.

A chuckle rumbled up from Haack's chest. "Not dead? This a gag?"

"I wish to hell it was."

David Haack stared unblinking. "How?"

"Got me. Got out of the water somehow and walked away. Family's giddy. Now he's looking for Aleta's child."

"But how did he know? About the boy?"

CB looked over Haack's shoulder as a man passed the end of the driveway; he was walking a fluffy little dog on a retractable leash. He hollered out holiday greetings. CB hollered back, gave a feigned friendly wave, and muttered something belittling about the man. "My mother, I assume. She's known about the birth for a long time. The only one who could have told Carson except for..."

"BeBe?"

CB nodded. "BeBe." He looked into Haack's eyes. "My mother spilled the beans to the whole family tonight. The fact that Aleta had a child was a big shock to the lot of them, let alone knowing where it might be."

Haack noted the word *it* rather than *boy* but said nothing; he'd learned to keep his judgments under wraps. "Must have been a fun evening."

"Double shocker: Carson's alive, Aleta had a child. So yeah, you might say it was fun."

"So Carson, he's in Oklahoma looking for the kid?"

"And you need to get there ASAP. Make sure he never finds it."

"That right?"

"Yes. He can't have a clue where to look, so you have time. And David?"

"Yeah?"

"Remind our colleague where his allegiance needs to be on this."

"Allegiance? Pretty big word for the guy." Haack laughed.

"He'll learn it if he wants to keep the deal."

"I'll take a dictionary."

"David? Tonight. Find a flight. If there's nothing out of Sea-Tac, get Siegfried out of bed. Use that Cessna Citation he's always bragging about to get you there fast."

"A charter jet?" Haack said, his eyebrows up. "Lots of coin."

"Just get it done. Clean this up."

David Haack watched CB until he entered the house. It was going to be a long night engaging once again in the least favorite task he'd ever been given by the man who paid him. He wasn't happy with it, but that didn't matter.

-25-

Late Monday morning, Saffron Taylor opened the door to her small
bungalow, a squat building in an old neighborhood at the edge of
Tonkawa, and calmly assessed the two men standing shoulder to
shoulder with their backs turned to her looking at the yard. There
was no lawn; the yard was filled in with hardy plants and an array of
birdbaths, maybe ten of them. She was a long-legged slender woman
in her late fifties with shoulder-length charcoal gray hair wearing a
red flannel shirt behind faded blue bib overalls.

"You fellas gardeners or birders?" Her mellow voice rose behind
them. Before they could turn and answer, she said, "The birdbaths
are all made by a friend of mine. He's in the yard art business. I
buy the ones that have a flaw—cheap. Birds, they don't know the
difference."

"I like 'em," Ezzard said. "Very...very birdie."

Saffron Taylor laughed out loud. "Very birdie. You Mr. Dale?" she
asked with the tease of a smile on her lips.

Ezzard Dale grinned. "Good question, being as we're nearly
twins." Everyone chuckled. "That'd be me, Mrs. Taylor. Ezzard Dale,
nice to meet you."

She took his hand. "Not missus, just call me Saffron. And you'd
be?" she asked of Carson.

"Carson Barrus. Thank you for your time."

"We'll see about that after I get clear with what you gentlemen are
after." She didn't budge or ask them into her house. "Ezzard, you
were a bit cryptic about that. Something to do with a child born a
few years ago?"

"That's right," Ezzard said. "We're trying to find a child, a boy, who would have been born back in 2003."

"Here in Tonkawa?"

"Not sure," Carson said. "That's the rub. Could be anywhere in Oklahoma, but we think he was born somewhere in this area of the state."

She looked between them, seeming to take stock. "Why me?"

Ezzard cleared his throat. "Like I told you on the phone, I've been hired by Carson here to make inquiries about the child in question, and I have narrowed down our initial search to..."

"Some old midwives," she laughed. "What the hell, come on in. I'll put on some tea water, and we can kick this thing around. It's a quiet day, might be fun."

She invited them into her small kitchen. They sat at an old chrome-legged table topped in marbled red laminate and watched as she brought water to boil on an electric range, gathered pottery mugs, a container of loose tea, and brought it all to the table.

"So, while this is steeping, fill me in," she said. "You're looking for whoever birthed this child you want to find, right?"

"That's right," Ezzard said. "Were you delivering babies here in 2003?"

"I was. Not very active these days, but I was busy back then."

"Are you certified?" Carson asked.

"No, I am not certified." she answered. "That a problem for you?"

"No, no," Carson deflected. "I...in fact, we're actually looking for midwives who are not certified."

"I'm what they call a direct-entry midwife. Came in through the backdoor by watching then doing. It was the mid-seventies on The Farm. You heard of The Farm?"

The two men shook heads in unison.

"Famous commune in Tennessee. Started back in 1971 by an assortment of San Francisco hippies. They all called it an intentional community. You know, raise their own food, share and share alike, a back-to-the-land lifestyle. I was young, wide-eyed, and got drawn

199

into the whole thing. Piled onto a bus and ended up in middle Tennessee and whatta you know, soon enough with all the affection floating around women were swelling up. That's where I learned. My apprenticeship of watching other women delivering babies. That was, what? My stars, it was thirty-four years ago. So no formal training. We direct-entry midwives feel it as a calling."

"I'm sure," Ezzard said, ignoring his tea.

Saffron laughed. "I can tell you're moved by my story. So you want to know if I delivered a boy child in 2003? I probably delivered a few boys that year. It was a pretty steady year, as I recall."

"You have records?"

"Of course. Give me a name and a date."

"The mother's name was Aleta," Carson said. "Aleta Barrus."

"I can look, I guess, but can tell you right now I've never heard that name before." She tapped the side of her head. "And I have a steel trap up here for the names of my mothers."

"Probably used an alias," Ezzard offered.

She coughed a short laugh. "An alias? Now this is getting interesting. Explain that."

Carson looked to Ezzard. "Go ahead. You gotta tell her the whole thing."

"Right." Carson looked into the woman's questioning eyes and said, "You would probably have been contacted by someone who wanted you to deliver a baby that was to be adopted. I assume that would have been the approach. Child was born in December that year."

"December?"

"That's right. December 2003. Close as we can figure," he said, recalling his grandmother's best guess back when she first told him about the child. "Not sure when but maybe a couple of weeks before Christmas that year."

She leaned back and looked between the two men. "You mean the baby would not have remained with the mother?" She was getting the picture. "Well, that happens. Young woman decides to give up her baby for whatever reason: too young, father disappears, rape—you name it. So yeah, I've had mothers not wanting their babies over the years, not many and not for quite a spell. In fact, last one of those I had was back in 2001." She shook her head. "I remember 'cause that little gal wasn't more'n sixteen. Scared out of her wits. I put out the word on the grapevine, and some pretty decent folks took the child—a little girl."

"Pretty decent?" Carson asked with an edge.

Saffron Taylor folded her arms. "And damned fortunate she and the child were, too. One of my colleagues located a couple in Oklahoma City who covered all the costs, had a favorable background, and asked no questions of the girl."

"No questions? That supposed to be a good sign?" Carson asked.

"Look, Carson," Ezzard interrupted, "we're going astray here. Let's keep focused." He leaned on his elbows and gave the woman his favorite-person smile. "So Saffron, I think we can wrap this up quicklike. Just let me ask you one other question."

She nodded. "Fine."

"All right then. In this particular case, you would probably have been offered a sizable fee for this delivery, with the stipulation that it would be kept quiet. And likely the parties in question would've wanted minimal paperwork, if you get my meaning."

"Stop right there," she said, holding up a hand. "I can tell you that I would remember clearly such a ploy, especially the big money part. Didn't happen."

"You're sure?" asked Ezzard. "Sometimes circumstances can seem different. Maybe we're not describing it so it fits your memory."

"You listening to me, gentlemen? It did not happen, not with me. That clear enough?"

Ezzard held up his palms in surrender. "Clear as glass. Think we're done here, right, Carson?"

The men rose stiffly, as did Saffron. She asked, "Just for curiosity's sake, mind telling me why you're looking for this child?"

"He's my nephew," Carson said. "My little sister's child."

"She wants him back? Little late and hard to do."

"She's deceased. Suicide."

They left Saffron standing on her porch staring after them, pulling at the straps of her overalls, and drove back to Sapulpa with their hopes now resting on a woman named Inola Jeffcoat in a place called Tahlequah.

The bed in the Falcon Motel was as hard as a pool table, but the room was clean, the plumbing up to date, and a flat-screen TV sat where an old black-and-white RCA might have been in years past. He took a hot shower hoping that by washing away a long day of following the scent he would feel more hopeful. But he questioned their chances of tracking down who delivered Aleta's son by interrogating one midwife at a time all across Oklahoma. He considered if Ezzard Dale had the real know-how to get the job done. But he trusted the man's instincts, and after all, it had only been one day.

After his shower, Carson wandered up the street to a diner that had once been a gas station, satiated his hunger pangs with a cheeseburger, fries, and root beer shake, and returned to his room. And there he sat, alone, feeling oddly out of place in a motel room in Sapulpa, Oklahoma, staring at a television while his stomach argued over his choice of food. He watched the last half of George C. Scott as *Scrooge*, offed the television, and picked up his cell phone. Her number was in his contacts file: hers, his grandmothers, and Vince Horne's. The call kicked over into voice mail. "It's me," he said, "just checking in, no big deal."

A minute later his phone rang. "What do you mean, no big deal?" she erupted. "I've been on tenterhooks." Marla's voice was several decibels higher than he'd ever heard. "Why'd you call if it's no big deal? Is everything okay? You all right?"

He laughed. "Nice to hear your voice."

"You too."

"Which question should I answer first?"

After a pause she chuckled. "Yeah, well I've been wondering, is all. Curious."

"Curious?"

"Of course," she said. "Going off on this surreptitious...whatever you call it...so yes, whatever have you found out?"

"I'm curious too," he said. "Did you get all your candle orders shipped off?"

"Doggone you, Carson. Now get serious. Tell me..."

"We're still looking," he answered. "I just called to hear a familiar voice."

"Oh." She hesitated. "No luck, then?"

"Not yet. Just getting started." He inhaled and held his breath and considered his own uncertainty. "We'll find him, I think. No, we *will* find him."

"Sure."

"Met up with a hippie midwife today, name of Saffron."

She laughed. "Saffron. She know anything?"

"Not really. Dead end. Like I said, just getting started. Going to see another midwife tomorrow, name of Inola, Inola Jeffcoat."

"Another great name."

"Yeah." He paused. "So what you doing for Christmas?"

"Let's see, my calendar is so full I'll have to think on that." Her laugh was playful. "Have my little artificial tree up, lights blinking and all. Oh, bought some eggnog. Going down fine with a splash or two of bourbon." When he didn't react, she asked, "You there?"

"What else?" he said.

"What do you mean?"

"Christmas, that it?"

"Let's see. Ola Mae and Cecil have invited me over to Christmas Eve dinner. That what you mean?"

"Sounds nice."

"Yeah, Cecil got a spiral-sliced ham. I'm taking over my favorite baked yam dish and a bottle of wine. And like that. Quiet time. No gifts, just good friends and comfort food."

Carson felt the warmth behind his eyes. He squeezed his lids down as the wetness began to seep out. *Silly*, he thought, and sniffed.

"Carson? You okay?"

He forced a laugh. "You know what?"

"What?"

"This will be the first time I've ever not been with family on Christmas. Just came to me. Silly damn lump in my throat, can you believe?"

"Actually, I can," she answered. "First Christmas after Glen died, I was sitting here in The Dalles, just me and my memories and my sorrowful disposition. Didn't know anyone, there were no invites from family—nada. Talk about pathetic. Tell you what," she said, "Why don't you fly home?"

"God no," he said. "They'd probably lock me up. Besides we may be close by then to finding the boy. Anyway—"

"No," she cut in, "I mean home *here*. Fly back and have Christmas with us." When he didn't respond she added, "You could, you know."

"Thank you," he said, "that makes all the difference."

"Difference?"

"Being wanted somewhere. I can't, of course, but still feels good being asked."

"No charge," she said.

He paused. "Well, we're heading off to a town called Tahlequah tomorrow to meet up with Inola Jeffcoat."

"You have all the fun."

They fumbled around trying to say good-bye until she finally disconnected. He held the phone to his ear, the line dead, and questioned again what the hell he was doing.

-26-

It was the next day when the charter jet lifted off from Boeing Field in Seattle just after daybreak. David Haack arrived in Tulsa around midmorning; he bid farewell to Siegfried, picked up the Lincoln Town Car he had waiting at Hertz, loaded his favorite Dave Brubeck CD into the sound system, and set out on the one hundred miles ahead of him. He would arrive unannounced and nail the philistine with a dose of reality before Carson Barrus could even find him. It was only six days until Christmas Eve, and here he was in Oklahoma, accelerator down on the Cimarron Turnpike, carrying his marching orders, a stash of cash, a 9 mm Beretta, and wondering what the boy would look like by now. The coffee from the espresso drive-through was souring on his empty stomach, but that wasn't the only reason he was off his feed. He'd never wanted in on this and now he hated what he was supposed to do. But he knew that pleading his case with CB would have gotten no traction, no give, no understanding.

In the years he had worked for the man, Haack had known he could never reveal his human side to him, as sparse as it was, if he wanted to keep this job that paid so well. It paid well if he continued to carry out CB's orders precisely and with cold effectiveness. This he had done even knowing that his only purpose was to be his superior's iron hand, that there would be no tasks for him other than those requiring him to be the intimidator; his was to be the physical force to be reckoned with, whose mere presence usually brought compliance without foolish resistance.

There had been many times when he had gone down the well to hell when his orders had taken him there, maintaining order as prescribed, whether through forced collection, eviction, intimidation, humiliation, or physical pain. At those times when he had finished each act, he'd walked away big and gone back to his free luxurious apartment where he felt small even after showering and attempting to drink away the guilt. It had never worked, of course, but still and all that was the only way he could survive. This was the job he would never give up even though it had cost him his marriage, several friendships, and the loss of respect among those who had mattered once. The darkest day of fulfilling CB's dictates had been when he accompanied sweet Aleta to Oklahoma.

She sat beside him on the plane, quiet, uncommonly quiet, and said nothing the entire time. She was sedated of course; Haack had to guide her around the concourse, holding onto an elbow between flights in Dallas. When they landed in Tulsa, they were there to meet them. Unsmiling faces with an unhappy task for which he handed them a thick envelope for their troubles. He had watched them lead Aleta away; she looked back at him once, her beauty and innocence entering his chest like a blunt splinter, before she got into a waiting car. Her expression had been flat; she didn't wave or smile—nothing. Haack had watched until the vehicle was out of sight then returned to the terminal and waited for his return flight. He had too many drinks and felt no better about it all by the time he landed in Seattle.

Fifty-three miles out, after Brubeck's opening keyboard for "Blue Rondo", about the time Paul Desmond's sax solo came in, Haack took a ramp off the turnpike and drove through a Sonic drive-in for a chicken sandwich and soda, food he rejected unless he was on a countdown mission.

———————

Ezzard's Crown Vic rolled into Tahlequah around ten the next morning and made a swing down the main street, Muskogee Avenue. Using the directions he had written down, wound his way up into the older neighborhoods. It was a small box of a house sheathed in clapboard siding painted brick red with white trim. It sat on a brown stone foundation and was fronted by a bare stoop of four concrete steps beneath a simple porch overhang. A window air conditioner, unneeded in the cold weather, hung from a side window.

Ezzard parked alongside the house and they approached the front door together looking like multi-cultural door-to-door missionaries. Ezzard stood on the small concrete porch while Carson waited below, his hands fisted in coat pockets. After the second knock, the door opened a crack, and a woman's face appeared, suspicion emanating from her eyes. Ezzard tipped his head and said who he was; the door opened, and they stepped into a tiny living room and she invited them to be seated.

Inola Jeffcoat was a short woman. Her hair was gray-black, pulled back, and her face one reflecting the years and her Native American heritage: broad nose, high cheekbones, olive coloring, a mask of wrinkles that Carson thought almost beautiful, and eyes sad but with no hostility. She took a chair opposite the two men and held her hands in her lap.

"I remember your call, Mr. Dale," she said on quiet voice. "I'm not sure I can be of any help, but I will try. What is it about again, a birth several years ago?"

"Yes, Mrs. Jeffcoat. This is Carson Barrus. He is looking for a boy who was born in Oklahoma in 2003, December 2003. We know you have been a midwife in this part of the state for a long time and thought you might remember the circumstances of this particular birth."

Her expression turned solemn, and the prominent wrinkles of her face deepened. "Tell me about the child you seek. Who was the mother, and why is she not with you?"

By the time Carson had fully explained the story, Inola Jeffcoat was looking beleaguered and saddened. She shook her head and studied Carson's face for a long moment before speaking. "This story you have told me is a sad one. I am sorry for you, Mr. Barrus, and especially for your sister, but even more so for the child."

"Does what I've told you cause you to recall such a birth?" Carson asked sitting on the edge of the couch.

207

"No," she said, shaking her head a bit. "Nor would I have agreed to such a thing. I would never trade a happy birth for money. Or be party to separating a baby from its mother in such a disgraceful manner. There have been many adoptions I helped along, but none like that."

"I understand and hope we didn't offend you," Carson said. "May I ask if you can think of any who might be willing to assist in the manner I describe?"

She turned her head and looked in a corner of the room. "I have given many years to assisting mothers in bringing their children into this world, healthy babies, happy mothers. That there is my birthing chair." She nodded toward a small four-legged wooden stool with a seat that resembled a commode; open in the front but with no chamber pot. "Had it made nearly thirty years ago by a friend of mine, a Cherokee craftsman. He is gone now, but the chair goes on. It is maple and built to comfortably aid my mothers in their deliveries. It goes with me wherever I am asked to go. It is a part of me." She smiled.

Carson and Ezzard sat respectfully listening as she spoke, nodding and holding their questions.

"My answer to you, sir, is no. I know of no one among the community of midwives who would participate in what you suggest."

"No disrespect, Mrs. Jeffcoat," Carson said, "but not even if they believed they would be helping a desperate young woman?"

"You ask a hard question," she said. "A hard question. But not even then. No."

They left Inola Jeffcoat in her sadness over what they had suggested occurred to Aleta.

Carson was hoping that whoever helped his sister deliver her baby had the kindness and soul of this woman.

They drove out of Tahlequah, home of the Cherokee Nation and the United Keetoowah Band of Cherokee Indians, and out of obvious next options. No words were spoken on the return trip to Sapulpa. Ezzard lobbied for lunch at Chuck's Café, a block from his office on

Dewey Avenue, and convinced Carson that he hadn't lived until he'd eaten Chuck's hand-breaded chicken fried steak with hash browns and two eggs over easy. Carson acquiesced and indeed found the food tasty and enjoyed about half of it before putting his fork down.

"So now what?" he said to Ezzard. Those were his first words about it since leaving Inola Jeffcoat.

The investigator shrugged and continued to devour his food. "We start over," he said between bites. "We've only talked to two people, so we go back to that old drawing board. We might have to do this a dozen times, even twice that, who knows? That is, unless you want to call it a day." He held his fork in midair. "Do you? Want to call its quits?"

Carson drank from his coffee cup and stared into Ezzard's eyes. "What do you think?"

"Not my call. If it was me, I'd keep turning over rocks. We've only rolled but a couple. Comes to rock rolling, that's not many. Like I said, could be a long pull. But then, I'm not the one calling the shots, now am I?" He finished his meal and wiped his mouth on a red checked napkin. "It's your time and your money."

Carson looked at the remnants of chicken fried steak on his plate for a long moment. "Can't stop," he said finally. "Don't know what to do next, but I can't stop looking for him."

"Let's go on back to my office and kick it around some," Ezzard said, shoving his chair back and standing up. "Maybe Scooter's come up with something else. I kept her digging around."

Carson paid for their lunches and followed Ezzard Dale's wide behind back to his storefront office whose next-door business window had large white letters on the glass proclaiming it to be the office of one Cristal Swanson, Attorney at Law. Private investigator, attorney—all they needed was a bail bondsmen and a collection agency to round out the menu of options. Scooter was having lunch at her desk when they entered. She looked up at the two men when they entered, her eyes looming large through her glasses. Her face formed itself into a question mark; she folded ups the remains of her sandwich and asked Ezzard what he wanted to do next.

David Haack had a mouthful of food when his cell's ring tone, sounding exactly like an old rotary dial phone, interrupted his meal. He snagged the phone out of the cupholder, stuck an earpiece in, and grunted his presence on the line.

"Where are you?" It was CB

"About halfway."

"Thought you'd be there by now."

"Well, I'm not. Been on the move since I landed, but the miles are what they are."

"Yeah, okay. Just get this taken care of."

"It will be. Any idea where Carson is?"

"Hell no," CB grumbled. "That's the risk here. Could be anywhere in Oklahoma, but I think he was put onto the northeast part of the state somehow."

"Still a lot of ground. Besides, the boy and his keepers are way off the beaten track."

"Unless he gets tipped where to go."

"How could that happen?"

"Food chain. Food chain is always the weak link. We had to bring that riffraff into this confounded affair. That's our soft underbelly."

Haack swallowed a bite of bun and meat. "Hell, we paid them off."

"Yeah, well, we may have to again, along with some motivation."

Haack knew what that word meant. "If you say so."

"I'll say so when the time comes. You haven't tipped off our colleague, have you?"

"No. I'll be a big Christmas surprise. Wish I knew where Carson is, though. Hate to run into him unexpected-like."

"I'm working on that, may have an answer for you real soon."

"That could still be too late if I run into him at the end of this little ride here."

"Not likely. Besides, you're supposed to get a call from our man if anyone ever comes sniffing around with the wrong questions. Right?"

"Correct. What's the plan if by chance I do come face to face with your son?"

"You won't, not yet anyway."

"Still…"

"Nothing, you do nothing, David. Walk away. Just walk away, because that is the line where your motivational methods stop."

"Do I sense a gleam of sentiment here, CB?"

CB snorted into Haack's ear. "Hell no. Just don't want to have to justify anything like that to the family. Talk about hell."

"I'll let you know how things are after I make the stop."

"You do that."

Dicky Fain had never been to The Dalles; he'd barely been out of the state of Washington in his thirty-three years. Dicky Fain had never been good at much of anything, either, which had been a source of disappointment for his parents, both hard-working people, never rich but always decent. Much to their regret, Dicky had dropped out of school in the tenth grade, never to return. His search for something gainful to occupy his time and pay his way only took on traction after his parents evicted their only child for what in essence amounted to nonperformance. The act left them heartbroken and scarred; eventually his mother prevailed on his father, and they let him return and live in a basement room—if he applied himself. With great disappointment, they observed their son wander though a very long string of meaningless jobs, each coupled with an early discharge; it became a pattern of life until the day he was hired on by Barrus Properties to be on the clean-up crew. Soon he was given his first "dirty work" assignment by David Haack, and had felt right at home. He was sent on jobs beneath David Haack's standards. Sick acts of a threatening nature became his forte: rousting tenants that CB wanted out by banging on their doors in the wee hours and demanding to know when they were going to leave; slashing tires, which left an understood message; collecting past-due rents with a heavy hand was Dicky's specialty. For his perverse skills he earned some job security.

While David Haack drove across Oklahoma that day, Dicky Fain was driving up and down the streets of The Dalles. His instructions from CB Barrus had been emphatic: *Find where his son was living in the town, approach whomever he had to, and find out where Carson was in Oklahoma. Do it fast no matter what it took.* The only lead Dicky had was that Carson Barrus was living somewhere in the small city—that was it. Dicky put on his most pathetic smile and started asking if anyone knew of a man new to town because he was looking for a cousin who'd moved here, but he didn't have any address. He started his nearly futile task down on First Street going business by business asking the same questions, bowing out gracefully when heads shook, and most did, then moved on. By the time he entered the travel agency on Washington Street, his face was a stiff mask of feigned politeness, and his message had been reduced to a few words. He was stunned when the woman waved an arm adorned with a clatter of bracelets in a direction that indicated generally where he might find his cousin. And just where was Mile Creek Road, he'd asked, and did she have an address? He practically quit breathing when she told him both. Not only that, she proudly proclaimed that she had recently booked Carson a flight to Tulsa, Oklahoma. The woman had literally bubbled her pleasure in helping Dicky reunite with his cousin.

Dicky thanked her profusely and actually ran to his car feeling a sense of euphoria; he was sure that his successful sleuthing would win him big points with Mr. Barrus. But when CB Barrus answered on his direct number, he did not heap praise on Dicky Fain. He did not say *Well done, my good and faithful servant.* Instead, Dicky was told that what he'd found out was little more than useless, that Tulsa was where the airport was; Carson Barrus could be anywhere within two hundred miles of it. The scorching rant was still ringing in his ears after CB Barrus had left Dicky with a dead connection: "Listen, you putz, find out exactly where he is, and don't come back until you do."

-27-

Marla Snow was enjoying an afternoon nap afforded her by the holiday break when she was roused by a knock at the front door. She brushed the sleep from her eyes and strolled slowly from the couch to find a wiry young man on her front porch. He was grinning and standing with his hands jammed into pants; he stood hunched over as if apologetic. She thought perhaps he was lost and needed directions. But he wasn't lost, and the first words out of his mouth froze her in place.

"Sorry," she feigned buying time, "I was just napping. Could you repeat your question?"

"Yeah sure," he said on a nasal voice. "I was wondering if you know of a fellow name of Carson, Carson Barrus?"

Her heart began to beat faster. No one around there knew him by that name, not yet anyway. He'd been Bill Tolliver from the very beginning. Who was this guy, and what could he want?

"Barrus?"

"Yeah, Carson is his first name. Lady down to the travel agency in town gave me this address. Thought maybe you folks might know where he is? Guess he's out of town right now though."

Marla cleared her throat, again vying for time. "I don't know…"

"Gol dang," the man said and did a turn on the porch, brushing a hand over his close-cropped red hair. "You mean he don't live here? The woman, she sold him airplane tickets. She said this here was his address. This is the right address, isn't it now?" He pulled a slip of paper from his pocket and held it out.

"What is it you want, actually?"

The man's eyes narrowed and he stepped closer. "Look, lady, what I'm wanting to know is just where he is."

"He's not here," she said. "He's gone."

"Hell, I know that. I didn't come all the way down here to be told something I already know."

"Where are you from?" she asked.

"Never mind that." He smiled again. "Just help me out, and I'll be on my way." He paused, stuffed the piece of paper back in his pocket, and folded his arms across his chest. He was determined to get what he'd come for and show old man Barrus what he was made of. It was his first assignment out of town, and he had to succeed.

"I'm sorry," she said on a wavering voice. "I don't know you, and I'm not going to give out such private information. Besides, the man you seem to be speaking of is called Bill Tolliver."

"Bill Tolliver?" Dicky wasn't told anything about a different name.

"Yes, Bill Tolliver. Never heard of this other person you mention," she lied.

Dicky Fain stood transfixed for a long moment but stepped forward when the woman started to close the door and pushed his way in. "Had me there for a sec," he said, showing his teeth in a tight smile. "That'd be some kind of fake name," he said. "Whatta they call it, alias, yeah, an alias. Same guy though, right?"

"You can't push your way into my house," Marla snapped, gaining some sense of her need to exert confidence.

Dicky giggled. "Hell, I just did. Now look, lady, we can get this all done and over if you just tell me where Carson Barrus is at." He shoved the door shut and looked around. "Nice house. My folks have a nice old house kinda like this. Grew up in it."

"I want you to leave right now," she asserted. "If not, I'll call the police."

"No, no, no," Dicky chanted. "You're not going to do any such a thing. You're going to get yourself something to write on and put down all you know about where this Barrus fellow is: town, phone number, where he's staying—all that."

Marla was shaking her head. "No."

"Look," Dicky said. He laced his fingers and stretched his arms out in a show of strength. "I don't want to be getting physical or anything. Sure don't want that, do we?"

Marla felt fear pooling in her stomach. She looked around for something that might be a weapon but knew that would likely only make things worse. The man noted her eyes scanning.

"Now don't be thinking of trying to hit me or something. Bad idea. Bad idea. Go on, get some paper and a pencil or pen, and we'll get this done."

"No. Get out!" Marla raised her voice.

Dicky smiled some more and stepped over to her and gripped an arm. He squeezed; she sucked in a shaky breath. "You're going to do what I say or…"

At that moment her landline phone began to ring. They both stared toward it and stood stark still as the phone went on for six rings then stopped. Marla was still using an answering machine rather than voice mail. The machine clicked, and a voice said: "Marla, it's me. Just wondering how you're doing. Ola Mae and me are looking forward to having you over for Christmas Eve. Food'll be great. I'll be stopping by later this afternoon to get some of your firewood so we can have a rip-roaring fire that night. Bye."

"Who was that?" Dicky asked.

"Friend. You better be gone when he comes by."

"Scary guy, is he?" Dicky laughed. "Tell you what, lady. You and I's gonna walk up behind this house here. I scoped out things before knocking on your door. I think we'll just go on up to that old tin building out back where we can get this bit of business over in private. Just in case your big bad friend or somebody else drops by."

When she resisted, Dicky took her by the arm in a hard grip and directed her out the front door and up the slope to the Quonset. He shoved her inside and shut the door.

"Where's the light switch?" Dicky asked, looking around in the dim light. Marla stepped over to the wall and flipped a switch. When the cold light uncovered the room, Dicky looked around, curious, and wrinkled his nose. "What's that smell, that sweet smell? What is it?"

Marla walked into the shop, thinking of how to bide her time and get out of this fix. She picked up the remnant of a candle and held it up. "Candles. Bing cherry is the aroma."

"Candles," Dicky said as if it was a gag. "What, you make candles?"

"That's right."

"Crazy, man. Here, gimme that." He reached out and pulled the candle piece out of her hand and sniffed it. "Nice, I like that. Cherry, huh?" When she didn't respond, he threw the chunk of candle across the room. "Well who gives a shit? Now girly, you're gonna write down what I want, or something bad'll happen."

Marla stepped back slowly a few paces. "Look, I don't know where he is. I don't."

"Liar!" Dicky slammed an open hand down on a work counter. "You...you're making me mad. Now goddamn it, tell me where he is." He came toward her. "Where. Is. He?"

"Why are you doing this?" Marla pleaded.

Dicky grinned. "'Cause I'm being paid real good. So no way can I go back to my employer without what he sent me for. Get it? Now where the fuck is Carson Barrus?"

Fear caused Marla's throat to constrict. She reached out and placed a hand on the work stool next to her. She'd faced down some pretty tough characters as a teacher; she had been tough and assertive, and usually she had prevailed. This was different. How much was she prepared to endure in the face of this cretin? She knew her eyes were wide and her face filled with fear and that he saw that, too.

"What's it gonna be girly? You ready to give up the guy or take a bit more convincing?"

"Oklahoma," she said, throwing out a useless line. "He's in Oklahoma."

Dicky Fain screwed up his face. "Hell, I already know that. Quit playing games now."

"That's all I know." Marla threw up her hands and shook her head. "Really, that's it. Whatever he's doing, he didn't want anyone knowing about where he'd be or how to get in touch. I swear."

Her further denial brought a cloud over Dicky's face. He was out of his element; this was the first time he had been given a job this intense with an expected outcome that *had* to be fulfilled. Returning without completing his assignment just couldn't happen—at least in his mind. With his eyes blinking rapidly and his breathing becoming hyper, he approached Marla and took her by the arms. He stared into her eyes and hummed out a grumble then shoved her to the floor and stood over her.

"You are going to tell me what I want, you bitch."

Marla began to regain her strength, to regain her sense of who she was, and that meant giving no more ground—no matter what. "I know nothing more than I've told you," she said, looking up at him.

Dicky Fain's stance changed from menacing to bizarre. He roared a loud explosive howl and began throwing anything he could get his hands on: tools, molds, candle glassware, boxes—everything. Finally he stood, breathing in gulps, leaning over, hands on his thighs. Marla had managed to rise onto her knees and then stood, hoping to burst past him to the door, but he grabbed her again and pulled her close to him. She was repulsed by his sour breath and body odor, but she remained outwardly calm.

"Okay," he breathed into her ear. "Okay. Have it your way. We'll do it hard." He looked around from side to side. "You know, I'll just bet this old building would make one hell of a bonfire. You think?" She didn't respond. "Yeah, it will. You want that? I'll even bet you have matches or some lighters in here to test them candles you make." Dicky was feeling in control again. "Yeah, this old tin barn with its wood frame and all, it'll go up fast and hot." He pulled her behind him and started scouring the building. He found a box of wooden matches and cackled with glee.

"Whatta you say, lady? You ready to give me what I want, or do

217

you want this here place to go up, with maybe you in it?" He saw the fear in her eyes with that comment. "Oh yeah. Either I get what I need, or I leave no trace when I leave. Can't be leaving any evidence that I was here, right?"

Marla yanked at his grip on her. "You can't be serious," she said. "Are you crazy?"

"You'll think crazy when this place is in flames and you're still in it." He dragged her along to the back of the shop, looking and looking. "What you got in here that'll burn real good? Need something to get the fire going."

Marla felt a spasm in her stomach with the thought of the volatile fermentation heads in the plastic drums. The heads solvent was 170 proof; it wouldn't ignite with the explosive force of gasoline because it still contained water. Still, it would burn enough to do what the wild man was threatening.

"Last chance, Lady. I get what I want or poof!" He pulled her to the back of the shop, searching for something to start the fire. Marla's heart sank when his eyes found the plastic drums "Hey, what's in these here barrels?"

"Nothing."

"Ha! I think there is something in there that'll burn. Am I right?" He pried at a drum lid until it came off. "What is this stuff? Smells funny, sort of sweet like." He dipped a finger into the clear liquid, smelled it first, then tasted it gingerly. "Wow, that's high proof. Bet it'll burn like bejesus." He yanked her up close to him. "So what's it gonna be, princess? Pencil and paper or a bonfire?"

Marla drew in a ragged breath. "I've told you all I know."

"Tilt!" Dicky yelled. "Wrong answer. So watch this." He yanked at the blue drum until it tipped over, and the pungent liquid spilled out and spread across the floor. "Lookie there. Guess we're gonna have a fire. You think so?"

"Stop this," Marla shouted. "Burning this building down still won't get you what you want because I don't know. Can you get that through your pathetic head?"

With her caustic outburst Dicky's head shuddered, and he looked at her with eyes that had turned to marbles. "Pathetic? Last person to say that to me was my father. Never said it again, let me tell you. I'll show you pathetic, you bitch." He opened the box of wooden matches he was holding and began scratching one match after another and dropping them into the spill until several caught and a silent flame began to make its way back to the drum.

When Cecil Nash drove up to Marla's house, the Quonset building was fully engulfed in flames. He leapt from his car as it was still rolling and ran as fast as his big body would let him up the slope. Marla was sitting on the ground away from the fire watching the blaze reduce the building to its lowest common denominator. Cecil dropped to his knees, gasping for air and took her by her arms. She turned her head slowly, tears moving down her cheeks, and mumbled something.

"What?" Cecil shouted. The surging heat of the fire was muffling her words.

"I didn't tell him," she said on a raspy voice. "I didn't." With ashes drifting down onto her head, the intense heat painting her face orange, and the sound of sirens growing closer, she had a thought—Tahlequah. What did it mean?

Just then the Quonset gave up and collapsed in on itself.

-28-

Carson agreed. Start over. His acquiescence was stifled, but he said yes—of course there could be no surrender. Ezzard and Scooter went back to work picking over the loose threads of the search. Carson waited around impatiently—that is, until three days later when Cecil called. He caught the last Delta flight out of Tulsa, paced about for the hour layover in Salt Lake City, charged off the plane when it set down in Portland, and was on I-84 east to The Dalles by eleven-thirty. He pressed the Camry hard through the dark and rolled up Mill Creek Road and the drive to Marla's house near one o'clock Wednesday morning. The first thing to hit him when he stepped out of the car was the harsh smell of wet ashes. The stink hung in the chilled air; he rubbed at his nostrils and looked up to where the Quonset building had stood. All he could make out in the weak illumination from the house's porch light was a silhouette of the charred bones of the building, a sad pile of pick-up-stick remnants amid a heap of warped corrugated metal. The sight and the smell sickened him.

The house was dark. Her car was there, but he wasn't sure if she was; Cecil and Ola Mae might have insisted on her staying with them. He stood flat-footed, staring at the house, riddled with regret, and unable to move. After wrestling with his resolve, he dropped his bag and willed himself to walk to the front door. He took in a few deep breaths before knocking, first a light rap; then he pounded. The door rattled in its frame. Shortly a light came on upstairs and flowed down; then a hallway light flashed on. He held his breath.

Her face appeared and looked at him through the glass of the door. He raised a hand until she recognized him, threw the deadbolt open, and let the door swing in. She hid her hands in the patch pockets of a floor-length bathrobe and studied him before turning without comment and walking away. He followed her into the kitchen. Neither knew quite what to do: she was still recovering from her horror story with Dicky Fain, and he was raging with guilt over what she had endured and lost. He stood back watching while she went through the ritual motions of putting the teapot on the range burner, filling the void with activity.

"How about something stronger," he said in an attempt to lighten the moment.

She froze when he spoke and leaned on the stove, arms extended. When he saw her begin to shake, he went over and placed his hands her shoulders. "Marla, I am so..."

Before he could finish she turned and collapsed against his chest. They held each other and cried and took deep breaths until there were no more tears available. The smiles they put on their faces were so pitiable that they had to laugh.

"Well, I was tired of that bloody candle business anyway," she said, and they laughed some more and hard. "Guess you took me serious about that, huh?"

"God, Marla, when Cecil called I nearly collapsed."

"I asked you to come have Christmas with us, didn't I? Went too far, maybe?"

They laughed again. He watched as she pulled a bottle of Jim Beam and two glasses out of the cupboard; he took the bottle from her outstretched hand and poured them each a splash of bourbon. They sat at the kitchen table. He raised his glass; she smiled and did the same. "This is beyond the pale," he said.

"Who was he?" Her eyes were wide. "He wanted to know where you were. Who sent him?"

He said, "I don't know who he was. No idea. But I know who sent him."

She sipped from her glass and blinked when the alcohol hit her throat. "Who?"

"My father."

Her glass dropped onto the table; some of the liquor sloshed out. "Your father? No."

"Yes." He wrapped his hands around the glass. "Certain of it."

"But why?" She watched his head droop and waited.

"To keep me from finding the boy. He's paranoid about keeping Aleta's child a secret, buried forever."

Marla's expression was one of bewilderment. She cocked her head and said, "But why? Why go to such lengths now that you all know of the child's existence?" She held a hand to her mouth. "He...he burned my building. All because your father wanted to..."

"My father lives in another universe, one he controls, one where he sets the rules, rules that must be maintained at all costs. I grew up living on the outer edge of his universe and observed his hard-edged approach to business, family, to everything. He's been one cold hearted SOB. He's done some highly questionable things. I know that. But this, this is way beyond anything I know of."

She leaned toward him. "That creature would have hurt me. He would have. If he hadn't panicked when the building caught on fire, I might be dead." She wiped at a tear. "Do you hear me? Dead. And for what? My god."

Carson shoved his chair back and stood up. "I'll pack up and leave first thing in the morning. I'm going back to Oklahoma anyway. I'll clear my stuff out of the trailer and be gone."

"Sit down," she said. "Why do that? Sit down, Carson. I figure he won't be back after all of this. And I'm not evicting you. I need the rental income, especially now that I can't make candles." She laughed.

He lowered himself onto the chair. "Was the building insured?"

"No. I don't know, maybe. Owners may have."

"I'll pay to rebuild it."

"No way. I'm done making candles."

He reached out and touched her hand that lay on the table. She looked down curiously but didn't pull away.

She looked up and spoke very softly. "I made a deal with myself when Glen died. A contract, actually."

"A contract…with yourself."

"Yes. No new men in my life. Over and done with that."

Carson looked at his hand on hers. Touching her, the feel of her skin, reminded him of those first times he'd held Naomi's hand or when they happened to brush uncovered arms—those had been irreplaceable moments of sensory attraction. In the haze of those initial electric days he'd been like everyone in the throes of infatuation, he guessed: nothing else was on his mind, he could never get enough of her, everything about her was beyond description. All of that was true until it wasn't. All of that was true until she betrayed him. All of that was true until the thing he called his heart no longer responded.

He drew his hand back. The smile he gave her was a simple statement of regret. "Sorry," he said. "It was meant only as a measure of my concern." That was straddling the truth, but it was the best he had to offer. "In fact, I feel much the same. We are damaged goods, are we not?"

"Damaged goods. I don't like to think of it that way, but yes, I guess we are." She formed a fist with one hand and gave the tabletop a blow. "But damn it, I will liberate myself from that definition. I will."

"What part? Healing the scars you bear and holding your ground or also letting someone share life with you?" When her eyes flashed he added, "Because I'm asking myself the same question."

After a long moment she said, "I don't know. All I know is that the life I had with Glen was near idyllic. As close to perfect as any other chapter of my life." She closed her eyes as she spoke. "I had a happy childhood, college was great, but real life didn't kick in until I was thrust out into the world, first job, no backup crew to protect me, and then there was Glen. Life wasn't something stuck in between recess anymore. Life doesn't let up once you're expected to be a grown-up. Glen and I found each other somehow and decided to take it on together—this life thing." She raised her eyelids and met his gaze.

Carson smiled at the term *this life thing* and waited for her to continue even as he was having parallel thoughts about Naomi. When she spoke, he studied the topography of her face: her cheekbones, her gracile nose, the curve of her chin, the subtle lines at the corners of her eyes, even the gap in her teeth.

"But he left me," she said. "He chose to give in to his desperation without ever asking me to be a part of it." She raised a hand to her mouth and closed her eyes.

"Maybe he was trying to protect you."

"No, no it wasn't that. It wasn't that."

"What was it then?"

She picked up the bottle and set it back down. "That he'd never really given himself over to us. He just went off and left me. There was never an *us*, not like I thought."

"Maybe he wasn't himself. People who do what he did are usually ill."

She stared into his face. "But he never asked me to share in his pain. I would have."

"Pride maybe. Ashamed even. He was going to let you down and couldn't bring himself to be around when that happened."

"He left me with a mess and alone." She smiled a sad smile. "Not even a note saying good-bye—nothing."

Carson sighed and said as gently as he could, "He didn't have space in his angst to think of that, maybe."

"I wonder," she said. "Is it different from your wife, from Naomi, leaving you but hanging around as if she hadn't?"

He didn't know what to say to that.

Marla went straight on. "It's like she let *you* swing in the wind instead of doing it like Glen did."

"Game of gotcha here?" he responded.

She poured a bit more bourbon into his glass then hers. "Why not. Everyone else in my life was so sympathetic about the tragic loss of my husband."

He emptied his glass and stood up. "I'm sorry for all that's happened. Especially for that smoldering mess out there. But with that I will leave you and retire to the trailer—just Hazel and me. I left my suitcase sitting out by my car, guess my p.j.'s will be cold."

She followed him to the front door. "Get your suitcase. I think we can find a place for you to bed down in here where it's warm. Hazel can wait for you to be back home with her."

There were three bedrooms upstairs in the old house. Carson chose the smaller of two spare rooms, one that had corner sash windows with pull-down shades, a double bed with an art deco wooden headboard, and pale green wallpaper patterned with rows of little red roses. After an awkward moment, Marla wished him goodnight and disappeared into her bedroom. He pushed the door shut, sat on the edge of the coil-spring mattress, and leaned over onto his thighs, where he weighed the moment. He stared down at the braided rug beneath his feet on darkened fir flooring and shuddered. As had happened so often in the last weeks, the replay came up again, same as always but now with some added layers piled on top. Living in this parallel place, from which he could see where he'd come from but was unable, or unwilling, to cross back over, was so surreal that he didn't know who he was for sure—like right then. In a little more than four weeks, he'd gone from a life of predictability filled with revolving scenes: working at something he didn't much like, living with a woman who didn't much like him, a social milieu he didn't much care for, and being a person he didn't much like—all wrapped in wealth, position, and denial of his own aspirations.

Now here he was in an upstairs bedroom of an old farmhouse owned by a woman he hadn't known a month ago, brought here by a man who found him wandering around a fish hatchery, living in a trailer named Hazel, all so he could pursue his long-held guilt for neglecting his little sister. He rose and went to a window and raised the shade, but all he could see was his own silhouette in night-black glass backlit by the bedside lamp. He stood like that for several minutes, in the presence of his own image, before getting into his pajama bottoms and a tee shirt with a Nike Swoosh on it. He lay on his back in the darkened room but was unable to sleep. After an hour of repositioning heavy blankets and staring up at nothing, he turned on the lamp by the bed and got up. He remembered that Marla had quite a selection of books, so he went looking for something to read. An artificial Christmas tree, decorated for the season, stood in one corner of the living room, standing in for the real thing. A pine-scented candle sat on the coffee table; Carson smelled it and found that amusing—no bing cherry. He moved quietly to the wall of bookshelves, cocked his head to the side, and scanned the array of spines until he saw the title of a novel he had always meant to read and tucked it under an arm.

Her howl came as he reached the top of the stairs. She charged out of her bedroom wielding a baseball bat, swinging it back and forth. Carson held up the book in defense and had it knocked from his grip on a downward swing; he grabbed the bat from her before she could pull it back for another go.

"Marla!" he yelled. "What the hell!"

She choked and gasped and struggled to recognize him.

"It's me," he said. "Carson." He slapped his chest.

The way she looked at him was discomfiting. But the panic finally fell away, and the cramping of her face relaxed. She crossed her arms beneath her breasts and sucked in a deep breath. "He was back," she whispered.

Carson watched but didn't respond.

"That creature, he was back."

"A bad dream?"

"No," she said and shook her head. "No, it was real. He was in the house. I heard him coming for me."

"Marla." He held up his hands. "That was me. On the stairs. It was me."

"You?" She squeezed her eyes shut then opened them. "My god, it was so real." She looked at the bat in his hand and tried to laugh. "Are you okay? Did I hurt you?"

With the bat raised above his head he chuckled. "No but darn close to it. Thankfully I had this book to fend you off." He picked the splayed volume off the floor. "*To Kill a Mockingbird*. Apt title, considering."

She held a hand to her mouth and laughed. "*To Kill a Mockingbird?*"

"Yeah, always wanted to read it. I couldn't sleep...so, anyway you okay?"

"I don't know." She pulled her nightgown more tightly around her. "I don't know."

"He's not here, Marla. It was a dream. Really."

She nodded and studied his face. "Can I have my bat back?" He held it out.

"Just don't hit me." They laughed to abort the frightening episode.

"You'll be okay now?" he asked.

She reached for his hand. He followed along to her bed. She put the bat on the floor and they lay side by side; she faced away from him, pulled an arm of his over her body and held onto it tightly. Soon Carson felt her breathing become rhythmic. She was asleep, but he was wide-awake, taking in the sensory responses of being in the bed of a woman other than Naomi. Feeling the warmth of an unfamiliar body next to him—another female body—noting the scent of her hair and the sound of her breathing, it was strangely implausible. When he did finally drift off, the night was beginning to give way to a new day.

The world was fighting its way into his head, the morning light was prying at his eyelids, he gave in. She was awake, lying on her side just looking at him expressionless, but intently. He blinked and rubbed his eyes then turned to her. After several minutes he reached out and touched her face. She didn't react at first; then she managed the trace of a smile.

"Did he come back?" he asked.

She wiggled her head *no* on the pillow. "You saved me," she said.

"It was just a dream."

"No, you saved me. He was back, maybe only in my head, but it was excruciating."

He folded an arm beneath his head and looked straight into her eyes. "I know that feeling. Very well I know that feeling. In my dream I am back in the water and I see Naomi floating beside me and she's smiling." He paused. "I know she's dead, but still she's smiling at me, torturing me."

"Just like that creep is torturing me. And Glen. I still see him in the barn sometimes. He just looks at me, hanging there, no expression in his eyes."

With those things said, they fell quiet each with their own thoughts. When he started to get out of bed, she reached out and held onto his arm and gently pulled him toward her. How long had it been since he'd kissed a woman with other than spousal obligation or familial tradition—a long stretch. He could tell that for her this wasn't a moment of intense discovery but perhaps a moment between kindred souls. When he touched his lips to hers, it was a pure moment of something new. His expectation was that their mouths would be tense, unyielding because they were merely responding to their duel lives of damage and recovery. But her mouth was soft; she seemed to be inviting him to enjoy this moment. He relaxed his lips, and they held that connection until she leaned away, smiling. They kissed again, this time with less caution, and again. The early morning wandered on while they explored getting to know each other. And when they gave themselves to one another it was the first time in a very long time that either of them had felt the undiluted intoxication of being present for someone else.

They had a late breakfast, which they prepared together. And they laughed, really laughed more than they had since...well since then.

-29-

Dicky Fain had watched the flames grab onto the wooden shell of the building and begin to devour it until there was a roar in his ears. His heart pounding, he had shoved Marla Snow aside and run frantically from the Quonset building, through the billow of smoke rushing after him, and down the slope to his car. The last thing he saw before flooring the accelerator was the woman crawling out of the smoke and rolling away from the fire. He swore, pounded the steering wheel, and sped out of the driveway, onto Mill Creek Road and away from the chaos he'd caused. All the way back into The Dalles, he cursed and cried and drove recklessly through traffic until he found his way back onto I-84 headed toward Portland. He thought only about getting away, hoping no one had seen him at the old farmhouse. He would explain it all to Mr. Barrus. He'd tell him that it wasn't his fault and beg for another chance and that he wouldn't let him down ever again.

He would talk to him—that's what he'd do—before anyone else could. *I can convince him. I can tell him how it was and why I deserve another chance.* He fumbled for his cell phone and thumbed at his directory of numbers; there were only a handful. He didn't have many friends or essential contacts—he tried to laugh about that. With tears in his eyes, the car waddling side to side, he looked at the screen for the initials CB. It was in those moments of distraction that the car, his beloved Camaro IROC-Z, tried to straighten out a curve, met the center concrete barrier at high speed, rode up on its flanged footing, and began its roll: once, twice it rolled with Dicky Fain screaming, the cell phone flailing in his right hand, his left hand clinging to the steering wheel, and the unbuckled seatbelt whipping about. On the second roll his door flew open, and he was ejected still holding the phone, CB's number illuminated. When the EMTs placed his body on the gurney, one of them had to pry the cell from his hand.

———————

It was mid-afternoon the following day. CB Barrus was in discussion with his property lawyer over details regarding the purchase of a building near Pike's Street Market when his executive assistant, Mary Dickens, entered after a polite tap on the door. She didn't hesitate but walked right up to table where several documents were spread out, ignoring the other man. Her expression was all CB needed; he nodded to the attorney, who was used to such abrupt actions by his most demanding client. The man plucked his suit coat off a chair, said something about calling the next day, and left the office almost on tiptoe.

CB waited until the door closed. "What?"

"There's a call for you on line two," she said. "You'll want to take it."

"That right? Who is it?"

She held her hands at her waist, her way of distancing herself from matters she did not approve of, and said, "A woman who says we employ her son."

"Mary, spit it out."

"You hire a Dicky Fain?" she asked, knowing full well it was one of his off-the-book people. "If so, it's his mother." When he saw his eyebrows go up, she knew she was right.

"All right, I'll take it." He rose and went behind his desk. He and Mary Dickens exchanged eye contact until he tipped his head; that meant he wanted privacy.

Mary Dickens sniffed, turned, and left him to whatever circumstance called for secrecy.

"Hello, this is CB Barrus," he said into the receiver.

"Mr. Barrus." The woman's voice was choked with emotion. "I am Hilda Fain, Dicky's mother? Dicky Fain."

"I see. What can I do for you?"

"Dicky…he's been killed." Her voice broke into sobs.

CB felt a chill. "My goodness." He raised his voice in an attempt to match emotion he heard in others. "What happened? Where?"

"His car crashed." The woman could barely get the words out. "Out in the Columbia Gorge. Down in Oregon."

"I'm so sorry," he feigned.

"The police called. Yesterday they called. It was late. They's the ones who told me he'd died. At the scene they said. But, but they said that Dicky'd been involved in something bad before he crashed."

CB inhaled and clenched his teeth. "That so?"

"Mr. Barrus, Dicky, he was working for you, wasn't he? I mean, didn't he work for you?"

"Well yes, your son did work for us from time to time. At some of our properties."

"Was he working for you on that trip? They're saying awful things like he hurt a woman down there, in The Dalles, set fire to her place and all. Awful things. It ain't true—I know it ain't true." He heard her blow her nose. "He weren't no saint, but he was a good boy all the same."

"I'm sure. Sorry for your loss, but why are you calling me?"

"I was thinking," she stuttered, "with Dicky being one of your employees and all, I mean you could tell them people that he was on the job and that what they're saying he did, it's just not true."

CB stood at his desk. "Mrs. Fain, while your son may have done some work for us on occasion, on a job-by-job basis, he wasn't an employee, and we have no business interests in Oregon."

The woman whimpered a bit and said, "Well you see, I was wondering about that. I mean why he was down there and all. Thing is, the last time I saw him was here at our place. He has a room in the basement we fixed up and...anyway, Dicky, he was all so proud that he was going to be doing a special job for you."

"Is that so?" CB swallowed back a growing foreboding. "All I can say is that we have any number of projects going on where Dicky may have been scheduled to work. He was on a list of people we hire, like I say, job-by-job."

"Uh-huh. Oh, oh," she moaned.

"So while I share your grief," CB said in a flat voice, "your son's presence in Oregon had nothing to do with our company. I am sorry for your loss. Good-bye."

"Mr. Barrus?" the woman cut in before he could hang up. "I almost forgot."

"Yes, what is it?"

"The police, they may be calling you."

He gripped the receiver. "Why's that?"

"'Cause Dicky's phone, that cell phone of his, he had it in his hands when they found him. Guess they had to tug it out, he had such a grip on it." She sniveled some more. "Thing is when the police looked at that phone, they figured you were the last one he was trying to call."

"What?"

"Yeah, the policeman who called me asked if I knew who you were. 'Cause when they opened that phone, you know, it lit up with your name on the little screen. So anyway…"

He cut the woman off in midsentence and dropped into his chair. "Shit!" he barked and dropped a fist onto the desk.

It was easy enough to deny any connection to Dicky Fain and his presence in Oregon. When the police did call, CB was able to use his usual disconnected manner and disassociate himself and the company from Dicky Fain other than that he was on a list of day laborers Barrus Properties hired from time to time. If the authorities needed to know just when was the last time Dicky Fain had worked a job for them, he could find out and get back to them. No, that wouldn't be necessary, and the company had no business connections in Wasco County? That is right, no business there whatsoever. Nor any idea why Dicky Fain may have been trying to call him? No one asked how Dicky happened to have CB's direct cell number.

After that call, CB knew things were going too far, but then, he knew no other way.

———

Since her grandmother had stunned the family with the news that her nephew was alive, Purl had been anxious to speak directly with

232

Carson. But she didn't try to make contact because of Lillian's admonition to give him time. But on this day before Christmas Eve, she had decided that enough time had elapsed. She had retained the number in her cell phone from the night of Lillian's call, fully intending to use it at some point, if for no other reason than to prove to her own satisfaction this unbelievable story to be true.

So that afternoon she brewed coffee, very strong—she wanted the caffeine hit— and settled in at the kitchen table. She drank two swallows black and picked up her cell. Thumbing through the recent calls file, she found the number. Of course she knew that Carson might have already tossed that phone for a new prepaid version with a totally different number. No matter, she was doing this. Unlike most recent calls, there was no name given, just the number. She tapped the number and watched the screen morph into its calling mode; she held the phone up to her ear and waited.

It rang and rang, and just when she thought it would go to voice mail, there was a click and a voice: "Yes?" She froze an instant; it was his voice. "Carson? It's Purl."

"Purl?"

"Yes."

"What is it?" he asked.

She breathed out a laugh. "What is it? My god, what do you think?" They both paused. "I mean, we're all beside ourselves. First you're dead, drowned with Naomi. Then you're alive, wandering about somewhere. What do you mean, what is it?"

"Sorry," he said, "I just supposed Grandma told you everything."

"This is all about Aleta, then? It's true about a child?"

"Yes."

"And you're out there looking for her son? Somewhere in Oklahoma?"

"True, though I'm not in Oklahoma at the moment."

"So where are you, then?"

"I had reason to come back to home base."

"And where's that?"

233

He hesitated. "In Oregon."

"Home base. In Oregon. What's the name of that town, Dulles?"

"No, The Dalles."

"The Dalles," she repeated. "So you are done then, looking for the child?"

"No." He snapped out the word. "I had need to come back for a bit." He pondered a moment then added, "Something CB stirred up."

"CB? What has he done now?"

"Never mind. I'll be going back to Oklahoma right away. Besides, I have people working on this back there."

"Working on this." Purl repeated his words and wiped at the tears that suddenly came. "Carson, come home. Come back home, and we'll all see what can be done about Aleta's child. We'll help you. This is crazy what you're doing, don't you see?"

His deep sigh filled her ear. "Yeah, I'm the family nutcase who needs help. Don't you see, Purl, that we all ruined Aleta. She had no life. We all watched her try to blossom only to be stifled and wither."

"Listen, Carson, please—"

"No, you listen, Purl. My shame is that I've known for some time about Aleta's child and did nothing. After all, she was dead, the child was somewhere out of sight and mind, and when had I ever done the courageous thing? Well, I may not be courageous, and I may not be able to make this happen, but by god, I'm going to run at with all I've got, win or lose. Don't get in my way."

He disconnected before she could tell him she would stand with him. She tried to call back, but he didn't answer. She dumped the remainder of her cooled coffee in the sink and rinsed the cup, wondering if she truly would stand with him. The fact that Aleta had given birth was still bouncing around in her head, a fact that had driven great sadness into her mind. Katie, her only child, had presented her with a beautiful grandchild, the treasure of her mature years. How would she react if that child had been secreted away and unknown to her? What would she do to find that child if she suddenly became aware it existed? She knew the answer: *Anything and everything.*

-30-

It was midmorning of Christmas Eve day, and Marla and Carson were standing outside watching an arson squad from the fire department walk the scene of the Quonset fire. Barrier tape had been put up, someone was questioning Marla and taking down pertinent information, a photographer was firing away, and a couple of investigators were walking through the rubble collecting evidence—that was the story. It was all going to go nowhere. She had confirmed that the building was likely uninsured, and most significantly, the person who had started the fire had died in a car crash on the freeway less than half an hour after he'd sped away from the scene. But people had a job to do, and that was okay.

The stench of the fire hadn't left. Even though Marla never wanted to make candles again, the rubble of the fire and the loss of the Quonset, which had found a special place in her heart after all, saddened her. They left the arson investigators to their duties and went into the house, where she dropped onto a kitchen chair and cried softly.

Carson walked to the kitchen sink and began cleaning up their breakfast dishes and pans. With the first clink, she turned and told him to stop, that he didn't have to do that. He dried his hands on a striped kitchen towel and approached the table.

"I've been your worst nightmare, haven't I?" he said. "From the moment you saw me sitting on your porch with Cecil, you should have sent me on my way." She lowered her eyes when he sat across from her. "I'm sorry, Marla. You took a gamble, you rented Hazel to me, you took me into your life, and what has it gotten you? I swear I'll pay for all the damage."

"Will you please shut up," she said, again without looking at him. "And now I care about you. What do we do about that?"

After a moment she answered, "Nothing." She looked up. "Nothing, because we wouldn't be good for each other. Damaged goods, remember?"

"But…"

"That was nice, it was special, but two nights in a bed don't count. I'm scarred, and you're a newborn to this loss thing. Hell, we both have ongoing nightmares. Wouldn't it be fun to share our bumps in the night on a regular basis?"

"We'd fix that by being us."

"You are a babe in arms. Besides, Carson, you are on a mission. You have to find that child and make things right. Now I want you to please pack your things and move back up to the trailer while you're here, before going back to Oklahoma or whatever. Best thing."

The trailer was bone cold and not the least bit welcoming: he was a stranger all over again. The propane furnace was stubborn, but after several attempts it fired up, and soon the compact capsule was warm. Once he'd unpacked his bag and brewed some coffee, he looked in the fridge; it was bare except for a milk carton with souring dregs, which he dumped. He toasted two remaining slices of stale wheat bread and spread some peanut butter on them. That was lunch. In the quiet, what could he do but think? Think of the entangled threads that epitomized his existence these days? What had his life been before Thanksgiving? Was there anything back there that he wished to salvage, things he wanted to remember, even unfinished business he should revisit? He laughed out loud when he realized that he could decide to never go back to Seattle, move on with a new framework of life, send his family a Christmas card every year, and not miss anything of what had been. It was sobering to think that he had never been where he should have been in living his life. Wasted years, he thought—wasted by him, wasted because he had accepted someone else's decision of what he should do. CB had been the one to set the course for him and everyone else in the family, and he'd mostly gone along. They all had.

With the taste of peanut butter still in his mouth, he stepped outside, having decided to make a run into town and stock up on groceries before the stores shut down for Christmas Eve. Marla's Honda was gone. He was glad for that, wasn't sure what they could say just now, better to let the feelings of abrupt separation fade some. It wasn't as if they had been in a deep relationship anyway. Awkward to give up on something that hadn't yet been. He'd put the key into the ignition of his car when Cecil Nash's Taurus lumbered up. They met between the cars.

"Well now," Cecil said, "heard you'd come back to town. Some mess, huh?" He nodded toward the burned-down building.

Carson didn't look, just nodded in return.

"She coulda been killed."

"I know that."

"Almost was. I got here, she was outside but not by much. Guess you heard that asshole that did it died out on I-84. Rolled his car bunch a times."

Carson felt his heart thump. "I heard that."

"Paper said not more than thirty minutes after the fire alarm went out. Paper said was a guy name of Dicky Fain. You heard of him?"

Carson said no and turned his head toward the ashes. Thinking of a different outcome put a crimp in his stomach.

Cecil stroked his beard and zipped up his canvas coat against the cold. "Marla told us the guy was after you. That right?"

Carson looked steadily into the man's eyes. "That's right. Wanted her to tell him where I was in Oklahoma."

"Musta wanted to know real bad, way he roughed her up then torched the shop. Real bad, I'd say." Carson looked off into the adjoining orchard. "This all part of your odyssey?" Cecil asked. "If it is, getting mighty damn serious."

"I'll be leaving, get out of her way. There won't be any repeat of this. I'll see to that."

"So you know who's behind this thing?"

"I'll be paying for the cost of the building." Carson said, ignoring Cecil's question. "I'm just on my way to get some groceries before the stores close early."

"Want you to come on over to our place tonight. You don't want to miss Ola Mae's Christmas Eve spread. No sir."

"Maybe not a good idea. I can get me some eats, and that'll be good."

"No siree bob. Ola Mae gave me my marching orders to invite you. You don't come, I'll be in the doghouse." He stood quiet for a moment. "I'm getting vibes that there's something not right between you and Marla. That may be, but not tonight. You and your landlord can just play nice, and we'll all have a grand time. See you around seven then, or come earlier, and we'll have an early shot across the bow with my special eggnog."

———

It was a very nice time: good food, easygoing conversation with no mention of the assault or the fire, an amiable gathering until Carson's phone started chiming just when the mincemeat pie was being served. He hesitated, looked up to see Marla staring at him, then excused himself and stepped away into the living room. It was Ezzard Dale. Carson almost hit the End Call button but answered instead.

"You calling to wish me Merry Christmas, I hope," Carson said.

"Well, that too. I'll make this quick because, let me tell you, Rhonda will kill me if she finds me making a business call on Christmas Eve. We open our gifts tonight, not Christmas morning. The kids are in hyper mode."

"So what is it?"

"So Saffron, that's what."

"Saffron? The midwife we talked to?"

"The very same. Called me today."

"And?"

"Has had a change of heart. Seems she has something to tell us after all."

"Like what?"

238

Voices could be heard in the background. "I gotta go, man. You be at my office day after tomorrow. She'll be there. Whatever it is, must be weighing on her to drive all the way in from Tonkawa. Let's say around ten." Pause. "I'm coming, honey. Bye."

Carson rode out the rest of the Christmas Eve time with Ola Mae and Cecil while Marla kept studying him. After several rounds of eggnog laced with rum, he excused himself as graciously as he could, thanked Ola Mae profusely, and drove back home; Marla followed shortly thereafter. He met her when she stepped out of her car and asked to use her computer so he could book a flight to Tulsa the next day. It was an expensive ticket, but he intended to be in Ezzard's office the day after Christmas.

Once the ticket was confirmed, he packed his bag hastily and headed to Portland. The only flight he could get left early the next morning. When he drove away, Marla was standing at a window watching. They hadn't said much other than him thanking her for the use of the computer. He stayed at a hotel near the Portland International Airport and caught a less-than-full Christmas Day flight at seven-thirty the next morning. During a layover in Dallas, he walked the concourse still brooding over the mess he had left behind in The Dalles: the attack on Marla by an unknown assailant and the charred remains of the Quonset. He found an unused gate area and pulled out his cell. It was a phone number he'd memorized years ago; CB answered just using his initials.

"Just what the fuck were you thinking?" Carson barked.

"And a Merry Christmas to you," CB responded, "and from a watery grave yet."

"You sent a hatchet man to harass that woman? To shove her around?"

CB sucked back through his front teeth and said, "Don't forget the fire. Guess there was a fire, right?"

Carson grunted his disgust. "Where is your moral center? Do you even have one?"

"Good question. Never been determined."

239

"And you terrified someone just to find out my location?"

"That's right. Where are you, by the way, right now?"

"I'll find him, you know. I will. The boy. I'll find Aleta's child."

"My, such determination. I've never witnessed this kind of tenacity in you before. Where was all of this zeal when I wanted you to show more gumption? To be the heir to all I've built up. But you were a disappointment, weren't you?"

"Why the hell are you trying to block me?"

"Because," CB said, no more humor in his voice, "I don't want this to happen. And it won't."

"But why?"

"Why? Because, my resurgent son, it's history, history that can only tarnish our family. And I won't have it."

"That's bullshit, and you know it. It's her child. He belongs with us, with family."

"Not going to happen."

"Yes, it will."

"Search all you want. Scour the entire state of Oklahoma. I've sent Haack out to see that the child will never be found. You see, you're only making things worse."

"My god, what kind of deviant are you? My own father."

CB chuckled. "Let's not get too extreme. I'm really setting this matter to rest, as it should be. After all, Carson, I've always been the only one with the balls to protect the Barrus name."

Carson looked out through the large pane of glass onto the tarmac as a plane was being pushed into a berth. He exhaled, lowered the phone from his ear, and ended the call. He barely remembered boarding the plane for the short flight to Tulsa until a flight attendant reminded him to buckle his seat belt. When a young man seated next to him pulled out an iPad, Carson's eyes wandered to the screen and the flitting, brightly colored images of some game; that was all he saw until the plane jostled him slightly on landing. Since disconnecting from the insidious conversation with his father, all he had been able to think about was how his noble intention had become a nightmare. All he had to do to end the insanity would be to say uncle, cave in to his father, go back to Seattle, and pick up where he'd left off, just without a wife and without bringing Aleta's child home. He would also have to abandon this new self, the one that had discovered there were other ways to live than groveling to CB Barrus. He was certain that he could not go back to that controlled environment.

His bag popped out of the baggage chute and slid down to where he could grab it. It was quiet in the airport. Most of his fellow passengers, like he, had already missed most of Christmas Day. And like he, they left the terminal fatigued and plodding. Only a few were met by those still in the throes of celebration. Carson bypassed them boarded a shuttle bus and rode over to pick up a rental car. He stopped at a Quiktrip convenience store in Tulsa, the only store with food that was open, picked up some prepackaged food and a six-pack of beer, and headed for Sapulpa. He asked for the same room at the Falcon Motel and by late afternoon had settled in as best he could.

The sandwich he'd gotten, something called the Triple Stack, piled with turkey, ham, beef, and cheddar cheese went down pretty well. The beer helped. It wasn't a holiday feast, didn't match Ola Mae's spread or Thanksgiving. Thanksgiving. It came back to him: Thanksgiving at the big house in Sequim, the trip down the canal, the collision. It seemed so long, ago but when he added it up on his fingers, only thirty-three days had passed. A little over a month. It seemed as if he'd been around the world and back in that time. No, wait, not him, not that other person—that guy was still in the canal. He swallowed some beer and laughed out loud. Who was he now, Bill Tolliver? Maybe that's who he really was now, not that other person; not Carson Barrus.

On impulse, he dialed his grandmother but only got her answering machine. He figured that she was likely at Purl's house, where the Barrus clan now gathered since Lillian's house was no longer available. When Purl answered his call, he wished her Merry Christmas and asked her to tell everyone else the same once he had hung up. No, he didn't want to talk with everyone, and he wouldn't tell her where he was, but things were progressing; that was only a small white lie. He ignored her plea to say more and disconnected; he also shut off his phone. He wasn't in the mood for the pleadings or admonitions of the family, not yet anyway. If things went as he planned, they would all be part of what might transpire later on.

-31-

By the time Ezzard wandered up holding his door key out the next morning, Carson had been pacing impatiently outside the office for a good twenty minutes. Moments later, Scooter shouldered her way in carrying yet another bakery box of maple bars and her favorite sugar-glazed donuts. Carson turned hands down on the pastry but accepted a cup of coffee once it was brewed then sat down and drummed his fingers on Ezzard's desktop. Ezzard bit into a maple bar and launched into a detailed report of the calls they'd made to some thirty-plus other midwives since he'd been gone. How they lined up half a dozen appointments before getting the call from Saffron Taylor. But Carson wasn't interested; he was still shattered over the crazy-man incident in Oregon and not interested in small talk. Ezzard exchanged a knowing look with Scooter, and they went back to their computer screens.

Ten o'clock came then passed: no Saffron. At ten after eleven, Ezzard tried to call her. There was no answer. Carson was standing at the front window staring out when Ezzard guessed out loud that she'd been held up or got a late start. It was nearing the noon hour when the door flew open and Saffron Taylor burst in, breathing hard.

"My god, what a morning," she almost shouted and looked around at everyone. She pulled herself free from a shearling leather coat with brass buttons and a faux fur collar.

Carson stood stark still and noted the same shoulder-length charcoal hair and the same slender height, but this time she wore no bib overalls. Instead she had on a white blouse, dark blue canvas denims, and Ugg boots. "Thank you for coming all this way," he said calmly when he really wanted to blurt out *Tell me, now!*

"Sorry I'm late," she sighed. "My old Subaru blew a tire just out of Sand Springs, and me with no spare. Guy in a laundry delivery van gave me and my flat tire a lift—against company policy, bless him."

"Like they say," Ezzard joked, "no good deed goes unpunished."

Saffron Taylor laughed out loud. "Got that right."

Carson didn't join in on the levity. He remained standing, and when he felt he'd held back long enough, he said, "You have something to tell us, I hear."

The woman stifled her good humor, studied the seriousness written on Carson's face, and after a moment's hesitation said, "I do. Yes."

"All right. Please have a seat. Coffee?"

She said yes, draped her coat on the back of the chair next to Ezzard's desk and sat down carefully; it was yes to cream and sugar but no to a maple bar. Scooter hustled over to get the coffee. No one spoke then, no frivolous chitchat about her flat tire, the weather, or presidential politics. When Scooter set the coffee by Saffron's elbow on the desk, she took a hesitant sip, cradled the cup in her hands, and closed her eyes for a moment. The room was still. After she'd taken two more sips from her cup, she looked up at Carson standing over her.

"Would you mind sitting, please?" she said, smiling.

Carson pulled a chair over across from her and sat. His mind was whirling with thoughts of what this person had to say; would it be a breakthrough, or would it be a false alarm? He placed his hands on his knees and waited her out.

"You see," she said, setting the cup down on the desk and turning to face Carson, "I wasn't truthful when you came to see me." When he didn't respond, she went on. "You said

2003, right?" Carson nodded. "December?" He nodded again. "Young woman, pretty."

"She was beautiful," Carson said.

"Okay," she said. She hugged herself and tilted forward. "Okay. I lied. I did."

"Why?" Carson asked in a soft voice.

"Why do you think?"

Carson looked over at Ezzard, whose eyes were glued to the two of them. He blinked, and Carson said, "Money?"

"It had been a lean year, and I had debts."

"That right?" Carson said.

"I know that's no damned excuse." She choked on the words.

"So what happened?" Ezzard asked. "How were you approached?"

She turned to the investigator. "I got a phone call. In May, I think. A man. He asked if I could help a young woman with her pregnancy."

"Who was the man? He give you his name?" Ezzard had his detecting hat on.

"No, no name. He just made an appointment to come by and see me." She gripped her forehead with a hand and closed her eyes again.

"So did he?" Ezzard asked.

She bobbed her head. "He did."

"Name, description."

"He didn't give me his name, but he was a big man, very tall, ruggedly built, close-cropped hair, and forceful. I felt intimidated the moment he entered my house."

"What did he want of you?" Ezzard leaned back and laced his hands over his stomach.

"At first he asked some innocuous questions: How long had I been a midwife, how many deliveries had I assisted, did I provide prenatal care, and like that. All straightforward at first, like I say."

"Then what?" Carson asked. "What changed?"

"It all came out. How he was acting as an intermediary for a family from out of state. That a young woman would be coming to live in Oklahoma during her pregnancy and that they had need of some special services and would I be willing to provide those services. It became clear to me very quickly that this was to be a woman hiding her pregnancy away from her home base and perhaps giving the baby up for adoption."

"And you were willing to do that?" Ezzard asked.

"These things happen and, yes, I've assisted young women in such circumstances before."

"But this was different, wasn't it?" Carson said.

She nodded and caught her breath. "They wanted her pregnancy and the birth to be totally secret and for the child to be placed with some people they'd located who would take the child and keep it all off the record." She pulled a handkerchief out of a pocket and dabbed at her nose. "At first I said no I couldn't be part of what they wanted."

"They changed your mind with money, I gather," Carson said.

"God help me, yes. And I've been riddled with guilt ever since. When you two came to see me I wanted to yell YES I DID IT!" She dropped her head down then raised it and said, "You see, the midwifery philosophy is that the most basic human right for every woman is the right to choose her place of birth and who will attend her. Coercion about her birth is an obscene act. Obscene. And I was part of such an obscenity."

"Tell me," Carson said.

Saffron Taylor seemed to come to a new sense of calm as she revealed all that had gone into manipulating the birth. When she first met a young woman named Sarah, she saw what a sweet and lovely young woman she was. But then she did the bidding of the man overseeing things anyway and found a family that would keep Sarah in their home during the remainder of her pregnancy—for the right price. At term, Saffron delivered the baby: "A beautiful baby boy. She named him Thomas. Insisted." She witnessed the pain and anguish felt by Sarah, who knew she had to give up the child. It was apparent that she had no choice in the matter and that it was against her wishes. The big man came around three times prior to the birth to check on things and give Saffron further instructions—and of course more money. After the birth, Saffron made out a birth certificate, which the overseer insisted she give to him. Shortly thereafter he came again, gave Saffron and the host family additional large payments, and took Sarah and the Baby away.

"Her name was Aleta," Carson said. "Means truth."

The woman considered that. "I only knew her as Sarah."

"And the big man was David Haack, a fixer for things that need to be done on the dark side."

"He never ever said his name, and I was always paid in cash."

"Now, Saffron," Ezzard said, "the big question is where did they take the child?"

She didn't answer until she'd pursed her lips and pushed them in and out a couple of times. "I wasn't...I was never told specifically. It was obvious that I wasn't supposed to know. In fact, I was warned to keep everything to myself and never tell anyone. Actually, it was more of a threat. That's what it was, an out-and-out threat. All that was missing was *Or else.*"

"But you have no idea who has the child?"

"I didn't say that."

Carson felt a buzz; he sat up straight, all his senses full on. He and Saffron looked intently at each other. He held his breath and waited for Ezzard to ask the next big question.

"Are you saying you do know who has the child, Saffron?" Ezzard leaned forward; his chair springs squawked. "Is that what you're saying?"

"I think maybe. It's been four years," she said. "They could be someplace else. I don't know."

"I have another question," Carson said. "Who kept Aleta during her pregnancy? What would they know about who took the child?"

Saffron stiffened. "I can't tell you. Besides they had nothing to do with where the boy was taken."

"Still, I want to meet them," Carson pressed.

She looked back and forth between the men. "It was agreed," she said. "Promised, actually."

Ezzard bobbed his head. "To keep their name out of it, right?"

"They wouldn't have taken her in otherwise. Had to be kept secret...never to ever connect them with what happened. They took her in, harbored her." She wiped at her eyes with forefingers. "They were good to her."

"For a price," said Carson, "for a price they were good to her."

"Later, Carson," Ezzard broke in. "We can maybe meet them later. Right now, we need to keep our eye on the ball. We're in this to find the boy. To find Thomas. Right?"

Carson chewed on his lower lip for a long moment, listened to the soft-voiced coaxing from Ezzard, and finally agreed. Then came the disclosure Carson most wanted to hear: who took possession of Aleta's baby and where could they be found. By the time Saffron Taylor had divulged everything she knew, she was depleted in body and mind, but somehow tranquility fell over her. She wiped the tears away and smiled pathetically.

"So," she sighed, "it's over. Isn't it?" She looked between the men.

Carson's anger toward her had mostly subsided. "It is," he said in a composed voice. "For you, it is over."

"Maybe I'll sleep the night through. I haven't, you know, not since you came to see me. Not a single night."

She fidgeted for a bit then rose, breathed a soft good-bye as she pulled on her big coat, and walked out the door. The men rose and stepped side by side to the office window and watched her get into an old Subaru. When she'd driven away, leaving an oily cloud behind, Ezzard turned to Carson, hands clenched in his pants pockets. "That was something," he said.

Carson only said, "Yes."

"Woman was tormented." When Carson said nothing Ezzard said, "She was, tormented."

Carson said, "Self-inflicted."

"Hey man, give her a break. She's done right."

"You say so."

"I've snooped out some real lowlifes, and she's not even in the running. Look, this was gonna happen whether Saffron Taylor was involved or not, right? I say be glad she's the one who was around to look out for your sister's well being: had good folks take her in and delivered a healthy baby. The rest of it wasn't pretty but..."

Carson nodded and waved a hand. "Okay, okay. Get your drift.

Hell of a thing, though, and she went along with it. But...where was I back when it mattered? Nowhere, that's where, so I'm grateful she came forward, and who am I to judge anyway?"

Ezzard raised his eyebrows and decided he had nothing to add to the man's self-loathing.

"I've got them." Scooter had been clacking away at her computer and was beaming.

"Both names and possible locations."

-32-

It had taken David Haack much less than the hour and thirty-seven minutes his GPS had given to drive the hundred miles to Kildare out from Tulsa. That Saturday before Christmas, he drove the black Lincoln Town Car through the town of only one hundred people, cruised street by street, and reestablished his bearings: past the elementary school, by the farm co-op grain elevator, and finally out Pecan Road once his rote kicked in and he knew where to go. Somewhat over five miles out of the town's center, he turned onto Ferguson Avenue and eventually saw the house set back off the road up a rutted dirt lane. He slowed, and with Dave Brubeck's commanding piano in the piece called "Pick Up Sticks" filling the car, slowly rocked over the uneven surface, dipping in and out of gouges in the dirt road.

The house was a big box of a building, cheaply built, covered with T1-11 plywood siding, wearing institutional beige paint. Haack pulled into a wide yard of stunted weeds and packed dirt and parked next to an old Jeep Cherokee, its red paint oxidized, riding on high-profile thick-lugged tires. A family minivan sat beside the Jeep. Several children bundled for the cold were playing in the weed-infested yard around a stack of old tires; a wooden plank lay across the tires, and the kids were using it as a makeshift teeter-totter. Haack turned off the ignition and stepped out of the car while pulling on a light windbreaker; he stood behind the open door and took in the surroundings. The house was tired; everything about it was worn and neglected. Evidence of children was all about: plastic toys of all colors were scattered around, mostly faded or broken; bicycles of various sizes lay on their sides; a deflated basketball rested beneath a portable hoop that had no net.

A sudden childish scream emanated from among the kids at the teeter-totter. The front door of the house burst open after the crying went on; a man wearing a baseball cap came out on the rickety wooden porch and yelled for quiet. All went silent. He was huge, towering on an immense frame, sporting a gut that hung out behind a faded red tee shirt with the tail out. A little girl wearing a pink poly fleece coat came running up to the porch crying something about being wronged.

"You just shut the fuck up, Annie, or I'll give you what for," the man barked. "All ya's shut up if you know what's good for you." About that time he caught sight of the Lincoln, recognized David Haack, and uttered an oath. "Oh shit." The big man raised a hand and came stumbling down the stairs. He loped toward Haack, a forced grin stretching his puffy face. "Well lookie who's here." His voice had the scratchy tone of someone who'd yelled too much at a football game. "This here's unexpected."

Very seldom did David Haack have to look up to another man. In this case he did. Christopher "Kit" Brawner stood a good six foot seven, Haack guessed, and carried at least three hundred and fifty pounds around. "How you doing, Kit?" Haack said. A small cloud of white puffed out in the cold air when he spoke.

Kit Brawner bobbed his head too many times and hitched up on his pants. "Good, good," he bubbled. "We're doing good here." He glanced over his shoulder. "Kids, they can drive ya nuts, but other'n that, we're doing great."

"Glad to hear it." Haack leaned on the fender of the Lincoln. "You getting your payments okay?"

Kit Brawner's eyes lit up above fleshy cheeks. "You bet, sure are. Much appreciated, too. Yessir, get it regular as clockwork." His forehead puckered in creases. "So what ya'll doin' out this way?"

Haack smiled as if he really meant it. "Just came to see you, Kit. Yep, all the way from Seattle just to see you."

"Really?" The man yanked on his OU Sooners baseball cap. "Like I say, we're fine as frog's hair here."

"How's he doing?" Haack asked.

Kit Brawner's face tightened. "He's fine, doin' real good." He paused and toed a size sixteen Nike at a weed clump. "Hey, he had a birthday."

"December 15."

"Uh-huh, that's right. What's that...?"

"Week ago. What'd you do for his birthday?"

"Oh, well lemme think here...oh yeah, we had pizza delivered. Yep, had a big pizza party for him."

"That right, a pizza party? How did he like that?"

Kit Brawner's face reddened. "Swell, I think. He ate his share—that's for sure."

"Make's him how old?"

The huge man sputtered. "Gad, I got kids running out my ears. I sometimes forget." He laughed and rubbed his stomach.

"He's four," Haack said.

"Oh sure, four, that's right. Four. Cute little bugger, I'll say."

Haack looked over to where the group of children was playing. "He over there?"

"Lemme see." Kit Brawner pulled a pack of cigarettes out of his pocket and squinted in that direction. "Nope, don't see him. Probably in the house with Delores." After a pause the man said, "You didn't come all this way to check on the boy's birthday, now did you?" He thumbed a Bic lighter and lit the cigarette he'd stuck in his mouth.

Haack didn't like Kit Brawner; actually, he couldn't stomach him. When he'd located the Brawners as a possible family to take in the boy, he'd hated the idea, but there weren't any better choices at the time, not for what CB Barrus wanted. The Brawners, Kit and his wife Delores, had three biological children and usually around five or six foster kids running about the place. They squeezed them all into the five-bedroom house and mostly covered expenses with payments from the government and Kit Brawner's sometime seasonal job at the farm co-op. Aleta's son was living among them as another foster child but under special circumstances: he wasn't registered with the state, and his care was privately funded by CB Barrus on a monthly stipend. A substantial amount of cash arrived each and every month.

Haack had promised himself that he would visit the boy every year, but of course that hadn't happened, a fact he regretted. He had done one thing Aleta wanted; he had made sure the boy's first name was Thomas. Tommy, she'd said and smiled her wistful smile. He knew why she chose the name Tommy. He knew it was for the brief time in her life when she truly had someone, maybe the love of her life; no—forget maybe—he was. He was until he wasn't. He was until CB decided against him, and one day Thomas Shepherd vanished. Haack knew all those things because he had been the one to make sure her Thomas got the word that he wasn't to stay involved with Aleta. Had to give the guy credit: he resisted. He truly loved Aleta. Haack saw that in the guy. Her Tommy resisted right up until couldn't, right up until Haack took him out for a drink, passed him the envelope, and made it clear there were two ways to wind this thing up: one with what was in the envelope and a job opening elsewhere or two no envelope, no job, but a dark moment he really wouldn't want. In the end, an enraged and humiliated Thomas Shepherd took the envelope and left town for Atlanta but never ever made an appearance regarding the job opening. Word was the man got his real estate license and did moderately well, end of story. So the birth certificate made out by that hippie midwife had read Thomas, but the rest was just plucked out of the air: Thomas Allen Stevens wasn't officially anyone.

Haack stared into the brutish face of Kit Brawner and shuddered to think of what could possibly lie ahead, with Carson on the hunt for Aleta's child and Brawner holding the reins. It wasn't an uplifting moment in his life, but he would do what CB wanted, no matter the cold spike that was driving into his innards. He knew what had to be done; he just wondered if this buffoon was the person to pull it off.

253

"No, Kit, I didn't come all this way to wish Thomas happy birthday, or you Merry Christmas for that matter. You're right about that."

"I just figured." The huge man shrugged, hands in his faded jeans, exhaled a cloud of smoke, and grinned as if he were the brightest bulb in the pack.

"I want to see him."

"Sure thing." He turned. "Let's go on in the house. He'll be glad to see you."

Like hell, Haack thought. "He doesn't know me, Kit. And I want to keep it that way. Just bring him out of the house and take him over to the other kids. I'll watch from here."

Kit Brawner blinked his eyes several times, trying to understand Haack's instructions. Finally he waddled off toward the house his elephantine butt cheeks rising and dropping like hams. A few minutes later, the front door decorated with a sagging evergreen wreath opened and Kit Brawner and a woman emerged leading a small boy by the hand. Like her husband, Delores Brawner was overweight, had disheveled bleached blonde shoulder-length hair, and wore a denim jacket and khaki pants. She hustled the boy down the stairs all the while looking over at the man by the big black car. She led the child to where the others were playing and tried to get him involved, gesturing to the teeter-totter. The boy just looked up at her as if confused.

The boy was a towhead; his curly hair was overdue for a trip to the barber. From where he stood, Haack could tell the boy was fair of skin, as had been Aleta, and her hair had also been blonde. Probably had her blue eyes as well. His body weight seemed right for his age, though it was hard to tell for sure with him wearing a bulky plaid coat. Haack signaled Kit Brawner, and they walked toward the children where he could get close enough to convince himself that the child was being well cared for. Of course he would have no way of knowing how well Tommy was eating or how he was progressing with his social skills, vocabulary, cognitive development, and so forth. He cringed feeling that living in among the Brawner clan and an assortment of cheated foster kids was probably stunting the boy's maturation. How could it not, he surmised. Then again, that wasn't his responsibility, was it?

Up closer, Haack saw a small boy who was reluctant to get into the melee of the other children, a boy who didn't smile or yell out playfully. He stood by the woman, who glanced over at David Haack as she tried to encourage the child to get in the game, to mix it up with the others; she smiled sheepishly and shrugged. But he was a sweet little guy. Haack saw that and for a moment felt the boy's predicament, circumstances the child was totally unaware of. It was all so obviously unfair. He chewed over that for a bit before casting it aside and motioning Kit Brawner away.

"Boy seems okay," David Haack said. "You're feeding him good, right?"

"Uh, well Delores buys all the groceries, but yeah, we spend a ton food."

"Not what I asked. Are you feeding him right? His diet, is it healthy?"

Kit Brawner's brow wrinkled. "You mean is the food..."

"Damn it, man, don't you know what a balanced diet is? Are you feeding him junk food, or are you making sure he has protein, fruit, and vegetables?"

"Oh, I see. You're talking about a health nut diet. Gotcha. We feed all the kids good stuff."

"Like pizza."

"Yeah, we have a little place in town makes the best pizza. I mean, for a dinky town, it's really good."

Haack studied the man, his head tipped back to look up into the set of dimly lit eyes. He couldn't believe it. "Okay, I guess. Just make sure he eats right."

"You bet. Is there something else you came for?"

"Yes. It's getting cold. Let's get into my car where we can talk."

The Lincoln listed severely to the right when Kit Brawner settled into the passenger seat. Haack turned on the engine and set the heater thermostat. He rested his hands on the steering wheel and took in a deep breath.

By the time he had explained the circumstances to Kit Brawner three times in three different approaches, he felt marginally convinced that the man got it. He'd even pulled a piece of paper out of the glove box and had the man scribble essentials: Carson's name, relationship to the boy, his intentions, and when Carson might appear—that was a wild guess. Most importantly, he gave Brawner specific instructions about what he was to do next.

Kit Brawner had studied his scrawl of notes and slowly repeated everything back to Haack. Twice he did that. And yes, he could make sure that the instructions were carried out to Haack's satisfaction. When he was handed an envelope with extra cash in it, he was enthusiastically sure he could handle the job.

David Haack left the Brawner tribe behind and drove back to Tulsa where he checked into the Hyatt Regency and called CB Barrus. His orders were to stay put, keep in touch with the child's keepers, and call with constant feedback.

After the emotional outpouring with Saffron, Ezzard pressured Carson into letting go of his fervent desire to confront the people who had given sanctuary to Aleta during her pregnancy. He put an edge to his voice and directed the focus back to where the boy was now.

"That's what's important," Ezzard implored, while Carson paced. "Once we find Thomas, once you have him, if you still want meet with those folks, we'll do it. But listen up." He stood and leaned over Carson. 'We have to stay on target. You hear now? On target."

Carson looked into Ezzard's face, dropped onto chair and nodded. "Okay. You're right. Wasn't thinking straight." He knuckled his eye sockets. "What now?"

Ezzard sighed his relief and looked over at Scooter. "Scooter'll get to work on pinpointing the info Saffron gave us while we grab a bite to eat. That right, Scoot?" he grinned.

She blinked behind her glasses, gave her boss a dubious smile, and turned back to her computer. Carson wasn't hungry, so he watched as Ezzard devoured a hot Reuben sandwich oozing Swiss cheese and chattered about how sure he felt they were onto something. With Saffron's revelations, his instincts told him that very soon they would have a bead on where to find Aleta's boy.

"I can feel it," Ezzard said with sauerkraut juice dribbling down his chin. "It's a gut thing, you know? We're cooking, Carson."

Carson merely listened and shivered to think of being close to his intended outcome. After Ezzard wiped the last of the Reuben from his face, Carson begged off going back to the office and instead returned to the Falcon Motel; he had something else that was pressing in on him. He very much needed to check in with Vincent Horne.

Horne was in court when he called. Carson left a message, pulled off his shoes, and stretched out on the bed in hopes of recouping some lost hours from fitful sleep the night before. He was dead out when his cell phone began to ring. It was Vincent.

"You sound groggy," Vincent said. "I wake you old man?"

"Matter of fact you did," Carson yawned. "Didn't sleep last night. How are you?"

"Nix that, how are you? That's more important, and where the hell are you as well?"

"Back in Oklahoma. Vince? I know where he is."

"Really? My god, what now?" Vincent sucked in a breath. "This is getting eerie."

"I know. Gives me chills."

"I'll just bet. So what now? How are you going to, what, retrieve him, I guess is the word. How's that going to work?"

"Not a clue. Giving me a gut ache to think about it. But right now I need you to draw up a power of attorney agreement so you can take care of some of my business and personal needs."

"Sure. Where can I send the paperwork?"

"Overnight it to this private detective's office." He gave him Ezzard's address then instructed him about getting someone to check on the house, catching up on back mail, paying past due and current bills, and finally banking his paychecks from Barrus. "You may have to prod my father on that score, but I need my salary to keep coming through."

"I'll jump on this. It's going to cost you. You know that," he laughed.

"Well worth it, but those are the easy things. Where you'll earn your stripes is when I get the boy. This is going to be a snake pit. From what I'm learning, there's been no legal trail of birth certificate, adoption, or anything like it. What can I do about that will be the big question."

"Wow, that's out of my league, but I'll get some help, and we'll find a way. Jesus, Carson, you know how to juice up a guy's day. From dullsville to fireworks."

"And Vince?"

"Yeah."

"It's time to let the cat out of the bag that I didn't drown. Public disclosure, I mean. As my attorney I authorize you to issue a press release to the local media. It will announce that in the accident that took my wife's life, I survived but was disoriented and left the scene—something along those lines. I found a term on Wikipedia: post-traumatic amnesia. I think we can use that. Post-traumatic amnesia is a state of confusion that occurs immediately following a traumatic brain injury in which the injured person is disoriented and unable to remember events that occur after the injury. Got that? Okay, get one of your scribes to write up a release. Fill in the blanks, like you guys do all the time, and send it out. Okay?"

Vincent Horne exhaled and laughed. "Okay, I guess. What about your family? Shouldn't they be doing this?"

"No. Call my grandmother, Lillian Barrus, and tell her I've authorized you to do this, and she can alert the clan if she wants. Besides, I want it done right, straightforward with no outlandish quotes from my father about me being disturbed and shit like that."

"Okay. Carson what the heck am I going to do for thrills when this is over. Back to contracts I guess."

After Vincent Horne's call, Carson pulled out the piece of paper he'd folded and put in his pants pocket. On it he'd written the two words Ezzard had called over earlier: Brawner and Kildare. Scooter had Googled the town and found that Kildare was a tiny town just 17 miles from Tonkawa. Carson's eyes watered as he stared at the slip of paper and realized how close he was.

—————

Later, after he'd gone out for a steak dinner at an eatery just down the street, he returned to the anonymity of the motel room and showered. When he decided it was late enough in the Pacific time zone, he picked up his cell and pressed her numbers. She answered after two rings.

"It's me," he said.

"Who is this?" was her response.

"Ha, nice to hear your voice, too. How are you? Wild plans for New Years?"

"Sure, dancing 'til dawn and all that. How's Oklahoma?"

"Marla," he said unable to hold back. "I know where he is. The boy."

"Truly?" He could hear the excitement in her voice. "Where?"

"Place called Kildare little more than an hour and a half from where I'm sitting."

He could hear her suck in a breath. "Wow. Now what?"

"That is the question." He waited a beat then added, "My plan is to make whoever the people are an offer they can't refuse."

She chuckled. "That being?"

"Right. That being I don't know. Have to get a lay of the land and decide how to proceed: a straight-on approach or a clandestine maneuver."

"You make it sound like a military offensive."

"Sort of is. I have no straight shot, legally. The whole matter was handled off the books and under the table. I'm thinking the only way I can recover him is to go at it the same way."

"What about your father? Won't he try and stop you?"

"Yes. He's promised me as much. I don't expect to waltz into

Kildare, swoop up the boy, and drive away. In fact, he may have already been moved."

"You mean taken away?"

"Exactly. When I find this place in Kildare, he won't be there. My dad told me flat out that I would never find him. He sent his goon to take care of that."

"How old is this child?"

"Just turned four. A couple of weeks ago."

"Carson, this is awful. Do you have help?"

He smiled. "This private investigator I retained is all. Not sure how far he'll go with this."

"You better be finding out. Don't you go busting in someplace like the Lone Ranger. Could get your head handed to you."

"Nice to know you care."

She fell silent for a moment. "Well I do…care."

"I've missed you," he said in a soft voice.

After a moment she said, "We can get into that later. For now, you need to focus on that child. And for god's sake, get some help. A least a couple of people to ride along with you before just showing up in that town, what was it?"

"Kildare."

"Sounds Irish. Think there's a County Kildare in Ireland."

"Ah, the school teacher arises."

"Seriously, be careful."

He said he would; then they ran out of things to say. They wished each other Happy New Year, and that was it. The cell blinked off. He held it in his hand, feeling its connection to her before setting it on the nightstand and using the remote to activate the television. He found a M*A*S*H rerun, but he didn't really see or hear it with his mind roiling over what lay ahead: his promise to Aleta.

-33-

New Year's Eve rolled in with little importance as far as Carson was concerned. The young woman holding down the front desk at the motel recommended an Italian restaurant not far away, so at Cortona's Ristorante he splurged on a bottle of good Chianti and imbibed most of it over shrimp, mussels and scallops, served in tomato sauce over linguine. He witnessed the New Year begin to make its entrance as around him people celebrated, consumed his food as if it were oatmeal, and felt miserably alone.

Long before the midnight hour, he returned to his room with the unfinished bottle of wine, consumed what was left of it, and for a time flicked through the TV channels to take in the New Year's celebrations from New York, LA, and elsewhere. It tired him to watch all the tinsel and raucousness, and by the time the ball dropped in Time's Square, he was asleep on top of the bedspread in his clothes, TV remote clutched in his hand. The year 2008 was at hand; what lay ahead could only unfold layer by layer. During the night he shuddered several times.

He awoke with a reflexive twitch the next morning, still sprawled across the bed in his clothes; he jerked upright and rubbed at the crust on his eyelids. The television was flickering in the background; a news channel crawl line declared that the Taliban was threatening to escalate attacks in Afghanistan after a year of record violence. He merely licked his dry lips and held down the power button and the set blinked off. After showering away the dregs of sleep and too much wine, he dressed and danced out into frigid air to search for breakfast on the first day of the year. He finally found a gas station convenience store open, bought a large coffee and two egg and sausage things wrapped in a limp pancake, and returned to the motel. It wasn't gourmet, but he wolfed down his New Year's breakfast and was glad for it.

The motel room became an airless cell; the plethora of televised football bowl games were merely irritating; he wanted this holiday silliness to be over. He called Ezzard and caught him during halftime of the Capital One Bowl with Michigan leading Florida 21 to 14.

"Ezzard." Carson spoke on a hard breath. "I'm going out there tomorrow. Kildare. I'm going out there to find the boy. I've got to."

"Okay," Ezzard said easily. "Just like that? No plan, no support, just go."

"Thought you'd go with me. Will you?"

"Let me ask you, what you planning on doing if you find this place, where the child is? I should say where we *think* the child is. You just gonna waltz in, introduce yourself, and announce that you've come to take a certain kid with you? Then what? March off like it was an okay thing to do?"

Carson waited a few beats. "I guess not," he said.

"I would say *guess not*."

"I've got to do something. Going crazy just sitting here. I've got to go there and—"

"And what? And what, Carson?"

"Ezzard, my father told me I'd never find the boy."

"You don't think he's waiting 'til just when you show up before making good on that promise? Do you?" Neither man spoke until Ezzard said, "The boy's already gone, Carson."

Carson pounded a fist on his leg. "Damn it, I feel helpless. Here I am so close, but I can't do anything."

"We'll do something, man. We'll do something, but we have to do something smart if you want to get this thing done." Ezzard chuckled. "Tell you what, you let me watch the rest of my bowl games, and I'll see you in my office first thing—uh, make that around nine thirty in the morning, not too early 'cause I won't be there 'til about then. Then we'll get down to business. Don't worry, we'll find your little guy." He paused. "You got anything to drink? Something to warm your innards and lower your anxiety? No? Okay, I'll run by before the Rose Bowl game kicks off and bring you a little something."

Twenty minutes later Ezzard was at his door. He handed off a bottle of Jim Beam bourbon about three-quarters full and a bag of potato chips then sped off. Carson had the Rose Bowl game on in the background but couldn't have told anyone later that USC beat the snot out of Illinois that day. He was sedated and drifting in a cloud that anesthetized his extreme sense of needing to be some place, to do something important, but he couldn't quite focus on what it was.

USC beat Illinois 49 to 17. So what?

Ezzard Dale was pissed. He was a big Illinois fan; an older brother had played football there once. He grumbled some about the game but saw that it was of zero interest to Carson so shrugged and picked up a stale maple bar. They were leaning over an AAA Oklahoma state map spread out on Ezzard's desk.

"See right there," Ezzard said. "There's Tonkawa, then Ponca City, and right there just a smidgen north is Kildare." He jabbed at the paper with a sticky finger. "Just a blip. Like we said, maybe a hundred people live there—at the most. Only minutes from Ponca City." He tilted his head and looked into Carson's frowning face. "Maple bar?"

Carson couldn't hold back. With the box of leftover maple bars being held under his nose by Ezzard as if for the first time ever, he began to laugh. Soon they were both laughing. Even Scooter was giggling.

"Why not?" Ezzard stood and pulled up on his pants. "Life is too short not to have your share of maple bars."

Carson shook his head at Scooter; she snickered and ducked her head behind the computer screen. "Ezzard..."

"I know, I know. Let's get serious here. Carson, sit down, and I'll tell you what we're gonna do." He waited until Carson sat across from him at the desk and said, "We have to do this right. First time. No mistakes. We misfire here, and there'll be no overs—the boy will be outa range. That's what my gut's telling me. Like I said the other day, he's probably not going to be at the first place we look. But we have to start turning over some rocks and make somebody scurry for cover. Once they do, we'll begin to maybe figure out where they don't want us to go."

"I'm not giving up on this, Ezzard, no matter if we mess up first crack at it or not."

"I'm just telling you, Carson, from what you've said about your father. Seems like if he gets wind that we're anywhere close to the boy, he'll vamoose the kid for good and ever. Never find him." He leaned forward, eyes wide. "Isn't that what you think? Isn't that what you told me the man's capable of?"

Carson studied Ezzard's shiny face and exhorting eyes and considered the question: Was CB capable of spiriting Aleta's child away for good? Forever. Was he that twisted? Then again, why would he not go to those lengths? He had done all the rest: hidden her pregnancy, taken her away from family, taken her away from whomever the father was, concealed the birth, hidden the child, and let Aleta suffer until she reached bottom and had nothing left. He nodded to Ezzard.

"Okay then," Ezzard responded, looked at the last maple bar but didn't take it. "So we're gonna do this right from the get-go. Now Scooter and me, we haven't just been sitting on our bottoms over the holidays. Scooter, what ya got?"

Scooter wiped at her nose with a tissue and dropped it in a wastebasket. She smiled at Carson self-consciously and returned to her keyboard. "I spent some time searching for the name Saffron gave us: Brawner?" More typing. "I focused on Tonkawa, Ponca City, Kildare, Newkirk—all around that area. Came up with a passel of Brawners, mostly located in Ponca City and Kildare."

"How many is a passel?" Carson asked, smiling.

"Scientifically speaking," Ezzard laughed, "we investigators have found a passel to be somewhere's in the vicinity of half a dozen. Sometimes a bit more."

"I found five Brawners up in that area," Scooter said. "Two out of Ponca City and three right in around Kildare."

Carson turned to each of them, question in his eyes. "And?"

"And we're on it. Right now we're on it. I have two operatives out there nosing around while we're eating sweets. Couple of gals from Tulsa who specialize in blending in and gaining background info for me. Sometimes they come across as soccer moms, other times maybe legal secretaries—you get the idea."

"Who are they in Kildare?"

Ezzard grinned. "They're lost—that's what. Cover is that they came in from Oklahoma City looking for some folks they don't know, friends of friends they promised to look in on while taking this little trip they're on. They're looking for some people with names they are not quite sure of: could be Brawner or Browner, maybe Donner. Places are so small they can't go in like they belong, be picked out and kicked out soon as they opened their mouths."

"How long have they been on the job out there?"

"They've been out there since last weekend, missed New Year's with their families. Expect to hear something today."

"Who are these women?"

"You'll never know, never meet them. This time tomorrow they'll be back home doing laundry, selling houses, doing data entry, who knows?"

"How much?" Carson asked.

"Not cheap, but I decided we have to move. Okay?"

Carson pulled out a credit card and tossed it on the desk. "You use this?"

"Absolutely." Ezzard held the card up. "By the way, our billable time has used up your retainer as well."

Carson shrugged. He hoped Vincent Horne had received his power of attorney back and was taking care of his bills and all the rest.

The morning passed slowly as they waited for the Tulsa women to report in. Carson had a quavering sensation imagining himself approaching a house where the boy might be. Seeing him for the first time. Would he look like Aleta? What would he say to the child when he took him away from the place he knew, no matter how terrible it might be—or might not. What if it was a place he belonged? When he expressed his fears, Ezzard calmed him as best he could and persuaded him to go out for lunch. They went somewhere close, a café they'd been to before. Carson didn't recall, just ate a cheeseburger and questioned Ezzard repeatedly about what they were going to do. Ezzard responded each time with: "Don't worry. We'll get to that."

Scooter was on the phone when they returned listening to someone while typing what she was hearing. Occasionally she would say "Uh-huh." Finally she said "That it?" and hung up.

"That was her," she said to Ezzard. "I've got it all down."

Ezzard asked. "Print it out."

Scooter hit a few keystrokes, and the printer behind her desk began to whir. "You know Sylvia," she said, "matter of fact. Said they stumbled around, two goofball women who didn't know their way out of a parking lot. Got what you want and left a bunch of dufus males thinking they're the smartest guys in Oklahoma." Scooter laughed behind her hand.

"Damn," Ezzard said loudly, "what a piece a work those gals are. Worth every penny."

Scooter retrieved two pages from the printer. Ezzard scanned first one page then the other and snapped a finger against the top page with a pop. "We're rolling," he said. "The gals have given us a jump start. Lookie here." He waved for Carson to come closer, and they hunkered over the printout. "See these two names at the top: Kyle Brawner and Christopher, nickname Kit, Brawner. Sylvia and her partner are pretty sure these two are the hottest leads. Why? Right there: Kit Brawner and his wife Delores are known out there as long-time foster parents. Sylvia says here that they're usually housing five or six foster kids at any one time. Kyle Brawner seems to be a cousin or some other shirttail kin to this Kit fellow. The ladies liked Kyle for their list because there were kids running around his place that didn't act like they belonged. The guy kept calling them *Hey you.* No name, just hey you. Or telling his wife to *Do something with that kid.*"

Carson took the page from Ezzard and studied it. "How'll we do this?"

"I've got some ideas, but I tell you, with these domestic gigs, they can turn flaky real fast." He retrieved the page from Carson and examined it again. Ezzard sat down slowly in his swivel chair and tilted it back until it grunted. "Okay, here's what I've been cogitating on. Sit down, will you please? All right," he said then said it again, "all right." He massaged his hands. "Here's what I'm thinking. It's more than likely that the boy has been with Kit Brawner and his wife all this time. It is also likely, even certain, that he is no longer with them, having been moved at your father's mandate."

"And might be with this Kyle Brawner?" Carson said. "That what you're thinking?"

Ezzard nodded. "Could be. But if these boys are smarter than a pump handle, they might already be moving the child—place to place following orders. Then again, if they can't pour water out of a boot, we might get lucky. The good news is, we know where they are within a few miles give or take. We don't have 'em cornered but dang close if we move right quick."

"When?"

"Today's Wednesday, mostly already shot, so I'd like tomorrow to pull some details together. I say Friday morning we take the drive to Kildare. You ready for that?"

"Damn yes." Carson's response was hoarse.

Ezzard laughed and glanced over toward Scooter. "There's no perfect way to do this. We can't go in there like a Navy Seal team and just snatch the kid. Then again, we don't want to send these folks an engraved invitation in case they don't suspect we're around. 'Course we think they do know we're coming because of your father's involvement." Ezzard threw his arms up in the air. "So those are our major obstacles."

"Leaving what options?"

"I've been kicking this around ever since you first contacted me. Once the child was located, I wondered how to get him safely away. Someway short of kidnapping, else ways we'll run afoul of the law. I'm not willing to do that. Got to protect my license."

"And?" Carson asked.

"First I figured I'd have to send in scouts. Do ground-level surveillance. That we've done with the ladies from Tulsa."

"Then what?"

"Hell, then we go in. Friday, I'd say about midmorning. We'll go directly to this Kit

Brawner's place and make our initial contact. You'll go in alone. I can't go with you 'cause this Brawner hates blacks, known racist according to our gals' research."

"Wait, you're sending me in alone?"

"Yeah, I thought about that. Our ladies' report says this guy is one big dude, sounds huge. Don't know if that means capable of inflicting great harm, but we have to assume that to be the case. Now hold your horses. I have two fellas I call for this kind of work. They'll be going out ahead of us to Ponca City tomorrow, stay the night and be in position when you go out to the Brawner's place. You won't see them, but they will be around."

Carson's skin tone paled, his eyes focusing on nothing. Finally he raised his head and said, "Okay, I'm ready."

The drive to Ponca City Friday morning took a tad over an hour and a half. It was just shy of ten o'clock when Carson pulled his rental car up at a Starbucks near the Ponca City Medical Center. They each got a large coffee; Ezzard was disappointed that there were no maple bars but was content with a cinnamon scone. Carson couldn't eat anything; he hadn't even had breakfast before leaving Sapulpa. They sat in the car while Ezzard broke off pieces of scone and pondered what he thought would be Carson's best approach; after all the talk, there wasn't one, he thought.

"You sure you want to do this?" he asked.

Carson put his paper cup in the armrest holder. "No. But I have to. You've known that all along, Ezzard."

"I know. So we'll drive out there. You leave me off before driving up to the house. Remember the photo Sylvia sent us: long lane, big barn of a place? I'll drop out before you drive in, find a place to stay out of sight. My guys, they'll be somewhere in the background ready to come in if necessary." He laughed. "If you see two really big guys running in, don't shoot them.

You don't have a gun, do you?"

"Of course not. Are we ready?"

"I am if you are."

Carson swallowed the last of his coffee and started the car. In less than fifteen minutes they were in Kildare. Ezzard navigated following the directions given by the operatives: first finding Pecan Road then locating the turn onto Ferguson Avenue. A few miles out they found an extra large mailbox listing backward on a rusting metal post; the name Brawner could just be made out in faded black lettering. Ezzard gripped Carson by the arm, nodded, and slipped out of the car, pulling on a red and black plaid Mackinaw. He walked across the road to where three oak trees were clustered and stood in among them. Carson watched until Ezzard was hidden before moving at idle speed jouncing up the pockmarked drive. He coasted in and eased to a stop a ways back from the big squarish house. His heart was racing when he turned off the ignition and stared out through the windshield. At that moment, the front door of the house opened, and two boys, maybe eight or nine years old, burst out and down the stairs of the listing wooden porch. One boy carried a football; the other ran out, arms raised yelling for a downfield pass.

Carson smiled recalling his own boyhood backyard football games with the inherent scrapes, the bruises, the puppy dog sweat; those had been unforgettable days. He stepped out of the car, observed the two boys for a moment longer, and approached the house.

At the foot of the sagging porch he paused, his mouth dry and head swimming and looked out again to where the boys were playing. Seeing that they had taken no note of him, he climbed the few steps and rapped on a cheap metal-clad door. There was no response, so he knocked again, a bit harder. Finally the door opened a crack and a girl of about twelve peered out at him. She had brown hair in a ponytail, wore thick glasses and had brown eyes and a receding chin; she was wearing a washed-out red tee shirt with a Coca Cola logo on it, jeans with frayed cuffs, and flip-flops on her feet. For a long moment they just looked at one another.

Carson smiled broadly and leaned at the waist. "Hello there," he said. "Is your mother home?"

Before the girl could respond, a loud female voice yelled, "Who is it, Crystal?" The girl flinched as a hand grabbed her by the shoulder and pulled her away. An overweight woman wearing a stained gray sweatshirt and corresponding sweatpants, filled the doorway. Brittle blonde hair framed her reddish pimpled face; she looked at Carson with blue eyes that peered out through mere slits above fat cheeks. "Whatever yer selling, we don't want none, and we don't want no religious baloney, either," she said, resting a fisted hand on her right hip. The tight nasal tone of her voice was grating.

Carson took in a slow breath and kept his smile fixed. "I'm not here to sell you anything nor proselytize," he said calmly.

She squinted. "Pros-a-tize? What's that?"

"That means I'm not here to try and convert you to a specific religion."

She raised her head. "Damn good thing," she retorted. "Our family's been Baptists forever and always."

Carson nodded.

The woman calmed for the moment. "So whatta you want, then?"

"Mrs. Brawner," he began.

"How you know my name?" Her chin jutted out.

He turned and pointed back down the drive. "Name on the mailbox. Is it right?" Her face reddened even more, and he went on. "My name is Carson Barrus."

At first her bland expression remained intact, but then a quizzical look came onto her face. "Barrus? That what you said, Barrus?"

"That's right. Carson Barrus."

The woman shuffled back a step, and her eyes grew from behind their narrow openings. "I'll need to get my husband," she said.

"But don't you want to know why I'm here?"

"I know why yer here, mister. You just stay right there, and I'll get Kit." She turned and grabbed at the girl named Crystal who was still standing behind the woman. "Crystal." She shoved her out the door. "Go get Kit. He's in his work shed."

"I'm right here, Delores." A well-deep male voice came from behind Carson. "What's all the fuss?"

Carson turned quickly and looked down onto the biggest man he had seen in a very long time. He wore tent-sized striped bib overalls over a long-sleeved red and yellow plaid shirt and a maroon baseball cap that was positioned backward on his enormous head; the word *Sooners* was stitched on the back of the hat.

"Who are you, fella?" He raised the can of beer in his hand and drank. "Selling something?"

The wife slipped out the door onto the porch. "Name's Barrus, hon. What was it, Carl Barrus?"

"Carson," Carson answered. "Carson Barrus."

Kit Brawner crumpled the empty beer can and threw it on the ground. He took a step forward. "That right? Barrus. And just what the fuck do you want, Barrus?"

Carson felt a chill as he stepped down and faced Kit Brawner. At six-one he was still a good half-foot shorter than Brawner and less than half his body mass, if that. He took care to stand two arm's lengths away and far enough back that he didn't have to crane his neck to see the man's face.

"I think you know, Mr. Brawner. I'm here to see my nephew."

Kit Brawner stuck his big arms in behind the bib of his overalls and looked down at Carson with a grin that revealed a row of discolored piano-key teeth and one missing eyetooth. "Nephew? That right? Now why in hell you think your *nephew* would be here?"

Carson took two more steps back. "Look," he said, "I know the boy's been in your care since he was born. Four years ago now."

"Hear that Delores, thinks some kid's been *in our care*." Brawner laughed, coughed, and spit out onto the ground. "Fella, I don't have a fucking clue what yer talking about."

"I think you do. In fact, I know you do."

The man pulled his arms out and reached for a pack of cigarettes in his pocket. He eyeballed Carson as he lit up, not quite sure how to respond. "That right?" Brawner puffed and blew smoke out. "Who is this kid? We have a lot of kids around here. We's a certified foster home." He swung an arm around toward the boys playing with the football, except they weren't playing anymore; they were standing stark still watching the scene before them.

"Like I said, he's my nephew. I've come to take him home to his family."

Brawner dropped the still-burning cigarette on the ground and stepped on it with the heel of his boot. "Yeah. He said you'd be co-min' around. Claiming shit like this."

"He?"

"Yeah, he. You know who I mean now, don'tcha?"

"Maybe. Mainly I just want to see the boy and discuss his future. And I'm sure you know the child I'm speaking of."

"Nope. Whyn't you describe him to me?"

"He'd be four. Just turned four as a matter of fact—in December."

"Gotta name, this here kid?"

"Thomas, nickname Tommy. He was born just down the road in Tonkawa. December 2003. Then he came here, as a baby, a newborn." Carson's voice was rising. "But you know that, don't you?"

Brawner looked up at his wife, who was shaking her head. The man sucked in a big breath and snorted out a derisive laugh. "Got no kid here by that name. No Thomas or Tommy. I think you'd better get on outa here now."

"That what *he* told you to do when I showed up? Deny the boy's existence and push me on down the road?"

Brawner took a step forward. "Look fella, I just said we ain't got no kid like that here."

Carson smiled. "Then why did he, why did David Haack tell you I'd be coming and in your words *claiming shit like this?*"

With the mention of Haack's name, Brawner's eyes widened. He looked up quickly at his wife. Delores Brawner had gasped and wrapped her arms about herself. A staring contest went on for a long moment: Brawner moved his eyes back and forth between Carson and his wife; Carson locked onto the man's face.

"He's my blood," Carson said. "He belongs with his family. Let me have him."

Once again Delores Brawner was shaking her head at her husband. A quizzical expression formed on Kit Brawner's face, and he began to walk in a circle, muttering under his breath. After several turns he came at Carson and jabbed a hammer handle forefinger into his chest. "You, now" he said. "Now here's what yer gonna do. Yer gonna get in that car of yours and drive the hell off'n my property. You got that? And...and just keep on a driving."

Carson blinked away the man's beer breath and swatted at the finger Brawner still held out. "You are in big trouble, Brawner." Carson felt his chest grow tight and his heart beat harder. "You're being paid to harbor the boy, right? Am I right?" He lunged forward toward the big man. "Damn it! Am I right?" he yelled.

Brawner stood his ground, planted two hands on Carson's chest when he got close and pushed him back. Carson stumbled and went down on one knee. "Where is he? I want to see the boy. I want to see Tommy. Now."

Kit Brawner took three steps and stood over Carson as he rose up. "We ain't got no four-year-old kid named Tommy living here, I tell ya." He grabbed Carson by one arm and pulled him upright. "Now mister, unless you want me to put some hurt on you, get your ass off my property, and don't come back."

273

Carson swatted at the dirt on his pants, his breathing coming in heaves. "Listen, Brawner, both of you," he said, looking at Delores Brawner and back. "The gravy train is over. Not only will you no longer be getting the big payday for keeping Tommy, my guess is that this whole operation will be closed down." He waved a hand around. You better start looking for real work instead of being paid by the taxpayers to warehouse kids. Now where is the boy?"

Kit Brawner's face had turned bright red. He came for Carson, his hands folded into bowling-ball fists. Without a word he grabbed Carson by the arms and picked him up off the ground and shook him, Carson's feet dangling in midair. Holding Carson aloft with one hand, he punched a fist into Carson's face and let him fall to the ground. Carson crawled away as best he could, his head ringing. Brawner came after him and was pulling back a big boot when Delores Brawner let out a yell.

The men were large, not nearly as big as Kit Brawner, but there were two of them. They managed to get ahold of the huge man and drive him down onto the ground, where he grunted and cursed to no effect.

Carson rose and stood over Brawner. "All right, you son of a bitch, where is he?" When the man only grunted and glared at him, Carson turned to his wife. "Where?"

Delores Brawner drew herself up for a brief moment then sagged and said, "He ain't here."

"Where, then?"

"Delores," Kit Brawner growled. "Keep your mouth shut." One of the men holding him down put a knee in his chest; Brawner grunted and quit talking.

Delores Brawner shook her head from side to side when Carson looked to her again. He ran up the stairs and past her into the house. Several children of various ages were standing about in a big living room with clutter all around and a television blaring cartoons; they were in shock and mostly unresponsive when he asked if they knew if Tommy was in the house. An older girl, maybe fourteen, finally said no; he had been taken away.

Back outside, Carson stood over the still prone Kit Brawner. "Tell me where you've taken him."

He looked up into their faces. The two men holding him down were impassive. Carson was not. He got down on a knee and leaned over Brawner's fat face. "You know, Brawner, they cannot protect you from the penalties for what you've done. Their money won't outrun the law. Best you tell me where the boy is. Maybe that would be looked on favorably."

Brawner smiled; none of that had sunk in. "Fuck you," he said just before sending a wad of spittle into Carson's face.

Carson wiped his face with the back of his hand and watched as the two men pulled out a pair of plastic restraint handcuffs and managed to get them over Brawner's fence-post wrists and strapped his ankles with duct tape. They left him there, hog-tied and struggling in the driveway. The two men had never spoken and only nodded to Carson before they left, moving away as easily as they had appeared.

Carson questioned the Brawners one more time as to the whereabouts of Tommy but got nowhere. He left Kit Brawner tied up on the ground and warned Delores not to attempt to have the boy moved again from wherever he was. She glared at him for a moment before dropping her head and nodding her acquiescence. It seemed that his warning of possible reprisals had gotten through her stubborn head. Before driving away, Carson stood over Kit Brawner again and warned him that if he discovered that he had harmed the boy in any way he would pay for it. Brawner merely stared through tiny slits and said nothing.

It was at the end of the driveway, where he intended to pick up Ezzard, that the old man appeared.

-34-

He was almost skeletal compared to the enormity of Kit Brawner. Wispy white hair was fly away in the breeze, a weathered and cracked leather jacket hung on him as if he were a wire hanger, and the cold sunlight reflected off steel-rimmed glasses that rested low on his very thin nose. He was caught up in an animated conversation with Ezzard Dale next to the big mailbox out by the road. Ezzard raised a hand as Carson slowed and pulled up. He ran the window down, and Ezzard ambled over.

"We're done here," Carson said. "Have to follow up on the other leads."

"I know," Ezzard said, turning to the old gentleman. "Like you to meet Strother Larsson. That's Larsson with two esses." Carson offered a greeting, and the old fellow gave him a short wave. "Strother's been filling me in on what all went on up there at the house. My guys did all right, I guess."

"Saved me from bodily harm, so yeah, they did good," Carson said. "Gone now. Never said a word, doubt if I could ID them in a police lineup fifteen minutes from now."

"That's the way they work. Now Strother here is the father of Delores. Brawner?"

Carson stepped out of the car. "That so?" He looked back up the long drive. No one was in sight.

"It is," Ezzard responded. "He lives with his daughter and son-in-law."

The old man muttered something.

"What did he say?" asked Carson.

Ezzard grinned. "Think he referred to Mr. Brawner in a pungently derogatory manner."

"Pungently?"

"Colorful, huh? Anyway, Strother was just starting to tell me something mighty useful. About the boy."

"Like what?" Carson asked, somewhat dubious.

The old man raised a lumpy arthritic hand to his nose and honked into the weeds. "I know where he is, Tommy," he said, bobbing his head up and down. "Sweet little tyke. Been living with us since he was but a babe." He drew dry lips in and looked toward the house. "The boy, he should be away from this place. All them kids should be gone from there. The fosters."

When Carson started to ask what he meant, the old man kept right on. "But listen now, you don't have no time to waste." He coughed hard a of couple times and spit into the weeds again. "As I was tellin' this fella here," he pointed a finger at Ezzard, "he ain't here. Tommy ain't. Kit, he moved him last night. But I know where they took him."

Carson said, "He with that cousin, Kyle Brawner?"

"Forget Kyle." Strother Larsson waved a hand dismissively. "Not there either. Boy's been stashed with a hunting buddy of Kit's over to Ponca City. Here." He shoved a slip of paper into Carson's hand. "You'll find Tommy there, but you gotta kick ass. Kit won't figure you know about this, so you may have some time. But stupid as he is, that door'll close quick like." When Carson just stood deciphering the scribbling on the paper, Strother Larsson raised both arms and shouted. "You waitin' to be invited? Get a move on now!" He watched until they hustled into the car before he walked off into the scrub and began circling in around to the back of the house.

Once Ezzard was in the car, Carson sped off back into Kildare and on toward Ponca City. Ezzard pulled out his cell phone and began entering Google Maps driving directions between Brawner's place and the address the old man had given them.

"Come on, come on," he fussed, waiting for the download.

Carson chewed on his lower lip, waiting for directions. "You getting it?"

"It's coming, but damnably slow. But just keep driving. Address he gave us is on Pine Street. Okay, I've got it. Here we go."

"He showed up, all right." David Haack was driving with one hand on the wheel while holding his cell up with the other. "Surprised the hell out of me. Don't know how he did it. Then he had a run-in with Brawner."

"Run-in? Thought you said the guy was a brute." CB said. "Carson hurt?"

"No. He had help. Couple of characters corralled Brawner for our hero and cinched him up with plastic cuffs. Guess all Carson got was a bruise on his face."

"Where's the boy?"

"Brawner stashed him with a buddy of his in Ponca City. Not far. Brawner says no way Carson can know where the kid is. Moved him there yesterday on the Q.T."

"I'm not liking this, David. First you said Carson would be wandering the state of Oklahoma for a lifetime and not get close to finding the boy. Then he shows up in Brawner's front yard."

Haack gritted his teeth and inhaled. "I know. He's obviously hired himself some help. Didn't count on that. He's on a mission. Easy to misjudge a man on a mission. Guess I did."

"Mission, hell. He's just about making trouble." CB paused a moment. "Listen to me, David. You pull this out of the fire—you hear me? I don't care what you have to do. Stop this now."

Haack drove the Town Car past a school bus with several goofy kids waving or giving him the finger. He smiled then stared back ahead and asked, "CB, just how far you wanting to go here? This is your family, man. Maybe it's time to call it a day."

The bray into his ear caused Haack to jerk the phone away. When he held it back, CB was barking at the top of his voice, "Listen up, you fuck, this is over when I say it's over. You hear me?"

"I hear you."

"You do whatever it takes. You get the boy and drive into Kansas. I'll call you with the name of someone to connect with when you get there."

"Kansas?" Haack couldn't believe his ears. "You kidding? Where in Kansas?" He had to control the urge to laugh.

"You leave that to me. Now go get the kid. When you get it, you know what to do."

"Yeah, I know what to do." When the line went dead, he tossed the cell phone on the passenger seat, loaded another Dave Brubeck CD, and gripped the steering wheel with both hands, and drove on.

It was the middle of the noon hour when Carson drove the rental car along Pine Street in Ponca City. The house they sought was in a block where a long row of bungalows, probably built in the forties, was clustered for a block or so. Weedy yards, crumbling sidewalks and driveways, wide front porches that may have once been a big selling point were cluttered with broken-down wicker chairs, an occasional forlorn recliner chair, empty flower pots, and even an errant Hibachi cooker. They saw the jilted lawn mower sitting among the weeds in the yard before they saw the house number they were looking for.

Carson drove by slowly. He stopped at the end of the block and put the transmission in neutral. "What are these people's names again?"

Ezzard referred to the scrap of paper. "Tyler. Doobie and Cindy Tyler."

"Doobie?"

"That's what the old man wrote down. Doobie. No *Do*, just Doobie." Ezzard guffawed.

Carson ignored the joke. "The old man say if this Doobie works or not? Will he be home?"

"Guess he works for Phillips 66 at the refinery here. Mainly swing shift, according to Strother."

"Could be home then?"Ezzard nodded. "Suppose so."

Carson tapped a finger on the steering wheel. "Okay, let's do it."

"We just gonna take the boy if he's there?" Ezzard planted his hands on the dashboard and ducked his head. "We could get ourselves in a world of hurt. Could be accused of abduction. I might…"

"Lose your license, I know." Carson looked at Ezzard. "Okay. You stay in the car, and I'll go it alone. Let's see how it rolls out."

At first Ezzard shook his head then nodded. "Okay."

"Besides, this is about family saving a blood child from illegal abduction."

"Doesn't matter what you think. It's what the court thinks."

"We'll deal with that after I have Tommy."

Carson drove back up the block and parked in front of the house and slid out of the car without hesitation. Ezzard watched him approach the front porch with the certainty of a Jehovah's Witness out witnessing, stepping over missing chunks of sidewalk, finally standing on an askew welcome mat at the front door. He looked over his shoulder at Ezzard staring back at him from the car and raised a closed hand. After a moment's hesitation, he rapped almost politely on the door; when nothing happened, he knocked again, harder. Doobie Tyler was home. He opened the door in bare feet wearing jeans and a sleeveless undershirt. Carson was relieved that he wasn't anywhere near a big as Kit Brawner.

"Mr. Tyler?" Carson asked.

The man rubbed a hand over his closed-cropped hair and studied the person standing on his front porch sporting a bruise under his left eye. "Yeah. Who're you?"

"My name is Carson Barrus."

"So?" Doobie Tyler squinted. "That supposed to mean something? Look, I just got up. Worked swing shift last night."

"Sorry to trouble you, but I believe you have a boy named Tommy staying with you. I'm his uncle."

The man stifled a yawn and his eyes widened. "Uncle?" He cast a quick look over his shoulder.

Carson feigned calmness. "If I'm not mistaken, Kit Brawner

brought the boy here and asked you to take care of him for a bit. Right?"

Doobie Tyler scratched at his cheek. "Look, man, we was just trying help old Kit out, you know. You really the kid's uncle? Kit, he didn't tell us about no kin coming by or anything." When Carson merely nodded, the man turned and yelled, "Cindy! You all better get on out here. Cindy!"

The men faced one another, each with a lifeless smile on his face. A few moments went by before a young woman, slight of build, came up and stood next to her husband. Her bright blue eyes studied the man with a contusion on his face.

"What?" she said.

Doobie Tyler jammed his hands into his pockets. "Fella says he's the kid's uncle."

At first she looked quizzical before it sank in. "Oh." She took hold of her husband's arm and looked up into his questioning face.

His eyebrows went up and he shrugged. "Oh? That all you got to say?"

Her blonde hair was pulled back into a ponytail. She folded her arms across the front of a blue and white checkered blouse and tightened her lips. And there they stood, each one considering the circumstance that had orchestrated their meeting.

"Kit never told us about anybody coming by," she said finally and looked up at her husband again. "Just to keep Tommy until he come for him. Right, Doobie?"

"Yeah, supposed to get him today some time, maybe tomorrow. That was the deal."

Finally Carson smiled and said, "Maybe we should go inside and discuss this."

Doobie Tyler tilted back and lifted his chin. "I don't know, mister. Like I said, we're supposed to watch out for the kid until Kit comes for him. That was all we agreed to. You say yer the kid's uncle. How do we know that?"

"You don't. Any more than you know if Kit Brawner has any right to the child. Seems to me that you two are caught in an awkward situation here. Of course, it could all be sorted out when the authorities get involved."

Cindy Tyler took in a quick breath. "Authorities? Doobie, we don't want to be caught up in something like that. What have you got us into?"

"Me? You agreed to it right along with me."

"Yeah, but all you guys said was it'd be sort of like babysitting was all. Watch the boy for a day or two until they come back for him. That was all we agreed to, right?"

Doobie Tyler stepped back. "Yeah, guess we better go in the house and talk." He waved Carson into the house.

Carson glanced out toward the curb. Ezzard's face was framed in the car window; he gave no discernible reaction. Carson followed the Tylers into the house's living room and sat in a puffy faux leather recliner. A very large-flat screen television was tuned to a shopping channel touting nonstick cookware. Cindy Tyler picked up the remote, muted the sound and sat beside her husband on a couch that matched the recliner. The room looked like it was furnished on a package deal: full room for a flat price, no interest for six months, that kind of bargain.

Carson looked around, feeling a chill go through his body, anticipating his first sighting of Aleta's child. The woman saw him.

"I've got him down for a nap," she offered in a soft voice. "He's had lunch, too." When Carson looked over, she added, "We've been taking good care of him."

"Nice kid," Doobie Tyler filled in. "We ain't got any of our own yet. But we're planning too, right honey?" His grin was toothy.

Her smile was shy. "Doobie," she admonished gently.

Carson turned the recliner on its swivel base to face the couple. They nervously watched this man they'd never seen before, looking like he had been in a fight, claiming to be the uncle of a little boy they'd offhandedly agreed to babysit for a couple of days. They had no clue why Kit Brawner had asked them to watch the child or why the man was in their living room.

"Look," Carson began, "I can see that this is all very confusing to you. You are just being good friends. You agreed to take care of the boy and I'm sure you are doing a fine job."

Cindy Tyler smiled and nodded.

"Let me tell you a story," Carson said. He clasped his hands together and rested them on a knee and gave them an edited version of Aleta's story: the birth, her death, and his search. The Tylers were still lifes when he finished, staring—deer in the headlights.

"So I hope you can understand," Carson continued, "why I'm desperate to find the boy and return him to his biological family. I'm not sure how all of this will shake out with the child welfare agencies or the courts. I just know I have to do this. And I don't want you to get yourselves into any hot water over what you thought was only being neighborly. Right?"

At first neither one answered; they were stark still. Doobie Tyler finally cleared his throat. "I don't know," he said. "I figure I oughta call Kit. I mean, I hear yer story and all. But hell, I don't know you from swamp gas."

Carson forced a laugh and pointed at his bruised cheek. "Kit, he's the one gave me this. Would have been worse if a couple of men hadn't helped me. So I can imagine you might not want to cross a man with his mean streak and physical strength."

"It's not that," Doobie protested. "It's, well, this is…it's crazy, that's what. Jesus, you could be a kidnapper for all we know."

"I could be. I'm not. But you're right, I could be." Carson reached into his back pocket and pulled out his wallet. "Let me show you something," he said. "A picture of Tommy's mother." He fingered around and withdrew a small photograph, crinkled from his plunge into the canal. He looked at it and said, "I've never seen Tommy, but take a look at this and see if he resembles the woman in this photo." He stood and stepped over to the couch and handed it to Doobie Tyler. "That was Aleta, my baby sister."

He stepped back and watched their faces. It was a gamble. They leaned into one another, shoulder to shoulder, and studied the picture together. They looked into each other's eyes and back at the photo.

"The picture is wrinkled because it got wet. Does he look anything like her? Tommy?" He held his breath.

Cindy Tyler kept looking at the picture. She raised her head after a minute more. "Yes." She nodded and smiled. "His eyes and nose are like hers. Were her eyes blue?"

Carson sighed in relief. "Yes. And her hair was blonde. Is his?"

Cindy Tyler bobbed her head up and down.

"Can I see him?" Carson asked.

Doobie Tyler leaned back and folded his arms. He frowned. "What the fuck has Kit got us into?"

"Yes, you can see him," Cindy Tyler said and got up from the couch.

Carson followed her down a short hall where she paused before a closed bedroom door. After a moment she turned the knob and pushed the door open. The shades had been drawn so the room was dark. Carson felt glued to the floor as the dim light from the hall flowed in and the image of a small body beneath a cover came into focus. A tousled head of light-colored hair showed above the blanket hem. Cindy Tyler looked at Carson's face and smiled sympathetically, witnessing the intensity written on his face.

"He's a sweet boy," she offered, seemingly a verification.

Carson's mouth was a tight line. "May I go in?"

"Sure. He's been asleep for a little while, but you can wake him, I guess."

"No." Carson shook his head. "No. I only want to get a closer look."

She stepped back so he could enter the room and watched as he approached the sleeping child on tiptoe. He leaned over and gently pulled the blanket down below the child's face. Then he kneeled and for the first time saw his baby sister's little boy. He knelt like that for some time: looking, meditating over the moment. When he rose and came out into the hall again, Cindy Tyler saw the tears in his eyes and trails of wetness on his cheeks. It brought her own tears on.

He pulled a handkerchief from his back pocket and wiped at his face and eyes. "Oh my god," he gasped, "this is incredible. You can't know. It is really him, and I'm with him now."

Cindy Tyler reached out and patted this stranger on the arm. "It must be wonderful."

"Hey." It was Doobie Tyler entering the hall. "I called Kit. He's on his way over."

-35-

Carson and Cindy Tyler stared at Doobie as if he'd just confessed to assassinating the town mayor. On top of that, he was holding a pistol in his hand, a small black thing he held down beside his leg. For a stunned moment, neither Carson nor Doobie's wife reacted; they stood transfixed, eyes staring.

"You what?" It was Cindy Tyler who spoke first. "Doobie!" she yelled. "What were you thinking?"

"Only way to settle this," Doobie responded. "Now Cindy, don't look at me that way. Can't just let this guy run off with the kid. Gotta square things with Kit first."

"You fool," Carson spit out. "You'll have a war right here in your house."

"Says you," Doobie smirked. "Kit, he ain't like that. It'll be cool."

"Doobie. Doobie," Cindy said, shaking her head. "We was doing the right thing. Tommy, he's this man's kin."

"Says you." Doobie lifted the gun up and pointed it at Carson, not as a weapon, more like a pointer. "We don't know him. But Kit, we've been friends since...well forever."

Carson forced himself to remain calm; he didn't want to excite Doobie into using the weapon. Instead he tried to assess how things might play out once Kit Brawner arrived, likely all agitated and ready to get physical. And Ezzard was outside totally unaware of what was about to play out.

"Doobie," Cindy admonished. "You stop waving that darn gun around now. Could go off accidental and hurt someone."

"I's just pointing." He lowered the weapon. "It's just in case, anyway."

"In case?" Cindy said. "In case of what?"

"Hell, in case this guy and the other one out in the car just try and take the kid."

"What, you're gonna shoot 'em?" Cindy laughed.

Carson assessed the situation and decided he had to alert Ezzard. He suddenly stepped forward and walked past Doobie out to the front door. He heard Doobie telling him, "Just a darn minute," but kept going. He shoved the front door open and started waving toward the car. For a moment, Ezzard didn't react, but when Carson kept waving a calling his name he came out of the car quickly.

Ezzard hustled up the walk. "What?"

Carson trotted up panting. "Damn fool in there called Kit Brawner. Told him we're here to take Tommy."

Ezzard's face turned hard. "Not good," he said. "Want to get the boy and leave now? Before Brawner can get here?"

"The husband has a gun. Don't think he'll use but I don't want to spook him and get somebody shot."

Ezzard looked out on the street. There was no sign of Brawner's Jeep Cherokee. "Damn, this isn't good. Guy in the house with a gun and that huge bastard ready to mix it up."

They stood looking down at the sidewalk for a long moment. "Husband just came out," Ezzard said looking past Carson.

Carson turned to see Doobie out on the porch. He wasn't carrying the gun. He came down the walk toward them, arms swinging. "Best you fellas clear out," he said, jutting his chin out defiantly.

"Where's the gun?" Carson asked.

Doobie's face reddened. "I put it away. Cindy, she was throwing a shit fit."

"That's good," Ezzard said. "No need for guns."

Doobie looked at the chubby black man. "Who're you?"

"He's with me," Carson said.

"He yer muscle?" Doobie laughed.

Just then, the sound of an engine under strain interrupted.

The three men looked out on the street as the red Jeep roared up, bounced over the curb and came to rest on the sidewalk. The driver's door was flung open and the immense body of Kit Brawner came out. He hesitated and looked at the three men until Doobie waved for him to come on. Ezzard spun around and squared his body; Carson, under a rush of adrenalin, began a shuffling dance. Brawner went into a lurching run; a guttural sound came out of this throat as he closed on the men. All three men looked wide-eyed at the charging behemoth; even Doobie sucked in a breath.

It was immediately clear to Carson that Brawner was focused only on him, the one who had humiliated him. Carson started to dance faster with no idea what he'd do when Kit Brawner reached him. Before that happened, the big man went down like a side of beef and began howling.

"My knee, my knee," he yowled. "You bastard. Damn! Damn! Damn!"

Ezzard had kicked Brawner in the side of his right knee, sending the man down in excruciating pain. Ezzard stood back, out of reach knowing that Brawner was still very dangerous. With Brawner down, Doobie Tyler suddenly felt compelled to get into the fray. He lunged at Carson; the two of them went down in a tangle of arms and legs, flailing at each other with little damage inflicted. Even though down and crying in pain, Brawner was able to reach out and grab onto Ezzard, who had turned his head to watch the scrum, and pull him into a bear hug. Ezzard gasped when Brawner began squeezing with his huge arms. With the one arm he had free, Ezzard reached around and tried to jab Brawner's eyes, but he couldn't do it and was losing strength until all at once Brawner loosened his grip and fell back. Ezzard sucked in a ragged breath and rolled away.

David Haack stood over Brawner. He held the Beretta he'd used to knock the man unconscious. Across the street an elderly man, who had witnessed the entire incident, took the burned-down butt of a cigarette from his mouth, flipped it into a weed-filled flowerbed, and retreated to his house; it was none of his business, evidently.

Everyone froze. Doobie and Carson had disentangled, Ezzard was getting his wind back, and Haack was calmly slipping the nine-millimeter beneath his belt at the small of his back. A car slowed out on the street; two faces could be seen gaping.

"Let's get him in the house," Haack said. "Before someone cares enough to call the authorities."

Haack and Ezzard each take an arm and drag Kit Brawner's bulk up the walk. Cindy Tyler held the front door open and stood aside as the lifeless body is dragged inside and laid out on the living room floor. Doobie stood back, wide-eyed and pale.

Carson looked at Cindy. "The boy?" he asks.

She was staring, her face in shock. Finally she came around and said, "Still sleeping. He's still asleep."

Carson nodded, reassured. He studied the comatose body in the floor, then looked at David Haack; he was in his usual black denims and athletic-cut black tee shirt. His face held the cool, passive expression Carson had witnessed so often in the face of tension.

"So," Carson said, "thought you were running interference for CB on this."

Haack smiled. "Good to see you alive after all."

"I'll just bet you were all broke up when you thought I wasn't."

The others in the room looked between the two men and listened to the curious discussion, wondering what it all meant. Only Ezzard understood most of the stream of words.

Haack extended his iconic dry smile. "You really stirred things up. Didn't think you had it in you."

"The boy is here," Carson said.

"I know. I told dufus to make sure he couldn't be found. Best he could do, I guess." Haack looked Carson straight in the face. "Been impressed by your recon and investigative work on this. Didn't think you'd even get close."

"Forget the passive praise, Dave. We've found him, and I'm going to get him back to where he belongs. So if you're planning on..."

Haack held up a hand. "Before you start making threats you can't back up, even with your colleague here, let me say something."

Carson glanced at Ezzard. "What can you possibly say that will make any difference?"

"Just this. I'm done. This is as far as I go."

"Done with what?"

"All of this under-the-table crap over the boy." When Carson looked stupefied, Haack said, "Like I told CB, this is family. How far was he willing to go with his warped obfuscation over Aleta's child? This has been a hall of mirrors that should never have begun in the first place."

Carson took a step back. "You're getting out of the way on this?"

"Correct. You do what you think is right, and I'll be on my way back to Seattle."

"CB will have your neck."

"Screw CB, I've had it. Should have bagged it with him long ways back. Sure, he'll try to cut my balls off, but I'll tell him to stuff it." A cold smile emerged. "I know too much for him to give me any grief."

"This means no interference with Tommy?"

"Right."

"This is unbelievable."

"Tell me about it." He looked at the faces in the room. "Let's go out on the porch so we can finish this just between you and me."

Once outside, Haack continued what he'd come to say. "I decided to drop out on my way over here after another warm fuzzy talk with your father. You had good help. And you'll need some more help for a bit. Now here's what you're going to do. Wait, just listen, then do what you want, but here is my advice. Okay?"

Carson nodded.

"Take the boy. You're hearing me, right? Get Tommy out of here. Drive straight to the airport and fly back to wherever you're living. Oregon? Okay, Oregon. Once you're there, do whatever legal stuff it may take to get custody of Tommy."

"But…"

"No buts about it," Haack said. "That will all work for one very big reason: everything and everyone having anything to do with Tommy won't say or do squat. Because Tommy doesn't exist in Oklahoma: no birth certificate was ever filed, no adoption ever took place, and he was never legally assigned to the foster home he lived in those four years. And, Carson, everyone was paid off in cash. And not one of them will ever report any of this to the proper authorities." He raised both hands. "So take the kid, and beat it."

Carson stood open-mouthed as Haack unveiled his intentions and his admonition to move Tommy at once. "These folks here may make a fuss if I walk away with the boy."

"No they won't. Come on, we'll go in and set things straight."

The Tylers were waiting. They were nervous and uncertain. Kit Brawner was stirring. David Haack spoke to the Tylers in a manner they couldn't misinterpret regarding what was about to happen. When Doobie became agitated over what Kit Brawner might do, Haack kneeled beside Brawner and shook him fully awake and had him sit up and lean against the couch.

"You awake now, Kit?" Haack asked in a loud voice. "Kit?"

Brawner nodded his head and uttered a grunt.

"Say something," Haack said. "Say *I understand.*"

Brawner blinked his eyes and mumbled, "I understand."

Haack then gave Kit Brawner a termination speech, promised the buffoon one more payment, and advised him to look for other employment; the gravy train was over. Once he thought Brawner was clear-headed enough to drive, he told him to leave and never give the Tylers any grief.

Carson and Ezzard followed Haack out as he guided Brawner to his vehicle and watched the Jeep drive away. After that, he smiled, shrugged, offered Carson his hand, and drove off in the Town Car toward whatever his future would hold. Carson smiled at Ezzard, they laughed, and went back into the house.

They accepted a cup of coffee from Cindy Tyler while they all sat around a table in the small kitchen and waited for Tommy to wake from his nap.

Doobie Tyler was subdued after the melee. "This has been some day," he said. "A day I'll gladly forget about for all time. Don't even want the hundred bucks Kit promised us." He laughed uneasily.

When they heard the boy coming out of his nap, fussing a bit, Carson and Ezzard hovered at the bedroom door and peered in. Cindy stood back quietly. The child was sitting in the swirl of his blanket looking around, trying to figure out where he was.

Cindy Tyler slipped in and called his name. "Hi Tommy. Are you hungry?"

Carson stood by, anxious over how the child would react to being taken away by a stranger. He stood in the doorway as Cindy scooped the boy up and carried him out to the kitchen. She had a bologna sandwich all ready and a glass of milk. After a serious perusal of the new faces, the boy ate the food right down. While he was eating, Carson sat down at the table; after a minute or so he said hello and introduced himself. His sister's child looked at him and then at Ezzard with no discernible concern or acceptance. He didn't flinch or look fearful. He responded as he had evidently learned to.

"Guess he's always been a quiet kid," Doobie said. "That's what they said—the Brawners." He used their name reluctantly.

"No wonder, in that wild house he's lived in," Cindy reacted. "Well, Doobie, you been there. All them kids and Kit with his heavy-handed ways."

"Ain't for us to say," Doobie said. "Besides, cool it, little pitchers have big ears." He nodded toward the boy.

"I'll get his things," Cindy said. "Not much, just what he's got on and some pj's."

"I'll get him some more things later," Carson said.

After he had eaten and Cindy had put his things in a paper grocery sack, she got down real close to the boy and told him that this nice man was going to take him on a vacation. Would he like that? For a long moment Tommy studied the smiling man who was looking at him intently. Did he even know, Carson wondered, what vacation meant? When the boy finally nodded, it was the stiff motion of obedience. Carson raised his eyebrows at Cindy Tyler in surprise. He'd been expecting some reluctance, even tears.

Cindy shrugged and smiled. "I know," she said. "But like I said, think it's because of that place. He musta learned to follow orders, you know. Or else," she whispered over the child's head. "He's been living in a zoo." She mouthed the words.

Doobie Tyler frowned at his wife but didn't say anything more.

Carson waited while Cindy brought a washcloth and wiped the sandwich residue off Tommy's face and hands before taking him by the hand and walking him out to the car. Ezzard followed carrying the paper sack carrying everything the child owned. At the car, the boy stopped, looked alarmed for the first time, then turned and grabbed onto Cindy's leg. She sank down and held his face between her hands and whispered quiet assurances to him. After a few minutes, he sucked in a shaky breath and looked up at Carson. The unknown man was smiling, and holding out an open hand. Carson was wishing that he could tell this child who he was so that he would understand why he was there for him, but of course he couldn't.

Finally, the boy took a step away from Cindy Tyler and reached up, his small fingers extended toward Carson's hand. The sensation of touching the child and seeing traces of Aleta staring up at him was almost more than Carson could take in. Several moments passed between them before he lifted the boy into the back seat and got in beside him. It was right then, holding him, being next to him, and accepting responsibility for him that Carson shuddered in the face of that reality. His hands shook when he tried to buckle a seatbelt over the small body. Finally he made it work. Ezzard drove.

Just short of seven o'clock, Ezzard pulled up to the Falcon Motel. Carson carried a sleeping little boy to his room and lowered him gently onto the bed. The two men stood looking down on the sweet innocence of slumber and didn't speak for a long moment. Finally Ezzard grabbed Carson and swung him around into a bear hug.

They laughed soundlessly and shook one another in their unrestrained joy, tears glistening in their eyes.

A short time later, Ezzard's wife arrived to pick him up. The two men hesitated out in front of the motel room, hands in their pockets, clearing their throats and muttering in self-congratulatory intonations until Rhonda Dale tapped the horn. Carson watched until the Crown Vic disappeared around a corner and returned to his dream come true. Seeing the sleeping child on his bed made his emotions well up again. He took his wallet out, extracted Aleta's photo, and leaned it up against the lamp on the nightstand. He pulled a chair up next to the bed to be as near as possible to Aleta's child and watched entranced by the rise and fall of his tiny breaths. He swallowed at the knot in his throat, and his chest bucked up against gulping sobs. How he wanted to pluck the boy up and crush him in an embrace without end and tell him of his mother; to tell him that he loved him beyond any force of love he'd ever felt. To assure him that his life from now on would be one where he was safe, loved, where he could be unafraid and where he would grow into the son his mother would have been proud of.

By the time Tommy awakened, Carson had rebooked his return flight to Portland and added a child. They would lift off at 7:50 the next morning and be in Portland around 2:30 Pacific Time. He was apprehensive about how the boy would accept being with him: would he be afraid? Would he suddenly reject Carson? But what he discovered instead was a child who was calm, perhaps overly so, who didn't fuss and had little to say when asked. His responses were yes or no. He agreed to get food and some more clothes with no real reaction. He got into the car with this new person in his life as if it was the most normal thing to do. They had hamburgers at a Burger King before driving into Tulsa to buy clothes at Target.

Tommy seemed to like his new clothes, holding them up to look at when they were back in the motel room. It was then that Carson saw the first hint of a smile. "Do you like your new clothes?"

The boy nodded. "Never had new ones before," he said.

"Never?" Carson found that incredulous.

"I get Roger's stuff."

"You mean hand-me-downs?"

When Tommy looked confused Carson added, "You got clothes already used by another kid?"

"Yeah. Roger. Or sometimes Kenny's stuff. They weren't new like this. Old stuff. Had to wait 'til they got new stuff."

"From now on you'll have new stuff."

"Can I take these new clothes home with me?"

Carson paused, unsure how to answer. "Yes, they are your clothes. But first we will go on vacation, right?"

"Are we on the vacation now?"

"Not yet. We'll get on a plane tomorrow and then go on vacation. Have you been on a plane before, Tommy?"

He sobered. "I've only been where I was. 'Cept for car rides. No plane. How far is a vacation?"

Carson hesitated. "It will be a long way."

"How long is that?"

"Nearly two thousand miles. Do you know how much a thousand is?"

He shook his head. "Is it more than ten? I know how to count to ten. Crystal showed me how." He held up both hands, his fingers spread. "See ten."

"That's very good. Yes, a thousand is way more than ten, a lot more than ten fingers. That's why we have to fly in a plane, because it will be a long way. And since we have to get up early to get on our plane, we need to go to bed. How about wearing your new pj's?"

The boy found his new striped pajamas. Carson watched as he undressed himself and let him wrestle into the pajamas on his own. His mind was awhirl with all that had happened that day. But more than that, he was stricken by what lay ahead, the responsibility for the life of Aleta's child was now more than a dream—it was an absolute. He was concerned about what would happen when the vacation idea played itself out and Tommy asked about maybe going back to the only place he had ever known. Or would he want that? Carson hoped that would never happen.

When Tommy had drifted off to sleep once more, Carson got out his cell phone. "Marla, I have him."

"You do?" Her voice choked. "Oh, Carson. Really? You mean he's with you...right now?"

He looked at the bed. "Asleep right here in my motel room. God, he's a sweet child. Not without scars, but...he looks like her, Marla. He really looks like my baby sister."

"How is he taking all of this? Suddenly being with someone he's never known?"

"I don't know, really. He is okay for now. He's been told that this nice man, me, is taking him on a vacation and wondering if that was all right with him. From his childish perspective, it evidently seems okay."

"What now?"

"We're going home. That's our vacation."

"Seattle?"

"The Dalles."

"Really?"

"Yes, that's where I want to be with him. Where I want to start his new life." He paused. "Will you help me?" When she didn't respond immediately, he said, "I need to create a new world for him, you know? It will take having other people around: positive people who are good and kind and responsible and happy even. Different than what he's been immersed in these past four years."

"And you want to do that here? In The Dalles, not in Seattle?"

"I do."

"I see."

"Marla, you have no idea the environment that Tommy has been caught in. I'm sure it has been repressive and sometimes abusive, surviving in an atmosphere of ignorance. For him, being happy will be a new learned skill. And I thought..."

"You thought I'd jump at being a surrogate mom?"

Her reaction stunned him. "No," he faltered, "it's...I'll need the healing norm of females in his life is all I meant. He has been nothing but chattel, housed for money. Only one among a herd of foster and biological kids." He stopped and swallowed the knot in his throat. "I'm sorry," he said. "I guess I didn't think this through." He pressed End Call and stood stark still, bewildered that his best-laid plan had just been upended. Or admittedly it hadn't been a plan at all just an expectation that he could arrive back in The Dalles and she would help bring the boy out of the quagmire of his short life. He was in the bathroom washing his face, rethinking his future, *their* future, when he heard his cell ringing. He rushed out and snatched it up before it could ring beyond two times. Tommy hadn't stirred.

"Carson." Marla spoke his name like she was facing down something fearsome.

"Yes."

"You blindsided me."

"That right?" he said.

"Don't be mad."

"I'm not. I wasn't thinking, I'm sorry."

"So are you still coming...here?"

"Have to, tickets paid for and all. We'll be there tomorrow, maybe around five or so. Would you mind turning the heat on in the trailer?"

"Forget that," she said. "You'll both stay in the house."

"That would be nice, thank you."

"Stop the nicey-nice. Yes, I'll help you."

"No need for that. We'll make out."

"Shut up, Carson! Listen." He could hear her breathing. "Let me say something, okay?"

"Okay," he said.

"Glen and I, we were planning on having kids. But it never worked."

"Marla, you don't have to..."

"Yes, I do." She inhaled and went on. "My biological clock was running down. It never happened. Couldn't get pregnant. It was a lead weight in our marriage. Then he was gone." She paused again. "So…when you called just now with a—with Tommy—it was strange. My mind flew into full-blown resentment. How dare you bring a child into my life and expect me to fulfill a role I never had of my own. I was cheated."

"So what now?"

He could hear her crying. "You bring Tommy, you hear. You bring him home. I'll be waiting."

-36-

Lillian Barrus sat in her platform rocker tilting it back and forth in precise little movements. Across her living room sat a small lamp, one with a porcelain base and a bell-shaped shade with antique eggshell fabric casting out a soft circle of light; her eyes weren't seeing the lamp, only the unfocused glow of the light. Likewise her clarity of thought was obscured. She wasn't in the present. How could she be when all her mind wanted to do was replay over and again the voice of Carson? She was dressed for bed in a flannel nightgown when he called and blurted: *I have him, Grandma. Aleta's little boy. Tommy, he is with me now.*

She held the crushed handkerchief in her hand, damp from repeated dabs to her eyes. The tears had come flowing without stop; they were joyous tears and at the same time were tears of regret. When she roused from her mesmerism, not knowing how long she had been out of the moment, she went first to wash her face in warm water and then to smile at herself in the mirror above the sink; at last she couldn't restrain her joy. When the whoop emerged form her throat, she put her hands to her face as if in shock at the outburst but then laughed out loud. Now she had to share.

Purl's cell phone screen announced that Lillian Barrus was calling. She took in a deep breath before answering; she loved her mother but for some odd reason had never liked being chatty with her. "Mom," she said, attempting to have a lilt to her voice.

"Oh, Purl. It is so wonderful."

Purl dropped into a kitchen chair. "What is? Can't be the weather, raining again."

"He has him, Purl. Carson. He has the boy. Aleta's Tommy"

"What? You're kidding!" Purl sat up straight.

"No. I'm not kidding. He just called me. From Oklahoma."

"Oh my god. He actually found him?" A lump filled her throat. "Aleta's child? This is beyond surreal. Now what, is he coming back here with him?"

"No, at least not yet. He'll take him tomorrow to Oregon to that place...what's that town?"

"You mean The Dalles?

"Yes there." There was a pause between them. "Purl, I called to ask your advice about all of this."

"Wait, does CB know yet?"

"No. But that's my dilemma. This child is...he's their grandson, his and BeBe's. Their daughter's child. They need to be told."

"Mom, if you're trying to decide between BeBe and CB, no contest. BeBe is your only choice. Forget CB. My brother is the bastard in all of this. Call BeBe right now. I'll call the others, if that's okay?"

"Oh my yes, you must. Rove and Stuart will be astounded. Oh, Purl, this is so fantastic, isn't it?"

Purl was grinning at her mother's joy, now mixed with her own. Though she wasn't sure how such an astounding tale could ever come to a rational culmination. The darkness around the life of a small child was all twisted up in the bizarre intentions of people totally unknown to him. And now he had been rescued from the only life he knew. *My god*, she thought, *how could he ever be brought out of that past? Is he damaged? Has he been so marred that he will forever and always be behind in the world? Aleta, you were damaged yourself, weren't you?*

After agreeing with Lillian that it was indeed a fantastic revelation, she called her brother, Rove, and Carson's brother Stuart, bursting with the desire to knock them for a loop with the news. She felt a chill as she dialed each one. Rove was first; his gasp was that of someone who had just seen a child snatched out of the path of a speeding car. Stuart was more celebratory: "All right, way to go Carson." They all wondered: What now?

———————

David Haack had taken the last flight out of Tulsa after his face time with Carson in Ponca City; he was relieved to have the entire matter behind him. He landed back at Sea-Tac after midnight, picked up his Escalade from long-term parking, and drove to his dark and lifeless condo. He knew what lay ahead. *No matter,* he thought, and slept as soundly as a babe warm and full from its mother's milk.

He awoke early, astoundingly clear headed, loaded the coffeemaker with French Roast, popped some dried-out wheat bread in the toaster oven, and considered what next. Wait for the predictable CB mugging or hit first? That's what he'd do. After his cup of coffee and toast with grape jelly smeared on it, he stepped out onto his covered balcony and stood looking out at his spectacular view of Lake Union. He balanced his cell phone in one hand, considered the end of his comfortable and profitable employment, and made the call.

CB Barrus was already at his desk and answered his direct line. The bellowing response he gave to Haack's greeting made David smile; he almost laughed. "Because I had my phone turned off, CB, that's why."

"Listen you prick, you never block my calls, ever. You got that?"

"I hear what you're saying, sir."

"Don't you sass me. I've made arrangements to move the child. Kansas City."

"The child," Haack said in a condescending tone. "Why not use his name? Tommy."

CB paused before speaking more. "You been drinking? I don't like your tone. Where are you? You have the…you have Tommy?"

"No. I'm here in Seattle. Carson has Tommy." The explosion on the line was a joy to Haack's ears. It was right then, listening to his employer's verbal fusillade, that Haack knew he had done the right thing. For once in a very long time he'd made an honorable decision. "I have no idea where he will take the boy, nor do I care. Yes, you heard me correctly."

The vitriolic exchange between to two men, partners in so many questionable deeds, ended with Haack reminding CB Barrus that no, he would not make life miserable for him because of a certain file folder Haack had in a safety deposit box.

"I'd always thought that I would be vulnerable and knew without a doubt that I could never count on you to back me up. Am I right, CB? Thought so. Now here's the deal: I will be staying in this condo for the next year at your cost, and my services to you are hereby severed effective today. If you attempt to go after me in any way, I will open that file. My attorney has a letter in his care to be opened if anything should happen to me. Yes, you are a threat I take very seriously. After all, I've seen you operate and have done much dirt for you. Are we done?"

The only sound from CB's end of the line was hoarse breathing; then the call was ended. Haack did fifty push-ups and went out to a nearby snobbish diner for breakfast; he hadn't felt as clear about things in many a year.

Lillian wasn't prepared for the shriek that emanated from BeBe Barrus when she heard the news. Minutes went by. Lillian held her landline receiver to her ear and listened wide-eyed to the gasps and sobs that came out of BeBe's throat and mouth. Lillian absorbed the tumble of moans and wiped at her own tears until her daughter-in-law's joy wrapped up in the sounds of grief finally subsided.

"Oh, Lillian," BeBe said. "It's really true? I'll get to see my grandchild after all?"

"Yes, I believe so, and soon."

"And Carson too. It's almost too much to take in. When will they be here?"

"They won't be here. Carson is taking Tommy to that place in Oregon where he's been living. The Dalles."

"The Dalles? Why?"

"Carson has his reasons."

BeBe sniffed and could be heard blowing her nose. "Well, we will just go there, you and I, to this place, The Dalles. Won't we now?"

"I say yes to that," Lillian responded. "Emphatically. How are you going to handle CB?" The sound BeBe made was sort of a gurgle; her joy was so great she hadn't thought of the most obvious impediment. After a moment of drawing breaths she broke through.

"He's out for the evening—again, doing something. Whatever he does. Besides, to hell with CB," she tittered. "Lillian, did you hear me? Oh my."

"I heard you well enough. Tough talk. You mean it?"

The quiet in her ear left Lillian thinking that BeBe would cave in as she had so many times over the years. "By heavens, I do!" She laughed. "Lillian, I do mean it. When should we leave?"

Lillian felt a flush course through her body. It had been so very long since she'd been faced with something vital, something thrilling, or something that reached into her core and made her tremble. The adventure of it and the joy of it were wrapped together in one reckless package.

"How soon can you be packed, BeBe?"

"Oh. Oh. Really?"

"Really. Carson and Tommy will be in The Dalles tomorrow. You game on leaving first thing in the morning? Wait until CB leaves for the office. Then pick me up, and we'll get out of town." She laughed, and BeBe responded.

The sound of BeBe fussing made Lillian smile. Finally her daughter-in-law erupted. "Okay, girl. I can be there first thing. We'll set the GPS in my car and hit the road. You have an address?"

"You bet. I'll be ready and waiting downstairs."

Another pause. "Oh, Lillian, this is so thrilling." She cleared her throat. "Now I've decided. I'm going to leave a message for CB in the morning with Mary Dickens, his assistant. We'll be out of town before he knows about all this."

———

Mary Dickens took the call from BeBe Barrus the next morning with her usual good nature. She had always been fond of the woman who

303

had for so long endured having CB for a husband. On this morning she listened attentively to BeBe's message; a wide smile filled her face as she took down the essentials and agreed that she wouldn't pass on the message to her employer until one hour had passed. She promised to wait. Mary Dickens had to laugh thinking of two older women, who had had to put up with the subjugation of their son and husband, collaborating on a clandestine mission. She could imagine the fulmination she would witness when CB was given the word. She dutifully watched the clock and did not deliver the message for sixty minutes.

"Good morning, Mr. Barrus." Mary Dickens's tone carried a not-too-subtle bit of sarcasm.

CB looked up from a contract that had been driving him crazy. "I can do without the snide tone, Mary." He looked up into her silly smile. "What? I have jam on my tie?" He looked down and wiped at the rep tie he had on.

"No, sir. You are in your usual sartorial splendor."

"Damn it, Mary. What the hell do you want? Busy here."

"Sorry, just came to deliver a message from your wife."

"Really? What triviality is she wanting to foist on me now?" He looked down when Mary Dickens laid the message on the desk then went back to his papers.

"She said it was important."

"That right? Important? Let me have a look then. This will be vital, I'm sure." His eyes scanned the handwritten note. He blinked twice before exploding. "What the fuck!" He jumped up and reread the message. "She and my mother are on their way to The Dalles?"

"That's what she said. Gee, CB, didn't know you had a grandchild. Big surprise to me."

He glared at her. "Yeah, well, we'll just see about this. Cancel my appointments for the next few days."

"Going somewhere?"

"You know, Mary, you can be a real bitch at times. If I didn't…"

She laughed. "What? You want to fire me again? What would this be, number six? With David Haack and me both gone, how would you function?"

"What do you know about Haack?" he snapped. "Just happened."

"He called. We chatted some. Told me where to send his final check."

He stood leaning with both hands planted on his desk and glared at this woman who kept his business life and personal affairs organized and under wraps. Her smirk made him cringe; how he would love to give her a smack across those grinning lips.

He inhaled and held his breath until his lungs complained. "Whatever," he grunted. "All I want is for you to put all my appointments on hold for a week." When she raised her eyebrows, he added, "Never mind the mockery. Just move everything out a week. Got it?"

Mary Dickens raised her right hand in a stiff-wristed salute, turned on her heels, and marched out of the office. CB took no notice of her theatrics; he was already picking up the phone to call Siegfried and charter a plane.

-37-

The boy took in the airport and getting onto the plane as if experiencing a parallel universe. How had Tommy said it? *I've only been where I was.* Those words had stunned Carson and frightened him; he was now this little human's tutor, his guide to the outside world and his protector. He watched the boy looking at things seemingly strange to him and felt a small hand clutching his fingers very tightly as they walked the concourse. The child's eyes flitted from scene to scene: from other children laughing and tugging at small wheeled luggage to clusters of passengers inexplicably crowded at a gate. His head would jerk around when the speaker system yelled about some ensuing flight, but most often he stared straight ahead, daunted by the frenetic environment.

They at last entered the Jetway ramp, walked its length, and stepped through the wide doorway into the plane, where they were met by a cheery steward: but for none of it did Tommy smile or verbalize any curiosity. He was a sober child likely used to masking the starkness of things he was exposed to; in this case things and circumstances totally foreign to him. Carson hovered and guided the boy down the aisle. They had been assigned the window and middle seats in a row of three; the aisle seat passenger was a scrawny young man who donned headphones and dozed off. Carson stuffed his bags in the overhead bin and put Tommy in the middle.

He buckled Tommy in and asked if he was okay; for that he received a tight little bob of the head and a firm line of the mouth. When the plane started to taxi, the boy's eyes widened, and he hung on tightly to the arm rests. Takeoff caused him to look around apprehensively at Carson, who assured him it was okay and put his hand over the small hand next to him. Everything was a new experience: the roar of the engines, the video messages about safety, the pilot messages from the speaker above their heads, and the constant parade of passengers and stewards in the aisle. Carson recognized that to this four-year-old the ordinary was extraordinary.

The connecting flight out of Dallas landed in Portland a little ahead of schedule; Tommy had slept most of the way after eating half a sandwich during the layover. Carson kept him close as they walked through Portland International. Everything so mundane to Carson was new and confusing to a child who hadn't been exposed to life beyond the confines of what Carson had deemed the *foster farm*. His heart swelled every time he turned to observe the boy's reactions. There he was, Aleta's little boy, the child she saw only briefly before he had been taken from her. Her grief had been deep and irresolvable; her only way out had been the one she had taken. He had so wanted to pick the boy up and hug him again and again—but he didn't, not yet. After all, to Tommy he was only this man who was taking him on a vacation; he had not earned license to embrace the child. But he would. He vowed that he would soon be able to rightfully hold him.

At the long-term parking, the Camry balked, but finally the engine rolled over and ran smoothly. Then at last they were driving out I-84 east. Tommy fell asleep almost immediately in his car seat, awakening as they were passing Hood River. Carson could see him rubbing his eyes and looking out the side windows.

"Hi, Tommy," Carson said with a lilt in his voice. "You have a good nap?"

"Uh-huh." He was quiet then asked, "Where are we? Are we still on the vacation?"

"Yes, we are. We're in Oregon."

"Oregon? When will we go back? Where we came from?"

"I don't know," Carson answered. "We've just started our vacation. Do you want to stay on vacation?"

There is no response at first. Then, " Stay on vacation?"

Carson swallowed and slowed behind an eighteen-wheeler. "That's right. We could both stay on vacation."

"Oh."

"Is that okay?"

"I guess maybe."

Marla had been up since six o'clock. She and Ola Mae Nash had told their boss at Boyd Organics that they both needed the day off for personal reasons. Cecil and Ola Mae agreed to come over and be with her while she waited for Carson to arrive with the boy; they came by around one o'clock. There wasn't much to do but sit around, discuss Carson's odyssey, and marvel that but for Cecil's trolling of the freeway in Marigold none of this would have become part of their lives.

"God, I'm a wreck," Marla said. They were sitting around the kitchen table nibbling on a plate of fresh-baked chocolate chip cookies over tea and coffee.

"Come now," Ola Mae said, "he's just a little boy. Give him some cookies and milk and show him he's welcome. He'll be fine."

"He's more than that," Marla said. "He is the vestige of a tragedy. He has been retrieved from horrible circumstances, and now he is Carson's responsibility. What can he do? How can he claim him so he can help this child develop into a fully-formed human being? And he's asked for my help. That's why I am a wreck."

She had always known that if she and Glen had conceived the learning curve would have been steep and unending when their own little creature arrived. She had been resentful of her husband's abandonment, first as her soul mate and then for the lost-forever chance to have children together.

Now, damn it, she was expected to take in this child who was not her own; take him in and disregard her empty womb; take him in and offer affection because that was what he would need most; take him in and then what? And of course she was terrified. She could not fathom why she was so apprehensive, so timorous about meeting a small child—but she was.

Ola Mae decided they should bake another batch of cookies, this time oatmeal raisin. The aroma of the just-emerged tray of fresh-baked cookies had filled the kitchen when Cecil sprang to the window.

"They're here," he said pulling aside a curtain. He turned to see Marla standing rigid, frozen in the middle of the kitchen, an oven mitt on one hand. "You ready?"

Ola Mae waved a hand. "Oh, Cecil, don't be so dramatic. Of course she is." She put a hand on Marla's back and circled it around in a calming motion. "Glad we made more cookies, right?"

Marla stood still for a moment before pulling the mitt off her hand. "I feel like a goof," she laughed. "Why am I so nervous?" Ola Mae patted her back.

"There's Carson," Cecil said and turned toward the women with a big grin on his shaggy face. "Man oh man, he really did it, Marla."

"Yeah," she said on a breath. She tossed the mitt onto the kitchen counter and went to the window to look out. Carson was standing beside the car looking toward the house. After a minute he opened the back door, leaned over, and reached in. Marla's heart began to throb with expectancy; it seemed to take so long. Finally when he stood back up he was holding a child in his arms. She saw a curly head of yellow hair and a little face turning and looking around wondering where he was.

Marla smiled and felt tears forming in her eyes. Ola Mae patted her on the back again; Cecil was chuckling. They saw Carson draw the boy close and press his face into the sweet head of hair before he approached the house. Finally they all broke loose in excited verbal declarations and rushed to the door and out onto the porch. There they stopped, and Carson stopped. It was Cecil who finally let out a whoop and rushed down the steps. The child's eyes grew when he saw a big man with a hairy face running toward him. He drew back into Carson's arms and ducked his head against Carson's neck.

"Hello, hello," Cecil said clapping his hands together. "And who do we have here?" he said, leaning forward.

Carson saw Marla watching. They studied one another until she couldn't hold back and came down the stairs. She approached, her arms folded across her chest. "Hi," she said to Carson. "Hi," he said back.

She smiled into the blue eyes of the child and reached out to touch his arm. He didn't flinch or draw back. "Hello, Tommy," she said. "I am so happy to meet you. My name is Marla. Let's go get you some cookies just out of the oven."

Everyone traipsed into the house and gathered around the kitchen table. Tommy's eyes grew when he saw the plate of cookies. Ola Mae set a glass of milk in front of him and held the plate out. He looked up at Carson, who nodded; then he took a chocolate chip cookie into his small hand took a large bite. Everyone chuckled. While the boy ate one cookie and then another, the adults sat in observance, their joy complete.

Later they all ate together from a meal prepared by Ola Mae and Marla. Tommy's anxiousness over the unfamiliar began to melt away; he wandered about the house and would return to the kitchen, see that Carson was still there, and go off some more. After Cecil and Ola Mae had gone, Marla and Carson sat at the kitchen table over fresh cups of coffee and let the quiet envelop them. When she finally reached out and put a hand on his arm, he felt a warm flush of confirmation.

"You did it," she said. Her voice was husky.

He nodded. "I have him, he's away from where he never belonged, but it isn't over. I have to remake his life in some way."

"Carson, do you know how unique it is for a child who has been removed from the only place he's ever known to accept you as he has?"

"I know. I only hope he isn't locked in a shell of his own making and we only think he's doing okay with all of this."

"He's a lovely little boy," she said. "You'll find a way to make it right."

At that moment Tommy came out of the living room needing to use the bathroom. They both looked at him then smiled at each other, noting that the extreme saga of finding and retrieving him was now putting on the trappings of normalcy. Later when Carson had gotten his bags from the car and Tommy into his pajamas, they both tucked him into the rollaway bed Marla had set up in the spare bedroom right next to the bed Carson had slept in before. They stayed in the room until he drifted fell asleep holding onto one of Carson's fingers.

Marla brought out a bottle of red, and they settled on the couch in the living room. She poured them each a glass then raised hers smiling. "Salute," she said.

They touched the bowls of the glasses with a gentle thunk. "Salute," he echoed. Then he laughed, set his glass down, and laughed until he cried. "I can't believe it," he said, his voice thick.

"You made it happen," she said.

"I *wanted* it to happen But you want to know the truth? I may have sounded determined and unshakable, but in my gut I didn't think I would succeed. Not really. I figured I'd run around like a fool, pitied by my family but not taken seriously, and come up empty. My only option after that would be to return to the clan. They'd take me in and tell the world I'd been disoriented all the while I was thought dead." He paused and looked into his glass. "And now part of my sister is here with us."

"What you did is amazing, Carson." She put a hand on his shoulder. "I mean staggering."

"We'll see."

"Yes. Now what?" Marla asked.

Carson had inhaled in preparation to respond when his cell began to vibrate in his pants pocket. He stood quickly and pulled it out. He recognized the number. "Hi Grams," he said.

"Oh Carson, there you are," said Lillian into his ear. "We're here!" Her voice was enthused and loud.

"What?"

"BeBe and I, we're here—in The Dalles. Your mother and I, we just got here. We drove down, left early this morning." Her voice faded, and he could hear mumbling. "We're downtown, I guess…what's the street?" More mumbling. "We can't see a street sign, but we're in the Chamber of Commerce parking lot. Can you come get us?"

He hesitated then smiled. "Sure. You just wait right there, and I'll drive down. I'll be in a silver car."

"Silver. Okay. Carson?"

"Yes."

"He's with you? The child?"

"Yes. He's sleeping."

Lillian could be heard passing the word, and the two women laughed in joy. "Oh, come right away, Carson. We can't wait to see him…and you!"

-38-

When Carson returned to the house with his mother's big Lexus right behind, he saw an unfamiliar car parked next to Marla's Honda, a white Buick he'd never seen before. When he and the two excited women entered the house, they were met by the sound of Marla shouting: "You will not!" followed by a responsive throaty male voice. The verbal exchange was coming from the kitchen. Carson moved quickly ahead of the women and entered to see Marla, her face red and agitated, nose to nose with his father. A slender man, maybe in his fifties, stood behind him. The women following in his wake gasped simultaneously.

"CB," Lillian said in a firm voice. "What are you doing here?"

CB turned quickly on his heels toward the three of them. His expression was grim, frozen in rage. "Carson," he said, his tone flat as iron. "There you are, damn you. What a fucking mess you've made of things."

Carson stepped forward. "Dad. What the hell are you up to?

"Tommy," Marla said. "He wanted me to give him Tommy. Threatened me."

Carson's eyes opened wider. "Where is he, Tommy?"

Marla patted the air with an open palm. "Still asleep upstairs." She turned back on CB. "He shoved his way in here. He and whoever this person is." She pointed to the other man.

"Who is this?" Carson asked.

CB didn't look over his shoulder, just said, "My pilot, Siegfried."

"He your muscle?"

"If need be, if need be."

The man Siegfried raised his hands in surrender. "Hey, Mr. Barrus, I'm not in on this. You just said to keep you company. I'm no enforcer."

CB turned to the man. "You're whatever I say you are."

Siegfried looked from face to face, shaking his head. "Hey folks, I'm a charter pilot—that's all. Not sure what's going on here, but I'm going to go on out and wait in the car, Mr. Barrus. Once you get things worked out, I'll fly you back."

"You fuck," CB said, his hands fisted. "You'll never work for me again."

Siegfried exchanged eye contact with CB. "So be it," he said finally. "You want me to wait and fly you back or not?"

CB stood still, his jaw muscles flexing. "Just wait until I come out." Siegfried nodded, pursed his lips, and eased past Carson and the two older women.

When the front door closed, Carson approached his father. "Dad," he said, "I want you to leave—now. Your pilot is waiting."

CB's mouth formed into a mocking smile. "I'm taking the boy with me. You know that."

"Are you crazy!" Carson stepped back. "Tommy is back with the family where he belongs. After the contemptuous way you treated Aleta, forcing her to literally give away her baby, how can you even show yourself here?"

"You are in deep shit," CB said. "You kidnapped a child, took him from his legitimate home, and stole him away. The courts look down on such behavior."

Carson reached out and pushed a forefinger into CB's chest. "No, you are the one in deep shit. Everything having to do with Aleta's pregnancy, the birth, putting the baby with that disreputable couple—all of it—was illegal. And you know it."

CB shook his head. "Wait until I get the authorities in on this."

"You have nothing to show them," Carson said. "Remember? Everyone along the way was paid in cash, birth certificate destroyed, no official assignment of the boy to the foster home—you have no legal trail. No legal trail because you needed to cover your tracks."

CB squinted. "David Haack."

"Yes. Not everyone you work with is without a conscience."

Lillian came up behind Carson and stared at her oldest child. "Cadence," she said. "What have you done?"

"Mother, stay out of this." When she continued to glare at him, he said, "Aleta went astray. Had to clean it up."

"You mean that young man, he was the father? What was his name?"

CB blinked, rubbed a hand over his close-cropped gray hair, and looked toward his wife. BeBe stood stone-faced. "Thomas Shepherd," she said. "That was his name. Aleta adored him."

"Bullshit," CB said. "He wasn't good enough for her."

Marla, still standing a ways from the two men, caught a glance from Carson. His expression was one trying to assure her in spite of the familial fray. She nodded.

"This Thomas Shepherd," Lillian said. "He was the father, Tommy's father?"

"Of course," CB said and looked to the side then back. "Had to be."

"Where is he?" Carson asked.

CB hesitated. "I don't know. Last I heard in Atlanta."

"So he ran out on Aleta?" Carson said.

"No." It was BeBe who responded. She walked over and stood next to Carson. "Thomas Shepherd was a good man, a decent man," she said, emotion filling her voice.

"BeBe," CB said, his tone condescending. "Stay out of this. You don't know a damn thing."

Carson watched as his mother drew herself up and squeezed her hands together. "Of course I do," she said. "You know I do."

"BeBe, shut up."

The crack of the slap that hit CB's face caught everyone unaware. BeBe had put every ounce of strength she could muster into the blow. CB's head jerked to the side. When the shock drained away he glared at her and opened his mouth to denounce her but not before she struck him again.

"What the hell," CB said with a growl. BeBe hit him one more time.

"I should have done that so many times," she said. "I have hated myself for all of the times I looked the other way from your abhorrent behavior. I allowed you to act out your perverted view of life again and again."

"Allowed me?" CB erupted.

"Yes, allowed you. I should have challenged you for being the mean-spirited person you are: for your lack of a conscience, for lacking the ability to love, to care. I'm as guilty as you. But now we have Aleta back with us in Tommy, and it goes on no longer. You hear?"

"Stop it," he responded. "BeBe, just stop it, I say."

BeBe's smile was not warm, not loving, not even nice. "I hate this," she said, "but I have to do this. It is time."

Carson saw his father's face fall slack and begin to lose color. He took a step forward, stopped only by Carson's hand on his chest. "No," Carson said.

BeBe turned toward Lillian, who stood transfixed, mouth ajar, and looking back and forth between husband and wife. "Lillian," she said, "Thomas Shepherd wasn't the father. He's not Tommy's father. He was only accused of being so in absentia, after he'd been run out of town. You and I now have to share the disgrace as mother and wife that our son and husband took his own daughter into his bed."

"BeBe!" CB roared. "Stop this insanity."

BeBe sagged to the floor on her knees and began to sob out her grief. "My baby, he ruined my baby's life and my own."

Lillian blinked in bewilderment as BeBe hunkered at her feet. She looked at her son in disbelief. The room grew quiet. They all stood stock still absorbing the sudden revelation of a long held depravity. No one spoke for long while.

Finally CB looked to his son and said, "I suppose I should feel what is described as shame, perhaps even grief. But then again, I've never used those emotions."

"I know," said Carson.

"It always seemed so counterproductive and weak," CB tried to explain. "Whenever I observed such reactions to whatever circumstance had presented itself, I saw only wasted opportunity to use problematic moments to one's advantage. Don't you see?"

Carson studied the man he called father and was saddened and enraged in one breath. Of course, if he were to tell him of his feelings, he would receive nothing commensurate in return. It was an impossibility but he had to try. "No, I don't see," he answered. "I'm guilty as well, guilty of watching you assume unfair advantages again and again, of corrupting your dealings with the trusting and the vulnerable just to win."

His father was staring at him, a man perplexed by what his son was accusing him of. "I saw you as my mirror image," he said. "You know that? The one to carry on. But then…"

"Then what, Dad? I wasn't what?"

"You weren't going to…"

"What? Ruin people like you did? Cut anyone to the bone who stood in your way and look upon any woman as yours if you wanted her?" Carson lunged forward and grabbed his father's coat front and yanked him up close. "Like fucking my wife but worst of all impregnating my baby sister—your own child. My god, how evil." He drove a shoulder into CB's chest, and they crashed to the floor together sprawled in a flailing entanglement of arms and legs. Amid the gasps and heaving breaths the two men crawled about, grabbed and clawed and punched at each other before struggling back onto their feet. The women stood back wide-eyed and shocked, mouths agape.

CB swiped at his coat with first one hand then the other. His breathing was unsettled and raspy. He touched a bleeding scratch on a cheek. "Feel better now?"

Carson inhaled and shook his head. "You don't get it, do you? We're through with it, through with you dictating our lives. And we are through with you. You no longer matter. We're going to rebuild. There's goodness in this family—that's what the world will see in us now. Tell me, you bastard, do you now think that bedding your own daughter, destroying Aleta, was an opportunity used to your advantage?" Carson's voice rose. "Well, do you?"

CB took in a deep breath, shoved past his son, and moved toward the door. Before going out he turned and said calmly, "She loved me in that way, you know." And then he was gone. The departure was almost serene; there was no evident trauma connected to his leaving, no clear signal, no reverberation sent up that a dominant force had been eviscerated. But it had.

They stood in the dead quiet, each one looking to the others in turn; no one spoke or maybe knew what to say. The sound of a car starting was all that broke the silence. When it had driven away, Carson held his mother in a long embrace and cried with her. He gave his grandmother a big hug and kissed her parchment cheek. And then they begged to see the boy, to cast their eyes for the first time on Tommy, who was in a deep sleep and had been spared the chaos.

Marla and Carson stood back as the light from the hall played fingers of light into the bedroom and across the twisted blanket covering Tommy's small body. BeBe and Lillian slid into the room as if on glides and stood over the rollaway bed and looked down, arm in arm. When they came out, there were smiles and tears alike on their radiant faces. And of course they weren't ready to retire. Marla brought out the remaining cookies, and they all sat around the kitchen table nibbling and quietly discussing what had occurred. Carson finally, and with a blush of shyness, introduced Marla to his mother and grandmother; the two women instantly fell in love with her as the one who had saved Carson—which she denied.

At last, fatigue fell on all of them. Marla made up a bed for BeBe and Lillian in the remaining spare bedroom, and soon the house was quiet. Tommy awoke with cry in the night but responded to Carson's comforting arms and cooing words and drifted back to sleep.

———————

Word about CB came after two days, time those in The Dalles spent getting acquainted, Tommy becoming comfortable with the women in the house and they with him. But he mostly wanted Carson to always be nearby. It was a love fest, and Carson was sure the boy hadn't felt as much affection and attention ever.

That pool of affection was suppressed suddenly when Purl reached BeBe on her cell; CB had perished at sea. The story was that he had gone directly to the family compound in Sequim after Siegfried had returned him to Seattle. The following morning, in spite of small craft warnings, CB had put out into the Strait of Juan de Fuca in one of the kayaks kept there. Winds rose, and swells increased; no one with any savvy was out in a small craft let alone a kayak. He never returned. A full-time resident and neighbor had seen CB's departure and noted he wore no life vest, nor did he have a spray skirt attached to keep seawater out of the kayak. As the day wore on, the neighbor grew increasingly concerned and eventually reported him to be considered missing to the Coast Guard. At first a search turned up nothing until an empty red Kevlar-hulled kayak was discovered floating off the Dungeness Spit. It was identified as belonging to CB. It would be nearly a week before his body washed ashore.

BeBe and Lillian absorbed the news as if they'd just been advised that an immense oak tree that had once dominated the neighborhood had fallen, it's roots exposed and its limbs awry—a legend no more. The women sat together with Carson at the kitchen table over cups of tea that cooled without being consumed; they mostly asked themselves how it could have happened and what had he been doing and was it suicide? After quiet speculation among them, BeBe offered that he had taken his own life. She was sure of it. She shed no tears; neither did Lillian. Carson had no such feelings left, certainly not enough of a reserve to be devastated, even one last time.

"It is best," BeBe said finally. "Our mutual suffering is at an end. Besides, CB could never have tolerated his hidden transgressions being given the light of day. Even though he could never see them as profane himself, he had to know others would." She did at last dab away a few tears before saying, "Well, Lillian, it's up to you and me to put on our sackcloth and write the final chapter for our son and husband. You up for it?"

Lillian had been listening to her daughter-in-law as if she were a stranger. Where had this woman been all the years of enduring the ridicule and disrespect from the man she had once loved enough to marry? She had to smile, for she had loved this woman and bled for her torturous existence at the hands of her eldest. "Yes, BeBe, I'm with you. One more time, and then we're done. Then we can stand in for Aleta and her child. It will be grand."

The women spent a little more time with Tommy, gave him big hugs, which he seemed not to mind, and drove home to make arrangements to finalize Cadence. As they drove away, Carson felt that something vital he'd set out to do had actually come full circle.

Tommy had stood between Marla and Carson, with the assurance of a child who was right where he belonged. He had reached up and taken Marla's left hand in his right and Carson's right hand in his left and held on watching with them as the car with the curious old people in it had driven off.

EPILOGUE

That night, after Lillian and BeBe had gone and Tommy had been put to bed holding onto a stuffed animal Marla had dug out of a closet, an elephant with a long snout, which he loved, she settled down on the couch with Carson and considered the hand they had been dealt. They wondered about the happenstance of how they both ended up in that place, with comparable senses of loss, with equal layers of rage behind the forfeiture of their mates, and with equal drives to recreate who they were in spite of the destruction of what had been.

"You know," Carson said and squeezed her hand. "I could take Tommy back to Seattle."

She was quiet, her face curiously blank. "I thought you asked me to help."

"Didn't think you heard me."

"I heard you. Scared the hell out of me, if you want to know. What you're asking would come with a lot of other stuff, too."

"Like?"

"You. And me." She sat back and folded her arms. "I decided after Glen. After I left that place, told myself that there wouldn't be any more of that. Ever. Would be just me living a life I wanted. No slicing off bits of myself for someone else's self-persecution."

He leaned forward on his knees and clasped his hands together. "You're not up to taking any more risks? On other people?" She didn't respond. He said, "I feel that too, you know. I was dumped on just like you. I ran out just like you. I had something to prove just like you. There's just one thing."

"What's that?"

321

"I care again. Didn't think I would but I do. Outside of Tommy you're the one I care most about." To her incredulous expression he said, "It's true. How's that go down?" He laughed and leaned against the cushions.

"Carson," she said on a soft breath. "We can't go there just because..."

"Because we had a roll in the hay? I know that. Thing is, I love you. And now I love the little life in the other room. I'm responsible for him for always and ever. I'm asking if you'll to take on two handsome dudes and grow a life together. That corny enough for you?"

"Pretty corny."

"And it isn't over yet," he said. "There's going to be crunch time with the courts sorting out who Tommy can legally belong to. Starting tomorrow I'm turning my lawyer loose on this with no holds barred. And we're going to go for it right here in The Dalles. I want to raise him here."

She smiled. "Here in the cherry pit capital of the world?"

"I like it, feels good."

"Okay, so feels good, but what about your family and the business?"

"I'll work that out." He stood and looked down at her. "So, you game or not? I know you'll need time to think on all of this. And Tommy and I'll need more space than the trailer so I'll look for a house."

She stood and stepped up to him and put hand against his chest. "This, right here, is your house. Come on." She took him by the hand.

Carson remembered the erotic brittle sex he and Naomi had—a hard coming together that had satisfied their baser instincts. But it hadn't been love. He had no way of knowing how it had been between Marla and her man, and he didn't care. All he knew was that when their bodies touched it was a mutually enjoyed sensuality; it was not a demanding performance. They willingly gave themselves to each other with no holding back. Afterward, he held her close, smelled her hair, and knew that he had to keep on sharing this life next to him. When Tommy was heard fussing, they laughed and decided which one would go take him to go potty. It was Carson's turn.

_____

Beginning the next day, Vincent Horne moved forward on Carson's signal with the legal process to sort out how to acquire legal custody of Tommy for Carson. Contact was made with the Wasco County District Attorney's Office and a time to meet arranged. Horne, who was licensed in both Oregon and Washington, made the trip down to The Dalles himself, where he met with a Wasco County deputy district attorney and a child support specialist. The game had begun.

Later, when the Circuit Court judge assigned the case looked upon the gathering before him, Tommy, Carson, Marla, the boy's court-appointed attorney, Vincent Horne, and representatives from the DA's office, he considered the recommendations from the official parties, queried them at length for clarifications, nodded his head in agreement, and granted temporary custody of Thomas Barrus to one Carson Barrus. It had been decided to begin using Barrus as Tommy's last name; he didn't seem to mind or perhaps even take it in.

_____

It was a week after Tommy had arrived when the Barrus family convened at Purl's house and waited anxiously for his arrival. The loathsome story of CB's incestuous violation of Aleta had staggered his siblings and progeny beyond belief but it had already played itself out. CB was cremated; there was no service. Rove drew the short straw and drove to Sequim to dump his father's ashes along the Dungeness Spit, which he did dutifully. On that blustery day, he stood on the rocky shore, poured the powdery residue into the lapping water and watched the ashes spread out and gradually disappear; he felt nothing.

The news media had already picked up on CB (Cadence Leland) Barrus's death and were soon comparing his drowning with that of his son Carson Barrus's near drowning and temporary amnesia. It made an interesting human-interest story and hit page one below the fold and was the second lead story on local television for one day. There was speculation that death by drowning, even though one had arisen from a watery grave, seemed to run through the notable family's gene pool.

The family contingent waiting at Purl's house on that Saturday morning included all of the out-of-town children who made the trip to meet Aleta's miracle child firsthand. Magic was in the air, tainted only vaguely by the unthinkable. When at last they had arrived, all chatter fell away and the everyone clustered around the wide front window, their murmurings a chorus of sighs. They stood shoulder to shoulder watching, waiting to see the child, to actually see that he existed. Their collective breathing seemed in suspension until the car door opened and the driver stepped out; it was Carson. It was substantiated; it was truly he.

He stood still behind the open door of the car and looked toward the house. He saw them; he stared but didn't raise a hand or smile. After a long moment in which no one moved, Carson stepped back, opened the back door of the car, and leaned in. In the house, there was an inhalation of expectation. The boy came out on Carson's arm; his curly hair mussed, his blue eyes awakening, his small lips mouthing something—he was there for all to see.

Then the passenger door swung out, and a woman emerged. She was slender, had long brunette hair, a narrow face, and high cheekbones; she wore no makeup. Her expression was one of curiosity tinged with a bit of apprehension.

"There he is," said Lillian. "There's Tommy."

"Who's the woman?" asked Purl.

"That's Marla," BeBe said. "Marla Snow. She is amazing."

And then they flooded out of the house into the chill and a light mist. Tommy at first reared back and clung to Carson until he saw the smiles and heard people saying his name. He looked up at Carson who, smiled and nodded that it was okay; then he relaxed in Carson's arms. Marla came quickly to Carson's side and gripped his free hand. He squeezed back and forged ahead into Purl's house.

After an excited round of introductions, Carson invited everyone to gather so he could tell them the complete story. Tommy sat on Marla's lap while Carson spoke to the people he'd known all his life.

"Accounts of my death have been greatly exaggerated," he began. Everyone laughed in great relief. "It was Mark Twain who first said that, but it is apropos. The rest of the story is true, and the evidence is right over there: Thomas Leon Barrus. I think Grandpa Barrus would approve us using his name. Aleta chose Thomas after her son was born, so Tommy it is.

"Marla, who is holding Tommy, has been a pillar of strength. She even accepted a derelict off of the freeway and let him rent her trailer while he got his act together. She saved my bacon. But more about her and Tommy in a bit. But first, settle back and I'll tell you everything."

———

The telling came out of Carson the way a boy confesses a wrong-doing to his parents—haltingly and uncertain of the repercussions. His rapt audience responded with wonder, gasps, and laughter as he unwrapped the continuum of the story. When at last he held out his hands and said that was it, his family applauded. The cheering woke Tommy, who had been asleep on Marla's lap; he looked around startled but calmed when Marla patted him and whispered in his ear.

"And now," Carson continued, "I have something more to say. First, I didn't go through all of this to return to the status quo. I love you all, but I will not be living my life as before."

He went on to explain that while he would remain as a principal in the company, he would be living in The Dalles and making regular trips to Seattle for business; he urged that Stuart and Rove assume key leadership roles with Barrus Properties, decided by whatever method they deemed best.

"The reason for this change must be obvious to everyone. And he's sitting there on Marla's lap—my baby sister's son. Tommy will be my primary focus from now on. My attorney is working with the court down in Wasco County. I have been given temporary custody and as soon as the legal matters can be attended to, I intend to adopt him." He turned to look at Marla. "I'm hoping that Marla will be my partner in raising Tommy. She's considering an offer I've made to her and has agreed to not take in any more road warriors—just look what it's gotten her into." She blushed and pulled Tommy tighter amid the laughter.

After a quiet moment of shared smiles and nods, Carson asked the family to concur that he assume the responsibility of raising Tommy on Aleta's behalf and with their blessing and participation as his extended family. They did, unanimously, and for the first time they were able to celebrate without the specter of CB's control or interference.

On Tuesday, Barrus Properties gained a soul when Stuart Barrus became CEO and Rove was appointed Chairman of the new Board.

On the second anniversary of Carson's arrival in The Dalles, Cecil, Ola Mae, and Vince Horne stood in as witnesses when Marla and Carson were married on the second-floor stairs of the Wasco County Courthouse juxtaposed by majestic marble pillars. Two months earlier, Marla had accompanied Carson to see Tommy Leon Barrus enter the first grade. After watching the boy disappear into a classroom, she shed tears and on the drive home at last agreed to be his mom and Carson's wife. The presiding judge noted with a smile the presence of Tommy standing between the bride and the groom holding a small bouquet, which he gave to Marla just before she and Carson embraced. He belonged to them now, so the court had ruled.

ACKNOWLEDGEMENTS

For their assistance, knowledge and goodwill, I wish to thank: Steve McCarthy, Clear Creek Distillery; Fred Coler, psychiatrist; Camelia Moss, Camelia's Candle's; Larry Leverette & Faye Tayler, child welfare specialists; William S. Doenges, who drove me all over Oklahoma; David Stelzer, Azure Standard Natural Foods, Dufur, Oregon; Sandy & Bill Perkins, veteran over the road truckers; Stan Swan, flight instructor; Melissa Wiseman, midwife; Jim Hess & John Shultz, proud owners of a vintage Avion Travelcade trailer; Lynn E. Long, Wasco County Horticulturist (for all things cherry;) Hood Canal resources: Hood Sport & Dive Shop, Mason County Fire District 1, and Mason County Transit Authority. And thanks to David Haack who in a weak moment at an auction for the Portland Pearl Rotary Club donated enough to claim naming rights for one our characters; watch for his namesake in the novel.

Special accolades go to my editor, Karen Brattain, (she always makes it better) and to Dennis Stovall, a good friend who designs my books with great care and unique creative skill.

And as always, to Betsy Wright, to whom this book is dedicated for her loving support as my first reader and my life partner in all things.

GEORGE BYRON WRIGHT is the author of five previous novels: *Baker City 1948, Tillamook 1952, Roseburg 1959, Driving to Vernonia,* and *Newport Blues, A Salesman's Lament.* He lives with his wife Betsy in Portland, Oregon.

CPSIA information can be obtained at www.ICGtesting.com
Printed in the USA
LVOW12s2256160115

423136LV00006B/10/P